Shadow Hunters of Helaman

M.D. House

Cover art and interior design by David Provolo
Editing services by Cassidy Skousen

Books by M.D. House

The Barabbas Trilogy
I Was Called Barabbas
Pillars of Barabbas
The Barabbas Legacy
Sophia: Daughter of Barabbas (Spin-off #1)
The Barabbas Companion Volume 1 (Study Guide)

The Patriot Star series (Science Fiction)
Patriot Star
Kindred Star

The End Times Convergence series (YA Fantasy)
Crossroads of Awakening Memory

The Servant of Helaman series
The Servant of Helaman
Shadow Hunters of Helaman

Amulek: Revenant

Introduction to
Shadow Hunters of Helaman

Very few people have heard of the heroic man called only by the label "the servant of Helaman" in what The Church of Jesus Christ of Latter-day Saints considers ancient scriptural record from the Americas. His name is never revealed, but his briefly chronicled role among the thousand-year history of a long-deceased Christian-majority nation—from about 52-50 BC—is dramatic and inspiring.

In the first book of this series, aptly called *The Servant of Helaman*, I gave him a name: Kihoran, or Kai for short. Telling Kihoran's story was an entertaining and inspiring experience for me, and I knew I wanted it to continue. This volume builds on the original story, following the main characters through the continuing challenges posed by both individual circumstances and societal struggles.

In particular, I try to open the window further on how and why the Nephite people struggled so profoundly in remaining faithful to God and his commandments, even after he had performed so many miracles on their behalf. We face similar challenges today, driven by the same factors: the difficulty of our mortal existence, the pride of our hearts, and the temptations of Satan.

As you will see at the end, there will be a Book 3 (with a fourth probable as well). Next to *Sophia: Daughter of Barabbas* and *Amulek: Revenant*, this was my easiest book to write. The planning was a bit more difficult, but the ideas flowed naturally onto the page, with the early drafts coming out relatively clean.

Many thanks to Cassidy Skousen for her helpful edits and comments, and Dave Provolo for his skilled design work on the cover and interior.

Like its predecessor, I love this story, which increases my faith and determination to follow the living Christ. I hope you will, too.

M.D. House
July 2024

PROLOGUE

Verily, verily, I say unto you, ye must watch and pray always,
lest ye be tempted by the devil, and ye be led away captive by him.
And whatsoever ye shall ask the Father in my name, which is right,
believing that ye shall receive, behold it shall be given unto you.
—3 Nephi 18:15, 20

Kai turned the fateful dagger over in his hand again. No traces of Kishkumen's blood remained. The weapon seemed to glitter, even inside the antiquities shop, out of direct sunlight. He squinted, remembering that moment of surreal destiny with piercing clarity. His hand trembled slightly, and he suppressed a shiver.

"The price is acceptable?"

Kai's gaze snapped up to the neatly-dressed shop owner, and he couldn't fully disguise his emotions.

The man's forehead wrinkled, and he nodded slowly. "I can see it has some sentimental value to you. I'll give you a senine more for it, but that's my final offer. If it's too precious to part with, then don't."

The knife became hot in his hands, and he nearly dropped it. There was no way he could keep it, and not just because of the promise to the kindly Merga and Orofin in Bountiful. Unbeknownst to them, he had slain a man with their knife. Though Kishkumen had been a cold-hearted murderer, Kai still hated the fact that he had needed to kill him. On top of that, he desperately wanted to keep his role in the whole matter a secret. Helaman and Dan knew, of course, as did Siarah, his betrothed. Arayah, too, former Gadianton spy and Kishkumen's love interest, though she had courageously rebuffed the assassin's advances.

The knife marked Kai. Not only was it visibly distinctive; it was now unmistakably tainted—to the spiritual eye if not the physical. Helaman had offered him a fair sum to make it a public relic, but Kai wanted no part of such a display. He had traveled to Manti—a good distance from the capital of Zarahemla—to avoid prying eyes while making the transaction. He had almost sold the blemished blade in Minon along the way, but he could get a better price for its original owners in a larger city like Manti. The old couple just wanted to find peace, and they needed the extra money.

"Agreed." Kai lifted the weapon, bringing his other palm up to caress the sharp steel as he handed it over reverently. Suddenly, the parting seemed difficult, but his determination hardened. The man cocked his head slightly, a question in his eyes, but he asked nothing. He just nodded, taking the dagger and setting it on the table. He reached into a bag at his waist, then counted the payment out into Kai's proffered hand.

Relief suffused Kai, as sudden as the inexplicable hesitation, and again he couldn't mask his emotions. Before the man's curiosity could overcome him, Kai thanked him, bid him farewell, and walked briskly out of the shop. It was done. He would return to Zarahemla and arrange to have the money sent to Merga and Orofin so they could make their planned emigration northward. And he wouldn't retain any commission on the sale.

———◆———

Vyim bore Kai swiftly back to his new home. As usual, Kai had to rein in the big, spirited bay stallion often. It seemed as if his equine companion's greatest wish was to die in the glorious act of galloping at top speed, and it made Kai chuckle. Vyim had already sired three foals to mares of his friend Aaron, who still mourned the loss of his wife during the most recent Lamanite invasion. One filly was Aaron's, as promised, and the other two—a filly and a colt—would go to Siarah and to Kai's sister, Neva.

Kai skirted Gideon, where his friends would likely delay him. Part of him itched to stop by the synagogue where Shemnilom, the wise old spymaster and priest, had his office. He would also enjoy visiting the barracks, where he could find Jeruzim, leader of the Gideon militia.

But he resisted.

He arrived at Zarahemla near noon of the next day, entering through Elijah's Gates on the south side. That would let him pass by the temple and its peaceful grounds on the way to the Santorem. His spirit yearned for heavenly connection in a way he couldn't adequately describe.

When he finally reached Helaman and Jerena's house, in which he had his room, it was late, well past dinner time. He wasn't hungry—in fact, he hadn't even stopped by his favorite meat pie vendor in the city.

Dan happened to be on duty at the front gates. He studied Kai carefully as he dismounted and led Vyim toward the stables in the back.

"Successful journey?" Dan asked, walking with him.

Kai nodded. "It is done. I'll send the money tomorrow."

"Helaman still wishes you would have sold the knife to him. You saved his life with it."

Kai kept his eyes forward. "I know. It still didn't feel right, and he would have made me keep a portion. I don't care where it ends up, as long as I never see it again."

Dan didn't say anything, but Kai knew he understood. The former stripling warrior exercised full stewardship over a well of wisdom Kai doubted he could ever attain.

Dan helped him get Vyim brushed down, fed, and settled, and then they entered the house through the back. Before they had taken two steps inside, Helaman materialized in front of them, causing Kai to take a step back.

"Kihoran, you're back! That is good." He slapped Kai on the shoulder with a friendly smile, then instantly turned serious as he looked at Dan. "Brother Dan, we may have found how Gadianton's band escaped the city."

Dan arched his eyebrows. "Oh?"

"Yes. Two doors down from Imrahiel's pottery shop, some officers found a shaft. It's deep. They haven't followed it yet, but they set a guard. Can you investigate? I don't mean now. In the morning."

Dan's mien intensified as he thought for several moments. "I'll go now." He turned to Kai. "Kai, I know you just got back, but will you accompany me?"

Kai didn't have to think about it—Imrahiel's name was a living scar. "Of course. I've been sitting on a horse all day; my legs are fresh."

Dan grinned. "Good, let's get some lanterns and light armor, and then we'll go."

———◇———

Kai's heart beat faster as they descended the ladder from the floor of the innocuous-looking flower shop. The shaft was indeed deep, and he wasn't surprised when they found themselves in hip-deep water at the bottom. This close to the mighty River Sidon, the water table was high.

Pretty soon, he realized it wasn't just water. "These breeches are ruined," he noted, nose wrinkling.

Dan chuckled. "I've seen worse."

Kai didn't argue. Dan had been through so much more than Kai, serving under Helaman's father in the Great War. He just grunted and began wading through the muck. The tunnel angled northwest, which gave him some hope that the water level would drop as they progressed.

"They started this tunnel a long distance from the north walls," Kai commented after one of his booted feet made a gross sucking sound under the water.

"They were clever," said Dan. "We've been searching closer to the walls, and all we've found are a few minor passageways, more difficult to traverse."

"It's hard to reconcile. Imrahiel always seemed so confident. People that confident rarely construct such elaborate escape plans."

"Well, Gadianton is the mastermind, and Imrahiel did what he was told. As did Kishkumen."

"May he writhe in torment." Kai pictured Kishkumen's face fluttering in the lantern light. Those harsh, cruel features. Nearly blond hair and dark, fiery eyes. Merga's dagger had snuffed out that spark, but the memories would linger forever.

"We are not the judges," said Dan, "but he will get what he is fairly due."

They waded for several minutes, each remarking on the careful and skilled crafting of the tunnel, which featured advanced shoring techniques to prevent collapse. As expected, the water became shallower, until it almost disappeared.

Dan suddenly stopped, neck craning as he looked up. "We should have reached the walls by now."

There was no way to know, of course—they hadn't brought marked string—and the tunnel continued on. They picked up the pace, which soon led them to a wall, the tunnel branching in opposite directions.

Dan swiveled his head several times, humming, then pointed. "That branch must go to the river. Follow it, but be careful. They may have the exit guarded, even now. I'll take the other branch."

Kai raised an eyebrow. "Why would they guard the exit? They're long gone."

Dan gave a slight shrug. "We don't know that all of them left. And if they wanted to get back into the city unseen, this would be a prime path."

It was a good point, sending a chill up Kai's spine. "They're regrouping already?"

Dan's frown took on a menacing aspect in the flickering flames of their lanterns. "We don't have any evidence of that yet, but we haven't found many leads to their whereabouts, either. Some may have passed beyond our borders, either up north or into Lamanite lands, but others might be hiding in plain sight, working in secret to undermine Helaman's government and destroy the Lord's church. Their goals haven't changed. And their master drives them ... relentlessly."

"Satan."

"Yes, and like frenzied beasts they heed his call."

Such a sobering, realistic assessment. "We can only be defeated if we weaken ourselves," observed Kai, remembering many of the lessons he had learned, some of them quite recent.

"Indeed," said Dan, "and we weaken ourselves by abandoning God and seeking happiness in selfish hedonism and the temptations of unchecked power. Gadianton's primary recruiting tools."

"Which don't work on you and your people. I wish we could all be more like you."

Dan scrunched his face in a way Kai hadn't seen before. "We're not immune, Kai. No one is—don't ever forget that. I'll meet you back here if you don't find an exit. If you do, head back to Helaman's house."

"After jumping in the river to get the stench off, I will." Kai chuckled, then turned to follow the branch heading toward the river. It angled slightly downward, and before long the water level began to rise again. Clean this time, thankfully. After leveling off for half a mile or so, the floor began to rise, gently at first, then more sharply. He slowed his pace, exercising the caution Dan had advised, trying not to slosh through the water, now only ankle deep.

He thought he detected a lightening ahead, so he extinguished his flame and paused to let his eyes adjust. Sure enough, faint glimmers of moonlight hovered in the distance, and after several more careful steps the water disappeared. Soon, muted sounds of the river greeted his ears, and nothing else. If anyone guarded the exit, they were silent … or asleep.

Several branches from a large bush obscured the angled opening. He moved them aside and found that the exit was not twenty yards from the top of a steep bank to the river. The orifice had narrowed considerably, so that he had to crawl out. When he was free, he paused again, then stood, observing the landscape around him as he listened intently. The moonlight brightened as clouds shifted, and he spotted a tiny boat, hidden among some rushes and tied to a tree root dipping into the water. The kind of boat Gadianton and his band had used, probably. They would have kept a number of them here. Had this one not been needed, or had someone used it to come back, as Dan suspected? From upriver or down? Upriver seemed more logical.

Either way, it was a great discovery. They could watch this place, day and night, and perhaps hook themselves a few fish.

Chapter I

*And now, my beloved brethren, after ye have gotten into this strait and
narrow path, I would ask if all is done? Behold, I say unto you, Nay;
for ye have not come thus far save it were by the word of Christ with
unshaken faith in him, relying wholly upon the merits of him
who is mighty to save. Wherefore, ye must press forward with a
steadfastness in Christ, having a perfect brightness of hope, and
a love of God and of all men. Wherefore, if ye shall press forward,
feasting upon the word of Christ, and endure to the end, behold,
thus saith the Father: Ye shall have eternal life.*
—2 Nephi 31:19–20

Siarah shivered, even though the summer night simmered with
warmth and humidity. She noted again how sore her feet were.
She and her government escort weren't more than twenty miles
from Bountiful, but they hadn't taken the smooth main roads.
And they zig-zagged … a lot.

"Are you sure we have to be this secretive? We *won* the battle with
the Lamanites—they're all gone—and Helaman is safe, too. The assassin
was, um, dispatched."

The tall, broad-shouldered man ahead of her stopped and turned,
crouching. She refused to follow suit, standing straighter instead.

"Helaman is safe for now, that is true. But Adonihah, your betrothed,
may not be. The game of spies is a dangerous one, and the battle is never
over."

She shivered again, thinking of her soon-to-be husband. Curiously,

Kai's fellow spy didn't seem to know his real name ... or maybe didn't want to let on that he knew it. She wasn't sure how to feel about that, though the man seemed earnest enough. He had treated her well, which made a difference given how completely out of her element she was. Lost and confused barely scratched the surface.

"Explain to me again why Captain Moronihah sent another spy to help me escape. Even if these 'bad people' you talk about know who I am, couldn't he have just sent a guard or two and let the chief captain of the city know?"

He blinked at her in the dimness. "You really have no experience with this, do you. Trust me. We'll get you to a safe place until the situation ... stabilizes."

"And ..." she almost said Kihoran's real name, "Adonihah will meet us there?"

The man who called himself Zoram nodded. "I don't know when, exactly, but yes. Helaman is being kept informed. All will be well."

That *did* make her feel better. If the prophet was involved, it had to be the right thing. Still, she sighed. "Fine. Lead on."

He gazed at her a moment longer before spinning back to his feet and pushing a tree branch away from his head as they continued along a narrow footpath. The woods were sparse here, but she felt almost claustrophobic.

"Have you met Helaman?" she asked in a voice well above a whisper.

His step hitched, but he kept moving. "No. I haven't even seen him before."

Something in his tone bothered her. "But you're a Christian, right?"

After a pause, he turned his head slightly. "No."

"Oh." Well, not all good people were Christians. And not all Christians were good people. Still, she couldn't help herself. "Why not?"

She detected a slight chuckle. "I tried it," came the faceless voice back to her, "and it was too much for me. Too harsh. Too ... constricting."

Harsh? Constricting? A lot of people said that ... and then constricted themselves with other things, mostly merciless vices. She felt sympathy for him. She hadn't seen him drunk yet, but they hadn't been inside a place that served anything strong. In fact, they hadn't been inside *any* place, not since Zoram had shown up at her house the day before with that strange letter, signed by Moronihah.

Another grudging sigh escaped. "Are we sleeping on the ground again?" She could handle it—any good Nephite woman could, especially a soldier's wife—but it wasn't her favorite type of adventure. It also grated on her, she realized, that she hadn't seen Kai in months, not since he had been scouting for Captain Lehi, whose armies had routed Coriantumr near Bountiful. Kai had never been good at sending letters, either.

"Yes," he admitted, "but we should reach Morianton in two days, maybe three, taking it slow and careful. I have plenty of rations, and we'll find all the water we need along the way."

"Why Morianton? You haven't explained that clearly."

He shrugged as he continued walking. "It's not a likely hiding place for good people like you … or Adonihah."

Again, his tone seemed a little off. Did Christians annoy him in some way? Instead of pursuing it, she remained silent, trudging along behind him, occasionally letting out a small gasp of pain to let him know how much her feet hurt. He ignored every last one of them.

——◆——

After two more nights of fitful sleep and a series of dry, tasteless meals, Zoram halted their progress at the edge of a stand of trees in the late afternoon. Before them lay a broad meadow and some low, forested hills. He pointed toward the tallest of the hills.

"Straight over that mount and just two miles beyond is Morianton."

She groaned in relief. She so looked forward to sleeping in a real bed.

"I need to ensure it's safe first," he added.

Her excitement dampened. "What does that entail?"

"We have a camp nearby, hidden from unwanted attention."

"Unwanted attention? And who is 'we'?"

He gave a sharp nod. "You'll see. Come on." With that he angled east along the tree line, moving too fast for her to continue the conversation; it was all she could do to keep up. After twenty minutes of that pace—and more than one new blister—they entered a campsite in a small clearing. Smoke wafted skyward from two campfires, most of it getting lost in the overhanging branches. But not all of it. Would it give away their location?

It dawned on her that her mind had volunteered that thought. She'd never had to notice such things before, though Nephite soldiers had. *Kai* had. She almost expected to see her betrothed sitting calmly at one of the fires, waiting for her. No such luck, though.

Zoram led her to a gangly man lounging on one elbow in the summer grass, far enough from the fires that the deepening shadows did a fair job of hiding his features.

"Inderum, this is Siarah, from Bountiful. We are on our way to Morianton, but I knew we should check in first. What have you heard and seen recently?"

The man looked her up and down, a process that took at least two seconds too long. She felt like a spider was crawling up her back.

"No change. We still haven't made contact with the right people. So we remain here." He didn't seem too upset about it.

Zoram turned to her, then lifted his hands, palms up. "I'm sorry. Everything is still very confused. Some people who tried to protect Helaman and prevent Kishkumen's foolish attack are being hunted by the government, while others who assisted Kishkumen are unwittingly viewed as allies."

"The lies are thick enough to cut with a dull sword," said Inderum in a lazy drawl, eyeing her indecently again. She would tell Kai about this man, and he would inform Captain Moronihah.

Zoram ignored him, still focused on Siarah. "Some of Helaman's men tried to attack us a few weeks back. We escaped, and nobody was hurt, but they wouldn't even listen to us. We had someone on the inside, in the building, the night Kishkumen tried to assassinate Helaman. We'd been tipped off, and our man was there to prevent it. He didn't end up seeing anything, but because his presence was noted by one of Helaman's servants, now Helaman suspects him … and anyone associated with him." His hands came up higher. "I get that he's concerned—I would be, too—but we should be united."

His tone was almost pleading, as if she could do something about it, which, of course, she couldn't. She knew the government was rife with factions, but she didn't understand them. Maybe they thought Kai could help, since he was close to Helaman.

"But Moronihah sent you," she said, "and he takes his orders from Helaman."

"Yes, but not all his captains take their orders from him. Gadianton succeeded in one thing—dividing us further."

That thought made her heart quail. More conflict. More pain. More death.

"Have you been able to locate Gadianton or any of his people?" she asked.

After a glance at Inderum, Zoram shook his head. "No, and we're not even sure Gadianton was behind it. He and Kishkumen may have split, with Kishkumen favoring … more violent paths toward change in the government."

This conversation was soon going to make her brain hurt, too. She didn't pay much attention to politics. Not that she couldn't; she just didn't want to. She worshipped God and led a simple life, and it was good. She knew marrying Kai and moving to Zarahemla would change her circles of activity, but she still hoped to keep things as simple as possible. Well, for being married to a national hero, his identity known by the Chief Judge and High Priest if no one else.

Inderum suddenly sat up, startling her. "Does your betrothed know anything that might help us?" he asked. The drawl had disappeared, his eyes flickering with intensity.

She slowly shook her head. She wasn't about to give strangers any details about what she knew. "No. He's still new, just a junior aide. When I see him, I will ask him, though."

Inderum was on his feet in an instant, causing her to step back with her arms tucked in close. The dirty man grabbed Zoram's arm and pulled him away. "A word with you," he muttered. They sidled toward one of the larger trees, much farther from the fire, leaving Siarah standing isolated in a camp of at least twenty men. Another new experience, and not one she ever would have chosen for herself.

The two whispered back and forth for at least five minutes. Finally, they came back, Inderum stalking like a hunting cat.

"Inderum is worried you're a spy," said Zoram.

"I'm a *what*?" she blurted in genuine surprise.

Zoram's eyebrows rose. "There *are* female spies, you know."

"Of course I know that." She didn't, actually. Well, until now. And she supposed it made sense. Her sheltered life continued to crumble around her. "But I'm not one of them. I mean, I just live with my parents. I don't go anywhere, and I don't talk with anyone interesting. You didn't know that already?"

Zoram shrugged. "I tried to explain it to him, but he makes a good point: I haven't personally known who you are for very long."

She tilted her head. "So maybe you caught me while I was ... *hibernating*?" She was proud of herself for coming up with that. An apt analogy to make these buffoons look silly.

"Well ..." he reached behind his head and scratched, then looked at Inderum. "That's not very likely, I know. But all of these men are rightly nervous." He swept an arm around the camp.

"And properly rude." She scowled at both men. "You'll just have to trust me, like I'm trusting you." Had she really just spoken so boldly? After marching for more than three days through the wilderness, she could forgive herself.

Her reprimand seemed to have gotten to Zoram, though Inderum remained unfazed. "You should go on into the city," he uttered after a tense few seconds. His tone had become neutral, which was worse than before. "We'll move the camp."

He might as well have slapped her in the face, and she almost reacted as if he had. Instead, she tightened her facial muscles and focused on Zoram. "Let's go now."

"Right now? Can't we wait until morning?"

She spared a glance at Inderum, who had folded his arms and was smiling smugly. "No, we can't. If you won't come with me, I can find my own way." She imagined Kai would be proud of her for saying it so forcefully.

"That just makes you look more like a spy," said Inderum with a trace of mockery.

That raised her hackles, but she forced them back down. After a loud "humph!" she added, "Fine, we can stay here tonight. But God is my witness that I've warned you not to touch me."

The mockery in his tone increased, sending another spider along her spine. "That's all right with me, princess. A bagful of venomous snakes would be more enticing."

She wanted to be incensed. She really did. But fear gurgled in her belly, spreading through her chest and then nearly strangling her. On instinct, she took Zoram's arm, turning them away from Inderum, who laughed. The cretin actually laughed!

"I'm sorry," said Zoram in a low voice as he led her away, toward a spot near the farther campfire. "I don't like him, either. He's effective, but definitely not pleasant."

She was tempted to ask what he could possibly be effective at, but she wasn't sure she could stomach the details. So she let Zoram lead on until he indicated a place they could set down their packs. She was grateful she hadn't packed much; but then, he had told her she didn't need to. He had promised she would soon be with Kai. That time couldn't come quickly enough.

---◇---

The morning arrived with impolite promptness, bringing with it more aches and pains. Her body protested as she stretched sore muscles. All the men in the camp were awake and moving about, and they weren't shy about bodily noises. They hadn't dug the latrine far enough away from the camp, either, and the direction of the light breeze wasn't kind. There were no women or children, but she hadn't expected to see any.

These weren't soldiers being moved on a permanent or semi-permanent basis to a new place. These were … well, she still wasn't sure what they were, despite Zoram's explanations.

At one of the fires—now mostly embers being used to warm their simple breakfast of corn meal and mutton—she sat as primly as she could on a stump, ignoring the many stares. Zoram sat on the ground next to her, chewing on a long stem of grass.

"Did you sleep well?" he asked after a long minute of gazing into the coals.

"Not really," she replied. She didn't tell him why, not with so many people watching them. How in the world did she get to be the lone woman in a camp full of stinky men? She couldn't prevent her nose from wrinkling at the notion, and her heart constricted again as she thought for the thousandth time about Kai's exact whereabouts. What was he doing at this moment? When would she get to see him? He would fix this. She knew he would.

"I kept watch," Zoram admitted in a near whisper.

She blinked, twisting her head to look down at him. "You stayed awake all night?"

He shrugged. "I've done it before. And," he rubbed his jaw, then the back of his neck, "we received some news during the night from one of our scouts."

One of their scouts? They were certainly acting like an army unit. She noted his tone, too. The news obviously wasn't good. She swallowed, then stared off into the woods, waiting patiently for him to deliver it.

"Some of Kishkumen's kin have been spotted in Morianton," he finally began. "They know of Adonihah and his connection to Helaman, and they want to talk to him."

"You mean torture him for information."

He raised an eyebrow but nodded. "Yes, probably. They know what he looks like, and we think one of them has seen you as well."

She shook her head in surprise. "What? How?"

He paused, not glancing up. "A little while back, you received a strange visitor at your house, did you not?"

18

The memory gave her chills. "Yes, but … how would you know that?"

He tossed the blade of grass away, then looked up. "We've been keeping watch for a while, suspecting you might be in danger. Your betrothed was receiving a great deal of scrutiny from the wrong people, though we weren't sure why."

An implied question hung in the rancid air, but she pretended not to have noticed. She wouldn't tell them *anything* about Kai, even if they claimed to have been sent by angels. Which, based on Inderum alone, clearly wasn't the case. Instead, she dropped her head, staring at her hands in her lap.

"So … what are you telling me? That we can't go to Morianton?"

"I'm not saying that," he replied. "But we have to be more careful. We need to go in disguise."

She jerked slightly. "Disguise? Like criminals?"

He gave a soft chuckle, plucking another long blade of grass and sticking it between his teeth. "No, but these are crazy times."

CHAPTER 2

And now I would that ye should be humble, and be submissive
and gentle; easy to be entreated; full of patience and long-suffering;
being temperate in all things; being diligent in keeping the
commandments of God at all times; asking for whatsoever things
ye stand in need, both spiritual and temporal; always returning
thanks unto God for whatsoever things ye do receive.
And see that ye have faith, hope, and charity, and then
ye will always abound in good works.
—Alma 7:23–24

Sword practice wasn't Kai's favorite activity, and the level of difficulty had quickly risen several notches under Dan's strict tutelage. The rest of Helaman's guards all knew now that Kai was more than an aide, so they didn't go easy on him. Swing, parry, dodge, feint, thrust. Dan told him he had natural ability, but Kai was much more comfortable with a bow, even on horseback—or with a dagger in tight spaces. He was also decent with sling and spear. Dan insisted he become proficient with the sword, though, so they practiced. Incessantly, in the large yard behind the house. Kai's hands, arms, and shoulders were definitely getting stronger.

He blocked a swing from another guard with his wooden practice sword, the impact reverberating up his arms. He pushed the man away, then feinted, anticipating a thrust, which indeed came. He thought about the tunnels he and Dan had found. Swords would be of limited use there; daggers and short clubs or spears would be required. They had presented their discovery to Helaman and some of the chief captains, and the search for tunnels had expanded—not just in Zarahemla, but in several of the larger cities, especially those known for their laxness in upholding the laws of Mosiah, which had their basis in God's laws.

He took a sword slap to his upper arm and grunted in pain and surprise. This was one reason he didn't like using a sword. He didn't seem to be able to exert the same focus with a long, unwieldy blade in his hands as he could with a bow—or just about any other weapon. He backed up a step, bracing himself for a strong reproof from Dan, who watched his trainees like a hawk. The former acolyte of Helaman the Elder also participated sometimes to keep up his own skill, which outmatched that of any soldier Kai had ever seen.

The criticism never came. Instead, Dan smiled as he approached. Was this a trick?

"A messenger just came to the house, Kai. Your family has arrived."

Kai let the tip of his practice sword drop to the dirt. "Finally! That's great news. And Siarah?"

Dan shrugged. "I presume so. The messenger didn't say. Helaman put them up at your favorite inn." He winked.

Jacob's Rest. He wasn't sure he could call it his favorite, but it had accrued many memories in a short period of time. "Thank you, Dan. I'll go get cleaned up."

Dan nodded. "Tell them 'hello' for me, though we haven't met. I'll step in for you."

As Kai handed him the practice sword, he heard a groan from his erstwhile sparring companion. The man would now be facing the master … and it would be painful.

———◆———

The venerable inn had taken some damage during the Lamanite occupation, but as far as Kai could tell, everything had been repaired, including the brown brick cladding the first of its three levels. The common room was grand again, the oak tables polished to a high sheen. The midday lunch crowd was numerous and noisy. With the most recent war over, and with political order reestablished, Zarahemla hummed with renewed commercial activity, and that meant great business for *Jacob's Rest*. Kai was surprised Helaman had been able to find rooms for his family and Siarah.

He approached an innkeeper at a desk, noting all the keyless hooks on the wall behind him. Before he could greet the man, though, he heard a squeal. Turning, he barely had time to brace before Neva launched herself at him, arms wide. It was hard to believe his little sister was eighteen. But even twenty years from now, she would probably greet him the same way. He hoped so. The former orphan siblings would always share a special bond.

"You look wonderful, Kai!" She squeezed hard, and he squeezed back before setting her on her feet. When she released him, he noted his parents, Gideon and Ishara, dodging a pair of servers as they approached, both beaming as they took him in. His emotions welled. It was so much better to see them here than he had anticipated.

Before he could greet them, Neva cast her first question. "So, when can we see Helaman's house? Oh, and the main market, and—"

"And the temple?" asked his mother, sliding between him and his sister to sneak in a hug.

Neva looked abashed for a moment. "Yes, the temple. Of course." Her eyes flitted around the room. "This is a big inn. You stayed here?"

Kai laughed. "Yes. A few different times. This whole city is much more, um ..."

"Frenetic?" supplied his father.

"Fun!" said Neva.

Ishara laughed. "Yes, it's different than Bountiful, that's for sure. But the Lord's church is headquartered here, and his prophet resides here. When Helaman has some spare time—I know he's very busy—we would love to meet him. Not that we have to, of course." She seemed to blush, and Gideon stepped in.

"It's enough to be here with you and Siarah," he said. "And we'll be able to see Helaman preach in person."

"Oh, he definitely wants to meet all of you," Kai reassured them. "So … where *is* Siarah?" His eyes scanned the area behind his family.

His mother laid her hand on his arm, and he noted her quizzical expression.

"She isn't here already?"

Kai glanced at his father and sister; they also seemed confused.

He shook his head. "No. I assumed she came with you."

"She didn't," said his father, eyes rounding. "We talked to her parents. She left before we did. We took our time, too, so she should easily have arrived first."

Concern spiked across Kai's shoulder blades, then twisted in his gut. "And you never passed her?"

They all shook their heads as Neva replied, "No, and we didn't hear anything along the way, either. You know, about any possible …" She glanced away.

Had Siarah suffered a mishap? Fell ill? He hadn't received a letter in more than two weeks, but he had assumed she was just focused on getting to Zarahemla, where they wouldn't have to write letters to each other. Or rather, her to him—he was still terrible at it. A familiar guilty feeling washed over him, overshadowed by a fresh fear that threatened to crack his calm, confident facade.

"I'm sure everything is all right," he said with a reassuring smile for Neva. "I can send messages to the cities and villages along the route. She may have taken ill and had to stop. We'll figure it out quickly."

Gideon nodded thoughtfully, eyebrows drawn down, and Ishara gave Kai a look colored with both empathy and amazement. "You really are an influential member of Helaman's household, aren't you? That is incredible. We're so proud of you, son."

In an attempt to avoid blushing, he laughed. "Too big for my britches is probably what I am. Helaman and Jerena have been very kind to me, and I don't deserve it."

"Yes, you do," said Gideon. "Trust me, the prophet knows what he's doing."

Leave it to his father to make an argument Kai couldn't refute. He cleared his throat, changing the topic, his voice still tight with concern for Siarah. "Where are your rooms?"

Neva answered. "Third floor, and we have a great view of most of the towers. The colors are amazing, especially on the thin, freestanding spires. I don't know how they made them."

Ishara patted her arm. "Neva has become much more curious about how things are constructed. We almost thought she was going to start working with designers of buildings and aqueducts and such, but then she decided to start making—"

"Don't say it!" Neva scolded. "I want to tell him. In fact, I'll show him. Find a place to sit, and I'll be right back." She raced away, darting between people as she headed for the east stairs. Kai watched her for a moment, then shrugged and turned, looking for an open table. He found one, and after they were seated one of the servers came by to see if they wanted anything to eat or drink. Kai remembered the menu, and he ordered for everyone, telling the young woman that Helaman would be footing the bill. She looked skeptical until he showed her the writ he carried with him, which Helaman had given him just the day before, to use for this very occasion. Then she appeared a little awestruck.

She hustled away as Neva returned, and Kai's eyes went wide.

"You made me a *bow*?"

Neva stood proudly before him, clutching the instrument to her chest with both hands. "Yes, working with the best bowmaker in Bountiful and using the latest techniques. It's not steel, but it's reinforced with metal at key points. The way the wood is shaped and strengthened … well, this bow shouldn't *ever* break if you take good care of it."

He studied her handiwork. It certainly looked impressive, and he noted it was just short enough to use from the saddle.

As if reading his mind, Neva added, "You can use it from a horse, and it's as powerful as a much longer bow. I promise. I'm not strong enough to unleash its full power, but you are." She seemed to notice his chest and shoulders, which had been growing. "I, um, didn't know aides spent so much time in physical training."

He couldn't avoid the blush this time, even though he knew his family was aware of his true role ... *and* what he had recently done to save the prophet's life. "Well, those old stripling warriors are taskmasters, that's for sure."

They knew about Dan, too, and his mother commented, "They aren't that old."

He shrugged. "I know. But with everything that has happened, the Great War seems much further in the past."

Gideon tugged at his chin. "That is true. And while it's good for the horrors to fade, we tend to forget the lessons, too. Which is why you had to come here in the first place."

That gave Kai pause. What if Kishkumen had failed to assassinate Pahoran the Younger? What if the Nephite government had remained strong and united? Kai would still be a scout and a spy in the army, based out of Bountiful. He would likely already be married to Siarah. They might even have a child. It was almost too surreal to contemplate. How and when had Zarahemla come to feel like his home? Was it because he had lost brothers here? Because he himself had almost perished on its walls? Because he had helped achieve a great victory in its retaking?

Their food and drinks arrived, brought by three different servers, each letting their gaze linger on Kai, obviously wondering at his connection to the nation's high priest.

"I think I need to go find Siarah," he said after the servers had left, causing his parents to freeze with forkfuls of food halfway to their mouths.

"Are you that worried?" asked his mother, setting her utensil on the plate. "The messages won't be enough?"

"Yes, I am."

"Then you should go."

"I'll have to clear it with Helaman first."

"Of course," said his father. "He will understand, though, I'm sure."

Kai's heel began tapping beneath the table, his whole body wanting to tremble. His concern for Siarah became a flood, and in the midst of the waters he saw a face.

Imrahiel's.

———◇———

"This indeed appears like it could be serious," said Helaman in solemn tones as Kai sat with him, Jerena, and Dan at their dining table. It was late, and the children were in bed. Dan hadn't gone home yet.

"Imrahiel is a very dangerous man," noted Dan as he cracked one of his knuckles. "And deeply evil. But you already know that."

Kai's mind had been stirring up haunting memories of interactions with Imrahiel for the last several hours. He'd made himself show his family a few of the Zarahemla sites, but they had finally prevailed upon him to go and prepare for his journey. He'd made those preparations while waiting for Helaman to return from the temple; today the relatively young Nephite leader had been mostly focused on his high priest duties, and those had kept him past dark, even on a long summer day.

"They had eyes and ears everywhere," said Kai, "so of course they learned about Siarah."

"They still do," said Dan, frowning. "The Gadiantons will know when you leave, and they'll try to follow you."

Helaman nodded gravely. "Most of the big players escaped. We've hampered much of their ability to remotely oversee activities here, but they can still cause problems."

Jerena took her husband's hand on the table. She certainly harbored deep concerns for Helaman's continued safety. Kai had killed the man who was likely the band's best assassin, but the wicked usurpers wouldn't give up. So frustrating. They were worse than the Lamanites and their high leader, King Tubaloth.

"I have Vyim. I can stay ahead of them, even while I search."

Helaman's brow rose. "He is indeed the finest specimen of horseflesh I have ever seen. Which begs the question of how the army ever got him. Have you asked Moronihah that question?"

Oddly, Kai hadn't, and he shook his head. It was beside the point anyway. He was just grateful to have Vyim now, and he would utilize the advantage.

"I'll walk him through the Mulek gates well before dawn. We can cross the Sidon farther upriver, then swing down to the main road. That should give us a good head start."

"A sound plan," agreed Dan, looking to Helaman, whose eyes had fixed on the empty chair opposite him.

After a few seconds, Helaman snapped his gaze back to Kai. "You will find her, but I cannot say how long it will take. Hasten straight to Bountiful with the Lord's blessing. Then send word back, and be patient."

When a prophet used a word like "hasten," Kai knew better than to take it lightly. He already felt the urgency, but Helaman's pronouncement enhanced it while also lending it more credence.

———◇———

He departed earlier than intended, just an hour after midnight, thankful for a strong moon unmarred by heavy clouds. He led Vyim through the gates, and for nearly half a mile afterward, then mounted and urged him to a gallop. The cool air rushing past his face both refreshed him and boosted his confidence. He was moving, doing something instead of waiting, and Helaman had given him his blessing.

The fording went smoothly, and it was light enough that they could move quickly along minor roads and paths. When they reached the main road east, he walked Vyim for a bit, then let him alternate amongst canter, walk, and gallop. Kai sensed the proud stallion's excitement for the journey, and he wondered if Vyim understood something of the intensity behind it. If the Spirit could influence humans, it could touch animals, too, right? He made a note to speak with Helaman on the subject.

By daybreak he was more than fifty miles from Zarahemla, and no Gadianton spies would know for sure that he had left the city's environs for at least half a day. Comfortable in that knowledge, he stopped at a way station and let Vyim rest, grabbing a few minutes of shuteye for himself as well. He already felt fully back in scout mode, moving at whatever time of day or night, grabbing sleep when he could, eating when necessary.

He moderated Vyim's pace, but they traveled well into the dark hours each day, rising early to begin anew. In that manner they swiftly swallowed the miles eastward to Bountiful, even while making multiple stops to ask questions of innkeepers, farmers, and traders. As each sunset passed, Kai became more concerned. It seemed as if Siarah had never traveled this way at all, and she didn't have any reason not to find passage along the main roads—another of Helaman's aides had even made the arrangements! If she hadn't, and she wasn't still in Bountiful … all remaining paths led to something bad.

When they finally approached Bountiful, early in the evening a week later, the city seemed less welcoming to Kai than it had on all his other returns. He entered through the western gates, then aimed Vyim straight for the house of Siarah's parents, Thandrum and Dinah. A Gadianton spy might be watching the house, but Bountiful was a safer place. If they weren't home, Kai would go straight to Captain Orihon. And if by some happy circumstance Siarah was with her parents—perhaps a brief illness had forced her to turn back?—well, Vyim had already shown he could carry two people long distances. They would be in Zarahemla before the Gadiantons could organize a response. He also had money to help Thandrum and Dinah relocate, if they so chose.

Dismounting in front of their house felt both foreign and familiar. How many times had he passed through that front door? After a couple of pats on the neck for Vyim, he stepped up and knocked. Given the time of day, the couple should be home. He hoped they were. Light peeked through the windows. He waited a few seconds, then knocked again, resisting the temptation to check around back.

He heard some shuffling noises from inside, and then the door cracked open, revealing Thandrum's face. His eyebrows angled as he stared a Kai a moment, and then he swung the door wide.

"Kihoran, what are you doing in Bountiful?"

It was exactly the question he had hoped *not* to hear. He had thought through several possible responses, but he kept coming back to the simplest and most direct. "Siarah didn't arrive in Zarahemla, so I'm trying to find her."

"She didn't?" Dinah had appeared by her husband's side. Their eyes became moons. "But she left weeks ago."

"Did she leave alone?" he asked.

Dinah shook her head. "No. A young man sent by Helaman came to escort her, explaining that the plan had changed and she would no longer be traveling with your family. Did ... did *they* arrive?"

The icy knot in Kai's stomach extended tendrils up into his brain, delaying his response. "They did, a little more than a week ago."

Thandrum squinted. "Are you saying you made the trip from Zarahemla to Bountiful in a *week*?"

He gave a tight smile. "I have a very fast horse. But I talked to a lot of people along the way. Nobody saw Siarah pass through. I'm worried."

"As are we," said Thandrum. "Please, come in and tell us whatever you can."

"This all seems so strange," said Dinah breathlessly, tears streaking down her cheeks. "I can't believe she didn't get there before your parents. What could have happened?"

"That's what I'm going to find out. I—" He wanted to say something reassuring, but he couldn't come up with anything. Dinah's lower lip began trembling, and Thandrum motioned Kai to a seat in the front room while placing an arm around his wife's shoulders.

The ensuing discussion was fruitless ... and exhausting. With each passing minute, Dinah became more distraught. After a while, Thandrum began to lose control as well. Fortunately, they were ultimately able to calm each other, at least to a degree. Kai finally extricated himself with more promises that he would figure out what was happening, even if he had to reach out to Captain Moronihah, who was due to visit Bountiful before wending his way back to Zarahemla. Or maybe General Lehi.

———◇———

After a restless night in the city's barracks, Kai found himself welcomed into Orihon's office the next morning. The man treated him as if he were an old friend. Kai's orbit had definitely changed.

"Kihoran, welcome. Please sit. You look like you've been traveling hard."

Kai winced at that truth as he lowered himself into a chair. "I have. I'm worried about my betrothed, so I made best speed. Helaman arranged for Siarah to travel to Zarahemla, but she ... has gone missing." He had chosen words and tone for dramatic effect, and it worked.

Orihon scrunched his brow as he popped up out of his seat. "Do you have any idea where she went missing?"

"No, not yet. She left her house about a month ago. That's all I know. Helaman allowed me to come investigate." He clenched his jaw, feeling determination like a well-forged spearhead, still hot from the fire.

Orihon placed his fists on the table, leaning over them. "Helaman has sent messengers?"

"Yes."

"But you beat them here."

Kai nodded.

"All right. I don't have many men to spare at the moment because of the new directive from Captain Moronihah to construct additional fortifications and increase our training regimen, but I'll arrange for some scouts to go out in all directions."

"Send them in pairs," said Kai.

Orihon blinked but then nodded. "A wise precaution, I agree, though it will slow the search."

Kai almost retracted the suggestion, but Imrahiel's face reasserted itself, searing his mind. This was *not* a routine, peacetime scouting objective. Perhaps a lone scout might find Siarah more quickly, but it did them no good if that scout ended up dead. "I know."

"Why your betrothed? Kidnapping is a serious crime."

"Because she's connected to me, and I'm connected to Helaman. I was also in the building the night the Gadianton assassin was killed. Somehow they know that."

Orihon gave a knowing nod. "The walls have ears, especially in the Hall of Judgment."

"Here in Bountiful, too, it seems."

"That is a sobering thought," agreed Orihon, lifting his fists off the table and straightening, "but not unsurprising. Gadianton's cancer has spread throughout the country. It's as if we've learned nothing from Ammonihah, or Amalickiah and the Great War."

He was right, and Kai wanted to shout his frustration to the heavens, right there in Orihon's office, decorum be damned.

———◆———

He went to Merga and Orofin's shop next. He didn't need a new cloak this time, but he wanted to make sure they had received the money from the sale of the dagger. And perhaps they had overheard something in the course of their business.

It turned out they had already left. The new owner, a middle-aged woman who wore a bright red apron, said he had missed them by only a few days. He knew they had been waiting for that money before emigrating north, but they had acted quickly. Is that where Gadianton, Imrahiel, and the other conspirators had gone?

As he rode the streets of his former home, he evaluated options. Should he journey north alone? He didn't have Helaman's permission, but he could send a letter. What would the prophet and Dan think about that? And what good would it do? He didn't have a lead, not even a faint one. Try as he might to obtain some sort of specific direction from the Lord regarding Siarah's whereabouts, none seemed forthcoming. Or rather, he probably wasn't smart enough or strong enough to interpret it. That raised his level of aggravation further.

He finally decided that with Captain Orihon doing all he could, his best option was to return to Zarahemla and marshal additional resources, again at best speed, depending on how Vyim held up. No horse had endless endurance.

Neither, it was clear, did his faith.

CHAPTER 3

And now, I, Moroni, would speak somewhat concerning these things;
I would show unto the world that faith is things which are hoped for
and not seen; wherefore, dispute not because ye see not,
for ye receive no witness until after the trial of your faith.
—Ether 12:6

Siarah had no idea how she was holding it together. Or maybe she wasn't. How had a month passed? A *month*! She'd already broken down twice that morning, and Zoram was avoiding her. After trying to travel to Morianton, they had apparently been chased by Gadiantons, though she hadn't actually seen any of them. They'd taken refuge in a village to the east, with Zoram leaving on scouting missions day after day, always bringing back bad news.

The villagers were kind, but it wasn't a thriving place. She had begun to wish they were back in that silly camp of cretins—an insane thought driven only by the fact that it lay in the direction of Zarahemla ... and Kai. Thankfully, they were again on their way to Morianton—and some semblance of civilization. She had to remind herself that Morianton was *not* one of the more spiritually enlightened cities of the Nephite realm—was, in fact, better known for specious land disputes with neighboring Lehi. At several points they had actually tried to assert their claims by force of arms. What kind of people—besides hardened Lamanites and fanatical, delusional Nephite dissenters—did that sort of thing?

"Are you all right?" asked Zoram, causing her to yelp as he popped out of the trees near their resting place, supposedly two or three miles from the city. He added, "Remember, crying will damage your disguise."

Their stupid disguises. She sniffled as she nodded. "I'm fine. This isn't much of a disguise anyway."

"It's enough," he replied. "A few well-placed grease marks on your face make more difference than you might think, especially to people who don't interact with you on a daily basis. And we didn't dye your hair because they would expect that."

The infamous 'they.' He had explained all this before. He must think she was a child. Truth be told, she was acting like one, which admission brought her to the verge of another breakdown.

They started trudging along again, following a minor path used by some of the local farmers. It meandered like a lost sheep, making the journey tedious. She took a deep breath, said a silent prayer, and felt a tiny bit better. Then she sighed. "Who is this person you're supposed to meet again?"

"Zemnari. He can help us. He has many contacts in the city, including in the government."

"And what about the Church?"

He turned and cast her a slight scowl. "There are few members of your church in Morianton, and Zemnari isn't one of them. He is a good man, though."

"I wouldn't assume he isn't, so quit acting so annoyed." It felt good to let some irritation spark. She reminded herself again how wonderful things would be when she was reunited with Kai. And they were married. And she could meet the prophet and his wife. They would have a nice home in Zarahemla, in a quiet neighborhood where their children would make many friends. "People in 'my' church know things, too."

She stomped ahead of him, feeling her well of tears dry up. No more emotional breakdowns. They needed to get to the city, where she would find some answers.

He caught up too quickly. "I know they do," he said, barely breathing hard, "but they aren't perfect."

She spun and glared, nearly tripping over a root. After catching herself, she replied, "Of course we're not perfect. We don't claim to be.

Whoever thinks we do is an overripe melon."

He remained silent for several paces, then surprised her with a question. "Don't you think it would be good to have a king? To bring more order and justice?"

She wanted to turn her head again, but remained focused on her footfalls. "No, I don't. That's what got our ancestors into so much trouble. Samuel the prophet warned the people of Israel against it, but they persisted, like spoiled children." She had meant that to sound harsh.

It didn't seem to faze him, though. "That was a very long time ago, and in a distant land."

"So? People are still the same. We haven't magically changed into better creatures over the years, or by living in a different place."

"A good king can accomplish great things," he persisted. "Israel reached the height of her power under David and Solomon."

"And the inevitable bad kings who followed led the Israelites into one ruinous disaster after another. By the way, how were successors normally chosen? Direct line of descent. That's a terrible way to choose a king."

"You do that with high priests," he challenged. "Helaman is the son of Helaman, who was the son of Alma, son of Alma."

"True," she conceded, "but that isn't always the case. Alma the Elder's father wasn't a high priest, and hardly anybody even remembers his name. Mosiah could have remained the high priest but didn't. And we don't assume that one of Helaman's sons will be the high priest after him. The Lord will choose, and if his sons turn out like … well, Eli's … then *none* of them will be chosen."

"So you say." Silence returned, but only briefly. "It could be a member of your church."

"A king?"

"Yes. Or a queen. Unless your god is opposed to women leaders."

She stopped again and fixed him with a stare. "You don't have to pander to me. He's not. Priesthood administration is assigned to men, but the women are just as important in leading."

He folded his arms across his chest, puffing it out a bit. "That doesn't make sense to me."

She responded with hands on hips. "Well, the rest of our society treats women worse, so I'm happy where I am."

His eyes narrowed. "So you agree your church treats you as less than equal?"

She shook her head in exasperation. "No, I don't. And the Lord certainly doesn't treat women as less than men. Do *you*?" She squinted tighter than he had, her accusation slicing the air between them.

He sloughed it off, which was maddening. "You don't know me well enough yet."

"Yes, which is why I'm starting to not trust you."

Somehow, *that* seemed to get to him. A muscle in his face twitched, his eyes widening slightly. "You *can* trust me. I swear it."

"With what? Will you show me the message you're planning to deliver in Morianton?"

Redness rose along the sides of his neck. "I can't. I'm sorry." He swallowed as his eyes darted around, finally resting on her again. "But what about your betrothed? Has he shared all his secrets with you?"

She puckered her brow. "We haven't seen each other for a long time. But I know the important parts."

"Does he write often to you?"

That hurt. "No, he doesn't have much time. And he's often in danger."

"Hmmm." That non-syllabic response struck deeper than a real knife, but he didn't press it all the way home. Instead, he began walking again, faster, his long strides testing her to keep pace. He didn't seem angry, but he certainly wasn't jovial—not that he generally was anyway. And she couldn't have cared less.

——◇——

"We're here," Zoram announced as they paused a quarter mile from one of Morianton's gates. The main road lay just a hundred yards away.

"I can see that."

"Remember your new name?"

"Of course I do. Zarell." She almost rolled her eyes, as she had when

36

he'd first told her to use the false moniker. "And yours is Teancum."

"Yes. He was very brave, right? People look at me differently when I use that name."

"Zoram was very brave, too."

"The original one? I suppose so. A little naïve, though. Not that I don't like my name, but there have been many Zorams. Not many Teancums."

Why they were bandying about names, she had no idea. She most favored the name Kihoran for a man, of course, but she wasn't going to appear needy bringing *that* up. A gust of wind swirled around them as she pointed toward the city. "Where do we go first?"

"A spice maker's shop, near the main market. The woman there will know where we can find Zemnari."

She gave him a puzzled look. "We can't go straight to him?"

He shrugged. "He is a busy man and moves all over the city."

"And she keeps his schedule?"

"Yes. Well, sort of."

She blinked, then quirked an eyebrow. He ignored the implied skepticism as he motioned her forward, adopting that unfairly fast walk. She lifted her skirts as she hustled to catch him.

"Slow down," she demanded, sure he would ignore the request. Oddly, he complied, and she was able to walk beside him. Ah, that was it. He wanted them to look like a normal … couple? She nearly rolled her eyes again. All the skullduggery was—in a base sort of way—enticing to think about, bringing a rush once in a while. But mostly it was tiresome and dull. And too often pointless. How could Kai stand it?

They nodded to the lone man—a child, really—who watched the gate with a lazy expression. He wasn't even armed, unless the spindly stick he tapped against the ground counted. Zoram turned left at the first intersection as Siarah noted the general lack of upkeep in the city. Clearly, the garbage wagons didn't run often enough and the sewers weren't well maintained—both smell and sight bore witness. That matched her vision of the city from various tales she had heard, though the spice maker's shop they entered after two more turnings did not. It was immaculate and tastefully decorated, rivaling the best Bountiful had to offer.

The woman, introduced to her as Lita, matched the space. Her clothing was some of the finest Siarah had ever seen, fashioned mostly of multiple colors of silk. Very expensive, the stitchwork top-notch, probably even better than Siarah's own. Her hair, too, impressed, structured in layers with thin ribbons and fine silver chains. It had been dyed recently, the sheen of the root-based tincture unmistakable. She was trying to look mid-thirties but was probably past fifty.

Siarah gave a small bow after Lita rose, not knowing how much deference she should show. Some, at least—these were people trying to help her get back to Kai. And standing in a civilized room again seemed to have altered her mindset, calming her frayed nerves.

She realized with sudden fright how terribly out of place she must appear. Glancing down at her wrinkled dress, bearing the obvious stains of travel, she nearly winced.

"You have a fine shop," she said in a soft voice.

Lita smiled as she resumed her seat, which occupied the prime spot in an open corner at the back of the shop. No customers were present at the moment, and the lone attendant had retreated to the storeroom at a signal from Lita.

"Please, sit, both of you. I'm fascinated to hear your story."

"We're here to—" began Zoram, but Lita raised a hand to stop him. She nodded toward a chair, and he dipped his chin before sitting. Siarah took one of the remaining two seats, eyes catching on the opulent circular rug placed beneath the setting.

Lita pinned Siarah with a friendly but somehow disconcerting gaze. "You are Siarah, is that correct?"

Siarah's eyes widened, and she barely resisted glancing at Zoram. Why should she be surprised, though? These people were well beyond her abilities. She nodded. "Yes, ma'am."

A smile tugged at the corners of Lita's thin lips, lightly colored with a glossy pigment. "And you are betrothed to a man named ... Adonihah?"

Hesitantly, she nodded.

"That is not his real name, though," Lita added. "How long have you known Kihoran?"

She couldn't resist glancing at Zoram this time, noting his surprise; so, he really *hadn't* known. "All my life. Or, well, since he came to live with Gideon and Ishara."

Lita nodded knowingly. "Yes. He and his sister were orphans, I understand. That nasty business with the king men." Siarah wasn't sure if the disgust coating the woman's tone applied to the king men themselves or to what had happened to them. Fierce debates still broke out occasionally regarding whether their treatment had been too harsh. She'd never asked Kai his opinion, presuming he opposed the punishment, since it had made him and Neva orphans. But did he? He revered Captain Moroni, and he had great respect for his son Moronihah, too.

Siarah offered a weak nod, and Lita turned to Zoram.

"Are you calling yourself Teancum again?"

His cheeks reddened as he nodded. "Yes. It's a well-respected name."

"Not so much here."

"True," he conceded, "but not as bad as Lehi."

Her tone grew more serious. "You are looking for Zemnari?"

"Yes. I need to deliver a message from … the men trying to clear their names."

She flicked a finger toward Siarah. "And you escorted her here why?"

"To keep her safe, of course."

"Of course. Your destination is Zarahemla, I presume."

"Yes." His brow furrowed, as if he suspected some trick from her. Who *was* this woman? So strong. So in control. Siarah caught herself admiring her. Maybe she could become strong, like Lita. Kai would like that. Or he would learn to.

Suddenly, Lita focused on Siarah again, sitting straighter in her chair. "How well do you know this Kihoran? I mean, who he is *now*, not who he was as a boy."

"I …" she stuttered "I'm not sure what you mean. He's a good man, a hard worker. He has a good reputation with the Merchant Guild."

"He's no merchant, or rather, merchant scout."

"What?" She tried to appear perplexed but doubted she had pulled it off. Lita's next words confirmed it didn't matter, and she should have just assumed that. She was looking more foolish by the second in front of this impressive woman.

"He was a spy and a scout for Moronihah's army for several years," said Lita. "And now he's in the service of Helaman, who has a very large target on his back. Your betrothed is inviting you into a dangerous life."

She swallowed, but only because of Lita's penetrating stare. She had already thought all of that through, and it didn't matter. She loved Kai. She would stand by him. And God would protect them. He would.

"He is a good man," Siarah repeated, maintaining eye contact with Lita until the heat became too much and she looked down at her hands, resting meekly in her lap.

"Hmmm," mused Lita. "That may be. But I advise you to be careful."

An uncomfortable silence ensued until Zoram spoke again. "Helaman bears watching, too. He is too young to be the Chief Judge. The politics of Zarahemla will either corrupt him or tear him apart."

Siarah cast a hard frown at him. He returned it, then addressed Lita. "He seems to feel entitled. That is dangerous. But … I am loyal."

Why did he feel the need to say that? Because of her, or because of Lita? Confusion addled Siarah's thoughts as Lita made a vague comment about the value of his loyalty. Then she screwed up her courage and lifted her chin toward the woman.

"I need to get a message to Kihoran, and quickly. You obviously have the means to make that happen."

Lita raised an eyebrow, then gave a slight nod. "I can. He has been expecting you. He must be worried. Though perhaps not as much as you think. We have already sent some reassurances that you are safe and that the situation is … resolving itself."

That sounded at least somewhat satisfactory, and she nodded, lowering her eyes again. Lita's next words were directed at Zoram.

"You need to lie low for a bit. I've already arranged a place for you to stay, with an older couple, on the outskirts of the city. Zemnari will come to you, and you can pass along your message to him. But first, you will let me see it."

Zoram frowned. "Those weren't my instructions."

"They are now." Her expression brooked no argument, but Siarah suspected Zoram would refuse. Slowly, though, his resistance melted, and he finally grumbled, reaching into a pocket Siarah wouldn't have thought was there. He handed Lita a folded parchment, which she received with a flourish. She unfolded it, then spent the next minute reading, eyes moving rapidly over what must have been tiny script.

"Curious," she said, then handed the message back. "Zemnari definitely needs to see this. The prophet is clearly in more danger than he realizes." Suddenly, she rose. "I have somewhere to be now, but my assistant will tell you where you need to go. Be careful. Morianton is a dangerous pool in which to swim." With that she was gone, leaving Siarah feeling mentally and emotionally exhausted.

Zoram's next grumble turned into a growl, and then he rose, too. "Let's go find that assistant. I'm not waiting for her to come out of the storeroom." Siarah felt a thrill of pleasure that Zoram was so unhappy—and that a woman had made him so. Lita made her uncomfortable, too, but she couldn't be all bad.

After getting directions, they left the shop, and the first thing Siarah noticed was a pair of mounted soldiers trotting their horses down the street. She instantly thought of Kai, her heart constricting as she studied their faces in the vain and silly hope that one of them might actually *be* him. Zoram seemed annoyed they had to wait to let the soldiers pass; or perhaps his mood had carried over from inside Lita's shop.

Siarah watched the soldiers' backs forlornly until Zoram broke her out of the trance by tugging on her elbow. She twitched and followed, sensing a numbness expanding from her chest. Everything seemed peaceful here. Why, then, was she not yet with Kai? She couldn't be in *that* much danger, despite his prime role in dispatching Kishkumen the assassin.

"I'm coming back here to give Lita a letter to send to Helaman," she stated, "so he can get it to Kihoran."

She expected Zoram to respond with, "That wouldn't be wise," or, "We have to be careful," but he just grunted as he led them to the first intersection. She determined to write the letter that night, then return in the morning, whether he liked it or not. And if he tried to stop her, she would scream at the top of her lungs that she was being held hostage. Even the people of Morianton would respond to that sort of plea, wouldn't they? Doubts gnawed at her brain, but she still resolved to see it through.

It took nearly twenty minutes to reach the old couple's home, which sat so near the city's main defensive wall that she could make out tiny cracks in the stone near the wall's base. The fortification was nothing like Bountiful's—or Zarahemla's, surely. Bountiful's walls were made entirely of stone, while this one was stone and wood, and even piled earth in some places below the wood. Its haphazard construction and slovenly appearance matched the city and its people, she decided. And who would want to invade Morianton anyway?

Her mood had hardened considerably by the time Zoram reached up and rapped on the door, stepping back and clasping his hands in a slightly peculiar way, as if he were preparing to give someone a boost over a hedge or a fence. In a few seconds the door opened, and a hard-eyed older man with unruly wisps of white hair and a pronounced hunch showed his face, the interior behind him dim. His eyes flicked down to Zoram's hands, and then he studied Siarah, eyes moving up and down, almost leering. She wasn't sure which urge came stronger—to run away or to punch him in his crooked nose.

"Lita sent us," said Zoram in a low voice, the tense silence that followed presenting Siarah with another choice—roll her eyes, or ... well, run again.

"Very well." The man's face disappeared, and the door opened wider, though only enough to let them squeeze inside. The man shut it firmly. "Come to the back," he said.

The running option grew more attractive every second, until they passed through a pair of floor-length curtains into a much brighter space comprising the kitchen and some storage. The woman of the house stood with her hands cupped just as Zoram's had been, and she was the spitting image of Kai's mother. Except for the jagged scar running from chin to cheekbone.

This time Siarah didn't seem to have a choice. She burst out in tears, flopping her face into her hands, sobbing uncontrollably for at least ten seconds. The dam had broken. This was too much. She couldn't do it. What in the world was happening?

She heard shuffling, though nobody said anything; she had clearly caught them all off guard, even Zoram. Finally, it was the woman who spoke, but while she looked like Kai's mother, her voice held none of Ishara's soothing kindness.

"You'd better pull it together, girl. Your future husband would not be impressed."

What an awful woman. Siarah calmed herself a little, took a deep breath, straightened, and refused to look at the harsh mistress. Instead, she glared at Zoram. She caught a glimmer of reaction in his face—guilt maybe, finally—but then it was gone.

Chapter 4

And it came to pass that I, Nephi, said unto my father:
I will go and do the things which the Lord hath commanded,
for I know that the Lord giveth no commandments unto
the children of men, save he shall prepare a way for them
that they may accomplish the thing which he commandeth them.
—1 Nephi 3:7

"This stew is delicious, Jerena." Kai didn't dare say more—his parents were sitting at the table in Helaman and Jerena's home, and his mother made a very fine stew, of which she was rightly proud.

Jerena laughed, as did one of their daughters. "Not as good as your mother's, I'd bet."

He didn't know how to respond to that, just scooped in another mouthful. That wasn't the only reason to focus on his eating, of course. No news had arrived yet concerning Siarah. The cooler months were almost upon them, and it was as if she had dropped off the face of the earth. Nothing had come from any of the messengers—not even the officers Helaman had sent across the country. Nothing from Captain Orihon in Bountiful, either. Kai continued trying to pray about it, but what more could he ask? He didn't feel comforted, and he wasn't getting any clear answers. That made him irritable on his best days. He was happy his parents were here, and Neva had taken to Zarahemla like a foal to its mother's teat, but he wasn't complete. Not without Siarah. Was she dead? He had begun to seriously entertain the possibility.

Dan had made attempts to counsel him, along with Helaman, his father, and one of the other priests, but none of it really helped. Kai had saved Helaman's life, and the Lord had helped him do it. Was he being abandoned now? Was his usefulness at an end?

Helaman cleared his throat, causing Kai's eyes to meet the high priest's intense but somehow gentle stare. After a long second, Helaman took a deep breath and spoke.

"I will not keep you here, Kihoran. Try as I might, my soldiers and spies have been unable to locate your betrothed. *You* can find her, though. Perhaps that is what the Lord intends."

Kai had no idea if the Lord intended such a thing, but his heart promptly thrummed with energy. He would much rather be doing *something* than nothing. In fact, he was ready to leave that instant. If failure awaited him, so be it.

"I've asked Dan to accompany you," Helaman added.

Kai straightened in his chair. "Don't you need him here? And what about his family? He shouldn't be away from them on my account."

Helaman shared a brief look with Jerena. "He made the suggestion himself. He feels it strongly. And those stripling sons of my father are hard to argue with." A small smile emphasized the truth of that statement, and Kai's heart leaped with joy. He always felt better with Dan around.

"Do you ..." Kai began hesitantly, thinking back to particular moments in Nephite military history that probably didn't apply to him, "know where we should start?" He glanced away, then looked at his parents, feeling embarrassed for having to ask Helaman, especially in front of them. Neva gave him a vigorous nod, though.

"Lehi," said Helaman with confidence, and Kai's eyes snapped back to him as his eyebrows rose, then scrunched.

"General Lehi, or the city?"

"The city."

"Why there?" Again he felt ashamed. Did it look like he was openly doubting the prophet? His face warmed.

"It is a good starting place," came the reply, and Helaman reached over to grasp Jerena's hand. "But eat your stew first. It has magical properties."

Kai's jaw nearly dropped at the deadpanned, seemingly blasphemous joke, and he stole a peek at his mother to see how surprised she was. Instead, she beamed at the prophet. She wasn't starry-eyed, either, not that Kai would have expected it. She was too steady, too grounded.

"I've only seen Lehi once," said Gideon. "What a magnificent city. So creatively unique in its design. And the waterworks, they are a wonder."

"Indeed, they are," agreed Helaman as Kai brought up images of his only visit to the city. It seemed an eternity ago. He had been a merchant scout then, and much less of a spy than he had presumed. But the connection he had stumbled upon there had changed his life. For the better? He wasn't sure now.

He coughed, appetite evaporating. He knew he would have to finish every last drop of the stew in his bowl, though, with his mother watching. "Can we leave tomorrow morning?" he ventured.

"Yes," replied Helaman. "Dan knows I was planning to tell you tonight, and he says he is ready."

"That is ... wonderful. Thank you, Prophet."

Helaman's smile filled his face, including his eyes. "You are most welcome, Brother Kihoran."

———◆———

Dan arrived at the house before Kai woke up, which earned Kai a good ribbing from one of the other guards. Perhaps he should have accepted his mother's invitation to stay with them, at least for a night. Fortunately, he had packed before turning in, so he was ready quickly. But when he set foot outside he found that Dan had already done all the work preparing the horses.

"I'm sorry," he said. "I should have woken earlier. I could at least have saddled Vyim."

Dan chuckled as he shook his head. "Don't worry about it. For some reason, I'm as excited as you to begin this trip, and it's not because Zarahemla isn't my favorite Nephite city."

Kai nodded, taking Vyim's reins from his faithful, battle-scarred friend. His confidence surged as he recalled all the miracles which had attended Dan and his brothers in battle after battle. How could he fail if Dan, who had a *real* connection with the Lord, was with him?

They mounted, then endured a brief chiding from a robe-draped Jerena for attempting to skip breakfast, which she brought out to them in two small sacks. Dan seemed appropriately chastened, while Kai, in his rare ebullient mood, found it amusing. He didn't let a smile slip, though. He wasn't that foolish. Jerena didn't worry him, but his mother would find out.

Through the gate they passed, saluting their fellow guards, then along the peaceful, ornate streets of the Santorem, the richest district in Zarahemla—and probably in the entire land. Few people were up and about, and Kai hoped it remained that way until they reached the Grand Gates in the eastern wall. He conducted another mental checklist as Vyim pranced along, the magnificent steed obviously happy to be doing something different again. Kai and Dan carried bows, swords, and daggers, along with spears strapped in vertical casings behind their saddles. Kai's pack and saddlebags contained three changes of clothes, extra boots, rations, water, tinderbox, fishing hooks and cord, a wound kit, plus plenty of funds. Dan carried much the same, though his saddle bags didn't bulge as much. Kai determined not to let him know how many garment changes he'd brought, knowing what Siarah would expect. He was becoming positively domesticated, and he wasn't even married yet!

After exiting the city, Kai let Vyim loose for a stretch. It felt good to feel the powerful horseflesh beneath him galloping with such joy. As those short minutes passed, however, his elation at the beginning of the journey began to evaporate. Worry crept in, taking firm hold. It would be a long, multi-day ride to Lehi, and how would he know what to do when they got there? Dan was definitely good at listening to the Spirit, but Kai wasn't, and this was Kai's mission, his responsibility. Could the Lord tell him how to proceed in a way he would recognize?

When he slowed Vyim to a walk, Dan and his sturdy horse caught up. He seemed to sense Kai's quandary.

"Patience, my friend. And faith."

Normally, Kai would have accepted such advice from Dan with humble gratitude. But frustration bubbled up again. "Gadianton has her. Or at least Imrahiel. I can't imagine what they're doing to her."

Actually, he could, and it sent shivers of rage from the top of his head to the soles of his boots. He wore military-grade boots, and he imagined one of them crushing Imrahiel's face in all its arrogant malice, blackening those piercing, condescending eyes.

"Likely true," said Dan, "but the Lord has proven often enough that what looks impossible to us is easily achievable by him. I truly believe he wants us to find Siarah, Kai. I wanted you to know how strongly I feel that. Not even Laban and his tens of thousands could stop us."

Kai was almost too ashamed to look at his wise, steady friend, but he finally did after his nerves had calmed. "Thank you, Dan. I trust you—a lot more than I trust myself."

Dan gazed stoically at him for a moment, then replied, "And I trust you, Kihoran. You are better than you give yourself credit for. I know how frustrated you are. Truly, I do."

Kai would never think to challenge Dan on such a sentiment, though he still struggled to believe it. He focused anew on how fortunate he was to have Dan with him, and that helped his mood a little. Besides Helaman, and maybe Moronihah, nobody else on the face of the entire land occupied by the Nephites and Lamanites could successfully help him find Siarah. Alive and well, the Lord willing.

——◇——

They would have traveled faster if Dan's horse could have kept up. Kai was careful not to let impatience show, however. Instead, he took care not to push them too hard, reasoning that if they needed to chase Gadiantons on horseback, they would both have relatively fresh mounts. He created numerous scenarios in his mind, and not just of pursuing the enemy on horses. Perhaps they would catch them hiding in the woods, in a house, in a shop, or even in a synagogue. Fear would flood Imrahiel's features as the mighty stripling warrior and Helaman's infuriated servant unleashed the very wrath of God upon him and his henchmen. Gadianton they would likely find hiding in a hole, and they would drag him back to Zarahemla for swift and public justice.

"Kai. Kai? *Kai*." The inflection finally caught his attention, and he looked over at Dan, who pointed ahead.

"Lehi. We'll make it by evening."

Kai squinted, bringing the shimmering city into better focus. He had known they were getting close, but surprise still coursed through him. He was sorely tempted to urge Vyim to a gallop. His heels even twitched, and Vyim flicked his ears back, as if wondering what Kai was thinking. Vyim had the stamina, and Dan could catch up. And once he reached the walls, if he shouted Siarah's name loudly enough …

Fool.

"Um … good."

Dan must have read his mind, which probably wasn't too difficult. "You can go ahead if you want. Just don't run him into the ground."

The offered choice made him feel even more of a fool. He was a professional soldier, and one of the prophet of God's trusted aides, not a fourteen-year-old boy with less sense than King Noah or one of his fatuous priests.

"No," he replied, heels still quivering. "We arrive together. I know one of the good inns in the city. We might learn something there." *If lightning struck twice in the same place.*

"I think we should go directly to the Chief Judge's office in the morning," said Dan.

Kai turned his head in surprise. "Not the captain of the law officers, or the head of the militia?"

Dan squinted toward the city. "Those were the most logical choices, as we discussed. But … visiting Omner first feels right."

Kai couldn't gainsay him, so he scrunched his brow and said, "I don't think I've ever met one of King Mosiah's sons, just seen a couple of them in passing."

"Well, they're very old now, and they don't travel much anymore. I'm surprised all still live, though that will inevitably change, and soon."

Kai let his eyes wander the landscape, pondering the way of the world. He himself was lucky to be alive. What if Kishkumen had been able to block his attack that fateful day? He surely would have been able to overpower Kai, given how much more skilled a fighter he was. Kai would have been the one lying in a pool of blood on those stairs, his spirit passed on to the next life. At least he could have shouted an alarm before dying. Helaman would still have been safe. He gulped. *Siarah, too.* Would that have been the better outcome? He kept his eyes forward, blinking to keep a rebellious tear in abeyance.

Dan let him think, or brood, or whatever it was he was doing, for at least a mile. Then he said, "I was surprised when Omner became a chief judge."

Kai frowned at him, grateful for the distraction. "Why?"

Dan shrugged. "Because none of Mosiah's sons wanted political power, not after their conversion with Alma. And that attitude remained strong."

"Omner must have found a convincing reason."

"Yes. He would only have accepted the position if he felt it was the best way for him to serve. The people of Lehi are good. And I believe his wife is from the city, though she has passed."

Kai considered the buildings slowly growing in the distance. "I didn't know that. They had children, I presume?"

"Yes. Several. I imagine most of them live in this area, along with grandchildren and great grandchildren."

"Another reason to serve as a righteous chief judge."

"Yes, indeed."

———◆———

They arrived well before full dark, as Kai had finally given in a little and increased their pace—nothing frenetic or foolhardy, of course. He had no trouble finding the inn he had visited before. The owner, an owlish man with a reedy voice, welcomed them with several flourishes once they introduced themselves as members of Helaman's household.

The décor of the common room had changed, a woman's touch obviously involved. Fresh flowers graced large vases on tall plinths in various parts of the space, and three colors of pastel paint in patterns gave the walls and ceiling a uniquely sophisticated look. Kai couldn't remember exactly what the tables and chairs had looked like before, but they were probably the same, of fine make and design.

They had eaten only a light lunch earlier in the day, and Kai was famished, so he was glad the cooks weren't overly busy serving a large crowd. The owner showed them to what he proclaimed his best table, next to a window, then gave them an impressive list of dishes to choose from. After salivating at all the options, Kai chose the duck, which he'd long ago taken a liking to when out in the field, while Dan asked for more vegetables than meat, choosing venison.

Kai studied the occupants of the room. Fewer than twenty people, and mostly men, all well-dressed. The conversations combined serious business and joviality, which made sense. Lehi was a prosperous place, and business was good.

He started when a large hand fell on his shoulder. Twisting his head to see whose hand it was, he felt his eyes widen as he recognized Captain Lehi, who gave him a gruff smile. Kai would have spun to his feet and saluted, but Lehi's iron grip kept him in place.

"It's good to see you again, Kihoran. And this—" he nodded at Dan, "is one of the two thousand?" The thin blue headband was a sure tell.

"Yes, this is Dan, the captain of Helaman's guard."

Dan chuckled. "I'm not sure 'captain' is the right title, but I serve the prophet with pleasure."

"Well met, Captain Dan." Lehi removed his hand from Kai's shoulder and extended it as Dan rose. They clasped forearms while Kai got to his feet, noting the keen attention they drew from the other patrons. Dan was almost as large as Lehi, the difference inconsequential. Lehi returned his gaze to Kai. "What brings you to Lehi? It wasn't named after me, by the way, in case you were wondering, but my father. And yes, he tried to name me Lehihah, but my mother argued it was too awkward to say. Thank the heavens for her common sense. This city is my favorite place to be when Moronihah doesn't have me traipsing around the countryside training troops, strengthening fortifications, or beating up Lamanites." He winked as he filled his broad chest with air. There was an extra chair at the table, so he sat, Kai and Dan following.

Kai commented on how the two esteemed warriors had never met. In the great war, Lehi had worked with Moroni in the east, while Dan and his brothers fought in the south and west with Helaman the Elder. Each thanked the other for his valiant service.

"Helaman sent us," Dan then said in a low voice. "It appears our good friends the Gadiantons have kidnapped Kai's betrothed from Bountiful. She never arrived in Zarahemla, after many weeks."

Lehi's face darkened as he nodded in acknowledgment, and then he turned to Kai. "They don't know your secret, do they?"

Kai almost blanched. "You do?"

Lehi's eyes intensified. He could probably win battles just with his stare. "Aye, son. I have been part of the search, and Moronihah answers my questions."

"He knows, too?"

"Don't fret. Helaman has entrusted this information to only a select few, and we would die before revealing it. I know how important that is to you, and to your family."

Kai muttered a pathetic "Thank you" as one of the servers brought the food he and Dan had ordered and set it on the table, along with large mugs filled nearly to overflowing. She asked anxiously if Lehi wanted something to eat, but the general declined. Kai himself didn't feel as hungry as he had just minutes ago.

"Eat up," admonished Lehi, "and I'll tell you what I know and think." He waited until Kai complied before continuing. "Gadianton obviously suspects you might have some information about who killed his precious assassin, and you're close to Helaman. I'm betting he hasn't made known that he has Siarah for two reasons: first, he wants you as uncomfortable as possible for as long as possible—a form of torture, I suppose; and second, he still doesn't have a firm base from which he feels confident operating, and I've been doing my damnedest to make sure that remains true. He is our greatest enemy, more dangerous by far than any Lamanite king. My men scour the land for his agents, and we've found quite a few. He fears us. Unfortunately, he is fully consumed with hatred and lust for power. He will not stop, which means we need to find Siarah and free her. If he finds out the truth about you, he will not rest until you're dead. You and all your family."

Kai had taken a few bites of his food, but all taste suddenly dissolved. He glanced at Dan before addressing Lehi in a cautious whisper. "Siarah knows what happened."

Lehi clasped his hands over his armor—did he wear it all the time? His voice became a small avalanche. "Then we have to assume Gadianton is aware of the truth. Once he has entrenched his gluttonous backside somewhere, he'll use her as bait."

Kai gulped. "We had thought of that. But I'm not afraid of Gadianton."

"Well, you should be, though I admire your pluck."

"Helaman felt Lehi was where we should start," interjected Dan, "and we plan to meet with Omner tomorrow."

Lehi's voice softened as he squinted at Kai. "Well, the Lord's prophet won't lead you astray. And Helaman couldn't have known I was here. I'm going to help, like you helped me. The way you turned that army toward our ambush has become a lesson I drill into all my scouts."

Such high praise, especially coming from the venerated Captain Lehi, made Kai uncomfortable. But before he could utter some sort of clumsy acknowledgment, Lehi continued.

"I'm giving you twenty of my men. My best men, mind you. They will not disappoint; that is a promise."

Twenty of his *elites*? That seemed excessive. What did Lehi think might happen? The thought sent new currents of fear pulsing from Kai's chest to travel along his limbs. He looked at Dan, who seemed to have picked up on it as well.

"You suspect the Gadiantons have already regathered some of their strength," said Dan.

"Yes."

"Do you have some ideas as to where?"

"Mainly the wilderness areas," said Lehi, "though they still have networks in many of the cities, especially among the wealthier class. They're making more inroads among the poor, too, by concocting extravagant and stupid promises. I believe some may have gone to Lamanite lands as well, others north."

"North?" asked Kai.

Lehi nodded. "Yes. Familiar, but less populated, and removed from Nephite authority."

That made some sense, and Kai felt a pull in that direction. It was hard to tell why, though. The north had fascinated him for a while, well before he had even heard the name Kishkumen.

"What about Morianton?" asked Dan.

"Still a den of thieves," spat Lehi. "They generally stay in line, especially when they know I'm close by, but I'm certain they're harboring at least a few of Gadianton's senior people. We should ask Omner. He may have received further intelligence since I was last here. Like you, I just got here."

What were the odds of arriving at the same time as Lehi? Kai offered a silent prayer of gratitude, feeling somewhat guilty that such prayers had become too rare recently. He had been raised to pray more often, in good times and hard. Most people prayed harder in the bad times; he was the opposite. Well, usually.

After more authoritative encouragement to eat, Kai finished his meal as Lehi described some of the rebuilding efforts across the Nephite heartland, which Coriantumr had devastated with his massive army. He also talked about the pride growing among some of the church members, especially those whose cities and towns hadn't been affected. Apparently, some of them thought they had been spared the destruction because they were more righteous. Lehi's opinion of them was poignant:

"Dumb as a cow's licker."

— ◇ —

The main audience room at the Hall of Judgment in Lehi had an odd shape, narrower at the main entrance with the far end curving in facets, giving the space the general outline of a cut gem. Seven alcoves punctuated the perimeter, each boasting a bright brass sconce. There was no dais, and the chair Omner occupied was no different than any other in the room. Several aides attended the chief judge, but Kai didn't see anyone who looked like a high judge.

Omner, sporting wispy hair whiter than snow and row upon row of deep wrinkles, welcomed them in a raspy voice as his aides arranged a few chairs close around him. Then he dismissed the aides altogether. He smiled at Lehi as the last aide closed the door behind him. "That will get some people talking."

"There are still eyes and ears here in Lehi?" asked the general.

"I know of at least two," said Omner, "and I make sure I know what they're doing."

"It's a complicated game."

"Indeed." Omner directed his attention to Dan and Kai. "You have traveled here from Zarahemla at Helaman's request? Dan notified me late last night."

"Yes," said Kai. "He thought you might be able to help."

"That I may," he said, then coughed into his sleeve. His face looked gray and drawn, though he kept his back remarkably straight. After clearing his throat, he continued. "We have received a new batch of intelligence, some of it from Shemnilom's network." He nodded at Kai. "I believe you know him."

Kai dipped his head. "I do. He is a great man."

"Yes, he is. I don't know when the Lord is going to take him from us, but I hope it isn't soon—for our sakes, not his."

"I would say the same about you," said Lehi in the most solemn tone Kai had ever heard from him. Not that he knew him that well, of course.

Omner chuckled. "We can all be replaced. The Lord is always preparing his people, those who will listen, and we cannot come close to conceiving the perfect complexity of his plans."

Lehi angled his brow. "Agreed."

Omner coughed again, then took a long breath. "We have been mapping out some of the hot spots of recent Gadianton activity. Of course, we can only do so much to thwart their influence. We operate under strict laws that demand evidentiary fairness, as God requires of us. Unlike many of the kings of old—or Gadianton himself—we cannot just cart people off to jail on suspicion of nefarious pursuit, or outright eliminate them. Such behavior would only feed the evil trying to consume us, as history has proven time and time again. Instead, we keep watch as diligently as we can, and we firmly uphold the law in circumstances where we have proof it is being violated."

While Kai shared wholehearted agreement with everything Omner had just said, he knew what the temptations felt like. To find and rescue Siarah, he often found himself desiring to do decidedly lawless things. Shemnilom wouldn't be proud. Nor would Helaman, or Dan, or his parents … or Siarah herself.

"We can employ stratagems, too," continued Omner, "as we often did during the Great War. Sometimes, if our adversaries believe we know either more or less than we actually do, they will slip up, and we can catch them in an illegal act, including the intimidation of potential witnesses. We use some of our own intimidation as well." He gazed at Lehi, his smile slightly crooked. "And we do our very best to keep God's commandments and follow his Spirit. We could not do this alone. He makes us superior to our enemies, gives us advantages we often can't even imagine." His eyes focused on Kai, clear and bright, undimmed by years. "And that is why we will win. We will find Siarah, and we will find her in good health. You will be reunited."

Warmth spread through Kai's chest, and he knew that the faithful missionary, priest, and now chief judge had spoken solemn truth by the Spirit of God. His confidence swelled, tears rebelling again. He hurriedly cleared his throat as he dropped his chin. "Thank you for your help."

"Where should they start?" asked Lehi. "I'm sending twenty of my best with them."

Omner nodded vigorously. "That is good. You should travel to Morianton, very close to here, but swing wide. Camps have been popping up there, moving around. We've mapped many locations. You may find some information among them, especially when you show up in such strength." He studied Kai and Dan in turn. "Be bold, but be careful to do what the Lord would have you do. He loves all of his children, even the wicked ones, and he wants us all to take a chance on him."

Kai swallowed as he nodded. Morianton. Yes, that felt right.

CHAPTER 5

Do not suppose, because it has been spoken concerning restoration,
that ye shall be restored from sin to happiness.
Behold, I say unto you, wickedness never was happiness.
—Alma 41:10

"We're at least ten miles past Morianton," announced Dan as they paused on a knoll to examine their surroundings.

"Welcome to the East Wilderness," said Kai in a tone of mock pride.

"You are familiar with this area?"

"Somewhat, but I usually traveled farther east or northeast, sometimes beyond our borders. I've visited Gid. Also Moroni, to the south."

"I'm still surprised there aren't more people here," mused Dan, "despite the lack of large, navigable rivers nearby."

"It's difficult to irrigate reliably on a large scale here," said Kai. "My father explained it in some detail. I didn't understand most of it. It looks pretty green to me." He smiled as he looked at his friend.

"Well, there's good game here. That's why it was popular with the Lamanites for a long time. Until Captain Moroni pushed them out. That was wise. This is strategic ground."

Kai wasn't sure about the strategic part, other than the fact that controlling it let the Nephites protect more sensible borders much farther south. It had its own beauty, though. Trees didn't blanket it the way they did other areas of the Nephite lands, but they were still plentiful. And though it didn't boast major rivers, it produced significant water through springs and creeks. An army, split into pieces, could easily hide here. Moroni must have realized that as well.

Kai twisted in his saddle to look back at their impressive troop. All rode large horses, most as big as Vyim. They were powerful men, seasoned in battle, some nearing forty years old. Lehi's elites. Each wore a thin purple headband, laced with gold, proclaiming them as such. Several had noted to Kai and Dan their preference not to wear them, for fear of boasting, but Lehi wanted people to know who they were, especially in battle or on missions like this. They were feared and respected. Kai felt like a child among them.

Dan fit in, of course. In fact, Lehi's elites showed great deference to him as one of the two thousand. It would take a long time for the stripling warrior legend to fade, if it ever did, and it was hard to imagine such a group existing again. Their circumstances had been so peculiar, the miracles too incredible.

Two of the elites came riding up from the north. Kai had sent them scouting, and instead of reporting to their own commander first, a man named Jerid, they came straight to Kai.

"We spotted a camp, sir," one began. Kai wanted to ask him not to call him sir, but he'd been doing that for several days now, to no avail. "Just two miles northeast, along a larger creek. They have good natural cover, and the location is defensible."

"How many?"

"At least forty fighting men, though poorly armed and without proper shielding."

"Can you tell why they're here?"

The man shook his head. "We couldn't get close enough to overhear conversations. They had a single patrol out, easy to avoid. The camp definitely isn't permanent. They've been moving."

"Lamanites?"

"No, sir. Not by their clothing or the weapons we could see."

"Any horses?"

"A few, and not in the best shape."

"We need to talk to them. What's your recommendation?"

The man looked at his companion, who nodded. They had clearly discussed it. "We ride hard and fast straight toward them, sir. Don't let them flee. We can blow a signal demanding surrender. They will recognize it."

Kai arched an eyebrow. "And if they mount a defense?"

"You tell us, sir. What are the rules of engagement?"

Dan chimed in. "They won't be looking for a fight … though they may *need* to be fought."

That was an insightful way to put it. But for their oath, Dan's parents might have said the same thing.

"Agreed," said Kai. "We treat it as a military engagement. This many armed men, encamped in the middle of nowhere, must be challenged, and engaged if they resist. They'll have the option of surrendering, and we'll give them fair warning." Part of him had wanted to follow the two elites' recommendation of charging in and catching them by surprise; perhaps Dan's presence influenced his thinking.

"Very good," said the elite. "I'll pass that along to Captain Jerid and the others."

"Thank you. I will lead."

"Excuse me, sir?"

"I will lead," repeated Kai. "I've been promised I will find Siarah. I have to trust that, right?" Part of him recoiled at the logic, but he glanced at Dan, who reassured him with a grave nod.

The elite finally gave a sharp, impressive salute that Kai didn't merit, then hurried off with his companion.

After a brief discussion on a strategy that would allow them to use their horses with maximum effectiveness if the contact turned violent—half for the actual fighting and half for the ingress, giving them a coordinated mounted and foot presence—Dan offered a prayer for the group. Even Kai clearly recognized the assurance that flowed from his humble, powerful words.

Within minutes they drew near enough to the camp to form a skirmish line, with specific paths mapped out through the trees. Kai took the middle, with Dan beside him to blow the horn notes calling for surrender when they were close. Then they let their horses walk.

Kai spotted the camp's patrol, about thirty yards ahead and to his right. The pair scampered toward the camp, and Kai gave them just enough time to reach it before halting the skirmish line and signaling Dan. His friend brought the ram's horn to his lips, blowing clear, beautiful notes. Kai raised an eyebrow at him in surprise. Dan just smiled when he lowered the horn. A hidden talent. Kai would have to tattle on him to Jerena. She would have him teaching music to her kids in no time.

Their line waited, Kai listening intently for any response, musical or otherwise. After nearly a minute, he started Vyim walking again, Dan staying beside him. He signaled the others to follow a couple of paces behind them, weapons ready. Instead of a spear, Kai took out Neva's new bow, nocking an arrow as he guided Vyim with his knees. Dan preferred his spear.

After a hundred yards, which put them about the same distance from the camp, Kai stopped again, raising his voice.

"By orders of Chief Judge Helaman and Captain Lehi, you will answer our questions! Approach unarmed!"

Again they waited, Kai allowing another full minute. He heard minor rustling noises, but most of the animals had gone silent. That worried him.

"If you do not show yourselves, we will assume you are hostile!" he added, shouting even louder.

Kai waited only a few more seconds before ordering the charge. The line surged forward in response. No shouts passed the lips of Lehi's elites. They didn't need vocal accompaniment to steel their courage or enliven their muscles. Kai's skin tingled as he thought about them. He had seen them in action before, and any army without a tip of the spear like these men was just pretending.

The group sliced through the forest, all ahorse until Dan shouted the signal. Half performed a running dismount, spears or bows at the ready as they followed behind their brothers. The hostile camp came into view, dozens of men crouched in defensive positions behind trees, rocks, and a smattering of their own horses. Kai pulled back his bowstring, targeting a nervous-looking fellow near the middle. He calmed his breathing, enjoining focus, letting the crescendo of impending battle fade.

Just then notes of surrender blared frantically from just beyond the camp. Lehi's elites halted their advance, the dismounted men coming to the front and setting up a defensive line. Two pairs on horseback began a small-radius scout of their flanks.

Kai eased his bowstring forward, then jumped down from Vyim, Dan following suit as one of Lehi's men grabbed the reins and led the horses away from their line. Kai suspected this wasn't a full surrender; it was either a trick or the camp was divided. Either way, he still felt the surety of Omner's promise surge through his veins.

He looked at Dan. "Be ready for anything. I'm going to accept their surrender, if such it is."

Dan nodded with a hard glint in his eyes, and Kai walked forward, bow still in hand. Just short of a small meadow at the center of the encampment, he stopped. The men he could see remained still, but he heard whispering in the trees on the other side. The crackling of a cooking fire provided a sort of cadence to the tension.

"We seek critical information," Kai declared. Several seconds of silence followed, and then a man emerged from the trees, about Dan's age, dressed simply and with nothing in his hands. After he had taken two steps, a volley of at least a dozen arrows whistled from behind him. Kai instinctively … froze? Strangely, he didn't feel fear, just anticipation. Even more oddly, every arrow missed him and Dan, though several came close. Dan and the Lehites immediately advanced, darting in and out of cover. Kai noted the varied reactions of the men in the camp—they were indeed divided. Some rose and rushed forward, while others looked around frantically, as if seeking a way out.

Kai fell back a few steps to assess. The men charging him hesitated, and that proved deadly for them. The men of Lehi seemed to rise up out of the brush like it was thick mist, cutting down several with practiced ease. More of the hostiles joined the fray, while others ran. Kai calmly targeted one fleeing man, aiming for the backs of his thighs. Though he had chosen a much more difficult target to hit, he wanted to make sure they had at least one person to question without conducting a treacherous chase through the forests.

The *thunk* of arrowhead in flesh preceded a scream as the man fell, sword flying ahead of him. It looked to be a good hit. Kai grabbed another arrow, searching for his next target and not aiming to injure this time. But the battle had already ended. A handful of men dropped their weapons and surrendered. The rest abandoned arms and ran. The man who had first emerged from the trees was gone.

Jerid stood from checking the status of a fallen hostile, turning toward Kai. "Do we follow?" he asked.

Kai shook his head. "No. We dress what wounds we can and question those we've captured."

Jerid gave no indication as to whether he agreed or not, just nodded and shouted orders. The men of Lehi quickly secured all the horses, set a full defensive perimeter, and began addressing the needs of the wounded. Only one was theirs, and his injury was superficial. Kai felt stunned for a moment, but then glanced at Dan. The hulking Ammonite stood near Kai, eyes searching all directions, protecting him. He and the other stripling warriors had seen this outcome before—the enemy soundly defeated, no friendly forces lost. Kai wondered if such miracles seemed normal to him now. He knew Dan didn't enjoy battle, that he abhorred killing.

Kai approached the man he'd downed. He had rolled onto his side, face twisted in pain as he grasped the area around the protruding shaft. The bleeding wasn't terrible, but he needed tending.

Kai had some bandages and a salve to prevent infection in the pouch at his waist, which he retrieved as he knelt next to the man.

"I'm going to pull the arrow out. It didn't go through, so it will hurt more."

Tears leaked from the man's eyes, which were nearly squeezed shut, and he nodded with a grunt. Kai went to work, using his knife to cut away a section of the man's breeches, which were well made for cooler weather.

Dan appeared on the other side, kneeling to offer the man a stick to place between his teeth. Kai placed one hand firmly around the entry point, the other grasping the shaft. He twisted it slightly, trying to get a feel for the arrowhead's orientation. If he could get the ridges aligned with the shape of the entry wound, it would be easier. And then … well, he had learned that once you were as set as you could be, it was best to move quickly.

The man groaned, biting on the stick, and Kai yanked hard. The stick cracked in the man's teeth, and he spit it out as he screamed. Several delirious invectives followed, though none were directed at Kai or Dan. It had been a clean pull, the arrowhead coming free, fully intact. Kai tossed it aside, then cleaned the wound, applied salve, and wrapped a bandage around the leg. After tying it tight, he rose, setting his hands on his hips.

"There. You'll live, and your leg should heal. The arrow doesn't appear to have damaged the bone."

"How do you know?" said the man after a few more painful gasps.

"The arrow came out easily, and you'd be in much more pain with how tightly I bandaged your leg if the bone were fractured."

The man didn't acknowledge that, just gripped the leg with both hands and gritted his teeth. Dan got him into a sitting position and dragged him to a tree so he could lean against it.

"What is your name?" Kai asked when the man had re-opened his eyes.

"N—Nephi," came the strained response.

"Hmmm." That name carried connotations, which generally didn't include skulking around in the woods trying to avoid lawful directives. "And what are you doing here, Nephi?"

Just then Jerid approached, and Kai turned. "We have five others we can question. They aren't wounded. A pair of the wounded might also regain consciousness soon."

"Good," said Kai. "Question the five separately, without letting them hear each other."

Jerid gave the same sharp salute, and when Kai looked back at his prisoner, the man's eyes widened a little. Probably because of Kai's age.

"So," continued Kai. "Why this camp? Who are you hiding from?"

The man stared at Kai for a moment, then switched his gaze to Dan. "Is he …"

"Yes," answered Kai. "One of the two thousand. And these others are part of Lehi's elite. You never had a chance."

Nephi swallowed as he gave a slight nod. His expression slackened a bit, but then suddenly hardened. Kai had seen that before. He was screwing up his courage to resist interrogation.

"Do you truly believe we're the enemy?" asked Kai.

The man didn't answer, just let his eyes flit among the other soldiers. That meant the answer was "Yes."

"Why did Gadianton send you here?" The slight tightening of the eyes and the hitch in his breath told Kai he'd struck true. But again, no answer came.

"He kidnapped someone recently," continued Kai, letting his voice grow cold. "Someone important to me. A woman named Siarah, from Bountiful. We need to find her. You can either help us, or you can rot in prison."

Nephi's eyes finally locked onto Kai. They were still filled with pain, but also defiance. "I've done nothing wrong."

"Oh? I'm positive that's not true, and it won't be difficult to prove. You attacked my men, for one. That is treason."

The "T" word caused the man to swallow again, eyes closing briefly. Kai knelt next to him, lowering his voice to almost a whisper, letting his glare bore into the man's skull.

"If I don't find Siarah soon, we will declare war on Gadianton and his band, and there will be no offers of surrender." That was bluff and bluster—he had no idea if Helaman would entertain such a strong stance, or even if it would be wise—but he was angry and resolute.

"It doesn't matter. We are more numerous than you think." The man didn't meet Kai's gaze, but insolence laced his tone.

"I know. I was once one of you." Not really, but he *had* infiltrated part of their organization.

Nephi's eyes widened again, flicking to Kai's face. He pressed his lips tight, though.

"We'll take him back to Lehi," said Dan, "the city *and* the man, and see what more we can learn."

Nephi blanched, then squeezed his leg as if to fire his will by reminding himself of his pain. Kai rose, looking down on him for several seconds. "Yes, good. We'll put this one on Vyim, who likes to trot." It would be painful, no matter how they secured him to the horse.

After another thirty minutes, they were ready to leave. Jerid and the other Lehites hadn't retrieved any useful information, either, so they began the trip back to Lehi, where they could drop off the prisoners and then return to Morianton. They had given a serious scare to the men who had fled, but also put them—and Gadianton—on alert. Would that help or hurt in the end? Kai's mind already felt sore trying to figure it out. Dan didn't seem worried, though, and that calmed his nerves a bit.

After delivering their prisoners, Kai's group returned to the lands of Morianton, this time directly approaching the city. Kai and Dan rode at the head of their column, and Dan commented on the unimpressive walls. "These fortifications seem as unreliable as the chief judge here. Tiberion is his name, and Helaman doesn't have a high opinion of him."

"What about the high priest?" asked Kai.

"Another sore point. Helaman trusts him even less than Tiberion. I don't remember his name. I don't think we need to visit him, though, just Tiberion, if only to put him on notice." He raised his brow, and Kai nodded. It would be more problematic to strangle a high priest, anyway, even if he was corrupt.

It was early afternoon, so they proceeded straight to Morianton's Hall of Judgment, which stood out boldly as the nicest building in the city. The gold leaf on the main double doors seemed a bit much, but they didn't get to see the interior straightaway, because the guards informed them they needed an appointment to see Chief Judge Tiberion. Kai almost laughed as he turned to look back at the twenty Lehite elites behind him, all wearing appropriately grim, determined faces. Then he addressed the guards.

"We come with a special task from Chief Judge Helaman, and you're telling us we need to wait for an *appointment*?" The notion sounded even more ridiculous coming out of his mouth. He glanced at Dan, who gave a slight shake of his head.

"Yes, um, sir," said one of the guards, suddenly sounding uncertain.

Curse it, Dan was probably right. Helaman didn't like to be ostentatious or bullying with his authority, and Kai was acting as his envoy.

"Fine. Make us an appointment for first thing tomorrow morning. We *will* be here." He might have skirted over the edge, but it was the best he could do. He led his group away down the broad main street, and then he had another choice to make—split the group among more than one inn, or keep everyone together? These were the kinds of decisions required when in enemy territory, and Morianton felt like it. A sad commentary on the current state of Nephite society.

He finally settled on keeping everyone together, in part to make a stronger statement of their authority. After asking around, he found the best inn Morianton could offer, and indeed, it wasn't bad. It was no *Jacob's Rest*, but at least the city treated its visiting dignitaries and wealthy traders well.

The soldiers had to squeeze three to a room, with Kai and Dan also sharing a room, but it was much better than sleeping on the ground. Home-cooked meals were always nice, too. Kai had to admit he had become spoiled serving with Helaman and living in his home.

Shortly after Kai and Dan had retired for the night, a soft knock came at their door. Dan swiftly rose from his bed to answer it, holding up a hand for Kai to remain seated on the edge of his. He grabbed his sword from where it leaned against the wall before pulling open the door a few inches. From his angle, Kai couldn't see who it was, but he recognized the voice.

"I need to speak with you."

Mistress Havah.

Dan knew her as well, and he opened the door wider. Her usual cool confidence swept into the room with her, and she regarded Kai with a penetrating eye.

"You are bold," she said.

Kai raised his eyebrows. He didn't know if her statement was meant to elicit a certain response. "Bold? How?"

"You brought twenty heavily armed men from Lehi into Morianton with no notice."

Kai stared at Dan a moment, but the Ammonite's face gave nothing away. "Why would we need to give notice? And it was Lehi's idea." He wasn't just playing dumb with the answer. He knew Morianton's reputation, too, but it wasn't *that* bad, was it?

She considered him, tapping fingers against her leg. "Tiberion isn't happy. I know he refused to see you."

"The guards said we needed an appointment."

The tapping stopped. "Pshaw. One of his aides saw you coming. He recognized the markings of Lehi's elite. There is bad history there."

Kai was aware of that; who wasn't? "So he just blew us off? We'll be back in the morning."

"And he won't be there," she said. "In fact, he's leaving tonight, ostensibly on a trade mission to eastern lands."

Kai jumped to his feet, hands balling into fists. "He's *fleeing*? Who's going with him?" He wanted to ask how she knew, even wondered if it was true. Helaman still supposedly had trust in this woman—this enigmatic master spy with questionable allegiance—but she was definitely no Shemnilom.

"His normal entourage," she replied calmly, "which includes three of his aides and ten guards."

Kai's anger was beginning to boil. "I need to speak with him." He was about to rush out of the room and rouse the men, tell them to get ready to ride, and Mistress Havah must have sensed that.

"Chasing him down isn't the answer, as I believe Helaman would advise you. He will have to return. You will get to speak with him then. In the meantime, I have good information that Gadianton was spotted in this area, perhaps even in the city, though I'm not sure on that part yet. There is also a camp, just a few miles north, that seems to be connected. Surely Gadianton is the one ultimately behind Siarah's kidnapping. I wish I could tell you I had some firm leads on her location, but I do not. It appears they have been moving her. I hear only vague whispers. He obviously recognizes your … value to Helaman. She is bait of some sort. Perhaps he is even trying to turn her."

Turn her? Kai hadn't considered that scenario yet. He couldn't imagine how she could be turned against the prophet, though. Not Siarah. He shivered as he visualized her already meeting Gadianton. He had never seen the man himself—at least, that he was aware of—and he trembled in rage at the thought of Gadiánton—or Imrahiel; or Ara's father, Nahom—laying greedy, ruthless eyes on his betrothed. His fists clenched again, his entire head heating.

"Now is not the time for panic or rash action," she cautioned. That just made him angrier, until Dan laid an arm on his shoulder. Instantly, he calmed, then gave his friend a grateful nod.

He gazed at Mistress Havah for several seconds without blinking. His voice came out cold. "Do you have any other information that might be useful?"

With a purse of her lips and a slight shake of her head, she replied, "Not yet. But I'm working on it. Trust me."

Trust her? How could he? But he didn't have much choice, and he would latch onto any hope. "Alright, we will stop by the Hall of Judgment in the morning, act surprised and upset when the guards tell us Tiberion isn't there, and then depart the city. For now."

She clicked her tongue as she nodded. "Very good. I'll be in touch again soon."

Chapter 6

O that cunning plan of the evil one! O the vainness, and the frailties,
and the foolishness of men! When they are learned they think
they are wise, and they hearken not unto the counsel of God,
for they set it aside, supposing they know of themselves, wherefore,
their wisdom is foolishness and it profiteth them not. And they shall perish.
But to be learned is good if they hearken unto the counsels of God.
—2 Nephi 9:28–29

The scene at the Hall of Judgment in Morianton played out as expected. Tiberion had left; the guards pretended ignorance as they explained it; Kai and Dan both berated them; the men of Lehi appeared aggressively disgusted; and then they all left, promising to return in a few weeks. That seemed to put the fear of God into at least one of the guards, which might be useful. Kai was certain Mistress Havah had at least one person watching who would report back to her.

They departed, using the eastern gates as if they might follow Tiberion's course, just to increase the tension further, though Morianton scouts would soon be able to report they were heading north. They moved swiftly, Kai wanting to make sure they reached the camp Mistress Havah had mentioned well before midday. He hoped her directions were accurate.

A pair of Lehi's men found the camp on one of their scouting sweeps, almost precisely where the woman had said it would be. They reported being spotted, that the occupants of the camp—numbering about fifty men and just two women, with no children—had begun breaking down the camp and migrating northeast in a hurry. They, too, must have recognized the elites' headbands, which definitely had their drawbacks, too.

After quickly hammering out a pursuit plan, Kai split the group into four. Then they let the horses run, Kai having to rein Vyim in to stay even with Dan and two of Lehi's men. Their path would be the most direct, which would allow them to catch up first. The scouts had reported no horses in the camp, though there could have been a few picketed farther into the trees.

Kai felt his adrenaline racing, even faster than when they had approached the first camp. He wondered again how many camps there might be, how well they were coordinated, what they were planning. Surely this was Gadianton's work, and his aim was still the overthrow of the Nephite government.

"Archer!" yelled one of Lehi's men, and Kai instinctively veered Vyim. "Where?" he shouted.

"Keep going, I got him!" came the reply.

Kai obeyed, zigzagging through the trees, noting that a broad stretch of open ground lay ahead. He leaned forward, head staying close to Vyim's neck. He expected to hear or feel the flight of an arrow from ahead or behind at any moment, and his blood pulsed quicker. His body moved in perfect rhythm with that of his horse. Then he heard a scream behind him. Likely the archer, who must have also been a lookout. With the camp already warned, the man had probably hoped to remain hidden and be passed by. Unfortunately for him, the men of Lehi had sharp eyes.

Kai didn't slow as he awaited confirmation, which came a few seconds later with the short blast of a horn. The threat had been eliminated. By then, he and Vyim had nearly crossed the open ground, the others spreading out behind. They bounded into the trees again, and within fifty more yards Kai encountered the remains of the camp, the cooking fires not even extinguished in the haste to escape. A few articles of clothing still hung on lines slung between trees.

Kai brought Vyim to a whirling stop, waiting for the others. Dan was the first he saw.

"Two groups this time?" Kai asked. "One north, the other northeast?"

Dan paused to examine the area, then agreed with Kai's assessment of the probable avenues of their quarry's flight. Several of Lehi's men joined them, including Jerid. "Jerid can take ten, we'll take the rest."

"Good." Kai waited, almost bouncing in his seat as Vyim pranced, eager to continue the chase. The remaining men of Lehi weren't long in arriving, reporting no enemy contact beyond the archer who had met his demise in the trees.

Kai didn't have time for those details. He spun, aiming Vyim northeast. "Ten of you, follow me and Dan!" They already had groups of various sizes pre-sorted, so there would be no lag to figure it out. Indeed, a thunder of hooves harried his wake, pounding through the trees and brush. Kai and his group swept across the open space, following an easy-to-spot trail. Most of the people were clearly on foot, and they occasionally dropped things. It wouldn't be long.

He saw the trail split into four not long afterward, and he picked the one that signaled slightly heavier traffic. If the Gadiantons thought such a tactic would slow his pursuit, they were wrong. He didn't need to capture them all—just a few for questioning.

After topping a small rise, Kai spotted three men gamely sprinting about two hundred yards ahead, just disappearing into more trees. They looked exhausted, though they hadn't abandoned their weapons. Kai urged Vyim on, and the stallion vaulted down the gentle slope, the grass whistling beneath his skimming hooves. The wind in Kai's ears soon carried shouts and grunts as their prey struggled to maintain their pace. Kai wondered if they would stop and make a stand, and he blinked, trying to focus harder, especially on the dim spaces that could more easily hide a man.

When he knew he was close enough, he yelled, "Surrender, by order of Captain Lehi!" His eyes darted around the available cover as Vyim leaped over a small creek and kept streaking forward. Finally, Kai caught a glimpse of a man, still running, head twisting back every few steps, eyes wide with fear.

"Stop!" shouted Kai, but the man kept going, suddenly angling to his right. Kai raised his arm and pointed at him, shouting, "Dan!" Then he ignored that target, suspecting another distraction. The two directly ahead were probably more important, the rearguard trying to buy them time.

Whoever they were, he closed quickly, catching them as their feet churned across another stretch of tall grass. He flew past them on Vyim, stopping twenty yards beyond and turning. Lehi's men burst from the trees behind the two hapless sprinters, surrounding them with a bristling cage of cavalry. The pair stopped, huffing and wheezing, one bent over with hands on knees. They did indeed appear more important than the third man he'd assigned to Dan, based on their clothing. These were no simple farmers or woodsmen.

Kai moved Vyim a few steps closer.

"Why do you flee?" he asked the one still fully upright.

That man, somewhat tall and probably in his forties, cast him a bewildered look amid pants for breath. Most of his clothes were a fine dark color, though dirty. His hair and beard matched.

Finally, he got out a few words. "You are chasing us!"

Kai raised his eyebrows. "Because you're *fleeing*. And you're armed."

"Everybody's armed," said the man, lifting his hands in innocence. His companion straightened, blowing heavily as he looked around.

"Not in large groups, they're not," responded Kai. "Who are you, and why are you here, obviously hiding?"

"We are not hiding," said the other man, shorter and of fairer hair and skin. "We're on a trading mission."

"Off road, and without any pack mules or wagons?"

"We're investigating opportunities." He made it sound like the most logical thing in the world, and Kai nearly laughed.

"You've lost some weight recently," Kai said to the taller man, who looked down as if to measure the fit of his garments.

"It comes and goes," came the deft reply.

"You're a decoy," added Kai before the man could respond. That was disappointing, but he had known they'd only catch a few.

The man's face went blank, but then he smiled. "If I were, it would mean you didn't capture who you hoped to capture."

Kai gave him a quizzical look, then said, "Why would I want to capture a trade delegation?"

The man's expression was priceless. He had disintegrated his own cover story.

Kai addressed one of Lehi's elites. "Let's get them tied up and roped behind the horses. Then we'll move out and find the others."

Two men responded with alacrity, jumping from their mounts and grabbing rope from their saddlebags. The process was remarkably efficient, especially since the prisoners didn't resist. They complained a fair bit, which would have been amusing had Kai's gut not clenched again at Siarah's continued absence.

When the two were securely tethered behind horses, Dan returned, nearly dragging a third man behind his. Kai dismounted and walked up to the more meanly dressed fellow Dan had captured. His voice bristled. "You had two women with you. Who were they?"

The man gave a nervous glance at his nearby companions, licking his lips before answering. "Just wives of two of our number."

A quivering pain worried itself up Kai's spine. Had Siarah been married off to a Gadianton already? He kept an even expression as he pressed further. "And they came with you voluntarily?"

The tall traitor Kai had captured answered. "Of course. What are you implying?"

Kai spun and snapped his gaze to the man, who flinched.

Then Dan spoke. "Let's get them to Lehi first, and we'll question them separately."

Of course he was right. Kai was letting his emotions overtake logic and training. He glared at each of the prisoners in turn. He hadn't even asked their names yet, and he didn't want to. It could wait.

"Don't trip," he growled, "because we aren't stopping."

◆

Kai kept the horses at a fast walk as they angled toward the approximate area where the other group should have caught their prey. The two

75

vocal prisoners continued to complain, but he ignored them. Lehi's men followed his lead, moving implacably forward, even when one Gadianton stumbled and got dragged along for a few yards before getting his feet beneath him and levering back up, spewing a string of curses. Kai decided they would gag all the prisoners upon reaching the others.

They encountered Jerid and his group with four men tied up and sitting on the grass. It seemed a ragtag bunch, though looks could be deceiving.

Kai steered Vyim toward Jerid, who had dismounted.

"Anything interesting?"

Jerid waved a hand casually toward the prisoners. "We got their names—or fake names—but not much else. They claim to be part of a trading group. All but one are terrible actors. They'd be laughed off the stage at one of the First Day reenactments."

"Maybe they're doing original work," Kai joked. "Those are becoming more popular."

Jerid chuckled. "They're not very original ... or smart. But Lehi will have fun with them." He had raised his voice for the last part, and the prisoners shifted, glancing at each other with fear.

"Sorry," Jerid added, lowering his voice, "I assumed we would take them to Lehi first. But we can question them here if you want."

"No, we need Lehi. He can get something useful from at least one of the seven. And there's no time to waste."

They were quickly moving again, all of the prisoners gagged, expressions undulating among fear, arrogance, and loathing. Kai situated them in the middle of their train, and he sent skirmish groups scouting in wide arcs ahead and behind. Within an hour, that netted them two additional prisoners. They grouped the hapless quislings in threes after that, each led by a single elite on his horse. Then they pressed on, Kai willing the ground to pass beneath them more swiftly. It would take two days to get to Lehi at this pace, and that seemed far too long.

━━◆━━

They finally arrived, early in the afternoon following two short, watchful nights. Kai had worried about an attack, though he hadn't really expected one, not with it known that Lehi's elites were in the area. They had spared little food for the prisoners but allowed them plenty of water. During those times they ungagged them, the complaints resembled a gaggle of grounded geese being chased by a bear.

The guards at Lehi's eastern gates exhibited a few raised eyebrows but asked no questions, so the group proceeded directly to the Hall of Judgment, the entire troop of Lehi's elites ringing their prisoners and raising murmurs along the streets. Kai's anticipation rose as they passed through the outer doors.

One of Chief Judge Omner's aides led them to a large, circular room, then asked them to wait. Several minutes passed before the aide returned, bearing the news that Lehi was outside the city on a routine inspection but that someone had been sent to notify him. Kai wanted to groan with impatience, but he forced himself to take it in calmly. Not so calmly that he didn't force the prisoners to the floor, however, growling as he did so. Dan didn't try to intervene, didn't even give him a look. Instead, he conversed with various of the elites, many of whom had fought in the Great War like him. Most sported visible scars from it. Given their general comportment, their spirits fortunately didn't seem to bear the same kinds of blemishes. He'd asked Dan about that before, and he was still amazed at the answers. Kai had seen battle, had swung a sword in the defense of his country. He had killed at least once, and he felt forever changed, somehow lessened. Not Dan, though. His faith was stronger, his ability to apply the promised atonement of the Savior without peer.

Hours passed, and Omner's aides arranged for dinner to be brought in. Kai ordered only half portions for the prisoners, and they glowered at him like he was the devil himself. But unless Lehi and Omner were going to put them to work, they didn't need their full strength. Plus, Kai's cold anger would allow him to offer only so much sustenance. Dan continued his conversations with the Lehites, occasionally drawing Kai in, but otherwise letting him brood.

Eventually, the door crashed open with a push from a thick arm covered in dark hair. Kai started, and one of the prisoners exclaimed as he wet himself. Dan, seated on a cushion on the floor, calmly rose, as did Jerid, turning toward the bear of a man darkening the doorway. It was Lehi, only partially armored but wearing a wide, heavy sword. His gaze sliced through the group of prisoners, and without a single word of greeting to Kai, Dan, or his men, he pointed at the tall, well-dressed one. "Get up," he commanded in a low, rumbling voice, "and follow me."

The man paled, eyes bobbing in a sea of hopelessness.

"Now!" The walls nearly shook.

The man lurched to his feet, then stared at his bound hands as he shuffled toward the famed and feared general.

"What is your name?" It was more demand than question.

"Um ... Asher."

In response, Lehi cuffed the Gadianton on the side of the head, his hand striking with surprising speed for such a large man. The so-called Asher crumpled, and Lehi bent over to grab the front of his tunic in a bunch and launch him back to his feet like he was a stuffed doll. "Try again. What is your name?"

The man wobbled a bit as he struggled to focus his eyes. "Nimrod."

Lehi's eyebrows rose, and he said, "Good enough for now." Then he pulled the man through the door and half-dragged him down the hall. An aide appeared from the hallway and quietly closed the door.

Kai looked at Dan, then at Jerid, who smiled and shrugged. Another prisoner lost control of his bladder, at which point Dan scolded the lot of them, his face stern.

"You are so pathetic that you cannot hold your water? So cowardly you cannot say your true names? So benighted you cannot let God's people live in *peace*? Well was your master described as a snake by Mother Eve and Father Adam. Your lies will find no root in this place, and unless you are able to acknowledge the truth and swear off your rebellion by solemn oath, you will languish here, in the deepest cells of the prison ... provided you aren't worthy of death."

Wow. Kai knew Dan could be fearsome, but he was generally calm and mild-spoken. He loved everyone, too, good or bad, though he was certainly no fool. If righteous anger had a physical description, Kai was staring at it in that moment. He imagined how Captain Moroni might have appeared in such situations. Kai had spent some time with the legendary general but had never witnessed him in his full fury. He had seen his son Moronihah approach something akin to Dan's display, though. He was half-surprised their prisoners didn't faint dead away.

The room became deathly silent, and it was getting darker. Broad windows had supplied them with the day's light, but that was waning fast. Two of Lehi's men lit nearly a dozen oil-fueled torches along the walls, the flames remarkably steady. Another innovative design. This city was indeed a noteworthy place.

Not half an hour later, the door crashed open again, and Lehi threw Asher/Nimrod onto the floor of the room before stepping inside and pointing at another prisoner. "You!" he bellowed. The indicated prisoner jumped to his feet, and Lehi turned and left, obviously expecting the man to follow, which he did. The same aide reached in to close the door, but paused, looking at Kai.

"More refreshment, perhaps? This will be a long night; he will speak with each man more than once. Oh, and he asked that those he has already talked to not be allowed to speak to the others."

Kai almost smiled. "Yes, please, and we'll sort the prisoners. Oh, and the chamber pots they've been using in the next room might need changing."

"Not necessary," said the aide. "They are connected beneath, and water runs through."

Of course. He should have expected that. Each station just looked so … isolated. And the privacy screens were impressive. "Thank you," he said, and the aide gave a slight nod before withdrawing.

The process continued in pretty much the same fashion as Lehi cycled through all the prisoners nearly three times. The only difference was that those who were more compliant didn't get dragged from the room and thrown back in. By the end, they were *all* compliant. Finally, the burly general lingered instead of beckoning another prisoner. He looked at Kai. "Brother Kihoran, I have a few scribes compiling notes. They will be up the rest of the night doing so. You can deliver the prisoners to the central prison—my men know where it is—and then you and Dan may return here. Omner has prepared rooms for you. We can speak later in the morning."

Kai bowed. "Thank you, general. For all your help."

That gravelly voice rumbled. "Don't thank me yet. And this is my job, to root out the sons of the devil wherever I can find them, so they can't prey upon our people and destroy our peace." He took a deep breath, and his tone softened. "Also, to rescue the oppressed from the jaws of the oppressor. Like your Siarah."

A tear pushed out of the corner of Kai's eye at the thought of his betrothed, and he lowered his head. "I couldn't do this without you," he mumbled in thanks as he fought back emotions.

"And neither of us can do it without the Lord. Don't give up hope, son. Don't ever give up hope, not even in your dying breath, because what lies beyond all of this is far better than we can possibly imagine—especially if we have done our best to follow God's counsels."

Before Kai could start openly weeping, Lehi turned and swept through the door, his fading footfalls lighter than his bulk would suggest. Kai turned to Dan and Jerid. He didn't have to say a word. They just began getting the prisoners to their feet. They didn't bother with the gags. In their current mental state, the blank-stared Gadiantons probably couldn't make a ruckus to save their lives.

———◇———

Kai barely slept, though he had his own room and the bed was large and plush, fancier than anything he had ever slept in. Curiosity assailed him without ceasing. How had the questioning gone? What had Lehi found out? How many of the prisoners had broken? Would any of the information lead them to Siarah? Had any of them actually seen her? How was she? *Where* was she right now? When would he see her again? And why was Lehi making him wait? Well, that part made sense, despise causing so much frustration. His scribes weren't just copying everything down. They were cross-checking and analyzing, trying to filter out the truth from the lies. Standard intelligence assessment.

He spent a considerable amount of time praying—sometimes on his knees, other times while lying on his bed. He prayed harder than he ever had, and while it eventually made him feel a little better, he didn't receive the strong assurances he sought. Perhaps the Lord was telling him to trust what he'd already been told, both directly and through others, including the prophet. Perhaps he was too mentally out of sorts to hear or make sense of a response. Or maybe he was just too weak. An orphan, the son of a violent extremist king man and his willing wife who had tried to overthrow the government … more like his natural parents than he was willing to admit.

Gideon and Ishara had raised him well. They had surely done their best anyway. And he had been very blessed. *Perspective.* That's what he needed: better perspective. An eternal viewpoint. Trust in God, who knew all things, great and small, and designed his plans for maximum future benefit.

Far easier said than done.

By the morning, when he awoke somewhat groggily, he felt the platitudes ringing hollow in his chest. But he would keep going. If nothing else, his anger would provide motivation.

He and Dan were summoned to Omner's small audience chamber after he forced down a fancy yet tasteless breakfast. When they arrived, they found Lehi already there, seated near Omner and conversing with him in low tones. Two aides occupied the room as well.

Omner rose, raising a hand to Lehi to interrupt him. "Kihoran, Dan, I trust you rested well?"

Kai hadn't been able to get a look at his eyes in a mirror—he guessed they were horribly bloodshot. He had washed his face, at least.

Dan answered. "As well as can be expected. Each additional day that passes is difficult." He was definitely speaking for Kai, and Kai knew his friend sincerely felt for him. He trusted *that* fully, at least.

"Well, please sit, and we can discuss what we know. Captain Lehi and I have been examining what we learned from the prisoners for the past two hours."

Two hours? And the scribes had been up all night. Kai suddenly felt guilty. All of this for Siarah, and for him. What if some other random person had been kidnapped? Kai and Siarah weren't better than anyone else. Still, he was grateful.

"Thank you," he said as he found a seat across from Lehi. A rich carpet in orange and red warmed the floor between them.

Omner looked at Lehi. "Please give us your evaluation, Brother Lehi."

Lehi nodded respectfully, resting his large hands in his lap, fingers interlocking. He stared at a point beyond Kai for a few moments, then began. "We're certain at least one of our prisoners has seen Siarah in the last two weeks, and she seemed healthy. She was also unbound." His eyes found Kai's. "That's the good news. The bad news is they don't know where she went. A man was accompanying her, and—"

"Imrahiel." Kai spat out the word, venom threading through his heart.

Lehi frowned, then shook his head. "Unlikely. The man was younger and built like a warrior. From what I've heard of Imrahiel, he is middle-aged and most definitely *not* a soldier. However—" and he raised a finger, "I'm almost certain Imrahiel was with this group. He was the one being protected by the decoy you captured."

Kai almost jumped out of his seat in frustration. If they could have captured Imrahiel …

Lehi continued, angled brow enjoining calm. "We have a reliable source who works for one of the high judges in Morianton, most of which are complicit in helping the Gadiantons move around and find new places to infiltrate and reintegrate. Many of these robbers—which is the most polite name I can give to them—have moved far to the northeast, it seems, and that would likely include Gadianton himself, though I'm positive he has plans to return. Others have ventured south, even into Lamanite lands—or Antionum, which is the same difference, the traitorous slugs. Imrahiel was in charge of the groups directly north and east of Morianton for a time. He's either in that city now, or he has chased his master northeast. Men like him are cowards, so I'm guessing the latter, though I will not discount the former."

Kai considered the information, leaning forward and squinting as he studied the carpet. He still wanted to scream at having missed Imrahiel, even though the odds hadn't been high of finding him. Oh, how he would love to see the villain put on trial, with himself as a witness. After getting information about Siarah from him, of course. Or watching Lehi do it. He brought his head up. "So, what do we do?"

"I've sent scouts northeast and south, and we have eyes and ears in Morianton. I believe you should wait until they report back, but if the Spirit tells you to do something different, do that."

On at least two counts, that was a frustrating answer. First, Kai couldn't fathom sitting and waiting. Every day that passed seemed to take Siarah further away from him. And secondly, how was he supposed to receive clear direction from the Spirit on what to do? Was he worthy? Was he capable? Was his mission even important enough? The bigger picture was that the Gadiantons needed to be found and stopped. Saving the lives of thousands was certainly more important than preserving the life of one.

Despite seething and panicking inside, he put on a brave, obedient front. "Thank you, Captain Lehi. I will do my best."

CHAPTER 7

*But behold, I say unto you that ye must pray always, and
not faint; that ye must not perform any thing unto the Lord
save in the first place ye shall pray unto the Father
in the name of Christ, that he will consecrate thy performance
unto thee, that thy performance may be for the welfare of thy soul.*
—2 Nephi 32:9

"We have to go. Now."

Siarah struggled to blink herself awake and dispel the heavy fog permeating her mind. It was still the middle of the night, wasn't it? They had found a relatively sheltered place to sleep under the stars, after haring north at news of the arrival in the city of a large group of Gadiantons and rogue Nephite soldiers and law officers. Three weeks after entering the city, and just two weeks after leaving it, she and Zoram had ventured back south to within a few miles of Morianton. Before she had fallen asleep, Zoram claimed they hadn't been followed. She didn't know how he could tell. If he wanted her perpetually confused, he was succeeding, and while she craved a healthy dose of civilization, she didn't want it to be in Morianton. Staying with that old couple near the walls had been horrible, and her skin still crawled whenever she thought of them. The night sky made a fine ceiling.

"What now?" she asked in a whispered croak, sitting up with difficulty.

"A Lamanite scout group," he replied, leaning closer so his whisper was barely audible. "I was lucky to detect them, but their search pattern will discover us within minutes."

"A Lamanite ... what?" She had spoken too loudly, and two of his fingers immediately covered her lips. His eyes seemed strained, even in the dimness.

"We can talk later. We must go." He helped her to her feet, and as quietly as possible they gathered their few things, which consisted of a pair of blankets, some simple cookware, and the tinder box, which they stuffed in their small packs with the little food they carried with them. Zoram checked his weapons, as he so often did, and patted his water skin.

"Is yours full?"

She stooped to pick hers up. By the weight, it was at about half. Given his urgency, she couldn't take the time to fill it in the nearby stream. "I have enough."

"Okay, follow close." He started walking, placing his footfalls carefully, and she tried to mimic his movements exactly. After less than a minute, he crouched, turning to hold up a finger. She pressed her knees into the ground, listening intently. All she heard were normal animal sounds. Trees still covered them, but she spied open space ahead.

After a few seconds, he whispered, "We need to cross that field quickly and quietly. Once we get to the other side, I think we'll be outside their search pattern."

"Search pattern" wasn't a phrase she had ever thought she would become accustomed to, but it had become as familiar as "dress pattern" to her. Oh, what she wouldn't give to bury herself in making clothes again. Especially for children. Her fingers were so out of practice!

She started as he jumped up and began moving again, still walking, but faster. She followed, and as they passed the tree line, he accelerated to a jog. She kept up, worried that her pack bouncing up and down on her back was making too much noise. She was about to slow when he ran faster still. What had he heard? Her heart beat in her throat as she matched his pace, panic prickling her neck and shoulders. They rushed into the trees on the other side, and he didn't slacken his pace for at least another fifty yards. Then they walked for several minutes, stopping occasionally for him to listen. She still heard nothing of discernable import.

At long last, he signaled a rest at the base of a broad, gnarled oak. She slipped her pack off and set it down, then plopped onto her rump, arms splayed behind her, breathing heavily and not caring how undignified she might look. He kept his pack on, because of course he did, carefully scouting a short distance in each direction, *his* breathing near normal. She took the opportunity to down at least half of her remaining water, thirst rising in her like an unquenchable flame. When he finally knelt next to her, she hid her waterskin by her other side.

"I think we're safe," he said. "We should only rest a few minutes, though. It would be good to put a few more miles between us."

She nodded, but again wondered how all of this was possible. They had been traveling through dark, confusing limbo for so long she was beginning to believe she was trapped in a nightmare. Her comfortable life in Bountiful may never have existed.

"Zarahemla," she said firmly. "We should head straight for Zarahemla now. I don't care if it's dangerous. Once we're there, it won't be. I promise."

His expressions at such proposals had been evolving, but they still weren't anywhere close to showing acceptance. "And I promise you we will. Soon. We should head south first, then west. I agree we shouldn't delay much longer."

Wait, he actually agreed with her on something? Perhaps she was making more progress than she thought. Praises be to God!

"Thank you." She pushed herself onto her knees. "Now, I want you to pray with me."

She detected his eyebrows retreating to his hairline in the splotchy moonlight. He cleared his throat, preparing his next excuse, but she pre-empted him by beginning her prayer.

"Our Father in Heaven, hallowed be your name. We are grateful you spared us from danger this night. Please guide us as we continue our journey, and help us get to Zarahemla, please, and soon. In the name of your beloved Son, amen."

There. Short and sweet. He couldn't complain. He gave a small grunt anyway as he got to his feet, and he didn't help her up this time. She didn't care if he was offended. He was a son of God. He would learn to pray. And someday it would do him some good.

They set out in silence, his walking pace moderate, and he didn't turn and stare if she made too much noise. They must really be safe, she concluded. Now, if she weren't so sleepy, or carrying a pack, it might be enjoyable to stroll through the woods in the early hours of the morning. The land around them seemed to be at peace, Earth herself calming and consoling the two peregrine travelers. That prayer had helped. She hadn't added Kai to it, so she silently petitioned the Lord on his behalf as well. *Please,* please *let him be safe.*

She must have spent a lot longer pleading for her betrothed's welfare than she thought, for suddenly Zoram was calling for a stop so they could rest and eat. She looked up, noting the considerable lightening of the sky. The land had opened up, with fewer trees, but far in the distance she spotted more thick forest as hills marched toward rugged mountains to the south. She had heard of that range—the Wandering Mists—but had never been there. Just beyond them lay the borders of the Lamanite lands, aligning with the River Moren. Her eyes strayed west and a little north. She thought that was the approximate direction of Zarahemla, still so far away. She had no idea where they were in relation to Morianton. She could see a few villages, but she wasn't studied in maps like Kai.

She sighed, then found a smooth place in the grass to sit as Zoram apportioned some rations. She took a long swig of water before biting into the hardtack bread and dried fruit. They saved meat for the evening meals. Zoram seated himself two feet to her left, silently scanning the horizon as he partook sparingly. He should eat more, she decided. She tore off a chunk of her bread and handed it to him.

He turned, staring for a moment, then frowned. "I don't need more. You must keep up your strength, too, and we aren't starving."

"I know. I just—" She just *what?* Sighing again, she withdrew the bread and changed the subject. "Where is Jershon?" He raised an arm and pointed, south and a little east. "There, just east of the Wandering Mists." His arm shifted. "We'll head southwesterly, like I said. Mulek will be a good place to stop and resupply."

Mulek. Well, it was closer to Zarahemla than they were now. And better than Morianton. Wasn't it? Her eyebrows came together as she thought about how much farther south they were heading. "Do you know someone there?"

"Yes. A jewelry maker. I can trust him, and he might have good information."

"Can he give us horses so we can ride to Zarahemla?" She knew that was a long shot, but her desire to make progress in that direction surged again as the bread became tasteless.

"Maybe," he replied, and her heart did a little dance. Really? She didn't let him see quite how excited she was, but she could savor the dry bread again, at least a little.

Within a few minutes Zoram had them up and moving again, making a beeline for the middle of the Wandering Mists. He explained they would veer west once they reached the forested foothills, following a minor road. That sounded good, because at the moment they weren't on a real trail, much less a road. The uneven terrain was starting to wear on her, especially her ankles. Maybe Kai enjoyed overland trekking, but she would be ecstatic for flatter surfaces.

It took until dusk to reach the road in the forest, and, as promised, they followed it west. As the nocturnal noises increased, Siarah's body became increasingly exhausted. Before long, her eyelids drooped as she plodded along, moving one foot in front of the other without any conscious thought. If it weren't for the occasional traveler who passed them heading in the other direction—mostly lesser traders—she might have crumpled into a heap and entered a deep slumber.

She didn't notice the multitude of stars blinking on in the heavens, barely registered the shouting that suddenly arose. It seemed to come from a great distance, and while part of her wanted to show curiosity and concern, she was too spent. Until Zoram froze, grabbed her arm, and pulled her close behind him. Crashes sounded nearby, and her mind awakened with a flush of adrenaline.

Three horsemen suddenly bore down on them, yelling incoherently. Was it some sort of … battle cry? She whipped her head to the rear, heart roaring in her ears; the road was deserted behind them. Then she peeked around Zoram's shoulder, noting the raggedly dressed men still coming, horses at a near gallop. Two brandished swords, while the third held a spear. She didn't think they were Lamanites, especially not on an open road. But who were they, and why were they attacking?

"Bandits!" Zoram said in a loud whisper. "When I tell you, run for the trees. I'll pretend to follow, but then I'll turn and defend."

Turn and defend? Her mind barely comprehended that part. When he told her to, she ran for the trees, heedless of the brush scratching her feet and lower legs, snatching at her dress. She heard Zoram following, and then he stopped and erupted in his own war cry. She paused, trembling, embracing the bole of a young maple tree as she strained to see him in the encompassing gloom. He carried sword, bow, and dagger, but the bandits were too close for him to make use of the bow.

The twang that followed proved her wrong. A bandit screamed as his sword clattered to the ground, and then Zoram's shadowy form dashed between the other two horses. With branches from other trees in the way, she had a hard time following what was happening, but Zoram seemed to be moving faster than was humanly possible. And he had somehow turned what seemed to be the disadvantage of being unmounted into an advantage. The two uninjured bandits clearly struggled to control their mounts, spinning them with crazy abandon as they sought to get at Zoram or bring their horses' front hooves to bear. One horse lost its balance, and a giant crash assaulted the night air, followed by both equine and human screams. A shaft of moonlight stabbed through the trees, illuminating the killing stroke Zoram administered, which froze Siarah's lungs and turned her belly over. Her hands left the tree to grasp her midriff. Her eyes watered, further obscuring her view. If only she were deaf and couldn't hear the awful sounds of the skirmish.

She couldn't tell if the third bandit escaped or not, and when she finally came to herself, she was sitting with her back against the tree, head in her hands, as Zoram knelt beside her, coaxing her back to reality. She finally lifted her head, blinking in his direction, noting the deafening stillness. Her mind started functioning again.

"The one you hit with the arrow … is he … ?"

"I finished him." His voice was a strange mixture of ice and fire, and she shivered in a wash of heat.

"Did you … kill all three?" She had to know, though part of her cowered from the truth.

"Just two. One got away. We have a horse, though. It should be able to carry us to Mulek."

"Is it … hurt?"

"Yes, but not badly, and I can't assess it fully in the dark. Come, we need to keep moving."

"Why?" she asked, spine suddenly stiffening. "They're gone. Can't we camp here? Let the horse rest?"

She expected him to brush off that suggestion with his usual professional scrutiny. She even recoiled in anticipation of anger, remembering that he had just slain two men in less time than it normally took her to wash her face in the morning.

"If we move farther into the trees, we can find a place to set up a camp. I might even be able to make a small shelter."

"A … shelter?" She realized she was trembling uncontrollably.

"Yes. It's going to rain soon."

Ara stood atop the western wall of Gideon, leaning against a stone parapet as she watched the sun sink into the horizon. She thought yet again how aptly the scene portrayed her fading hope. Gideon was a good place, filled with admirable people, and Jerena's letters had been helpful for a while … until they weren't. What was she doing here? She had a job, similar to what she'd done at the late High Judge Zerahir's house in Zarahemla. She rented a room for herself with a family that was nice but not all that warm. Her father, sister, and brother were God knew where, and she had no other family that she knew of. What real friends she might have claimed were either gone, dead, or still in Zarahemla. She hadn't tried to make friends in this place, and why should she? She didn't fit in. Most of these people were strong, faithful Christians, and she was ... well, she wasn't like them.

After the sun had completely abandoned her, she turned away with a heavy sigh. Then she sucked in a breath and froze upon noticing a rock of a man who had been standing just behind her. She nearly swallowed her tongue.

"Who ...?" she squeaked. "Oh, Jeruzim." Her heart started beating again, hand resting on her chest as she gulped more air.

"I've noticed that you come here often, and you never leave happy." His mellifluous tone carried no judgment, though she sensed some concern. She was used to ignoring that.

"To be fair, I never *arrive* happy, either," she deadpanned, looking down the wall, with its occasional sentries.

"I see. You miss Kihoran, I know."

Her eyes snapped back to him, narrowing. "Why would you say that?"

He gave a slight shrug. "Because it's true. And you aren't the only one who receives news from Zarahemla. Specifically, from the household of Helaman."

"You mean Jerena."

He nodded a little uncomfortably at that. "Yes. She is worried about you."

"She asked you to watch over me?" She put her hands on her hips to emphasize how insulting that was. Or how insulting she thought it *should* be, at least.

"We should all be watching out for each other, especially as followers of the coming Messiah."

Of course he would hit her with an unassailable statement like that. She huffed. "Well, I'm different. And I'm fine."

He studied her for several moments in the fast-fading light. "Whether you are or you aren't, Shemnilom would like to see you."

She gave him a puzzled look. "The ... old priest?"

She realized how she had inflected the word "old" by the wry smile he returned. "Very old, yes. Also very wise, more so than you might imagine."

What did that mean? Kai had made oblique mention of the grizzled cleric being somewhat unusual, but she hadn't questioned him about it.

"Now?" She replied.

He shrugged again. "Might as well. His work for the day is done."

She sighed deeply again. She could say no. She wanted to say no. And yet she felt a strange pull. "All right. He lives in the back of that synagogue near the center of the city?"

"I'll take you," he said.

"You don't need—"

"It's alright."

"Fine." She waved her arm forward, causing him to turn and lead the way. They walked along the wall for a short distance, then down narrow stairs with no railing. He took the first street leading away from the wall, then made a pair of turns before they finally arrived at the indicated synagogue. She remembered it, though she didn't spend much time in this quarter. She associated it too much with Kai. She never walked by the barracks, either, or the militia practice yards. *Especially* not the practice yards.

Jeruzim led her through the synagogue at a slow but confident gait, hands behind his back, head slightly bowed—in reverence, she guessed. She had gone to synagogue a few times in a different part of the city, but it didn't hold much meaning for her. She tried—she promised God she was trying—but what was the point? Jerena kept telling her things would get better, and a shrinking part of her still clung to that optimism. But, well, they hadn't, and she wasn't a patient person. At least, not in this.

It helped sometimes to stoke her anger toward Imrahiel and his thieving, murderous thugs. She reveled in all the torments they would eventually suffer, whether in this life or the next. Oh, how she wished she would be able to participate in their administration! She didn't know exactly how, but somehow *he* was responsible for her and Kai not being together. Yes, the logic fell apart whenever she tried to follow the threads, but some things a jilted woman just knew.

Amid a dreamlike opacity, she followed Jeruzim into Shemnilom's office, observing with detached interest as the two men greeted each other and shared a few informal words in the flickering lamplight. She closed her eyes and inhaled slowly. Some kind of incense was burning. It seemed to relax her a little.

Her eyes opened, then widened as she realized Jeruzim had already left, like a ghost. "What is that?" she asked.

"What is what, my dear?"

"The herb you're burning."

"Nothing special. It smells nice, though. My late wife loved it. Our daughters and granddaughters do, too. Our sons and grandsons—those who have survived the wars, anyway—not so much. The great-grandchildren are still undecided."

In a very kind way, he had just corrected her perspective. She resented that, and yet didn't. Not from him. He radiated kindness and compassion. Obviously, this was another of Jerena's schemes to cheer her up or make her forget the only man she could ever love. Silly to think that way, she knew, but what if it was true?

"Will you sit, please?" he asked softly.

She glanced at the only two rickety options in his office, across the tiny desk from him, then picked one. It creaked a warning as she set her weight on it, but it held. He'd better not tell her to try the other one.

"Arayah, I have some news for you."

She blinked in surprise. "News? About what?"

"About Kai. And Siarah."

Twin blades pierced her heart, one from each name. She stuttered, "What ... about them?" Was he going to let her know they had officially married? Did Jerena think that barrel of ice water dumped over her head would shock her out of her somber reverie? That it would somehow be a *good* thing? She gave a shrug, schooling her face into an expressionless mask. "Never mind. I know. They're married. I wish them every happiness." She barely got the last word out through the lump in her throat, and her mask felt like it had cracked in several places.

Shemnilom hummed deeply, glancing at his gnarled but strong hands clasped on the desk, which creaked as well. "No, actually. Siarah has been taken—kidnapped—by those who follow Gadianton, probably to lure Kai into a trap. They suspect he knows something about the death of Kishkumen, their top operative."

Operative? That was a word she hadn't heard used before … and she had been in the spy business. Mostly for the wrong side, to her eternal shame. "What do you mean? They infiltrated Zarahemla?"

The old priest shook his head. "They took her from Bountiful, many weeks ago, and we have been unable to locate her thus far. Helaman has men looking. Kai himself is working with Dan and some of Captain Lehi's men in the east, seeking to pick up the trail."

"How would they lure Kai into a trap? They're still on the run."

He took a long breath. "Well, by letting him pick up their trail at some point. They are still numerous, and they have many supporters, including in some of the cities. Those men of Lehi—members of his elite band, no less—surely give them great pause, so they'll try to split them up. Kai and Dan know that, of course, but … well, sometimes people don't make decisions using the best logic, especially in emotionally trying circumstances. Gadianton knows that well."

At least one of those daggers in her heart was being pounded deeper by a large hammer. Not only was Kai in serious danger again, but Shemnilom had just said he might do something stupid in his desperation to find Siarah. Not her, but Siarah. She swallowed, blinking back a selfishly reckless tear.

"Why tell me this? It isn't any concern of mine." Those words were difficult to say.

"Jerena thought you should know. I wasn't so sure at first, but she convinced me. I presume she believes you still might have some … um, useful connections."

Her face heated, and not with embarrassment. Anger flashed through her eyes. "I am not in contact with *any* of the Gadiantons, and I have no idea where they might be. She seriously thought I might still be connected to them?" She started to rise, but he held up his hands.

"No, my dear, no. Most certainly not. She and Helaman are deeply concerned for Kai. They only wonder if something you can remember might be leveraged."

"Well, I guess it was smart to get a priest to deliver that slap in the face, then."

His face fell as he stared at his hands again. Then he looked back up, eyes piercing and solemn. "I am not just a priest, Sister Arayah. I trust almost no one with this information, but I feel like you should know. I am Helaman's chief spymaster."

The muscles in her jaw went slack. "You're ... a spy?"

He chuckled, the sound tinged with discomfort. He scratched the back of his neck. "Yes, and I have been for a very long time. Twice your lifespan, easily. I have seen much, and these ... vicious thieves ... of Gadianton are probably the worst I've seen. They will utterly destroy this nation if we let them, and laugh while doing it. We must stop them."

She swallowed, looking away. "I know how evil they are," she muttered in a near whisper, then shivered as she recalled again how much she had helped them.

"Yes, I am sure you do. And so I'm pursuing this further than Jerena intended. I won't merely ask if you can recollect any contacts your father or others might have mentioned, or that you may have stumbled across. I want to recruit you. I would like you to work for me. Your first assignment, of course, would be to help us locate Siarah and protect Kai. I know that is a difficult task ... for obvious reasons." He squinted. "But I trust you—because Jerena and Helaman trust you—and I know you can help."

She studied the warped but polished surface of his desk. What had being a spy gotten her before? Granted, she had been on the wrong side, but ... well, it *had* introduced her to Kai. That was good. Or was it? What if she had never met him? Of course, if she had continued working for her father, and Imrahiel, and, by extension, Kishkumen and Gadianton, she would likely be hiding somewhere with them, waiting for the right time to return, crafting stories that the lawyers could use to help them ultimately evade the law. Disastrous for her either way.

"Gadianton and Imrahiel are patient and clever, and far more dangerous than you think," she said. She looked up to see him cock an eyebrow. He leaned back and folded his arms.

"Are they now? I try not to underestimate anyone, and I have stared pure, malevolent evil in the face more than once. They might surprise me with a tactic here and there, but the depth of their depravity, and their stubbornness in pursuing it? No, that will not shock me, young one."

"What if they find me before I find them? I don't think they'll just kidnap me. I took the second set of oaths."

"Indeed. That is a danger. And so I don't make this proposal lightly."

"Maybe they'll try to frame me, make it look like I was in league with Kishkumen. They could claim I was the one who convinced him to "go rogue" and abandon everything his famous grandfather—who founded his own *city*—stood for. They could turn a lot of people against me with such lies, using provable truths to support them. I *did* spy for them. And Kishkumen had made it known to a lot of people that he wanted to marry me."

Shemnilom grunted, then suddenly looked haggard. The abrupt change jolted her. He rubbed his face with both hands. "I'm getting too old for this. It's the same thing, over and over again. And our people, whom I love with all my heart—which is the *only* reason I'm still doing this—let themselves be led around by the nose so easily." His head shook slowly as he closed his eyes. When he opened them, he took a heavy breath. "Let us both think on this further. I do still believe you can be helpful, but I'm not sure at what cost. You have so much more life in front of you, while I am nearing my sunset. Perhaps my judgment is becoming clouded. Can we speak again the day after tomorrow?"

She found herself awash in what seemed like genuine warmth. But was it? Could she trust him? If not, who *could* she trust? Kai, most certainly, if that mattered. And Jerena, too. If she couldn't trust Jerena, having a lot of life ahead wasn't worth much.

She gave a shallow nod. "Yes. And … thank you." She rose and turned toward the door, hesitating as he said, "You are a good woman, Arayah. Don't let yourself forget that."

She didn't acknowledge the comment, just left the room and moved quickly through the synagogue, picking up more speed as she exited the building. She made a brief stop at her rented room. Then she was off to Zarahemla, begging whatever transport she could find. If she couldn't make it back to Gideon in time for that next meeting with Shemnilom, so be it.

CHAPTER 8

And he shall go forth, suffering pains and afflictions and temptations
of every kind; and this that the word might be fulfilled which saith
he will take upon him the pains and the sicknesses of his people.
And he will take upon him death, that he may loose the bands of death
which bind his people; and he will take upon him their infirmities,
that his bowels may be filled with mercy, according to the flesh,
that he may know according to the flesh how to succor
his people according to their infirmities.
—Alma 7:11–12

K ai couldn't decide whether to feel satisfied they were making progress or frustrated that they weren't. They worked a
standard, broad-sweep scouting pattern as they headed north,
and with twenty-two mounted men, they could scour a great
deal of territory quickly. On the other hand, those wide sweeps slowed
their forward progress, which often caused him to feel like he was losing
ground on Gadianton and his gang. *If* they had even fled north! What if
they had gone south instead?

"I have no idea if we're heading in the right direction," he complained to Dan during a pause. The horses needed frequent breaks given
how hard the men were running them.

Dan nodded, his responding tone sage. "We can only do our best
and let the Lord provide."

Kai's simmering vexations began to boil again. "Why doesn't he let
us know where to find Siarah? He's revealed many times where Lamanite

99

armies were going to attack, and also where to find prisoners. Is it me? Am I just unable to hear him well enough?"

Dan returned a sober stare. "You are too hard on yourself. And the Lord hasn't always told us where to go. The Lamanites have surprised us more than once, like at Ammonihah ... or, more recently, Zarahemla. Even then, the Lord made ways for his faithful people to escape those calamities."

"Exactly!" pressed Kai. "Siarah's kidnapping is a calamity, and she's one of the most faithful people I know. If the Gadiantons can get away with it—and they *are*—what kind of message does that send to every-one else?"

A sense of righteous fury flared in his chest, and he lifted his chin as he awaited Dan's response. As usual, the big warrior of stripling fame remained calm, his gaze exuding composure and reflection.

"The Lord knows what he is doing, Kai. Given the many things I've seen—some of which seemed wholly illogical at first but ended up being perfectly brilliant—I cannot deny that. Keep seeking after him. Keep doing all in your power, without worrying too much about what you can't control. This will all work out in the best way possible for us, because God cherishes his children and is always faithful to them. *Always*. And remember, nobody will ever 'get away' with anything. Not in the end. Justice and mercy will both be fully served. Pray to the Father that he will help you understand this better."

As usual, Kai couldn't argue against such powerful testimony. And truth be told, he relied on it. Maybe too much. He shuddered to think about how hard all this would be without Dan. He studied the ground near his feet, damp with recent rains. The half-year anniversary of Hela-man's rule as the nation's Chief Judge was coming up soon. And for nearly half that time, Siarah had been a prisoner. Or she was dead. That possibility reared its dark, demonic head more frequently of late.

Dan must have sensed it. "We will find her, Kai. Alive and well. The prophet has promised it, and he did so in the Lord's name, not out of pity for us. We can trust that."

Kai grunted as he leaned forward with his elbows on his knees and lowered his head. He closed his eyes, trying to reach out for any wisp of reassuring knowledge he could grasp. Keeping his head down, he asked, "How far to this new city of David we've heard about?"

Dan's reply carried sharpness. "It is a mockery."

"I know, you've already made it clear how you feel about it. But how far, do you think?"

"Two days, maybe three. And perhaps I need to moderate my feelings in that time."

Kai lifted his head. "Why? You're right to criticize them. By leaving us, they made us weaker, and many of them pretend they can make a new nation that will rival the power of King David's ancient one. But they're essentially slapping Helaman in the face. I know they don't say it, but they are."

"I don't care that they might have insulted Helaman," said Dan. "Neither does he. But yes. The prophet counseled them not to leave, urged them instead to stay and support him as he strives to rebuild the strength of the church. They adamantly refused. That carries consequences, and potentially not just in this life."

Kai thought again of Merga and Orofin. They were old. Perhaps they believed their departure to the north made no difference. They were good people who had lived through many wars, and they wanted to live out their remaining years in peace somewhere. But Dan was right. Following the Lord's prophet was more important, and for a host of reasons, even if Kai himself wasn't very good at articulating them. His adoptive mother Ishara was a shining example of that, and she wanted peace more than anyone else he could think of.

He thought of something. "What if Helaman eventually decides to lead all the faithful church members out of the land, like the first king Mosiah did? And even Nephi, hundreds of years ago."

"Then we will go," came the firm answer.

"What if your parents couldn't make the journey? They're getting old. You're a youngest son."

Dan shrugged. "We would work that out. Either I carry them on my own back, or they find another way to accompany us, or they stay behind to proclaim God to the unbelievers until the breath of this life leaves their bodies and they go to rejoice with their Savior. I don't worry about that, Kai. My mother, especially, taught me that there is no need to stress over what we think we cannot do, as long as we are on the Lord's errand."

Kai nodded with a small sigh. "Yeah, mine, too."

"It's a wonder we haven't introduced them to each other."

Kai caught a wink, and he suddenly realized how much better he felt. Hope rose anew in his breast, giving strength to his mind and muscles. They just needed the horses to feel it, too.

———◇———

It took three more days to reach the co-called city of David, and in that time they experienced all kinds of odd encounters. One small group of emigrants had decided to build a village entirely in the trees, including large boxes filled with dirt they had hauled up from the forest floor. Silly idea. Two other men, with their families, apparently fancied themselves the next Lehi and Ishmael, striking out for another promised land. After talking with them, it seemed they wandered on purpose, as if they could recreate the Lord's teaching experiences over the eight years their ancestors had roamed the wilderness before reaching the ancient area they called Bountiful and then departing on the specially designed ship. Kai and Dan even witnessed a loud, public argument about which of their sons would eventually lead them in the building of a boat.

The discovery of a group of young women, nearly twenty in all, training themselves to be fierce warriors, was startling. A few even wanted to brawl with some of Lehi's elites! They didn't ask for help in their drills, just wanted to measure themselves against acclaimed soldiers. Truly odd, and utterly foolish. A woman who was good with a bow might have some chance against a trained male soldier at a distance, but when that distance disappeared, the fight was over without a hearty helping of pure luck or angelic intervention.

They also happened upon two peculiar men driving a swaybacked mare pulling an old wagon filled with odd contraptions. They had set up a semi-permanent camp, complete with a small ore smelter. They called themselves inventors, and they claimed the Lord was guiding them toward remarkable new discoveries that would vastly improve farming, building, and even warfighting abilities. When Dan asked why they had left Nephite lands and pursued their work alone, they said they were tired of being rejected by those who resisted change.

As expected, Kai and his group also encountered several individuals and groups who had fled Nephite lands to escape the law. Some had been living beyond Nephite borders for years, mostly as nomads. The fear of God entered their eyes when they recognized Lehi's men, and most tried to run before they could be questioned.

Unfortunately, little information of real value came from any of the people Kai and Dan interviewed. And so, Kai pinned his hopes on finding some scrap of useful intelligence in David, the half-built city that couldn't hold a tiny candle to the once-mighty Jerusalem under the legendary David of old, king of all the tribes of Israel.

As they approached the entrance, Kai noted an archway that someone could pull a rope across. It was comically superfluous, since the "wall" was just a low berm that even the swaybacked mule they had seen could traverse. Kai voiced a question he, Dan, and Jerid had discussed before. "Shouldn't we be less conspicuous? If they're here, we'll alert them, and they'll run to ground."

"They're doing that anyway," said Dan. "And we need to impress upon these people how serious we are. They are not Gadianton supporters, and they also don't want the Nephite government interfering in their lives. They will understand that the quicker we can complete our mission, the sooner we will leave."

"They don't overtly support Gadianton, but they might fear him enough to hide him." Kai already knew Dan's response to that statement, but he needed to hear it again.

"They will respect us more than they do him, and they will help as they can. They might be going astray, but they are still good people."

Kai didn't lodge any further objections. He hoped Dan was right.

No guards watched them pass through the arch, but plenty of people stopped in the midmorning sun and stared, noting the accoutrements of Lehi's elites. Dan wore his distinctive headband, too, which drew whispered comments and pointed fingers. They probably had no idea what to make of Kai. He didn't stand out, except for being young. They must be wondering why he rode at their head with Dan.

They couldn't find an inn large enough to host them all, so they made a request of a man who seemed to be a longer-term resident. He led them to a large stretch of grass on which they could set up their tents. By noon the camp was complete, and while they probably didn't need to post sentries, they did anyway. Then they broke into small groups to canvas the city's inhabitants—maybe three thousand in total—for information on the movement of suspicious or secretive individuals through the area.

Kai insisted that Dan lead one of the groups himself, then took two of Lehi's men to find any leaders of the city.

They soon found that a single man wielded the vast majority of the influence in David and the surrounding area. As he introduced himself to Kai, he claimed he was just a humble servant granted an interim role by the people until they could decide how they wanted to establish a permanent form of governance. Kai had heard such claims before, on his many other trips outside Nephite lands, mainly to the east. The story usually ended up the same—the "interim" position became permanent, then evolved into an inheritance that could be broken only by violence.

"I thank you for your hospitality, Judge Angidah." The man had said he didn't want the additional honorific of the word "chief." "You are building an impressive city. How large was it when you arrived?" It wasn't truly grand, but Kai had learned a modicum of diplomacy as a spy, supplemented by his experiences with Dan and Helaman.

Angidah waved a hand before his face as they stood outside his modest but well-framed home, attracting notice from passersby. "You are too kind." Pride entered his tone. "We started out with five hundred. We hope to reach five thousand over the next year. We already do some valuable trading with cities both north and south of us—and even one to the east. People like the stability and opportunity we offer." It was starting to sound like a sales pitch, made even more obvious by the frequent, smiling glances at Lehi's men. Kai understood. Angidah would love to have a few such men to form the core of a defensive force. Or help with policing. At least he wasn't so naïve as to believe things would always be easy, especially when success would breed jealousies among outsiders and insiders alike. It was human nature.

Kai wanted to laugh, but that would be undiplomatic. "Are there many Lamanites in these parts?" He already knew the answer. He had been through the general area before, albeit briefly.

"A few. We found a small village nearby shortly after we arrived, composed of Lamanites and some people from the east. They created a mixed language many years back, but they all speak our language now. They are peaceful—tired of the constant wars, like us."

Kai tightened his lips. "Yes. We are all weary of war. And insurrections. I'm here representing Chief Judge Helaman, who, as you know, was almost assassinated."

Angidah shook his head slowly, eyes lowered for a moment. "Yes, we heard about that. In fact, for some of our recent arrivals, that was the final stone in their pack that toppled them. We welcomed them with open arms, of course, as we welcome you and your men. You all have families, too, I presume."

Kai swallowed hard. "All but me. And in part, that's why I'm here. You've heard of a man named Gadianton?"

Angidah frowned as he shook his head, and his eyes didn't reveal anything. He might be telling the truth.

"Well, Helaman's assassination was ordered by this man, as was Pahoran's. Helaman has search parties combing the land, trying to find him. Gadianton has kidnapped people as well … including my betrothed, from Bountiful."

Empathy flickered in Angidah's wide eyes. He looked away for a moment, as if examining one of his own memories, then returned his gaze to Kai. "You are not in Nephite lands, but I understand. You believe he may have come through here."

Kai nodded. "Yes, we do."

"Well, I suppose that is possible. Would he use his real name, though? Do you have a description?"

Kai had never seen him, but several judges and officers in Zarahemla had. "I do. He is middle-aged, of average height and build, with dark hair and eyes. None of that is distinctive, but he has a thin scar that runs diagonally across his left cheek. He is, by all accounts, very charismatic and persuasive, though also cruel and quick to anger."

Angidah gave a thoughtful nod. "He sounds like Morianton, that greedy fool who beat his servants, especially the women. But I have not seen such a man pass through our city. Others might have. I can make some inquiries."

"Thank you. He may be traveling with a man named Imrahiel. I'm certain that is not his real name. He is bald with a gray beard, also in his middle years, and he likes to dress like a lord. He is—or was—quite wealthy. Him I would know instantly on sight." He had injected more venom into his voice than intended, and Angidah seemed to take notice.

"He is the leader? Or is it this, um …"

"Gadianton is the leader. Both are the devil's own sons, though they pretend to be pious. The most venomous viper, hidden in your bed, is not more dangerous than these two, and Helaman knows it."

There. He had adequately impressed upon the man the urgency of the situation. Or at least, he hoped he had.

"I see," said Angidah, frowning again. "I will do what I can, though most of my people will not be interested in helping. We are safe here, far from the conflicts of our prior home, and we aim to maintain our peace by staying out of these … entanglements … as much as possible."

Angidah had essentially revealed that his 'help' would be minimal at best. He had also exposed his naiveté and selfishness.

Kai wasn't about to let him off the hook. "If Gadianton's group destroys the Nephite nation, they will come here next."

Angidah shrugged off that assertion. "They may expand east and west, maybe. South among the Lamanites. But not north. It gets colder here in the winter, and it is sparsely populated."

"But this area is growing," countered Kai, "both in population and in wealth. Many of the ore deposits farther north are exhausted, but this is still a rich land. They will come."

"God will protect this new Land of Israel," asserted Angidah.

Kai nearly gaped. "Land of Israel?"

"Yes, centered here in the city of David. We already have strong alliances formed with other groups who have moved to these north countries, and we may eventually band together more firmly. We Davidites are leading that process."

"And why will God protect you?" asked one of Lehi's men, named Gath, who took a step forward.

Angidah drew his shoulders back. "Because he led us here. And we are faithful in following the Law of Moses."

"As are we," said Gath, "but not all. Tricksters like Gadianton find and exploit the weak. His poison spreads quickly. What has happened in Nephite lands can easily happen here."

"I will not allow it," proclaimed Angidah, his haughtiness returning in force. "And you should strongly consider joining us. I know you are faithful men." His eyes rested briefly on each of the three. "Together we can keep this people safe from outside predators."

"Well," interjected Kai, "we can talk about that later. For now, you should realize that predators already stalk this land. We should cooperate on finding Gadianton and stopping him. That will benefit both your people and mine."

"So you say," said Angidah, rubbing his chin, "but we would be getting involved in Nephite politics. I will see what I can do, but I must be cautious. In the meantime, you are welcome to stay here and make more ... discrete inquiries."

That would have to do. Hopefully it would suffice.

———◆———

The people of David were friendly in a way that didn't fully mask their suspiciousness. They had left the Nephite nation for a reason, and the continued presence of a cohort of the legendary Lehi's men made them standoffish. Some wanted to be helpful, but only because the quicker the quarry could be found—or determined to be nowhere in the area—the sooner these heavily armed, brash Nephites would leave.

Though Kai hoped their stay in the area would be brief, he couldn't be sure. So he sent five of the Lehites home to visit their families, which would allow them to scout the group's back trail as well. They could rotate back in a couple of weeks to let others return home, unless the entire troop returned to Lehi. Kai led the longer scouting missions around David, taking four or five men with him at a time. Dan directed their activities in and close to the city. Each time Kai returned, Dan had at least one lead for him to follow on his next foray, and, given Kai's anxiety, he didn't sleep much.

He, Dan, and Jerid were sharing a meal at a small inn near the center of the city a few weeks later when Dan tapped his forefinger twice on the table. That meant he was suspicious about something. He didn't look at Kai or Jerid, neither of whom gave any hint they had recognized the signal. After a few seconds, Kai rose and walked toward the innkeeper, who was wiping her hands on her apron after depositing some dirty dishes in a basin near the kitchen entrance. He trusted his small distraction would attract the attention of the suspicious party and give Dan a few extra seconds to study whatever had caused his concern. As rehearsed.

"Do you have any of that pie left?" he asked as he approached the woman. He really didn't want any more food, but the pie *was* good.

She blew a wisp of hair from her eyes, which were rimmed with suspicion, just as they had been every other time he had interacted with her. "No, I'm sorry. We've run out. But ... I could make another one. Or one of my girls could. It's no trouble."

Kai raised a hand and gave her the most sincere smile he could conjure up. "No, it's okay. Next time. I guess I should probably get here earlier." He dipped his head in thanks before turning to head back to the table. When he resumed his chair, he glanced at Jerid, then Dan.

"I've got her," whispered Dan. "Jerid, pretend you're going to arrest that man by the door."

Jerid rose smoothly, placing his hand on the hilt of his sword as he stepped toward the false target, who was finishing up the last few bites of what turned out to be a piece of that pie. "I must arrest you," he said in a commanding voice, clearly audible throughout the room. Kai heard the innkeeper gasp, and his eyes flashed her way to make sure she didn't faint or do something foolish. The man jumped in his seat, dropping his fork to the hard floor with a clatter. Murmurs arose.

"Wha—?" stuttered the man. "What for? And by whose authority?"

Kai was impressed by Dan's stealthy movements. One moment he was seated across the table from Kai; the next he was halfway across the room. He drew his long knife as he sprinted like a lion toward his target, who went bug-eyed. The woman fumbled in her cloak for something as she scrambled out of her chair and placed her back against the wall. More gasps filled the air.

"Don't," warned Dan. He didn't have to utter more than the one word. She froze, and Kai studied her while Jerid explained to the man by the door that he was safe. The man seemed to be having a hard time believing it.

"Who sent you?" growled Dan. "And why?"

Kai narrowed his eyes, hackles rising as he got to his feet and drew his sword, scanning the other patrons carefully.

"I … I don't know what you're talking about." She looked around as if seeking sympathy. She wouldn't find any from this group.

"Show me that knife," insisted Dan, backing up half a step and lowering his own blade, almost daring her to attack him. She stared at him warily for a moment, then withdrew a long, thin blade, sharpened on both sides with a wicked tip.

"A woman needs protection," she explained, holding the knife loosely in one hand.

Dan nodded toward it. "Place it on the table, then take a step to the side."

She frowned, seeming—or maybe acting—confused, but then complied. In a split second, Dan had snatched her knife and moved between her and the table, his own blade raised again, a forearm just under her neck pinning her to the wall. The woman blinked, clearly surprised—and cowed—by the quickness of his bulk.

"Now, who sent you, and what is your purpose?"

She shook her head, long, dark tresses swirling. "I told you, I don't know what you're talking about."

Dan chuckled, playing the game as well as Kai had ever seen it played. "Well, we'll take you back to our camp and loosen your tongue." He glanced at Jerid. "Which of Lehi's protocols should we use?"

Jerid answered after letting his eyes wander in thought. "Four, I think. We don't have much time. And we'll send her to Lehi's headquarters if that doesn't work."

"Four it is." His fearsome gaze made her shiver. "Now, turn around. We need to tie your hands. Kai?"

Kai walked over, sheathing his sword.

"I'll let you do the honors," said Dan. "Be careful, though. She might have another weapon. If she resists, I'll give her a quick stab to the shoulder with her own knife. That worked for us before, with those assassins Imrahiel sent after you."

Indeed it had, and the woman took in a sharp breath. Kai knew Dan was serious, and the woman seemed to realize it as well, wide eyes darting between them. She may also have recognized Imrahiel's name, perhaps even the event mentioned. Her hands came up, palms out. "No, wait. I can tell you what I know. And I wasn't sent here to kill anyone." She gave a slight nod toward Kai. "Just to study how we might be able to speak to Kihoran privately."

Kai glowered at her. "You mean kidnap me. Like you did Siarah."

Though the woman tried to hide it, she clearly knew the name.

"No," she said, voice tinged with desperation. "Just talk. We have … a proposal."

"Does it come from Imrahiel?"

The woman gave him a confused look. "I … don't know that name."

"That's a lie, but all right. Gadianton, then. Where does he want to have this 'talk' with us?"

Her eyes widened momentarily as she glanced at Dan. "Just you,

Kihoran," she said, trying to sound defiant but failing.

Kai rubbed his hands in front of his chin, staring hard into her eyes. "Fine. I'm not afraid of your master. And I'm tired of chasing him. You lead. You have a horse, I presume?"

"Yes," she responded, seeming relieved but wary. He hoped he hadn't made it look too easy.

He turned to Dan. "Get a message to Lehi with all haste to prepare a battle group. If I'm not back in two and a half days, send another message for him to dispatch it."

Dan backed away a step. "Are you sure?"

"I am."

Dan nodded. He even added a salute, which made the woman scrunch her brow. She appeared a little more shaken, too. Good. What she didn't know was that Kai's use of the half day in his order signaled Dan and Jerid to lead the rest of their men at a distance behind Kai, spread out more than a mile in pairs, stealthily tracking him all the way to the destination. If they were discovered, so be it—the chase would continue.

"I'll bring your horse," said Jerid as he disappeared out the door. Dan followed after a few words with the innkeeper—probably about their bill. He kept the Gadianton woman's knife. Kai nodded to her and gestured toward the entrance. She gave him a look hovering between cold and cautious as she stepped by him.

"What do you call yourself?" he asked when he could see her back.

"Raven," replied the woman with a slight turn of her head.

Kai couldn't help but chuckle. "Original."

———◇———

This new Raven led Kai northwest from the city, then slowly curved all the way to the east. He supposed she thought she was being clever. Kai could be cunning, too, though. Every so often, he made sure Vyim stepped on softer ground, or brushed a bush that would bear the mark of their passing. He kept Raven ahead of him, too, and she could hardly complain about that. He was accompanying her willingly, and he didn't know where they were going.

She did look back quite often. Maybe she was worried he would leave and she would lose her prize. Or perhaps she suspected he might try to subtly mark the trail with his knife. Each time he stared calmly back at her, hands holding his reins lightly. It became more and more evident that she was much more comfortable in a city, terrible at tracking.

They traveled throughout the night, resting the horses infrequently. Kai was grateful for a strong moon—not to assist his own eyesight, but Dan's in keeping the trail. While the man was a phenomenal tracker, darkness presented a definite disadvantage. Kai often wondered how far back the men were, but he didn't feel too worried about it.

By the time the first soft shimmer of light glowed in the eastern sky, they must have covered more than twenty miles. That would put them close to one of the large lakes. This Raven probably didn't realize how much familiarity he had with the area, mostly through studying detailed maps, both trading and military. Not that it really mattered. He felt sure he was doing the right thing in following her—more sure than he had been in a long time, though doubts still nipped at his heels.

Before the sun could fully show itself above the treetops, Raven halted her horse. Kai stopped Vyim a few paces behind her.

"We have to go on foot from here," she declared, twisting in her saddle, which was much simpler than his, not made for war.

"Why is that?" he demanded.

"I don't make the rules," she replied with a slight tilt of her chin. She seemed much more confident now that they were near one of the Gadiantons' encampments. He took a deep breath, sniffing the air. Yes, the smoke of cooking fires, whether still dormant from the night or recently activated, was more concentrated here. The scent of bodies, too. He wasn't skilled enough to estimate the size of the nearby camp just by smell, but Dan or Jerid might be able to.

He stared hard at her for long moments, until she was forced to turn her horse toward him. "So, where do I leave my mount?" he asked sternly. "You're not stealing him." He looked around carefully, buying a little more time for Dan and the others while trying not to be obvious about it.

She clearly took umbrage at his remark. "We are not common thieves," she spat, throwing her shoulders back.

Kai blew out a half whistle. "No, you are definitely not that. You go for bigger game, with a ruthlessness born of the fires of Sheol." His father Gideon would be proud of him for coming up with that one.

She glared, then dismounted in a show of annoyance. He set his lips in a thin line, knowing he was being watched by more eyes than hers. Another question was in order. "And how far on foot?"

She didn't deign to return his gaze. "Not far. And don't try anything."

"Like what?" He allowed himself a small smile as he let himself down to the ground. He unhooked his bow from his saddle, looping the strap of his quiver over his shoulder as he checked sword and knife. He grabbed a short spear as well, just for good measure, then wrapped Vyim's reins loosely around a branch. The well-trained animal would be able to break free if needed, and he could find his way back to their camp in the city of David.

She ignored the question as she began hiking through the trees, lifting her skirts to prevent them from getting snagged. He caught a couple of curses regarding her attire. Apparently, she didn't like having to stalk somebody wearing a dress, but she would have looked out of place in David otherwise.

He followed, treading carefully, eyes scanning the trees and brush. He didn't immediately spot anyone else, but after about a hundred yards he caught movement in a tree that couldn't have been bird or animal. Then another, and another. Despite his earlier confidence in the wisdom of this journey, his adrenaline began to pump. Not fast, but enough. He became more alert, keeping his breathing steady.

Finally, he and the woman broke through the trees into a large clearing occupied by about twenty crudely made huts. Oh, how living in such primitive shelters must gall someone like Imrahiel. They were almost worse than tents! He wished to heaven the man was here, so he could witness it.

Several men materialized out of the shadows, armed with spears or long knives. The archers would still be in the trees. Kai stopped and set his feet.

"Who am I here to see?" he asked in a loud voice, causing Raven to hesitate and turn.

"His name is Lugran, and he already knows you're here." She made it sound like he should be frightened of the name, but he had never heard it.

He grunted in response, then pointedly ignored all the armed men as he walked toward the middle of the poorly organized cluster of huts. He noted two campfires aflame, the smells of roasting small game wafting in the air. That was another thing which would rankle Imrahiel—the food. He was used to fine dining at every meal, with only the best cuts of meat from cattle or large game. Eating unseasoned lesser creatures would come close to making him retch.

Kai passed Raven, then stopped when he reached the center. He tried to see inside some of the huts, though surely they wouldn't be keeping Siarah here. Would they? His heart beat a little faster, and his anger began to bubble.

He spread his arms wide, turning in a slow circle. "I'm here, Lugran, or whatever your name is. You wanted to talk."

Several seconds passed. Raven had stopped about ten feet away, studying him with an unreadable expression. At least ten men surrounded him, but they kept their distance. He itched to know how close Dan and the others were. No horn had sounded, so they hadn't been discovered. Still, they would have to be very cautious. How would they decide to deal with the sentries in the trees? He didn't spend too much time imagining—Dan and the elites knew their business well, and they were ghosts. He just needed to keep as much attention as possible centered on him.

A man stepped out of one of the huts, stooping low through the doorway. He was small and lumpy, his brown beard patchy and his hairline retreating, but he looked fierce. His eyes shone as tiny dark pebbles with fire in their core, and his hands clenched and unclenched repeatedly. A nervous tic?

He cast a glare at Raven. "This wasn't the plan."

She shrugged. "The plan changed. They knew I didn't belong there." She took a step toward Lugran. "The good thing is that he's obviously going out of his mind over his betrothed." A small smile accompanied her sidelong glance at Kai. "He seems willing to have a productive conversation."

The man grumbled as he squared up to Kai, rounding his shoulders and thrusting out his misshapen chest. "We'll see about that. I—"

"Where is she?" demanded Kai, his voice as cold and menacing as he could make it.

"Not here," Lugran snapped. "And you will not interrupt me again."

"Why is that?" challenged Kai, enjoying the purpling of the veins along the man's temples.

"Because we are not in Nephite lands. *I* am in control here."

Kai gave a slight shake of his head. "No. Gadianton is. Or Imrahiel."

"Neither of them are here, so it is I." The man blew out a breath and stamped his feet like a frustrated child.

Kai gave an exaggerated roll of his eyes. "All right, you're in control. So, where is she?"

"It's not that easy."

"Isn't it? You want information in exchange for her, correct?"

Lugran narrowed his eyes. "Yes. You're willing to provide it?"

"Perhaps. If you tell me where she is first, and show me proof."

Lugran's eyes popped wide. "Proof? How is that even possible, and why do you think you can demand it?"

Kai shrugged. "You've expended a lot of effort trying to lure me into a conversation … with or without your master's approval."

The man's cheek muscles twitched, and Kai continued. "What I have to say might really impress your bosses, but I must have proof *first*."

Lugran clearly didn't like having it pointed out to him that he wasn't in charge … or that he was an utter sycophant. He stamped his feet again, then raised his hands high and shouted, "Fine! How about we just torture you then?"

Kai laughed at that. The purple veins looked about to pop. "Unless you have several days to do it, torture won't be effective. I suspect you know that. And you don't have several days."

Lugran took two angry steps toward him, coming within three feet. "I have all the time I need, and I will not fail."

Kai laughed louder, and for several seconds. He had spotted some movement out of the corner of one eye, and he knew what it meant.

"Stop laughing!" screamed Lugran. "Guards!" He raised a fleshy finger and waved it in the direction of some of the surrounding men. "Take him and disarm him, and don't be gentle."

That's when Kai clubbed him on the side of the head with the butt of his spear. At the same moment, arrows whistled from cover, downing three of the guards and sending the rest into a mad panic. Lugran dropped like a sack of wheat, and Kai stepped away from him to engage one of the guards, getting a quick thrust into the man's hip before he could reorient to Kai's challenge. The man grunted in pain, then sat with a thump, dropping his sword. Kai didn't need to finish him off. In fact, he desired as little death as possible. This camp could be a bonanza of information.

He didn't surprise the next guard, but the man's fighting skills were rudimentary at best. A flurry of swings, parries, and thrusts with the spear put the man bleeding on the ground, just in time for Kai to fend off another guard, attacking from his right rear quarter. He tossed his spear at the man, causing him to back up a step in surprise while Kai drew his sword. This man was a better fighter, but a step, parry, and hard downward slash gave him some ugly marks. He would probably lose an eye, too.

As the man tried to stanch the blood and get away, Kai bull-rushed him, sending him sprawling. Then he sheathed his sword, picked up his spear, and searched for more targets. He realized that the clashing sounds of battle had already subsided, though screams and moans continued. Dan, Jerid, and several of Lehi's men moved quickly through the camp, searching for more hostiles in and around the huts. He heard more elites sweeping the surrounding trees, calling out to each other in a speech that was half normal, half code. Kai still hadn't fully learned it, though Jerid had been teaching him. It was effective.

Dan moved to his side, looking him up and down. "No injuries?"

Kai shook his head, tempted to brag to his master sword trainer how adept he'd just been with that weapon. But Dan wouldn't be all that impressed. "No. You and the others?"

"A sprained ankle, maybe. We took them by surprise, and most have never been real soldiers."

"Good. Let's bind the wounds of the survivors and see if we can get some information."

Just then Jerid emerged from one of the huts, dragging a disheveled and bloodied man along by the hair. "Dan, Kai, this one looks important."

Kai's face froze. Could it be?

"Nahom," he said, stepping closer.

The man looked around wildly, seeming unable to focus. Finally, his eyes settled on Kai, widening as they swam in pain. "No, that's not my name."

Kai took a couple more seconds to be sure. "Yes, it is. You are Arayah's father. I met you several times, in Zarahemla."

Nahom struggled harder, wrestling Jerid's large hand with both of his to escape the grip on his hair. He might as well have been trying to pull the horns off a buffalo. Finally, Kai slapped him, hard, and he stopped struggling, eyes going dazed again.

"Stop the act. You're Nahom, and you're here. You know Imrahiel, and you know Gadianton. Where are they, and where is Siarah?"

It took several seconds for Nahom to come to his senses, and then he gave Kai a blank look. "I don't know where they are. They don't tell me important things like that. Lugran might—" He pressed his lips tight as his eyes darted to Lugran, moaning on the ground. Dan stepped over and picked him up like he was a puppy. He could stand, but barely. He was clearly in worse shape than Nahom. Kai hadn't hit him *that* hard, had he?

"It might be a while before this one can form a coherent sentence," declared Dan after lifting Lugran's eyelids one at a time and peering closely.

"I'm ... I'm going to throw up." Nahom began to sway a little, and when he convulsed, Jerid turned his head away. The eruption from his stomach was an impressive sight, and he coughed and sputtered for at least twenty seconds. Then he wiped a sleeve over his mouth and stared at Kai, eyes slowly refocusing.

"You're ... Ara's boyfriend," he said, as if Kai had just appeared before him.

"I pretended to be that, yes," said Kai. "That got me into your home, and I learned some things that helped us save Helaman."

"You ... helped?" He seemed genuinely confused, and he definitely wasn't yet in his right mind. Perhaps a portion of his brain had exited in the rush of vomit.

"We all did," said Kai. "That's why Gadianton wants to talk to me. He wants to know who helped the most, and who was able to discover and overcome his prized assassin. That is a closely guarded secret, of course, and Helaman doesn't tell me everything. You know how it is. So, I can't say who killed Kishkumen, but I *will* accelerate the killing of Gadiantons if I don't get Siarah back. As Lugran helpfully pointed out, we are *not* in Nephite lands."

Lugran seemed to be recovering more quickly than expected. From his awkward position nearly hanging from Dan's iron grip on his upper arm, he spat toward the ground. "You're lying. You know something more."

Kai focused on Lugran for a moment, then looked at Dan. "We need to take him with us. Perhaps Nahom, too."

"No," pleaded Nahom with sudden clarity. "My son! I can't leave my son. My other daughter has already run away, and I can't lose my son. He's only thirteen."

Kai turned to Jerid. "Did you find any children or youth in the camp?"

Jerid shook his head. "No, but there is a secondary camp, where most of the women and children are. Two of my men identified themselves and then watched them pack up and flee, northward. Siarah was not among them."

Kai returned his attention to Nahom, thinking hard. After long seconds, he said, "I'm not like you. I'm not interested in ripping families apart in the mad pursuit of power and prestige. I'm also not arrogant and dumb enough to claim I know what's best for everyone. That's not even what a prophet does. A true prophet, like Helaman, speaks for the Lord, who *does* know. I can't comprehend why God lets pompous idiots like you make other people suffer while dragging his name through the mud. I don't even know how he can stand it."

"Rubbish," came another hissed retort from Lugran. "That's—" Dan's other hand clamped over his mouth and nose, and the man nearly choked on his own tongue, eyes going wide in both rage and desperation for air.

"Go," Kai said to Nahom. "Follow after the group with your son. Take this Raven with you." He gestured toward his erstwhile captor, who stood frozen in the same place Kai had last seen her, skin pale; she might not have moved during the entire skirmish. "Let them know of the mercy shown to you. And tell them that I *will* find Siarah, and anyone involved in taking her. If I have to bring an entire army up here, I will." That was a bold claim, but he wasn't going for honest accuracy. The threat certainly rattled Nahom; it even appeared to affect Lugran, to some degree. He stopped struggling against Dan, who let him breathe through his nose.

"Are you sure?" asked Dan. It didn't sound like he was objecting, and Kai nodded.

"Yes. Let him go, Jerid. Search him for weapons first, though."

Jerid did so, finding nothing, which didn't surprise Kai. Then Ara's father stumbled out of the ramshackle village and into the woods, heading north with a trembling Raven staggering alongside.

Kai took a deep breath, noting the look of expectation in Jerid's eyes. Then he nodded. "All right, let's see what we can find out."

CHAPTER 9

And behold, I tell you these things that ye may learn wisdom;
that ye may learn that when ye are in the service of
your fellow beings ye are only in the service of your God.
—Mosiah 2:17

The air was cooling rapidly as Ara walked her horse—borrowed from the Gideon militia—through the Grand Gates of Zarahemla, but that wasn't what caused the chill to run up and down her spine. She had been trying to forget the Nephite capital, had even told herself she would never step foot inside it again. It harbored too many memories—some sweet, some painful, some almost unbearable because they were sweet. She stared at one of the massive doors as she passed, remembering how she and some of her friends had tricked the Lamanite guards so Kai could escape to Gideon. So long ago, and yet fewer than two years had passed.

She refocused her thoughts on Jerena, and on her and Helaman's children. Ara had enjoyed immensely her time in their household, helping with the children however she could. They were wonderful kids, and only the eldest had some inkling of what was really happening. Their father was in constant danger, owing to the greed and arrogance of people like Gadianton.

She couldn't bear the sight of *Jacob's Rest*, the inn where Kai had stayed for much of his time in the city, so she cut north to avoid it, all the way to Lehi Street. Still, memories from the inn assaulted her in flashes. Their dinner, when she had dressed up for him. The beginning of the First Day festivities, when she had discovered he could dance. How exhilarating that had been. And their kiss, in his room. He had refused to go any further, and now she knew there had been more than one reason.

She avoided Imrahiel's former pottery shop as well. That snake of a man would rot in hell, and the day couldn't come soon enough. As she approached the wealthy enclave called The Santorem, she had to close her eyes for several seconds at a time as she moderated her breathing, letting her placid mare plod along the stone street.

She didn't remember steering toward the house of Helaman and Jerena, but she arrived in short order. She stopped, peering through the front gates at a guard who stared back at her. She didn't recognize this one, though the guards' numbers had likely increased after the assassination attempt. The one Kai had foiled, by himself. Well, with God's help. That's what he claimed, anyway, and she trusted him.

She just didn't want to think about him too much.

She dismounted, then approached the gate. "Arayah, to see Lady Jerena."

The guard looked her over, then ordered another guard to exit and check her horse. A third guard disappeared inside the house to pass along her request. While they waited, the first guard questioned her.

"From where do you hail?"

"I come from Gideon, though I am from here."

"What business do you have with Lady Jerena?"

"I believe she is properly Sister Jerena, and I used to work in this household. Dan knows me, and … Kai, er, Kihoran."

"Neither of them is here."

She nodded. "I am aware of that. They are hunting Gadiantons … among whom is my father. And I know they kidnapped Kihoran's betrothed." She nearly choked on that word, which wasn't lost on the guard. Mention of Gadianton's name had also caught his attention.

He addressed the guard searching her horse. "Nehemadin, anything?" She hadn't watched his progress, knowing he wouldn't find anything concerning. She removed a knife from its sheath hidden in a fold of her skirts, holding it up to hang from her fingers by the blade.

"This is all I have that might be dangerous. You can keep it, of course, while I'm here."

Nehemadin came up from behind her to snatch the knife. At the same time, Jerena herself emerged from the front door.

"Let her in, Josuel, let her in."

The first guard jumped into action, opening the gate and ushering Ara through. Jerena then rushed to her, the fierceness of her embrace startling.

"I'm so glad you're here, Ara." Jerena ended the hug but kept one arm around her shoulders as she led Ara inside. Josuel secured the heavy door behind them. "The children will be thrilled to see you again. It's been too long, but ... I don't blame you for not wanting to come." She didn't say more, and Ara knew she understood.

"Well, I couldn't stay away forever. You've been too good to me. And I miss your children, too. I probably won't recognize them."

Jerena laughed. "Oh, you will. It hasn't been *that* long. They're just as rambunctious as ever, by the way."

Ara let out a light laugh. It felt good.

———◇———

After an enjoyable evening with Jerena and the children—Helaman was away from the city on both government and church business—Ara found herself alone with the wife of the young prophet. Relatively young, at least. There was a guard stationed on each floor of the two-story house, plus a dozen more on duty outside. Thankfully, they were practiced at being unobtrusive.

The two women relaxed in the upstairs sitting room. Jerena had prepared tall cups of cool water sweetened with sugar and fruit nectar. They were delicious ... and apparently sleep-inducing.

"How is your faith, Ara?"

Ara hadn't expected such a direct question—not so soon, anyway—and suddenly she was wide awake. She curled her lips a little. "I can't lie to you. It's been difficult trying to ... I don't know, find my way. It's not just that I'm new to Gideon, and away from you and Helaman and your incredible family. I just …"

"I know," said Jerena, her empathy a palpable thing. "I should have found a way to visit you. It's still dangerous for me to travel, with or without the children. I wish it wasn't so, but I should have made the effort anyway. The Lord can protect me."

Ara shook her head. "I wouldn't be comfortable at all with you taking such a risk. Your letters have been enough."

Jerena gave her a tilted smile, raising one eyebrow. "No, they haven't, and I'm not accusing you of being weak. You are not. But we are friends, and we should help each other. We are surrounded by so much good, but also by tremendous evil. Helaman keeps assuring me it's getting better, and I believe it is, but the progress seems far too slow. Why, oh why, can't people realize that if they let God help them, their lives will be infinitely better? He won't force them, but why don't they just open their eyes and stop resisting his love?"

Ara felt the stab of truth convict her, and she lowered her head.

"I wasn't referring to you, Ara. In fact, I admire you. None of us is perfect. We all struggle sometimes. And your circumstances are far different than mine. Your father tied you to some foul actors, convinced you they were good people, and you … amazingly, you found a way to break free of that. I don't know how you did it."

"It was mostly Kai," she said softly.

"Oh, sister, I know the Lord sent Kai to help, but it was mostly *you*. I can promise you that. I've spent enough time around you to know. Don't lose sight of that. Don't talk yourself into believing you are less than you really are. Did I mention how happy I am that you're here?" Her grin broke the solemn tension, and Ara smiled back.

"That was the tenth time, I think."

"Well, it needs to be a hundred!" Jerena took a sip of her drink, then eyed Ara, subtly inviting her to ask the next question.

After enjoying a long draught from her own cup, which caused the regally composed Jerena to giggle, Ara asked, "How will I know when I truly have a testimony?"

Jerena hummed, considering for long moments. "That is an excellent question. It's one I ask myself sometimes."

Ara's eyebrows rose. "You? Why? I mean, how?"

Jerena shrugged. "We are mortal. We are weak. And yet, we can be so strong, if we seek the Lord and really want to be. Life is hard, every day, so for me, finding consistency is a constant task. Having children, I must say, is an unexpected blessing to me in that regard, in part because of how much I love them. I had no idea how much I could care for a child. I want to be good for them. For Helaman, too. He isn't perfect, by the way." She gave a smirk and a wink, in the way of wives speaking about their husbands. The knife struck deeper.

"I don't have anyone I need to be good for," said Ara, looking away.

Jerena didn't respond immediately, and silence settled over them. At length, she said, "You will. Your faith will be tested, but you will. And you have friends … like me, I hope."

Ara returned her gaze to Jerena and nodded. "Of course. But you're so much better than me. And I don't have anything to offer in return."

That caused Jerena to frown. "Yes, you do. I wish you recognized it, but you will in time. I feel even worse now for not braving a trip to Gideon to see you. I could have paid visits to other faithful sisters there as well. I really do have a duty to do that, and … darn it, I'm going to do it." She set her drink on the small table next to her chair and sat straighter. "I've been a cowering fool, Ara. And I will tell you that is another thing I admire about you. Your courage. Some of the things you've told me about … well, I couldn't do them. I'd faint, or lose control of my bladder, or some other such nonsense. But you … how are you so brave?"

Ara shook her head. She didn't picture herself as particularly brave. Stubborn, maybe. Proud, for sure. But brave? "I'm not that brave."

"Well, that's your opinion, not mine. And what if you stayed here for a while? I mean, a long while. We could arrange to have your things brought up from Gideon. I'm sure Helaman wouldn't mind. And it would be wonderful to have your help again."

Ara's mouth went dry. She doubted she could manage such a thing mentally, though it was tempting. "I don't think I could. I—" Emotion surged in her chest, and she squared her shoulders. "Besides, I'm going to help Kai find Siarah."

Jerena sat straighter as her eyebrows rose. "You *are*? How would you do that?"

She could probably guess the answer, but Ara supplied it anyway. "I have some connections, even outside Zarahemla. Many won't exist anymore, but some might, even if they're just names I overheard my father use in random conversations. I may even be able to infiltrate the band, convince them I've returned and want to reconcile with my father."

"Nahom," Jerena said before giving a swift shake of her head. "I doubt that would work. You'd just get yourself killed." She swallowed audibly.

"But part of this is my fault. And the Lord can help me, right?"

"How is it your fault?"

"Gadianton suspects Kai because of me. I'm the one who got him in."

"Moronihah called him here," Jerena countered. "He was a spy, Ara, and he had a job to do. He knew the risks. He is courageous, like you. And because of *both* of you, I still have a husband. Please don't forget *that*." Her eyes misted, and Ara blinked back a tear of her own.

"But ..." she faltered, and Jerena continued.

"But he did his job, and because he did, Gadianton and his people knew he was involved somehow in thwarting Kishkumen. They're not dumb. So, stay here. Helaman and Dan and others can help Kai. And we can exercise our faith together on his behalf."

Ara thought that over, but the more she pondered, the less right it felt. Or satisfying maybe, she couldn't tell. She was indeed stubborn. "I'm sorry. I have to try. I have to do *something*. I just ... I can't explain it, but I have to."

Jerena studied her intently for several seconds, eyes searching, then gave a slight nod. "It is your choice. I will support you in any way I can."

Ara couldn't hold the tears back this time. She nearly dropped her drink. "Thank you, Jerena." She took a deep, sobbing breath, composing herself. "I knew I needed to come here and see you before I set out on my task. Trust me, it's already helping. Now I need to get back to Gideon and return the horse I rode here, and then I can leave from there."

"Or," offered Jerena, "I can arrange to have that horse returned, and also bring your things here. I can also reach out to Kai's friend—Aaron, is it?—who lives across the river. I'm sure he will happily loan you a horse, perhaps even one sired by Vyim. Then you don't have to walk to wherever you need to go."

"That … would be wonderful," admitted Ara a touch breathlessly, then stared at the floor for several seconds. When she looked back up, Jerena bowed her head. Ara followed suit, and they prayed. It felt perfect.

———◆———

Aaron had said the young filly's name was Shefah, meaning "storm." Ara didn't ask why he had named her that, but she guessed it had to do with the manmade tempest of death and hatred that had taken his wife. He hadn't remarried yet, and he still looked sad. He gave her a new pack stocked with provisions as well. She thanked him profusely before leaving his home, promising to give greetings to Kai when she found him.

If she found him. Despite the prayers she and Jerena had offered together, one of which included Jerena's innocent, faith-filled children, Ara couldn't say with any certainty what would happen. She sincerely hoped the filly wouldn't get hurt, and she also determined to burn a brief note in a piece of leather and attach it under the side of the saddle. If something happened to Ara, it would let whoever might find Shefah know to return her to Aaron, or at least notify him so he could come and get her.

Shefah was an extremely fine horse, and that worried Ara. The temptation for someone to just keep her would be high. Most of her former friends and associates would, without a second thought. They might even claim they deserved it as a gift from God, though they knew almost nothing about Him. Not because they couldn't, but because they wouldn't.

But how much better was she than they? That question still niggled at her constantly. She had worked for Gadianton—indirectly, but how did that make her less awful? She had exhibited many of the same behaviors, and when she had first met Kai, she had seen him as just another fun conquest. Oh, but he was so much more than that. Fitting, then, that he wasn't hers. Siarah deserved him. *She* was the God-fearing woman Kai needed, the one who could nurture their children in faith and serve the Lord alongside him.

After several miles of travel, Ara realized she needed to change her focus or she would end up stopping by the side of the road and curling up into a ball. Which would be pathetic and wouldn't help anybody. She took out some small scrolls Jerena had given her. Some contained quotes from the brass plates, others various passages of Nephite scripture. One summarized a sermon her husband's father, Helaman the Elder, had given during the Great War. Ara had just turned eleven when that conflict ended, and shortly afterward her father started asking her to help him with certain tasks he claimed would help prevent such a war from ever happening again.

Now she understood how many people were expected to die to make that fevered dream a reality. She knew how impure the motives were, too. She could bear personal witness to the selfishness, depravity, and ruthless rage filling people like Gadianton, Imrahiel, Kishkumen, and— she shuddered to admit—her own father.

Shefah was just a yearling, but Aaron had already trained her well. Or one of his workers had. His farm and ranch were large and prosperous. Ara suspected he worked so hard to honor his late wife Nalani. It probably helped with the grief, too. The filly stayed to the road and navigated the flow of traffic with little guidance from Ara, so it was easy to read the scrolls as she rode. And they helped. Knowing Jerena had chosen them for her was of benefit, too.

Jerena had given her some money—which Ara promised she would pay back—so she didn't have to sleep under the stars each night. She did on a few occasions, anyway, but was usually able to reach a place with a decent inn. She didn't try to strike up many conversations, content to eat and ride alone. She did talk more and more often with Shefah, though, and by the time Morianton came into view, she was starting to worry about herself.

There it was, an ugly blotch of pestilence amid a beautiful, green landscape of trees and rolling hills. She had only been to Morianton once, when she was fifteen. Her father had dragged her there on some business or other she hadn't understood. By the time they left, she had taken the first set of oaths for the secret order that aimed to remake Nephite society from the ground up. She wished now that she would have been sick that week. Or run away. Then she wouldn't have gotten involved in any of Gadianton's treachery ... and she wouldn't have all these painful memories of Kai.

One of the gate guards leered at her, adding a weakly formed whistle that made him look more pitiful. She ignored him. She wasn't dressed finely, but she knew Shefah would turn heads. That was just one reason she needed to be cautious in approaching the man who used to be one of her father's main contacts outside of Zarahemla. He owned a tailor shop, and she had a general idea of where to find it.

She first stopped at the most reputable-looking inn she could find, dismounting and asking one of the men on guard outside to carry a message to the innkeeper. A few minutes later, a greasy-looking man with a wild fop of hair and an apron singed in several places stepped out through the main door, gaze following where his guard pointed.

The innkeeper approached, arching an eyebrow after carefully eyeing her horse. "What can I do for you, miss?"

"I need a room for the night—perhaps several nights—and I also need some information. I trust you know some things that haven't reached the ears of the high seat."

The man cocked his head slightly at the phrase, but almost anyone of at least middling influence in Morianton would know what it meant— she wanted to keep the conversation from anyone associated with the government in Zarahemla. Helaman's government. "And you are?"

"Starling. My father will have been through here recently, though I know he couldn't stay. Not yet."

"Yes, indeed," said the man, who was probably trying to figure out which of the cutthroats he'd seen pass through had been her father. "These are trying times."

"Trying times strengthen us for a better future. We will be victorious." That was a little bold, but if the man somehow turned out to be an agent of Helaman, she needn't worry. She had the best game piece on the board to play.

The man nodded, showing her some respect. That was good, though she knew she would have to do more to convince him. Gadianton's people everywhere had become understandably skittish.

"I need a safe place for my horse," she said, patting Shefah's neck. "Actually, I shouldn't say she's mine. She belongs to someone far more important than me." She locked onto the innkeeper's eyes. "You understand my concern, yes?"

The man squinted at Shefah, then nodded. "Of course. We will take good care of her. And you, of course."

"Thank you." She flashed a sign with her fingers, one she was pretty sure would never be changed. It was a sign for caution. The innkeeper recognized it, showing the same in return with practiced dexterity.

Within minutes, a groomsman—or what passed for one in Morianton—had come for her horse, and she had been shown to a respectable room. The bed felt lumpy, but it was better than the ground. Shemnilom had given her the names of various people she could stay with in and around Morianton, but she already knew she didn't want to be seen around those people. They were too risky for an untrustworthy castaway from Zarahemla.

Chapter 10

And whosoever shall believe in my name, doubting nothing,
unto him will I confirm all my words, even unto the ends of the earth.
—Mormon 9:25

"We're going to church," said Siarah in her most assertive tone. She swept her shoulders back, not letting her gaze wander from her target.

Zoram looked up from the knife he was sharpening in front of the small fireplace of the inn they had found in Mulek. Morning had just arrived, and she had known she would find him here, sharpening a blade, checking his bow, or exercising. He did all of those things to excess, though usually when other people weren't about. This early in the day, and especially on the Sabbath, the inn's great room was deserted.

He considered her for long moments, and she knew what he was trying to do. Intimidate her. Outlast her. Get her to back off. But she refused. Not this time.

"We've had this discussion. I swore I would keep you safe."

"No," she insisted, "we *haven't* had this discussion. I get that you don't want me going on my own, without protection. That's why I said 'we.'"

His expression came as close to a smirk as one could achieve while still being able to claim it wasn't a smirk. She raised an eyebrow in challenge, and then his face darkened.

"There's been another attempt on Helaman's life," he said, voice lowered despite the emptiness of the room. "It hasn't been made public, and

I don't think Helaman wants it to be, but Moronihah is worried that the Gadiantons have infiltrated the city to a dangerous degree again and have something bigger planned."

That stunned her for a moment. But then, surprisingly, her determination reasserted itself. "All the more reason to go to church, then. I must show my acknowledgement of God's wise beneficence and offer my prayers there for Helaman, his family, the good people in Zarahemla … and Kai."

"There are plenty of people praying for your prophet, so you needn't worry." His tone bordered on dismissive and harsh, but again she rallied.

"We're going," she declared with as much authority as she could muster. "Or, if you prefer to see it as *I'm* going, and you're following me there, then fine."

"Synagogue doesn't sit well with me," he said with a glower, but she spied a crack in his stony mien.

She nodded toward the knife. "You're man enough to handle it." Proud of herself, she twirled away and headed for the door to the back hallway, where they each had a room. She heard him rise, and she could picture the frustrated look on his face. That made her smile, and it felt good to smile. The smile was natural, too. She was going back to church today. After how many weeks? She had lost track.

After cleaning up the best she could, and enduring more of Zoram's grumbling, she chose the largest synagogue in the city, the location of which she had obtained through conversations with the innkeeper and several other guests. It was a beautiful, freestanding building of two stories. On the outside, a full-color carving of Moses parting the Red Sea spread across the entrance doors and to either side. The melding of stone and wood was magnificent, the fine artisanship even more apparent as Siarah and Zoram passed inside, where fretwork and masonry delighted her eyes and warmed her heart. None of it seemed too ostentatious—not to her. She basked in the ambiance, enhanced by the friendliness of the people, who were all dressed remarkably better than she was. That would be remedied soon, once she arrived in Zarahemla and Helaman the high priest himself welcomed her.

She also took some amusement from Zoram's discomfort, which had nothing to do with the design of the structure or the attire of its congregants. Though he tried to hide it, he was a fish flopping on the bank, gasping for air, the hook still lodged in his mouth.

A devious idea formed in her mind, and before she could talk herself out of it, she walked straight up to the man who looked to be the congregation's main priest, wiry and white-haired, with surprisingly few wrinkles. He nodded at her, eyes alight.

"Welcome, young sister. You are new to these parts?"

She bowed, then demurely studied his feet, clad in some of the finest sandals she'd ever seen. "I—that is, we—are just passing through."

A pause followed, presumably as the priest identified the other person in "we." She heard Zoram shuffle up behind her, the rhythm of his breathing already familiar to her.

"And this is your husband?" asked the priest.

She definitely had *not* thought this all the way through. Oh, the embarrassment! What could she say?

"Betrothed only," she blurted, keeping her eyes down, hoping the man didn't notice the heat in her cheeks. And it was true. She herself *was* betrothed. Just not to Zoram. "And we keep God's laws," she added, which was also true. She would feel doubly shamed if the priest thought they had engaged in … More heat rose to her cheeks.

"I see," said the priest. "Well, welcome. What are your names?"

This question she was prepared for, since they were already using assumed names. "Azrom and Rashia," she replied, feeling at least a little of the heat draining away, "from Jershon."

"Ah, a beautiful place. And what is your destination?"

She said the first city that popped into her mind. "Ammonihah."

"Hmmm," came the reply. She didn't dare look up to see the expression. The name Ammonihah bore a dramatic history. "That city is starting to prosper again, though it is still quite small. You may find many opportunities there. Including with the Lord's church."

She could well imagine Zoram's reaction to such a statement. She hoped he didn't appear queasy or sick in front of the priest. She wouldn't put it past him.

"Thank you," she replied, bowing lower. "We look forward to your sermon today."

"Excellent," he said. "Well, we're glad you're here." With that, he moved away to chat with others. She felt a tap on her shoulder.

"What was that about?" Zoram hissed in her ear.

A glare burst through her mask of embarrassed happiness. "I wanted to meet the priest."

"Clearly, but why?"

"I don't know. Why aren't we in Zarahemla yet? Or Gideon? That's a safe place, close to the capital, and Kai could come for me there. I'm positive that if we had just headed straight toward Zarahemla, everything would be fine, despite the Gadiantons and your paranoia. I would be safe, your mission accomplished. Then you could go home ... to wherever that is, because you won't tell me."

She couldn't help the rising of her voice at the very end, which caused him to look around in consternation to see who might be paying attention. She suddenly didn't care if everyone was. She was tired of this game. It was too much.

"Fine," he said in a harried whisper. "We'll leave tomorrow, but we'll travel fast, so be ready."

He probably hoped that sounded ominous, but all she heard were angels singing from the gates of the majestic principal city of the Nephites, welcoming her into its embrace. She would finally see Zarahemla! And meet Helaman. And be reunited with Kai.

They found seats on benches among the other congregants, near the front. The lead priest, along with two others, gave magnificent sermons, accompanied by several readings of both old and new scripture. Oh, how she loved to hear those words! She had scraps of a few holy passages with her, but those had become too repetitive. This ... this was like new life being breathed into her soul, and even into the very fabric of existence all around her. Thank the Lord for his church ... and for a proximate end to her nightmare.

She talked with several people afterward, again pretending that

Zoram was her husband-to-be. He didn't say more than two words at a time, but at least he didn't scowl at anyone, or growl like a bear, or flee outside. Any of those things would have been supremely discomforting, but especially the fleeing.

One old couple recounted the time the Lamanites had taken Mulek. Captain Moroni and Teancum had arrived, then lured the army of Jacob the Zoramite out of the city and liberated it. Their two sons, they said, had been part of Teancum's army, and both had survived the Great War. They owed it to God, they felt certain, so they made sure they remained active in their church responsibilities, supporting the priests in whatever was asked of them.

That story gave Siarah both comfort and heartburn. The Lord had indeed watched over the Nephites, preserving so many of them in the most extreme of circumstances. But many good people had died as well. She didn't ever want to receive a message that her husband Kihoran had been killed in battle, or on a scouting mission, or had disappeared while spying for Helaman.

When they finally returned to the inn, she remained quiet, introspective. Zoram seemed happy for the silence, and thankfully he didn't make any snide comments. She was ready to snap at him if he did, which bothered her a little. She didn't like being mean or rude to people, but she was leaning more that direction every day. She needed to pray more; that was it. And she would.

———◇———

Morning arrived, and when no knock came at her door for Zoram to lead her to breakfast, she ventured into the common room on her own again. She had taken especial care with her hair, to make it presentable but also suitable for a hard day of travel. She glanced around, not spotting Zoram.

The innkeeper's wife was serving breakfast to a patron when Siarah approached her.

"Excuse me, have you seen my traveling companion this morning?"

The woman turned to her, stared blankly a moment, and then snapped her fingers. "Ah, yes, the tall handsome one. He left very early—I hadn't even started the cooking yet—said he needed to run an errand but that he wouldn't be long. Would you like something to eat?"

"Oh." She really wasn't hungry, but she thought again of Zoram's admonition to be ready. She would need the energy. "Yes, please, thank you. Nothing special. Whatever you've already cooked is fine. Does it include eggs?" She had thought she wasn't hungry, but the craving for eggs leaped up and grabbed her.

"Yes, my dear. Eggs, sausage, bread. Some fruit, too. Dried, I'm afraid, but good."

"That sounds wonderful. Thank you." She turned to scan the room for a table, finding several unoccupied. Choosing one, she sat facing the front door, wanting to see Zoram's face when he walked in. Would he come in the back way, perhaps? No, more likely the front.

Less than a minute later, she stared at a generous plate of food. Her mouth watered. She began eating, slowly at first, even primly, but then faster and with less concern for manners. How was she suddenly so famished? And how had the woman cooked these eggs? Kai might like them this way. She would have to ask.

She almost didn't see Zoram walk in, but luckily she caught his first expression, as hoped. Surprise flashed, then was gone, replaced by something she couldn't quite define. Regretful determination? Was that it?

He crossed to the table and sat across from her. His hands were empty, so he clearly hadn't left to make a purchase.

He didn't say anything for several seconds, so finally she offered, "I came to breakfast without you, since, you know, we're leaving anyway."

He nodded, glancing at her food. "I know I said this morning, but we can't leave quite yet. I met with a contact an hour ago. Based on his recommendation, we're checking the trail ahead, all the way to Zarahemla. We should only have to wait two weeks, since the men are using horses."

She released her utensils and slapped the table, causing him to twitch. "What men? What are you talking about? Helaman's men? Instead of scouting the trail, they could just accompany us. We'll be safe."

"It isn't that simple."

"That's what you always say."

"Because it's true."

"Is it? I'm starting to doubt that. I think men sometimes exaggerate things. Most times, actually."

"And women don't?"

"Certain things, on occasion, yes, we do, I'll admit. But men are far worse."

A crease of annoyance furrowed his forehead. "Well, I'm not exaggerating. I'm doing my job. Two weeks, and then we go. I may have to leave by myself once or twice during that time, but you will be safe here at the inn; I've made arrangements."

"Which you won't tell me about."

"No, I will not, but I've kept you safe so far, haven't I?"

She had to admit that was true, but she lowered her eyes to her food so he couldn't fully witness the brief firestorm of frustration. She gritted her teeth. "Fine. Two weeks."

———◆———

Zoram left on a secretive quest two days later, and while part of Siarah was relieved, she also felt uncomfortable. She hadn't been left alone for so long she didn't know what to do. Zoram's constant talk of the dangers they faced—and those they had already encountered—resurfaced over and over in her mind. She even started to suspect the innkeeper and his wife of some sort of treachery. She finally decided she had to get some fresh air, notwithstanding Zoram's warnings not to leave the inn. However, despite her insistence that her feet carry her outside, it was supremely difficult to make them obey. In fact, she wasn't successful until her third try the next day, in the early evening. And she could only do it then because she promised herself she would go straight to the nearest synagogue and beg for some scriptures to borrow.

She tried not to walk too quickly, since that would be conspicuous, but she pulled a shawl tightly around her, despite the day's warmth. When she reached the synagogue, she paused at the entrance to peer into the relative dimness, then ventured inside.

After two steps, she dared a "Hello?" that seemed to echo throughout the small structure. It wasn't nearly as grand of a building as the one they had visited near the center of the city, and the colors seemed duller. No answer came, and after several seconds she progressed farther inside, eventually finding a bench and sitting, staring at the rostrum from which the priests and teachers would speak. No lamps were lit, and with dusk coming on, the gloom was deepening fast.

Finally, when she was about to get up and leave, she heard footsteps from the doorway. She rose and whirled, her heart suddenly in her throat.

"I'm sorry, sister," said a man, hands upraised. "I got done with work a little late today, so I wasn't here as early as usual for those who might want …" He stopped, cocking his head. "I apologize, but I don't recognize you." He was a youthful man, and lean. She wondered what kind of work he did when he wasn't attending to priestly duties.

"I am only visiting," she said, a bit nervously. Surely, this man couldn't be a danger, could he?

"Ah, well, excellent. Um, let me light some of the lamps in this room." As he hurried to complete the task, Siarah resumed her seat, watching him. When he was finished, he came to stand two benches in front of her, hands clasped between the sleeves of a robe he had grabbed from a peg on the back wall.

"Are you … well?" he ventured.

She paused before nodding. "Well enough, I suppose. My betrothed and I … our travel has been delayed for a few days, and I wonder if … well, if you have some scriptures you could lend me? Nothing much. Scroll, tablet, plate, parchment, it doesn't matter. It has been a trying time, and I need to be closer to the Lord."

He nodded, face etched with concern. "I see. You do seem … troubled and uncertain. Even … afraid?" He blinked, then bowed his head. "Yes, of course. We don't have an ample store—the larger synagogues can offer more—but we have a few copies of sections we can part with briefly. Your betrothed ..." he glanced toward the back, scanning the room and its entrance "... he didn't come with you this evening?"

It was obvious that she was alone, and that lent his question a sinister quality. Was he pleased she was alone? Was he planning something?

"He is taking care of some business," she replied carefully, "but said he would meet me here."

The man's face brightened, which lessened her fears. "Wonderful! I would love to meet him, too. Now, tell me, is there anything else we can do for you?"

She tilted her head. "We?"

"Oh, yes, there should be another priest along in a few minutes. A pair of the sisters as well. We don't have any classes or meetings planned for this evening, but there are always people who like to come and enjoy each other's company. Not all have families at home, and ... well, we are commanded to help each other, right?"

A warm feeling spread through her body. She suddenly felt safer here than she did at the inn, despite her previous paranoia. She hadn't expected that, except perhaps in her innermost thoughts. What was Zoram's attitude doing to her?

"I wonder if ... well, I, or rather, we, could get an urgent message to Zarahemla. We can't afford a private courier, but merchants and others from here travel in that direction, right? Do you know of someone we could trust?"

The priest nodded thoughtfully. "Yes, of course. I know of several. Good men, all. May I ask to whom the message needs to be delivered?"

She hesitated, wondering how much she could reveal, but found no other thing to say but, "Chief Judge Helaman."

The man's eyes widened. "Do you know him, or will this be a common petition?"

She lowered her eyes briefly. "We have not met yet, but he knows me. In fact, he is expecting me. I mean, us. Distant family relation."

The priest narrowed his eyes ... in disbelief? Finally, he said, "Well, I can do better than a merchant. We have regular communications with the church in Zarahemla, and one of our couriers is leaving tomorrow, as it happens. We can send the letter with him."

A jolt of excitement half lifted her from the bench, but she settled herself. "Oh, that would be wonderful. Except ... I'm sorry, but can I beg some parchment and pen? I promise I'll find a way to pay it back."

"Of course. I'll get that for you right now." He turned and disappeared into another part of the building. While she waited, the other priest arrived, along with two members of the congregation, older women who sat on the front bench and began to pray. She let their humble words caress her mind, closing her eyes until the first priest's voice shocked her fully awake.

"Here you are," he said, extending parchment and a thin charcoal pen encased in wax.

"Thank you, kind brother," she said, taking them eagerly. He backed away, and she set the parchment on the flat surface of the bench beside her, preparing her first words for the page.

———◇———

Zoram returned the next day, late in the morning. Siarah had slept in, and her dreams had been wonderful. She had split her letter to Helaman into two parts: one respectfully addressing Helaman, and the other directed to Kai. The priest had promised it would go out early that morning, so when she awakened her heart flew with the letter, following the roads to Zarahemla.

The knock on her door, followed by Zoram's low voice, caught her putting a last hair into place for the day. She turned, nearly skipping the few steps to the door. She flung it wide, smiling.

"Did you have a good trip?" she asked cheerily.

He frowned, obviously puzzled by her mood. "I don't know yet." He stepped inside and closed the door. "I need to leave again in two days. There has been a flurry of new activity. Some of the band of Gadianton who were responsible for this latest assassination attempt have been found, it appears. Others have been exposed."

"Well, those are great tidings for us, right?" She bounced on her toes. The day couldn't possibly get any better. Unless they could miraculously leave for Zarahemla.

"No, it's not. A cornered animal, especially one that is wounded, is extremely dangerous. And factions within Helaman's government make the situation far worse than I had imagined."

She put on a fake pout, still not believing he had delivered any sort of bad news. "Well, men like you and Kai will help put things right. I can't wait for you to meet him. I didn't mention your name in the letter I sent, but—"

He grabbed her by the upper arms with such suddenness she lost her breath. "You sent a *letter*?" His expression was a cross between anger and terror, and her shell of joy began to crumble. Fear spiked, too. What was happening?

"Um, yes? It left by church courier early this morning. One of the priests—at a different synagogue, one close to here—gave me what I needed to write it. I addressed it to Helaman."

He let go of her, then turned away and grabbed two handfuls of his own hair. "No, no, no, no, no," he muttered, with increasing volume. When he turned back around, she backed up a step.

"What's wrong?" she asked. "It's just a letter, and it's secure. You told me you've sent other letters to … I don't know, headquarters or something."

The muscles of his jaw hardened as he stared at her. Then he replied, "They were all intercepted. I just found that out, but I arranged to have another message sent through a different channel. That was part of what I was doing."

She shrugged. "Okay. So, what does it matter that *I* sent a letter?"

He stepped closer, and she could tell he was struggling not to look too menacing. "If both letters get through, they will cause confusion. That might not be bad for you, but it will be terrible for me."

"How?"

"Helaman might think I'm a Gadianton."

A laugh exploded from her chest. "You? No, he wouldn't. He's too smart. And, lest you forget, he *is* a prophet. The Lord doesn't tell him everything—that would be too easy—but he tells him a lot. Don't worry. We can trust him. It will work out." She had laid a hand on his upper arm without noticing, suddenly feeling confident. When he glanced at it, she hastily withdrew it, backing up again.

"So, you leave again in two days, you said?"

His look remained troubled, but he nodded. "Yes. And given what you just told me, I might be gone longer this time."

That didn't sound good. A needle of worry stitched along her spine. This next trip might delay their planned departure for Zarahemla. That possibility induced a faint pain behind her right eye, but she composed herself.

"Well, I trust you, Zoram. Be safe, and like I said, it *will* work out."

He grumbled. "I don't know whether to say your faith is admirable or annoying, but I'm going to get some food."

With that, he left the room, leaving the door open. She didn't follow until she had first closed the door and knelt on shaking knees to say a prayer.

———◇———

Zoram's next trip didn't delay their departure—in fact, it accelerated it by two days—but his dour, complicated news of spies and factions seemed calculated to dampen her hopes. She was better able to handle it, though, especially since she had spent considerable time at that small synagogue, getting to know the people. It was supremely uplifting to be nurtured by the good word of God in the company of fellow Christians.

Zoram had secured them better travel packs for the journey, and they were well stocked with provisions. No horses, unfortunately, but her feet felt light, even once the pack was settled on her back. His was much larger, plus he had all his weapons. He scowled when they were ready, and she was sure it was because of her optimism, not the weight of his own load.

After bidding farewell to the innkeeper and his wife, Siarah asked that they pass by the small synagogue on their way out. She doubted anyone would be there in the early morning hours, but she still wanted to see it one last time. Well, hopefully not for the *last* time. She would bring Kai here, introduce him to everyone, tell them the intriguing story of how she had been traveling with a spy and had to pretend he was her betrothed, and that the spy had helped her reunite with her real betrothed, who was one of Helaman's most trusted aides. She might even suggest that someone compile the story in long form. It could become a literary sensation.

As expected, they found no one at the synagogue, but she lingered a few moments just inside the doorway, hands running along the smooth and polished wood of the walls. She had returned the scriptures the night before. She smiled broadly as she finally turned away, taking a deep breath before addressing Zoram.

"I feel good about today, don't you?" The fractures in her hope had mended, and she basked in the growing warmth of the rising sun.

He grunted, glancing up the street. "We'll see," he said, then led the way out of the city.

———◆———

It was indeed a pleasant day, not too warm or cool, though she wished she had exercised more in preparation for the journey. She had become lazy in Mulek—at least, in some ways. After the first few miles, her feet were already sore, remembrances of treks past returning with vigor. But no matter. She was young. She could buck up, and her body would get used to traveling again.

Zoram didn't say much, though she tried to engage him in various kinds of conversation. He was content to plod along, his mood not quite so grim that he didn't acknowledge the occasional greeting from a fellow traveler on the road. That was a small positive, and she was convinced that the closer they got to Zarahemla, the happier he would become. It would certainly be true for her.

As dusk fell, he led them off the road to a small stand of trees watching over a broad, grass-filled plain stretching toward distant hills. Such open areas weren't the norm here, but it was beautiful.

"We can't stop at the way stations," he said.

She didn't need him to explain why; she had expected it. She gazed around the trees. "So, we sleep here tonight?"

"Yes. I'll make a small fire. It might get a little chilly."

"Thank you, but that's alright. We have blankets, and I'm tired."

He nodded, then tromped farther into the trees. She followed until he had found an area of flat ground that would accommodate them. In the failing light, they ate some of their dry rations, washing them down with water. Shortly after that, she settled down for sleep, and it came quickly.

Unfortunately, as soon as it came, it left. And not peacefully.

———◇———

With clouds scudding across a sky barely visible through the thick overhang of branches, and without even the dying embers of a fire to provide some additional light, Siarah's eyes opened onto a dark haze of meaningless melee. The sounds of a desperate scuffle assaulted her ears: punches, grunts, and shifting feet. Her voice caught, and before she could gulp another breath and call out, a strong hand clamped over her mouth, pulling her backward and upward as a man's arm crossed her midsection and pinned her arms. She kicked and flailed, making futile contact with the man's legs. He was too strong, and she could hear several others with him.

She tried to discern what was happening, eyes darting in a panicked pattern. The scuffling suddenly stopped, leaving the sounds of heavy breathing. Zoram. What had these ... bandits? ... done to Zoram? Was he dead?

"Bring him," ordered the man holding her in a husky voice. That gave her hope that Zoram wasn't dead. No reply came, but in the dimness she made out at least three other men lifting a form off the ground, two of them hoisting it onto their shoulders and immediately marching off into the woods. The man holding her followed, lifting her off the ground with one arm as if she weighed no more than a feather pillow. His other hand remained over her mouth, and it was starting to hurt. She thought about licking his hand, but that sounded gross, and besides, such a trick had only worked when she was a child. This was not a child's game.

After about half a mile, the canopy opened up, and enough filtered moonlight made it through to outline several horses staked in a line. The men carrying Zoram threw his limp form over the back of one, then began tying his hands and feet. She was taken to another one, and the hand came off her mouth.

"You can ride, or I can truss you up like your friend," came the husky voice.

"I'll ride," she squeaked. She wanted to scream, over and over until someone came to help. But she knew no one would. That option disappeared, anyway, as the man tied a thick cloth around her head to cover her mouth. After he helped her onto the horse—and she refused to give him the dignity of looking at him—he tied her hands, connecting that knot to a loop in the saddle. Then he took the reins of her horse as he mounted his own. In moments, they were away, moving back through the trees. She had no idea what hour it was, or which direction they were headed. The man had spoken so few words she couldn't place where he might be from, either. All she knew was that someone evil had captured her and Zoram and that she needed to pray.

Chapter 11

Wherefore, my beloved brethren, pray unto the Father
with all the energy of heart, that ye may be filled with this love,
which he hath bestowed upon all who are true followers
of his Son, Jesus Christ; that ye may become the sons of God;
that when he shall appear we shall be like him, for we shall see him
as he is; that we may have this hope;
that we may be purified even as he is pure.
—Moroni 7:48

Kai was tired of chasing thin leads coaxed out of Lugran and the other Gadianton prisoners, and it was making him churlish. How many people had they talked to? How many times had they covered the same ground after finally leaving David? They had spent a considerable amount of time in the city of Moroni, thinking they were close, only to learn they really weren't. The trail then led them to Mulek, and it was upon the outskirts of that city that Kai rested his eyes on a musty morning three weeks later.

Dan stood beside him, as steady and patient as ever. Jerid and his full complement of men, along with all the horses, sat a quarter mile back, out of view of the walls.

"We'll find either Imrahiel or Gadianton here," said Dan. "I can feel it."

Kai swallowed, the taste bitter. "I'm glad you can."

Dan didn't say anything more, and Kai was glad. He didn't need to be reminded again of how his faith was faltering.

"We talked about just you and me going in, disguised. Are you still all right with that?"

"Yes," replied Dan. "I'm not good at disguises, so I'll need your help."

Kai studied his friend's powerful bulk, his sharp brow and stern gaze. Dan would definitely be difficult to disguise. "Well figure something out."

An hour later, they both carried slight limps through the city gates, aided by crudely fashioned walking sticks. Dan had agreed to have his head shorn and his eyebrows trimmed, and he looked like a comically different man. Kai suggested he should let his mustache grow out as well … though that was more out of curiosity. Kai wore a thick, golden band around his forehead, along with a belted robe instead of shirt and breeches. Some of the things one could buy off a farmer surprised him. He had switched to sandals as well. A few tiny grease marks made him look at least as old as Dan, and they both hunched a bit in the hope that they wouldn't look like professional soldiers—just used-up ones, and there were plenty of those around. Kai added an unnatural curl to the fingers and wrist of his left hand. It served both to catch eyes and distract minds—from Dan—and he was practiced enough not to let his muscles slip out of character.

"We might be sleeping in barns or the back rooms of synagogues," Kai commented as they proceeded down the main street, taking note of each person they passed. "We don't look wealthy enough for a long stay at an inn."

"I know," said Dan. "And I don't mind."

"You lead," said Kai.

"Why is that?"

"Because I trust your instincts more."

"I trust yours, too, Kai, even if you don't."

Kai didn't respond, and Dan chose not to pursue the subject further. He took the next left, and Kai followed. They visited a shoe shop first, and Dan inquired how much it would cost to have the soles of some boots replaced. For a friend, he said, since his were obviously in good condition. He and Kai engaged the owner in some small talk angled subtly toward their quarry, but nothing significant came of it. They entered a small bakery next, where Kai purchased a long, flat piece of the cheapest bread. They had eaten a hearty breakfast, but it was good to nibble on something while they walked.

Several other shops followed as they wound their way along the well-worn streets. Mulek was a major city, and its relative proximity to Bountiful made Kai feel strangely homesick. He wasn't used to that, and Bountiful wasn't his home anymore. Zarahemla was. Magnificent, treacherous Zarahemla.

They had thoroughly searched an entire quarter of the city by the time the sun set, and then Kai found a willing owner of a barn near the walls. The man charged them next to nothing to sleep there, though he didn't seem overly friendly. The next morning they set out early, traveling to another area after enjoying a meager breakfast. Kai promised himself they would find a good seller of meat pies for dinner. His stomach grumbled loudly in agreement.

At one point, a pair of officers stopped them. He and Dan had known it might happen, and they had a plan for it.

"I saw you two yesterday," said one, "more than once. You don't seem to be employed, and I don't recognize you. What are you looking for?"

"We're searching for a runaway," said Kai. "My sister, from Bountiful. She's twenty-two and just lost her only child. Her husband was killed in the battles with Coriantumr."

The officers lowered their heads for a moment. Then the other one spoke. "I'm very sorry for your loss. If you can give us a description, we might be able to help. We'll share it with other officers, too."

"Thank you," said Kai. "That is appreciated." He was about to give a detailed description of Siarah, but hesitated. They would already have received such a description through official notifications, and Gadianton had his thumb on the pulse of some of those channels. So instead, he described a very average woman, admitting with apology that he didn't know what she might be wearing or even how she might be styling her hair. And with that, he and Dan were free to wander again.

A long, warm, frustrating day followed. They spoke with dozens of people who knew next to nothing, and the meat pies he eventually found didn't turn out to be all that great. They returned to the same barn for the night, and Kai couldn't help but complain.

"What am I doing wrong? Why isn't the Lord helping us? You said you felt good about this place."

"I still do," said Dan patiently. "I know the progress is slow."

"What progress?" Kai nearly shouted. "We haven't made *any* progress. Siarah might as well be across the Great Sea in Jerusalem. In fact, I'd probably have a better chance trying to find her there."

"Few ships can make that risky journey, but I get your point." He sighed. "Kihoran, I *know* the Lord is helping us. And I know he is helping her. There are things he knows that we don't. Do you think I believe that blindly?"

Part of Kai wanted to shout, "Yes!" but Dan's calm, supremely confident gaze disarmed him.

"We're going to visit one of the synagogues," Dan continued. "Right now. I don't know how it will help, but it will. Let's go."

He didn't give Kai a chance to object, just walked swiftly out of the barn, the heavy dusk swallowing him. Kai grumbled a bit, then followed. He didn't say anything as he matched pace, wanting his friend to know how angry he was. In part, the anger felt good. But it didn't fill any of the emptiness.

Within a couple of minutes they arrived, and Kai remembered having passed the structure the day before. The twin doors stood open, and lamplight shone from within. An old woman entered just ahead of them. Her eyes seemed both sad and full of hope; he knew his own eyes reflected only the sad part.

Inside, they found a place to sit at one of the benches. Snatches of conversation reached them from other rooms, occasionally punctuated by lively children's voices. Classes were being taught that night. A few other people meditated or prayed in the main room with them, and despite the muffled sounds from elsewhere, Kai felt a profound sense of reverence. In fact, he was surprised he detected it.

He glanced at Dan, who had bowed his head and closed his eyes.

What was the Ammonite thinking? Was he praying? Was he receiving any revelation? They needed it, because Kai's ability to access anything useful was next to nil. Finally, Kai closed his eyes as well, the vexations of the day roiling in his mind, then ever so slowly seeping away. He almost fell asleep, and he suspected that, for him, synagogues could only reliably be a sleep aid.

Dan nudged him after several minutes. "We should go," he whispered, "before the classes let out. We could visit an inn, perhaps, get something to drink, talk to a few more people."

Kai opened his eyes and nodded. "Yes, that sounds good to me. My throat is parched."

They rose as one and exited the building. Dan led them down the street, toward the center of the city, where the frequency of lighted lamps along the thoroughfares increased. Kai kept his eyes forward, pondering the uselessness of visiting an inn but craving the liquid refreshment. Anything but warm, stale water.

He noted movement ahead, to his left. A man exiting what appeared to be a jewelry shop. Kai's glimpse of his shadowed face struck a chord, but it was the man's gait that beat the drums. He stopped, holding out an arm in front of Dan, who turned to him.

"What is it?" Dan asked softly. The man was walking away from them, and he didn't turn his head. Kai nodded toward the receding figure, then mouthed, "Imrahiel."

He expected more of a reaction, but Dan just squinted in that direction, then nodded. "No drink. We follow."

"Yes," agreed Kai, his mouth suddenly moist.

They tailed Imrahiel carefully, making sure not to get too close or attract attention. Imrahiel never turned his head, for all the world a man who had absolutely nothing to hide, minding his own business, safe and secure in that knowledge. When he stopped at a house and finally looked back, Kai and Dan started swaying a little in their steps. Kai upped the performance by grabbing Dan's upper arm to steady himself. He kept his head down, too, to minimize the chance of recognition. They still had their limps.

They passed by just after Imrahiel entered the home, and Kai waited a full block before speaking. "I'm sure it was him. And we have two locations." He couldn't keep the excitement from his voice. Nor the red-hot steel.

"We should call in some of the men," said Dan. "Set up some discrete surveillance."

"Can they do it?" asked Kai. "I mean, be discrete about it? They're the best of the best when it comes to battle, and tracking, and sneaking through the woods, but this is different."

"I know. We can speak with Jerid about it. We can go tonight, if you wish."

"Yes, tonight."

———◇———

Jerid chose four of his men, but it took some doing—using contacts provided by a local priest—to acquire new clothing that would help them blend in as visiting travelers to Mulek. While Dan and Jerid handled that the next morning, Kai kept a close eye on the jewelry shop. He spent a fair amount of coin himself purchasing new outfits and other odd items for various disguises, but he felt confident he wasn't raising any suspicions on the part of Imrahiel, who received various visitors that didn't appear to be interested at all in jewelry.

Two days later, with nothing of import conveyed yet by Jerid's men, Kai and Dan settled into chairs in the common room of an inn a few doors down from the jewelry shop. Evening was beginning to settle. Imrahiel hadn't left the shop yet, but likely would soon.

"We need to get inside," said Kai after slurping a bit of surprisingly good stew.

"Agreed," said Dan, "though the residence might prove more useful."

"He shares it with others, and it's rarely unoccupied."

"True, but not never."

Kai pondered that as he took another bite. Dan had already downed all of his stew. "I could get in tonight. I've scouted it well enough."

Dan frowned. "I can't stop you, but I recommend more patience."

Kai sniffed. "I'm not sure I'm capable of that."

Dan took some time to respond. "I can understand that. Do what you feel is best. I will support you."

The stew lost some of its savor as Kai shook his head. "I don't know if what I *feel* is best. I'm just getting more desperate, Dan. That's shameful, and I'm sorry."

"Why would you feel shame?"

"Because I don't have your faith. And I should."

"But you *want* to have faith, and you're sincerely trying. That counts for more than you know."

Kai stared back, finding no adequate response and feeling no relief. Finally, he stood, the stew holding no more allure.

"Let's go now, while he's still in there, confront him directly. His reaction will tell us a great deal."

Dan furrowed his brow, his gaze hard. "All right," he finally said, "but let me fetch a pair of Jerid's men as backup. We can't afford to underestimate the situation."

"That's a good idea. I'll watch from just outside the inn. If he leaves, I'll follow and then find you later at the barn."

"Which I'm coming to love, by the way," Dan deadpanned as he stood. Kai couldn't tell if he was being sarcastic or not.

Kai stepped outside, sitting down with his back against the wood planking of the exterior wall, leaning his head back and closing his eyes to just a slit. As long as he was quiet and didn't make any trouble, the law officers would probably let him stay there for a while. He shouldn't need long.

Half an hour later, Dan returned with two of Jerid's men, the three of them making a show of being fast friends relaxing after a long day of work. Kai hadn't ever heard Dan laugh that much; he was also surprised at how naturally Lehi's hardened elites played their parts. If he were a casual observer, he would believe their act. Of course, Imrahiel was *not* a casual observer, and a wave of worry disturbed his concentration. He gave a loud yawn, trying to distract attention from them, then rubbed his eyes with the heels of his hands. That would also signal to Dan that Kai didn't want them approaching him.

After the group had passed, Kai rose, then moved back inside the inn and found a different table, knowing Dan would circle back to join him. He didn't have to wait long.

"They're in place," said Dan, sitting across from him.

Kai kept his gaze on the window, which showed him a portion of the jewelry shop. "Good, because we're looking more suspicious by the moment. If Imrahiel has eyes and ears here, we'll be found out very soon."

"Well, we'd best get on with it, then."

The walk from the inn was less dramatic than Kai had envisioned. They arrived at the jewelry shop within moments. It was too late for customers, and only a faint light emerged from somewhere in the back. After Kai closed the door behind them, they stepped lightly across the main space at the front. The floor was wood, which would creak loudly enough to draw attention at some point. So, halfway across the room, Kai increased his pace. The floor announced its protest at their intrusion.

"Who is that?" came a voice from the back, where light spilled under a door. Kai recognized it. The same demanding arrogance. The same determined self-assuredness.

Kai lowered his voice. "We received a report of potential thieves entering this establishment." What an ironic cover.

"You are mistaken, officers. Everything is well here. You need not worry."

Kai kept moving, anticipation driving his steps as his sword came into his hand.

"Officers?" said Imrahiel, his tone laced with worry and affront.

Kai kicked open the door, then entered and stepped right, while Dan followed to the left.

Two other men occupied the room with Imrahiel. The three had been seated around a small, circular table, but Imrahiel and the one who looked like he could fight had risen. Kai locked his gaze on Gadianton's lieutenant.

"You're under arrest, Imrahiel, for aiding the attempted assassination of Chief Judge Helaman … and for kidnapping Siarah, daughter of Dinah, of Bountiful."

Imrahiel blinked as if stunned. Then his eyes bored through Kai's thin disguise, anger mushrooming red in his face.

"How dare you challenge me. You are *mine*, according to your oaths."

Kai hadn't expected such a ridiculously haughty response, but he didn't skip a beat. "Those oaths mean nothing to me, but the life of my betrothed does." With that, he lunged at Imrahiel, who predictably raised his arms in defense. Kai went low, using his momentum to drive the man hard into the wall, hearing a crack that could have been wood, bone, or both. He backed up a step, though he had no worries about the other two men; Dan was there, and they would be foolish to challenge him.

A knee to the center of Imrahiel's gut missed, but only slightly. Then Kai brought the flat of his sword down hard on Imrahiel's now-uncovered head. He felt the impact reverberate up his arms, and he worried for a second that he had knocked him permanently senseless. That wouldn't help his cause.

He stood straight and turned, finding that Dan had herded the other two men into a corner, where he guarded them with his blade. Dan nodded toward Imrahiel, who lay moaning on the floor. A bit of drool dribbled from the corner of his mouth.

"I hope you didn't hit him too hard."

Kai nodded. "Me, too, though in truth he doesn't deserve to live. Who are these two?" He directed his gaze at the two accomplices, whose countenances had hardened.

"We are your betters, boy," said the non-warrior, who couldn't have been more than thirty. He was dressed nicely and sported one of the fancy new hairdos for men. He looked like a rooster.

"Great," replied Kai. "Sit."

Dan ordered them to chairs at the table. A trilling whistle came from outside once they were settled, and Dan trilled back. He looked at Kai. "Perimeter still secure."

Kai ignored the fop, focusing instead on his younger, more robust companion, who boasted a jutting double chin. "No rescue for you tonight. And by tomorrow you'll either be dead or on your way to a Zarahemla prison. Not the main one, mind you—that one isn't fully secure yet."

Whatever hope had glimmered in the man's eyes winked out, and Kai continued. "I won't ask your names, because you won't give me real ones, but I know your slobbering partner as Imrahiel. We had some interactions before the unfortunate death of your compatriot, Kishkumen. I wish I could have seen that serpent die, but I witnessed the gory aftermath."

The lie felt delicious, even tantalizing, given the way the men squirmed. Good. They hated him. Their rage might make them say something they didn't intend to reveal.

Imrahiel's groaning grew louder, especially as he tried to sit up. Kai got behind him, grabbing him under the armpits and hoisting him into another seat. His head lolled a bit, but he had stopped drooling, and his eyes achieved some success at focusing.

Now Kai ignored the other men. "Welcome back, friend. I apologize—sincerely, I assure you—for hitting you so hard. I don't know my own strength."

Imrahiel's mind wasn't back up to speed yet. He gave Kai a confused look, eyes blinking rapidly. He squinted at his two companions, examining them for several seconds. When his gaze traveled to Dan, he sucked in a breath. Yes, he probably knew what Dan looked like. He also knew Dan was one of the vaunted two thousand, and therefore to be feared … or at least respected.

"Over here," said Kai. Imrahiel jerked his head, eyes still watery. By the increasing lines of menace etching his face, Kai knew his faculties were returning at a faster pace.

"You will die for this," Imrahiel said in a slurred voice.

"We all die."

"You will die slowly."

Kai took a deep breath, ending in a low growl. "You think I fear your threats. I do not."

"You will learn to," Imrahiel snarled, though it came out more as a mewling.

Kai glanced at Dan. "My goodness, so dramatic. What did I ever do to him … besides knock him senseless and get him chased out of his posh pottery shop in Zarahemla?" He felt his anger churning fast and hot, and Dan held up a hand, enjoining calm. Kai tried to heed his advice. He truly did.

His open-handed slap to Imrahiel's face echoed through the room. He had held back, though; Imrahiel didn't fall off his chair.

"Where is Siarah, my betrothed from Bountiful?"

Imrahiel touched his cheek, then glared at him. "I have no idea who that is. I didn't even know you were planning to be married."

A second slap rang—opposite cheek. Imrahiel grunted, then growled, then shouted.

"You will *die* for this!" He started to rise from his chair, but Kai brought his sword up, and he sank back down, eyes boiling.

"You think I know something about who killed Kishkumen, the man you and Gadianton sent to assassinate Helaman."

Imrahiel kept his tone somewhat in check. "You have no idea what you're talking about, boy. We are patriots. We might have opposed Pahoran and Pacumeni—and maybe we weren't sad when they died— but we wouldn't have tried to kill them. And Helaman is better than they were. We do not oppose him as chief judge."

Kai studied him a moment. "Such lies slide so smoothly across your lips. You despise Helaman and all the Christians."

Imrahiel gave a wicked smile. "Not all the Christians are objection- able. There are many who support the true path of progress, presented by enlightened men like Gadianton."

Dan's clear, strong voice pierced the air. "Then they have broken their covenants and are not true Christians."

Imrahiel turned his head slowly toward Dan. "I would expect such tripe from an Ammonite. You will blindly follow your prophet through the gates of hell." His head snapped back to Kai. "But this one has the potential to be wiser."

Kai furrowed his brow, then cocked his head. The insult to Dan sharpened the edge to his voice. "Are you trying to recruit me, servant of Satan?"

Imrahiel's smile remained. "I am a poor recruiter. But perhaps you are recruiting yourself. You've seen the chaos caused by our divided government, with no firm hand to guide us. You are an orphan of such division, are you not? Yes, I know more about you than you might think. Your adoptive family, too. Perhaps I can even help you find Siarah. Have you considered that the reason she hasn't shown up in Zarahemla might be that she has seen the light herself?"

It felt like Imrahiel had slapped *him* in the face. His pulse quickened as bile rose in his throat. Dan spoke before he combusted, however.

"We are not interested in your contest of thrones. Our purpose is specific. A man matching your description was observed in Bountiful talking to a man who was later seen with Siarah. You either know where she is, or you can direct us to someone who does. The punishment for your crimes may be less severe if you help us now. If you reject that offer, you will most likely be executed. Kihoran here isn't the only witness to your treachery. Justice will be fair, but it will also be swift."

Kai was grateful for the time to calm himself a little and think, and he wasn't above a bold bluff. "The public doesn't know this, but before he died, Kishkumen admitted to assassinating Pahoran the Younger, and he implicated a few others by name, claiming that they would soon take over the Nephite government and avenge his death. Yours was one of those names."

Imrahiel narrowed his eyes. "I don't believe you."

"I was there as he was dying. So was Helaman."

"Kishkumen would never have broken his sacred oaths ... unlike you."

Kai laughed, the sound undulating in the confined space. "A man in intense pain, knowing he is on death's door, does unpredictable things. Surely you know that. And *sacred*?" He laughed again. Imrahiel's two compatriots glowered ... until Dan warned them with a steely glance.

Imrahiel's dark look made them bow their heads. "Don't be afraid of these two imposters. They—"

Kai's third slap carried the force of the prior two combined, and this time Imrahiel tumbled from his chair onto the floor. Kai sheathed his sword and crouched behind him, grabbing his forehead and chin and pulling back hard.

"Which city?" he growled. "And whose house?"

"Fool," mumbled Imrahiel. "You are too weak ... unlike *her*."

Kai twisted Imrahiel's head, hearing some pops from the vertebrae in his neck. "You're torturing her, trying to break her until she becomes your willing slave."

Despite his face being scrunched up in pain, Imrahiel's voice was smooth. "We haven't harmed her physically."

"I'll believe that when I see her, which will be soon. Is this elaborate chase part of your silly psychological game?" He twisted harder.

"We don't play games," breathed Imrahiel through clenched teeth, eyes squeezed tight.

"Nor do I," spat Kai. He looked up at Dan. "Let's get them to the Hall of Judgment. The officers there can prepare some cells, and we can talk to the chief judge in the morning. Maybe he'll have some ideas. We should probably bring the others from the house as well." He glanced down for Imrahiel's reaction to that. The man's features only hardened more.

Dan made a different series of whistling sounds, and within seconds Lehi's two elites were inside the room, helping them secure their prisoners. The Mulek Hall of Judgment wasn't far, and Kai felt a strong desire to kick Imrahiel all the way there.

———◇———

Kai and Dan retrieved their few things from the barn, sans the limps, and returned to the Hall of Judgment to sleep there, near the prisoners. By morning, law officers had brought several others in, and, though he was groggy, Kai led the first round of individual interrogations. Then he snatched a quick nap before he and Dan met with the chief judge.

"Chief Judge Manti," he began as they sat in a small chamber with a pair of guards, a low table between them, "I appreciate your willingness to meet with us."

Manti, who appeared ancient but whose eyes were still sharp, gave a slight nod. "Your commission comes from Helaman, is that right?"

"It does."

"And you both serve him directly?" His eyes landed briefly on Dan, exuding respect.

"Yes," said Kai. "We are hunting members of Gadianton's group involved in trying to assassinate Helaman and overthrow the government. Particularly, we are looking for those who have kidnapped my betrothed from Bountiful. It has been months already, and last night we got our first big break."

"Imrahiel. I have not heard of him. He is a senior member of the band?"

"Yes, he is."

"Then we must be careful. I will double the guards in the prison."

"That is wise, thank you. If we may, we'd like to move the rest of our men into the city and stay in your barracks."

"Of course. I'm surprised you did not ask before. Where have you and Dan been staying?"

"A barn," came the reply from Dan. "And we found it quite homely."

Again, Kai wasn't sure if he was being serious.

"Well," said Manti with a wrinkled smile, "you will find the barracks here much more comfortable, if not, perhaps, as *homely*. And rest assured, you can trust me."

Dan offered him a strange wink and a respectful smile, but Kai wasn't satisfied. He cleared his throat to get Manti's attention again, then asked somewhat boldly, "How secure is your prison?"

Manti's smile dissipated. "You mean, how well can I trust my officers? That is a question I often ask myself. I have many good men, Master Kihoran, most of them faithful in their church covenants. We are not perfect, of course, but such is the way of all the earth ... which, by the way, I am not much longer for." His smile returned. Kai had seen other old people express similar wistful sentiments.

"Well, thank you again for doubling the guard. These are extremely dangerous men, and I have personal experience with one of them. We plan to question them for a number of days and then send them to Zara-hemla. If you can arrange a message by your fastest courier for us, that would also be appreciated."

"Yes, of course. It will go directly to Helaman?"

Kai nodded, and Dan added, "He will send a select group of men to take over the escort partway. We'll send some of Captain Lehi's men with them to start that journey."

"Captain Lehi, you say?"

"Yes," replied Dan. "Our men are actually on loan from Lehi—a group of his elites."

"Oh, my. Yes, that is an impressive group, led by a wonderful, brave man. A true hero. You have both met Lehi?"

"We have," said Kai. "And I must admit that I haven't met a more … intimidating … person."

Manti chuckled. "That he is, indeed. Especially to our enemies. More than one army has soiled their collective breeches upon hearing Lehi was on the move against them." His eyes moved to Dan again. "The same can be said of you and your brothers, Master Dan."

Dan's expression was hard to read. "We are not the fighting force we once were. And our people tire of the constant conflict."

"Aye," agreed Manti. "I wish the Lord would deign to arrive on Earth tomorrow. Perhaps the signs of his coming in the Old Country would help our people remember their blessings for more than a handful of years."

"I am doubtful of that," said Dan, and Kai raised his eyebrows. Dan was rarely a pessimist. "Our remembrance is painfully short, our pride a rampaging beast."

Kai's mouth began to drop as Manti nodded. "I wish I could say you are wrong, my brother. But," he took a long breath, "we go along as best we can with faith in the Lord, and it will all work out in the end, right?"

"Yes, it will," said Dan, and suddenly he was the rock Kai knew again.

"So," said Manti, "we need to get some information from this

Imrahiel and his friends, and we have to do it ethically and legally."

Kai almost groaned as he nodded in agreement. A very insistent part of him wished he could do more than that.

"It will take some time," said Manti, "and probably won't bear much fruit before you send them to Zarahemla. But," he raised a finger, "we will try, and we will seek the Lord's help."

"Thank you," said Dan before Kai could object. "We know you have some capable leaders here. Kai and I will, of course, be involved."

"As you should be. We will prevail, brothers. We will prevail."

That seemed a brashly confident statement. Kai glanced at Dan, who nodded with somber determination, and forced himself to relax.

———◆———

Two mornings later, after several frustrating rounds of interrogation, awful but somehow inevitable news arrived at the barracks—Imrahiel and the two who were with him in the jewelry shop had escaped. Two guards had been killed, and three had disappeared. Collaborators. Traitors. *Demons.*

CHAPTER 12

And now, if the Lamb of God, he being holy, should have
need to be baptized by water, to fulfil all righteousness,
O then, how much more need have we, being unholy,
to be baptized, yea, even by water!
—2 Nephi 31:5

The scene felt too familiar. At least, this time, Ara didn't have to climb anything. She just needed a little luck. The back door of the woodworking shop had a metal lock. Not unsurprising, but deeply frustrating. Even with the semi-rigid tool she possessed, made out of a new plant fiber compound, it would be difficult to figure out the right pattern, much less mimic it. She had to try, though. With the darkness as her ally, she set to work, pausing to glance up and down the narrow alley every minute or so.

After the first hour, she almost gave up. Maybe there *was* a way in from the roof, even though she'd already scouted that as a negative. Her strained eyes were starting to cause a throbbing pain near her temples, and her fingers cramped occasionally. She took a short break, sitting with her back against the door, taking slow, even breaths.

"Psst."

The sound made her twitch, nearly stopping her heart. Her head whirled, and she saw a crouching figure slink out of the inky blackness. Female, it appeared, dressed in dark breeches and tunic, like her, with a cloth covering nose and mouth. Ara gripped the knife at her belt, getting her feet back under her as she prepared to defend herself. The woman drew nearer, and Ara detected wrinkles around the eyes that placed the woman in her middle ages, though it was difficult to be certain. Who was she, and what was she doing here?

The woman stopped just three feet away, then suddenly sat cross-legged, empty hands in front of her. "Helaman said you might come to Morianton. He asked me to help."

"Who are you?"

She gave a slight shake of her head. "That doesn't matter. You can call me Osprey, if you like. I know you've gone by Raven in the past."

That the woman knew that was disturbing. "How can you help me?"

"Well," began Osprey, "for starters, I'm a lot more experienced breaking through locks, even metal ones. And I have better tools, designed by a curious sort of man. A genius, really. It turns out he's a cousin of Hagoth. You've heard of Hagoth, of course."

"Yes, the shipbuilder. You ... you can get through this door?"

Osprey nodded. "I can. If you'll allow me?" As she rose, Ara straightened and stepped smoothly away, hand still on her knife. Her heart beat less rapidly than she would have expected, but it was still racing. She watched as the oddly confident woman approached the door, extracted a set of three tools similar in appearance to the one she had, and went to work on the lock, balancing on one knee. She closed her eyes in concentration, turning her head slightly, clearly focusing on what she could hear as well as feel.

Ara couldn't discern too much of what the woman was actually doing. But her eyes widened when, less than five minutes later, Osprey smiled, stood, and pushed the door open.

"How did you get that so fast?" Ara couldn't help but ask.

"Practice, my dear. Lots and lots of practice. We all have our talents. This is one of mine." She smiled, then entered, and Ara followed, shutting the door behind her and feeling around in the near-total darkness to relock it.

The woman called Osprey lit a candle—similar to the one Ara had used an eternity ago in High Judge Zerahir's home office—exposing a crammed, disorderly storage room. Wood scraps and half-finished projects dominated most of the space, a plush, gilded chair with the face of a lion etched into the seatback posing a sharp incongruence. No obvious repository for documents presented itself, so Osprey snuffed her candle before opening the interior door.

They followed a short hallway running along the side of the building, opening to the front area at its end and revealing one other door. Probably an office. Osprey opened it slowly, then stepped inside. It wasn't as dark, since it featured a thick, curtainless window. Raven immediately went to cover it, taking cloth and tacks from her bag. Then Osprey lit her candle again. Her tinderbox was an odd contraption, too, but it disappeared before Ara could get a closer look.

The office was almost as messy as the storage room, with just a small space cleared on a broad, lacquered desk stacked haphazardly with scrolls and parchment.

"A lot more paperwork here than a common woodworker could possibly generate in a year, or even five," noted Osprey. She sighed, but with a hint of glee. "Well, I suppose we should get reading."

They spent the next three hours poring through the stacks, well into the tenth hour of the night, and they only knew the time by the muted, half-strangled chimes from one of the city's bell towers. The sun would rise in less than two hours.

At first, the writings were interesting, but they quickly became repetitive. The shop owner was definitely a supporter of Gadianton, but nothing they found clearly incriminated him with the breaking of laws. Lots of harangues about the unfairness of this or that government policy; instructions about influencing this or that important person, or even the public at large; general disdain for all things Christian, including insipid insults about Helaman and his family.

"This looks interesting," said Osprey, thrusting a parchment at Ara, who blinked in surprise, realizing she had started to doze off. She took the document and began to review it, commenting aloud.

"The finding of Kishkumen's 'insidious' killer is still a top priority. Hmmm ..." Not unexpected, but given Kai's involvement, it sent a shiver down her spine. "New inroads have been made with several judges in various cities, along with some army captains, pursuing that same information." The chill intensified. She recognized a few of the names, but not all. And the list of army captains was disturbingly long. She had brought parchment and ink, and she pulled them from her satchel.

As she copied names, Osprey remarked, "The rot isn't decreasing—it's spreading. Slowly and cautiously, but it *is* growing."

"Why?" said Ara, looking up, "and how? Helaman has been pursuing Gadianton, his lieutenants, and many others. They scattered. Some fled the country."

Osprey nodded slowly, the candlelight glinting in her pupils. "Yes, but they were far more numerous than was known, and many returned when they confirmed there wasn't enough proof for the government to punish them. They know Helaman will uphold the laws fairly. Ironically, they despise those laws."

"They are willing to break *any* law if they believe they can get away with it."

"Yes, child, that is true. Which is why wise King Mosiah warned us that if we became wicked enough, no number of laws could keep us in line ... or free."

"Who are you, really?" Ara asked with some earnestness. "Do you know Helaman?"

The woman looked away for a moment. "I know him. I don't agree with him on everything, but he and others like him are a force for goodness, stability, and prosperity. Gadianton claims the same, but he is driven by hubris and greed. I think he may also be mad."

"You know *him*, too?"

After a pause, Osprey gave a tight smile. "We have met. He is brilliant, but dangerous. That touch of madness makes him even more so."

"I am a Christian now. I was even baptized. He hates Christians with a passion."

"Indeed he does, but mostly because faithful Christians hold so many powerful positions in the government and are generally more difficult to coerce. If it were otherwise, he would appreciate their hard work and tolerate them as foolish children."

"Are we foolish children?" Ara wasn't sure why she had asked that.

"What makes you think I'm part of the 'we'?"

"I … wasn't implying that." She lowered her head and began copying again, uncovering the next piece of parchment. Osprey didn't pursue the topic, just kept studying documents. After a few minutes, the older woman spoke again.

"Kihoran knows something about Kishkumen's death."

Was she asking, or did she know? Ara didn't meet her eyes. She felt a sudden need for caution. "He was in the building that night as one of Helaman's aides … but pretending to work for Imrahiel."

"Yes, Imrahiel. Arrogant arachnid. He's not even a Nephite. He might not be Mulekite, either, though that doesn't really matter."

How did she know so much about Imrahiel? Picturing the man's face nearly made Ara shudder, and she left off copying for the moment, finally looking up. "What will they do to Kihoran if they capture him?"

"Oh, they will most assuredly torture him for information, then kill him." Osprey said it so matter-of-factly Ara winced. But then her tone softened. "I'm sorry. I deal in realities. I know he means something to you. And I don't believe he's in all that much danger right now. They could try to hurt him in other ways, though."

"Like kidnapping Siarah."

Osprey gave a little shrug. "That wasn't just meant to hurt him, or lure him into a trap. She's also prey to be toyed with and tamed. They may ultimately be successful in using her to trap Kihoran, but there are other ways to destroy him, once they decide to move forward with that. They're experts at swaying perception, for instance. They can concoct lies about him, weave them into the public consciousness. They may even try to paint him as the killer of both Kishkumen *and* Pahoran, while claiming Kishkumen sacrificed himself to *save* Helaman. That might entice certain zealots to go after him."

"But that's ridiculous," Ara protested, too loudly, her hand coming unbidden to her mouth. Was Osprey trying to bait her into revealing something about Kai?

"It is. But you have known people to believe ridiculous things, have you not?"

Ara swallowed. "Yes, including me."

"Truth is an elusive quarry."

"But ..." Her voice trailed off. She had wanted to say, "But the Spirit will guide us," which is what Jerena had taught her. Did she *know* that, though? Was it really true?

Osprey held up a scroll. "They will continue to lie about the Church, too. We've seen more than hints tonight at the development of new plans for that in these documents. They will attempt to cultivate a façade of compassion and tolerance for themselves in the process. Do you know why the Nehors have been so successful, despite Ammonihah?"

Who could forget the Desolation of Nehors? "They ... don't believe in God?" She was already off-balance, and felt stupid as the words left her mouth.

"Well, they might not, though they certainly claim to. The temptation they dangle is that nobody need carry responsibility for anything they do, especially not with God, who accepts everyone, no matter how bad. All will be saved in His kingdom. What an alluring message. Rubbish, of course. Why would someone who has become hateful desire to live in the presence of love? They couldn't bear it. That's true on Earth as well. Can you imagine Imrahiel staying at Helaman's house? And feeling at peace with it?"

The question hit close to home, and in more ways than one. Ara had spent a considerable amount of time there. Precious time. *And* she had worked for Imrahiel. Her head drooped as her eyes blurred. Osprey seemed not to notice how the question affected her, or at least pretended so.

A profound silence ensued. Ara was able to start copying again. When she finished, she put away her parchment and continued searching the messy desk for more intel.

"You know," said Osprey, "we haven't been very careful about putting things back where we found them."

"I know," said Ara. "But they might not notice, since everything's such a mess."

"Hmmm. Well, even the messiest person often sees the clutter as organized in their own mind. No matter, though. In fact, it might be good to give them some discomfort. Any hitch in their plans is good, right?"

She nodded. Osprey had a point, but that wasn't why Ara had come to Morianton. She needed substantial clues about where Kai currently was and where he should search for Siarah. She grew less certain with each passing hour that she could actually help, but somehow, that served only to increase her determination.

A man burst into the room, jolting her out of that reverie. He was stupid, because he let his eyes flinch as the candlelight hit him. He had a knife in one hand, though. Ara reached for that wrist with both hands, clasping tightly and then pulling back, using her weight to supplement her inferior strength. He tumbled toward the desk, and she had to let go lest she break her own arms or get caught underneath him. She scrambled out of the way, reaching for her knife as she turned to assess. Osprey began beating him over the head with a pair of hard scroll cases, her assault swift and coordinated. That left his back—particularly his kidneys—wide open for attack.

Two years ago, she might have done it. Now, she couldn't. Why not? He was attacking them! With a knife! Angry at herself, she knew she had to do *something*. So she took a chance, stepping close and pushing the point of her blade through his shirt, piercing some flesh, too.

"Stand down," she hissed. "We're not who you think we are."

He tensed, and she prepared for ... whatever she needed to do. Good grief, she was becoming a ninny! That made her even angrier. But suddenly he relaxed. Osprey delivered another good bop on the head, and then all their eyes turned to the flames from the toppled candle, licking eagerly at several strewn pieces of parchment. Osprey stared for a moment, then looked at Ara and shrugged.

"My father will have you flogged for this," said the man, whom Ara realized couldn't have been more than seventeen. "I don't care who you are."

"Well," said Osprey, "we'll leave you to put out the flames, then. I'm sure there are important papers at risk. Do tell him to be more careful, though. Gadianton doesn't like carelessness."

With that she whisked herself out of the room. Ara stared after her in stunned amazement for a moment, then followed as quickly as she could, sparing another glance for the youth, who ignored her as he took off his shirt and started to slap at the fire. His torso wasn't as muscled as Kai's, but he would probably fill out nicely. Shooing that vapid thought out of her head, she reached the back door, which Osprey held open.

"You have your satchel. Good," she said.

Ara hadn't ever taken the strap off her shoulder. The papers with the names were safely tucked away.

"Take those to Lehi," Osprey continued, "then look to the north. Based on what I read, many Gadiantons have begun to concentrate there as they make plans to filter back into the country with manufactured proof of their innocence."

"Where would I find Captain Lehi?" she asked.

Osprey shook her head. "I meant the city, not the man. Chief Judge Omner will take them, and he can set some wheels in motion."

Ara turned as she noticed smoke wafting upward from the still-open door. The sky was lightening, too. That young man would have his hands full, though he might be able to save the building. Part of her wished him well. The other part still had the knife at his back.

"What do I tell him about you?" she asked.

"Why, nothing. Why would he even need to know I was here?" Osprey tapped her lightly on the cheek, then hurried off down the alley.

"What a strange woman," Ara whispered to herself. "And remarkable." She looked again at the open door to the shop. The smoke seemed to be lessening. Most of the documents in the office were probably destroyed. Not that she would try to verify that.

She went in the opposite direction from Osprey, aiming for her inn and a soft, welcoming bed.

———◆———

Evening came again, after a long and luxurious nap. She had one more stop to make in Morianton, and it would be a perilous one. She almost didn't go, but only partly because of the additional danger. She needed to visit her aunt, her mother's sister, who'd had an affair with her father shortly before her mother died. Her father had never talked about it, even though he had been discovered, and Ara never wanted to ask.

Nabish was married to another follower of the rising personality cult of Gadianton. Ara knew him to be a shrewd, cruel man, though he put on a much different face. Why her aunt had chosen Akrim she couldn't fathom, though he was wealthy. What she *could* understand is why her aunt might have sought the affections of Nahom, given the coldness of her husband.

She paused for more than a minute to regather her thoughts as she stood before their door. Then she raised her hand, poised it a moment, and knocked. Within seconds she heard footsteps approaching, and the door opened to reveal a servant in sharp white and scarlet livery, a man twice as old as she, with an oiled mustache. Those were rare. And odd-looking. Not attractive at all.

"Your name and business?" he demanded in an airy tone, chin lifted as if to emphasize the lofty nature of the threshold on which she stood.

"My name is Araya, daughter of Lanaina. Mistress Nabish is my aunt, and I wish to speak with her."

The man didn't seem impressed. "About what do you seek to speak with her?"

"The location of my father and brother. They may have passed through Morianton."

"Perhaps there is a reason they didn't tell you where they were going?"

"Of course there's a reason," she snapped. "Now, are you going to let me in to speak with my aunt, or am I going to start screaming until a law officer comes by?"

The man frowned deeply. "Rude. But, very well, you may enter." He stepped back, offering not even the tiniest of flourishes to welcome her entrance. Then he shut the door harder than would be considered normal or proper. He gestured toward a chair in the foyer before walking stiffly off, and Ara noted the finely polished stone of the floor. Zerahir's had been nicer, but this was expensive.

She sat, then reviewed again all the things she could remember about her aunt. Roundish, beady-eyed, always wearing trinkets in her hair, in addition to all her other jewelry. Pouty lips, like her mother's. Like hers, too, if she was being honest. Nabish and her mother didn't share the same personality, though. Nabish had always been more like their other sister, Tienvissah—vain, absent-minded, boring to talk to, and fake.

It took at least a quarter of an hour for Nabish to show up, and when she did Ara feasted her eyes on one of the finest formal gowns she had ever seen. She inhaled the perfume, too, noting the newest makeup style highlighting eyes and cheeks. Various ornaments dangled uselessly from hair that should have been graying. And the voice—oh, that awful, simpering voice, like the screech of a mouse caught by a cat and somehow happy about it.

"Arayah, my dear, how very nice to see you. You're so far from home! What brings you to Morianton?"

Her servant had surely told her already, but Ara restated it as simply and directly as she could. "My father and brother disappeared the night of the attempted assassination of Helaman, and I think they may have come through Morianton at some point. I'm trying to find them."

A hand to her breast signified Nabish's pretended surprise at the uncomfortable revelation. "Oh, my. I do hope they are all right. You … didn't go with them?" The tilt of her head seemed to signal genuine curiosity, and Ara decided to use it.

"The law officers weren't looking for me."

"Oh, dear." Nabish found another posh seat to rest her pampered rump. "Why would the law officers want to speak with your father? He is a judge, after all."

Ara narrowed her eyes. "You know he is a … silly man. I believe you liked him for it." She hoped she didn't sound too accusatory or impertinent; she needed the fish to stay on the hook. "I figured he may have come here to find some help."

"Well, anything for family, of course," said Nabish, hand to bosom again. "But we haven't seen him. It's been many months since that horrible business—are you sure he hasn't returned to Zarahemla? I presume he is innocent and would want to clear his name."

Perhaps her aunt was a little more clever than Ara gave her credit for. She was clearly lying, though, and Ara didn't feel like dancing.

"He is not innocent, and the government knows that." Well, maybe a little dance. "I need to warn him, and I have some information that can potentially help."

"Oh? What might that be, my dear?" She had never seen her aunt's eyes become so coldly calculating.

"I think he can make a deal."

"But that would vio—" Nabish's lips snapped shut, her painted eyebrows coming together. "What kind of deal?"

Yes, it figured her aunt had taken the oaths. "I still correspond with Helaman's wife. The axe is about to fall. But we can save a few."

Nabish recast her face to innocence. "Well, that sounds dreadfully ominous. I still can't imagine your father is in any *real* trouble, but sometimes the innocent get swept up in the schemes of the powerful." She sighed, and Ara could picture her wanting to fan herself—or commanding a servant to do it. "I did hear tell of your father and brother passing through the city. I believe they were … um, emigrating north. It still sounds strange to say that word."

North. It might not constitute a solid lead. But given what Osprey had said as well, Ara felt better about heading in that direction.

"Do you know where, specifically?

Nabish shook her head, suddenly seeming tired. "I'm sorry, my dear, I don't. But I'll give you some money. They may need it."

Ara dipped her head. "Thank you, Aunt Nabish. I will send word as soon as I find them."

"Thank you, my dear. Godspeed."

The last word seemed to curdle as it passed her lips, and Ara flinched inside. How much better was she?

Chapter 13

And now as I said concerning faith—faith is not to have
a perfect knowledge of things; therefore if ye have faith
ye hope for things which are not seen, which are true.
—Alma 32:21

Siarah shivered under her thin blanket, then peered into the early morning darkness at the spot where Zoram lay in their tiny, locked room, softly snoring. They had beaten him again last night. How could he sleep so well? Maybe he was just that exhausted—mentally as well as physically.

They hadn't beaten her yet, though every time they asked about Kai and she couldn't give them the answers they wanted, they beat Zoram. Poor man.

Them. Who *were* they, exactly? She had asked. They wouldn't say. Clearly they were part of the wicked group that had tried to kill Helaman, which attempt Kai had thwarted, but she had no idea where they were from, or who their immediate leader was; if they were part of a coalition of groups or all one body; and what their ultimate goals were, beyond overthrowing the current government. She was starting to understand a little more how politics worked. She hadn't focused much on it before, preferring to keep her mind on happier things while growing up in peaceful Bountiful.

From snatches of conversation she overheard, she understood they were in Antionum, land of the Zoramites, allied with the Lamanites for nearly three decades now. That meant she was outside Nephite lands for the first time in her life. How would Kai ever find her here?

A fresh wave of despair overtook her, and her shuddering somehow woke Zoram, who rolled over with a groan and looked at her with bleary, swollen eyes.

"It's all right," he said in a reassuring tone that clashed with their circumstance. *How is it all right?* Prayer. She needed to pray more, but she was finding it more difficult—at least to do it effectively.

She made a blubbering sound, her vision watering. "It's my fault they found us."

"No, it's not," he said. "You had just barely sent the letter."

His attempt to console her didn't work.

"I don't know where Kai is. Can't they *see* that?"

Zoram sat up on his pitiful straw mat. More groaning. "They probably know where he is. But maybe they think you'll remember something else."

She pushed herself up to a sitting position as well, pulling the blanket around her shoulders. "They keep asking about what happened the night of Helaman's attempted assassination. I *wasn't there*, and Kai is horrible about writing letters. How am I supposed to tell them anything?" She was proud of how she had crafted that deflection. "It's like I'm just a … cat's toy. They like watching me suffer. Both of us suffer."

"Maybe they're trying to lure him here," said Zoram, studying her closely.

"How? Nobody knows where we are."

"They can leak information to certain people. There are ways."

"Oh. Yes, of course. But Kai won't fall for something like that. He'll bring an army."

"To Antionum? And provoke a war?"

"Would it really start a war?"

Zoram's eyes widened, as much as they could, and she felt abashed. Of course it could start a war.

"Well, he could sneak in with a few hand-picked men. Moronihah or Lehi will lend him some. The very best. Maybe some of the Stripling Warriors."

Zoram frowned, studying the dirt floor, which had become easier to see with the sun rising. They didn't get a lot of light through the cracks in the windowless wooden walls, but they got some. "I suppose," he said. "That could be dangerous, though. We might get caught in the middle of the fighting. At some point, there *will* be fighting."

"Stop throwing cold water on my ideas." She wrapped her arms around herself, staring at the same spot he had fixated on.

An idea floated into her mind. "What if ... I gave them some false information? Pretended to remember something, sent them chasing after a hare. It would buy us some time. I mean, buy Kai and whoever he brings with him some time to come get us out. It might thin their ranks here, too, right?"

His brow scrunched as their eyes met. "I don't like it," he said.

"But the beatings might stop."

"And they might not."

"You don't deserve to be treated like this."

"You don't see the half of it," he replied, wincing, "but they don't care."

"Well, I have to try *something*." She felt her resolve hardening, her mind quickening. "I'll do it today. Help me think of something."

They had no time to deliberate, as the door rattled on its hinges. The lock clinked, and the door swung open, revealing a captor they hadn't seen before. He was tall, wiry, and wrapped in a cloud of calm menace. He made her insides turn to water.

"You are both summoned," he said. "Follow."

Siarah and Zoram looked at each other, then slowly got to their feet. As they stepped through the door into the anteroom of the building—Zoram limping markedly—she noted half a dozen men with long knives at the ready. These guards surrounded them as they followed Stormcloud outside into the brisk morning air. She glanced around. They definitely weren't in the capital of the land of Antionum. This was little more than a village, and she neither saw nor heard children. So, a war camp of some sort? They proceeded to a dwelling only slightly larger than the one they'd left, four guards remaining outside while two followed them in.

The simple structure was one large room, with a curtain suspended from the ceiling that could be pulled across on a taut rope to divide it in two. A man sat near the center on what could only be described as a throne—a broad chair, high backed, with intricate designs and leafwork in gold and silver. His hair was dark, and he sported a thin scar running diagonally over his left cheek. His eyes were nearly black, and incredibly penetrating. He looked to be in his mid-forties.

"Master," said Stormcloud with a low bow, "our guests." Then he glided with deadly grace to the side of the room.

Siarah almost forgot herself and protested at the laughably inaccurate term applied to her and Zoram, gritting her teeth instead.

The man on the throne studied them for at least a minute, his mien so lifeless and cold that Siarah soon felt she was floating in blackness. She had never experienced evil like this. She swallowed finally, and then his face brightened with jarring suddenness as he spoke.

"It is a pleasure to finally meet you, Siarah. I have traveled a considerable distance for this." His newfound charisma oozed over her skin like a dark, viscous oil, blocking her pores. She had no words. He tapped a finger lightly on one of the arms of his throne.

"I don't believe you have done anything wrong. But I'm just as sure your betrothed has. And whatever you may think of Nephite laws, those do not apply here, nor anywhere with me."

His tone had hardened. Siarah's mind froze as his words dashed her hopes of freedom. She looked at Zoram, whose jaw muscles twitched as he stared at the vile rebel leader, though he didn't seem as angry as she would have guessed. Her guesses were horrible anyway. She had no idea how to judge anything like this.

"Ah, you think me to be evil? You are so naïve. We can teach you, though. There is so much with which we can enlighten you." Lust filled his voice, fanning the flames of her despair. "I trust Zoram has already been useful in that regard."

She vaguely detected his lecherous smile, given how her eyes swam. Zoram? What would *he* be teaching her? And why? Then, realization crashed like the prison on the heads of Ammonihah's leaders. She jerked her head toward Zoram. He didn't turn to acknowledge her gaze. His jaw muscles were rock hard.

"You ... *kidnapped* me?" she whispered. "You betrayed me?"

"I did not betray you," he said, eyes still forward. "You should listen to Gadianton. He has a plan to forge all the lands of Lehi into the greatest nation in the world."

"The greatest ... what are you talking about? Does it justify murdering and kidnapping people? Am I going to be executed, too? I won't join you. I think you know that already. Maybe *he* doesn't—" she pointed a finger at Gadianton, not sure where she got the courage, "but you do. And I refuse to believe you're that evil. Not deep down."

Gadianton laughed. The sound was rich, sonorous, and deep. "I didn't expect so much backbone from this one. Perhaps she *will* be useful, once we break her." He suddenly scowled at Zoram. "It appears you have made a poor job of preparation."

Siarah squared her shoulders toward Gadianton and tried to stand straighter. "You cannot break me."

Gadianton harrumphed. "An empty, desperate claim. I have broken far stronger than you, and for less reason. You will remain here. Your betrothed—who nearly caught up with me recently, I must give him credit—will come. The clues will lead him here. He will underestimate both our numbers and our resolve, and he will come. It is only a matter of time. Until he does, I will enjoy getting to know you better ... *much* better." With a flick of his master's wrist, Stormcloud strode over and picked her up like a sack of wheat, throwing her over his shoulder and stalking out of the building. He returned her to the prison room, setting her down more gently than expected, then wordlessly locked her inside. Zoram—that nasty traitor and devilishly good actor—didn't return.

She was sobbing before her knees hit the floor hard, and she didn't care how much they hurt. Inside, she felt like she was being flayed, endlessly and mercilessly. Hope, if she had ever truly had any, fluttered in tatters just outside her vision, like butterflies massacred in a tornado.

"Father," she cried, "how is this possible? What have I done wrong? Why are these evil people allowed to do this?" She heard no answers, just her own bubbling and mewling. She wanted to scream, to wail in utter despair, but she didn't want her captors to hear that. Why, she couldn't define.

"Where is Kai, Father? Please, please, please keep him safe."

Before long, she fell to her side, shoulders heaving until she fell into a fitful sleep.

———◆———

Two days passed, and then Zoram mocked her by showing his face again. He stood outside the door, looking in through the barred opening.

"You haven't been eating," he said. "Or even drinking. Please, take some nourishment."

She pushed herself to a sitting position, heedless of her bedraggled appearance, gazing at him with narrowed eyes. For long seconds he held that gaze, then looked away.

"Are you worried I won't be healthy enough for Gadianton's *ministrations?*"

He seemed to blanch slightly, shaking his head. "Something happened. He had to leave. He'll be back, of course, but I don't know when."

A small mercy, or merely a delay of the inevitable? Or was he just lying again?

"I'm not hungry," she pretended, the arm across her midsection giving her away. She had never felt so famished in her life. She had been spoiled, she decided. But it didn't matter now. She would die here. Perhaps that's what God wanted. Maybe it would help Kai. All her visions of popularity and prosperity living in Zarahemla with Kai and their children, close to Helaman, the Lord's prophet, had vanished like wisps of smoke under a heavy rain. She would never have any of that. It wasn't fair, but she was powerless to change it. At least she could admit that.

"Of course you are," he said. "I came to make you a deal."

"I don't want any deals from the devil," she spat with a surge of vehemence, the hunger briefly dissipating.

"It's not from him," said Zoram with surprising softness. Then he opened the door and sat cross-legged in the entrance. "If you will eat a meal, I will let you teach me about this Jesus myth for an hour. And don't worry. Nobody else is here. Just me."

She stared, blinking. "I'm that pathetic of a prisoner?"

He frowned. "You are not physically dangerous to me. That does not make you pathetic."

She looked away, leaning hard on one arm, feeling the muscles wanting to give way for lack of nourishment. Part of her indeed wanted to die, but she also knew she was incapable of starving herself to death. She wasn't strong enough. Yes, she *was* pathetic.

"Fine," she whispered through cracked lips, "but I doubt it will do either of us any good."

"Do you hate me?" he asked.

Her jaw clenched. She wanted to. Oh, how she wanted to. But such a feeling—at least in its true form, which she now recognized—seemed foreign to her.

"I loathe and fear you," she replied. How close that was to hatred she couldn't be sure. Maybe, in time, she *could* hate.

"Hatred, properly channeled, is the gateway to Gadianton's influence for long-term, positive change."

Hatred was *what?* Her mind … wilted. She didn't want to have a conversation like this. She didn't respond, just stared at the floor near his crossed feet. He had acquired some new sandals. Crude, but sturdy.

He reached behind him and to the side, bringing a plate forward and setting it in front of her. Fresh legumes of a type some of the Lamanites grew, along with dried fruits and meat. He reached back again and produced a cup of water, placing it carefully next to the plate.

"Please," he said, and his earnest tone caused her to glance up. What was he trying to do? Lower her defenses? Fatten her up?

"I don't believe you actually care about me," she said, eyeing the plate but resisting. Her free hand twitched with the effort.

"I know," he said. "But I was—and am—doing my duty as I see it. I have no ill feelings toward you."

"Nor kind ones," she offered bitterly. "I am nothing but a tool, to be used and discarded, or to sharpen your lusts."

He flinched as if she had slapped him. "No, you are not. Gadianton believes I have ... had my way with you during our time together, but have I ever once acted dishonorably?"

"What would you know of honor?" she spat back. "And why didn't you set him straight about that? Because you're afraid of what he would think of you? Because you'd be embarrassed that you're not yet as depraved and heartless as he is?"

"He is not heartless," he objected, his mouth setting in a firm line.

"Why would you think that? Because he claims he can create the greatest empire in world? We hear rumors on the tides of Rome's continuing ascendance in the Old World ... does he wish to challenge Rome? At what cost? And why? For the benefit of the Nephite people, or because he'll be wealthy and powerful beyond all imagining?" She snorted. "You will, too, I imagine. Congratulations."

She surprised herself with such articulate vociferousness, but then her hunger struck with a vengeance, her mind and body knowing nourishment was within reach. She nearly doubled over.

Several seconds passed, the muscles in Zoram's face twitching in a spasmodic dance, and then he said, "Just eat, Siarah. Please."

Something in his tone gave her hand permission to move, and within another second she felt the sweet taste of food in her mouth. The dam broke, and she eagerly reached for the cup, nearly knocking it over, then thrusting it to her lips and drinking the water nearly gone. She went after the legumes, devouring them all, then the fruits, and finally, the meat. Her stomach reeled in ecstasy, and her thoughts became fuzzy.

When she fully regained her senses, Zoram still sat there, observing her shame as she pushed the empty plate and cup back to him. He picked them up without a word and set them to the side. She fully expected him to rise and close the door, reneging on his promise. But he blew out a shaky breath instead.

"Now it is your turn to ... feed me. That is what you Christians often call it, am I right?'

She brought herself to a more proper sitting position, cross-legged like him, and smoothed her skirt. Her throat no longer felt parched, but her voice still came out rough.

"We need to go back to the beginning."

"The beginning of what?"

"The world. Everything around us. This was all created by God. It isn't random happenstance."

He nodded. "I can agree with that."

"Good. But do you know who you are?"

He squinted, frowning. "I do not know what you mean."

"Where you come from, and why you have a … sense of yourself. Why you can reason, unlike the animals."

"Animals are aware of their environment. They have thought. They make decisions."

"But in a much more limited way than humans. Have any animals ever built a house like this?" She spread her arms in a wide gesture to drive home her point.

He knuckled his chin. "No, but I still do not understand your point."

"You, Zoram, as much as I loathe you … are a child of God. A son of God, made in his image, and with a potential that—" she coughed, "far surpasses what you can currently imagine."

"To God," he replied after a moment, "am I not just another animal, little better than the others, vying for supremacy?"

"That is not what God teaches us, through his prophets and the scriptures and the Holy Spirit. Even angels."

"Angels are not real."

"Whoever taught you that was ignorant." She hadn't meant to sound so disrespectful, but how much did it matter? He wasn't *really* listening to her. This was a game. She had nothing better to do, though.

His eyebrows rose as she continued. "Our first father and mother, Adam and Eve, were visited by angels who taught them the plan of salvation, or as it is also called, the plan of happiness."

"Why is it called that?"

The question flustered her for only a moment, and she thought back to many of the lessons she had been taught. She had conducted some herself, to small children. Which is what Zoram was. "When Adam and Eve were expelled from the garden for their transgression, they fell and became mortal. God knew that would happen, and this life became a way for them to unlock their true potential for both knowledge and joy by trusting in God and choosing to obey his commandments, which were delivered to them by ministering angels. Only spiritual progress brings true happiness; the rest is deception—temporary and illusory."

Her mother would have been proud of her; and perhaps even their priests in Bountiful. Zoram didn't seem impressed, though.

"None of this can be known. Have *you* seen an angel?"

She shook her head, expecting such a response. "No, and hopefully I don't need to. I have studied, and I have prayed, and I have felt the influence of the Holy Spirit testifying to me of truth. I have experienced a portion of the real, lasting joy God promises, but only when I have been obedient to his commandments."

"It sounds to me like he wants you to be a slave."

What an annoying response. So shortsighted and hypocritical. "Isn't that what Gadianton wants of you? Isn't that how his oaths are designed?"

He squirmed. She'd clearly hit a nerve. "God doesn't want slaves," she continued. "He gives us commandments to guide us along the treacherous paths of mortality, to help us avoid the horrible pitfalls of poor choices. He warns us, but he doesn't force us as one would a slave; as we follow his counsel, we become stronger, and freer, and more *individual* than all of Gadianton's motley band of miscreants. Your mind has been warped if you do not understand this."

Anger flashed in his eyes, but she didn't care. Again, what did it matter? Testifying of the truth suddenly gave her new strength and purpose, even if this turned out to be her last day on Earth. In a flash of insight, she realized how much her pride had been holding her back. She had hardly even considered such a thing before.

"Your priests have brainwashed you," he said, his voice low, "and you pay for their luxury."

"Nonsense," she retorted. "I know Korihor and others started those ugly rumors years ago, but that's all they are—rumors. Do we have priests who are not perfect? Of course we do. *None* of them are perfect. But they don't get paid for their service in the Church. They work regular jobs. If they deceive their listeners into giving them gifts, and Helaman finds out, they are punished. Some have even been expelled. But Gadianton doesn't tell you any of this. He wants you ignorant and hateful, a dumb weapon to sate his greed."

He sprang to his feet, and she recoiled, bracing for a violent action. Her bravery had just shown itself to be fake; she didn't want to die.

"Lesson over," he said in a hard voice. He backed out and slammed the door shut, rattling the entire building, leaving the plate and cup inside.

Over the next several hours, that simple dishware grew into a powerful reminder of the nourishment she had received, both physical and spiritual. Though she was still a prisoner—and a weak, fearful one—God had heard her prayers for relief and answered them in an unexpected way.

———◆———

Many days passed, and the weather grew unseasonably cool. Her captors continued to feed her, and she was given a newer blanket. She was even allowed to take some escorted walks around the village to keep up her strength. She feared this was all part of the psychological plan to break her, and that brutally harsh treatment would soon follow, but she set that impending terror aside and enjoyed the time as much as she could.

She never saw Zoram. He had probably left. She didn't try to strike up conversations with any of the others. She felt neither the need nor the desire. They all looked so hardened, anyway.

When Gadianton returned, the news spread like a summer brush fire, even to her prison. Her guards were noticeably pleased ... and agitated, which seemed an odd mix. She felt calmer than expected, and somehow more in control. At least a little. And her prayers had begun to feel more useful, which seemed a miracle.

Gadianton summoned her into his presence again, and anxiety naturally spiked. She prayed hard to keep it at bay. When she finally beheld his cruel, cold face again, she didn't quail. She did swallow nervously, though. Her guards had bound her hands in front of her. She almost laughed at that.

"I trust my men have treated you well?" said Gadianton with a sadistic undertone.

She looked at the floor. "I am alive," she said simply, with as little emotion as possible.

"Ah, that's no good, is it? Someone as young and alluring as you should live a happier life. You can, of course, if you desire it."

"I ..." she swallowed again "... am as happy as I can expect to be."

He gave a wry, mirthful chuckle. "That sentiment is not nearly as clever as you think. You're not the first to express such drivel. So much unnecessary suffering embraced by you Christians. And it's all fake. You play on others' emotions in order to bend them to your will and maintain your dominance. Such tricks do not work on me, nor on my people. We know where true, honest power lies, and we will take it—ruthlessly if we must—and employ it to improve the condition of *all* the people across this land. There's nothing you can do to stop us, either."

She kept her head down. He was right. There was nothing *she* could do. Even her tiny prayers would make little difference. God would do what *He* needed to do, and her desires had nothing to do with it. Not anymore, anyway. Which was all right. Many other saints had suffered worse fates.

After nearly a minute of silence, Gadianton spoke again. "You remember Amalickiah?"

She gave the slightest of nods. Who didn't remember the man who had caused so much destruction and anguish in his devouring lust for power? The Nephite general who had ended Amalickiah's life—Teancum—was a national hero, and she was understanding more and more why that was.

"Amalickiah was one of the most brilliant minds to ever grace this land, but the Nephite Christians, led by their prophets, priests, and teachers, rejected him. The Lamanites recognized his greatness—they just weren't strong enough to save him."

"He tricked them," she said.

Gadianton laughed. "Tricked, you say? No, he showed them greatness, and they chose to follow him. He almost succeeded in unifying the sons of Lehi."

"He would have made the Nephites slaves," she said softly. She still couldn't meet his callous eyes.

"Only those who resisted enlightenment. He graciously accepted those who changed, just as he did with the Lamanites. Many of them opposed him at first, too."

"He and his brother Ammoron languish in hell." She had said the words even more softly, and she glanced up to see him leaning forward. She caught his resultant expression of twisted rage and disgust.

"You will *never* say that again, or I will have your tongue removed. Is that clear?"

She gave a slight nod. She wasn't sure why she had said it in the first place. It was the truth, though.

Gadianton continued his tirade. "Do you know how many people your precious Helaman deceived in order to become chief judge? How many false pledges he made? How many favors he promised that he never intended to fulfill? There's a reason I have so many high judges behind me. If not for the usurpations of the military, Helaman would already have been put in his place."

What a thoroughly wicked man. She knew what he was doing. He could try, but he would fail. Suddenly, the heavens seemed to open. She felt a keen and joyous desire to live, an unexpected surge of pure confidence that she would somehow survive, and even see Kai again. It was truly incredible ... and unprecedented for her. She didn't spend time in wonderment, though. She merely shrugged, meekly, and didn't say a word.

"Well," said Gadianton with a small degree of satisfaction. "You will learn. You will dine with me every evening I am in this camp, and we will talk. I will teach you. You cannot save your betrothed, so you will forget him. Your future holds more promise than he could ever fulfill. Once you embrace the truth, you will be a powerful asset. I might even let you join my household."

She suppressed a shiver. She wanted to puke. She resisted the urge to run, and to keep running until her legs gave out. And then the peace, so completely unexpected, returned. Yes, she would survive, and not just physically.

CHAPTER 14

And I was led by the Spirit, not knowing beforehand
the things which I should do.
—1 Nephi 4:6

For some unfathomable reason, staying in Mulek for a while had seemed like the right thing to do. Dan agreed, though part of Kai wished his friend had convinced him to keep moving. He sent the men of Lehi home to their families again—also the right thing to do—though he sorely loathed to see them go. With them around, he felt invincible.

The days passed with agonizing slowness. He heard once from Helaman, apprising him of the stubborn futility of the search in and around Zarahemla. No messages had reached the capital from Siarah, and no promising leads from Shemnilom in Gideon, either. How could the best spy network in both major nations be so thoroughly thwarted? It didn't help Kai's mood that the body of a young church messenger had been found recently not two days from Mulek, on the road to Zarahemla, though that had no bearing on his predicament.

Finally, amid cooler weather, he and Dan received a missive from a high judge in Mulek. Apparently, one of his merchant friends had seen something while passing near a small village not far from Zoram, the capital of Antionum. A tall young woman with light brown hair and blue eyes, walking along a forest trail with two men following a few paces distant, both armed with bows and knives. The oddly resolute look on the woman's face had caught the merchant's attention.

Unfortunately, the merchant had visited many villages that week and couldn't recall which might have been the closest to the sighting. He had only mentioned it in casual conversation with his friend the high judge, not knowing anything about a young woman named Siarah who had gone missing and was being actively sought by Helaman and a select group of law officers. Fortunately, that particular high judge was a trusted ally of Helaman in Mulek, and he was aware of the situation.

After thanking him profusely in person, Kai immediately returned to the room at the inn and began packing for a journey through Jershon and into Antionum. Dan didn't like the idea.

"That's essentially Lamanite country," he cautioned. "And none of our laws apply there."

Kai grunted as he stuffed the merchant scout uniform he had purchased at a shop on the way back from the Hall of Judgment into a saddle bag. He would change into it once they arrived in Jershon.

"I know. And I know that neither you nor any of your brothers who have returned to Jershon can go with me into Antionum. The Zoramites hate you. But it's a golden lead. She's there—she has to be—and I have to go get her."

"I'll accompany you, then. Come up with a disguise for me."

Kai paused, cocking his head as he stared at his friend. "Your accent alone will give you away and send us both to prison. No, it has to be me. Just me. The Gadiantons won't expect that anyway. They know we've been traveling as a heavily armed fighting group. They'll expect us to sneak Lehi's elites in. They'll be watching for that."

Dan nodded with a heavy sigh, then raised an eyebrow. "You aren't going to try passing off a limp again, are you?"

"No, as a matter of fact, I'm not. I'm going to act like this is my very first merchant scouting mission, like I'm a complete novice. It'll be fun. Oh, and I'll shave my head and wear a cap. Grow one of those weird mustache and half-beard things, too."

"You'll shave …? Oh, never mind. I can't persuade you to wait, just a little while? We could get a different spy in there, maybe a woman. More intelligence is better."

"It is ... unless you don't have time to wait for it," said Kai, returning to his packing. "And I don't have time. *Siarah* doesn't have time."

"You're no good to her dead."

"If I can't save her, I'm no good to her alive, either."

———◆———

It was hard leaving Vyim behind with Dan, but a novice merchant scout wouldn't be riding such a fine horse, or even one as nice as Dan's. He would be walking, hitching rides along the way. Kai started with that approach, finding a merchant among the border towns south of Mulek who was willing to take him through Jershon and on to the city of Zoram, albeit for a modest fee. Kai's back story was silly, which hopefully made him seem even less of a spy. He said he had been rejected for the scouting assignment by a prominent trader in Nephihah but was going on his own to prove he could do it. He also wanted to court the trader's daughter. That part got a laugh out of the merchant, who clearly thought him a fool.

The ride to Zoram was uneventful, and painfully slow. Kai was tempted many times to urge the merchant to greater speed, or to at least ask him how old his horses were. They weren't young, and they clearly weren't accustomed to walking briskly. He kept his impatience in check, though, even covered it sometimes by talking about the imaginary daughter of the trader. He used Ara to describe her, not wanting to make her look like Siarah. The merchant would talk with friends and contacts, after all, and surely the tale of a forlorn, lovesick scout novice would get the man a few laughs around common room tables with plenty to drink.

Twenty-five years had passed since the Zoramites had separated from the rest of the Nephites. Kai had seen the capital city once, on a legitimate merchant reconnaissance. He had also submitted his observations on political mood and military fortifications to his spymaster, but there hadn't been much to tell. After being utterly humiliated several times by Captain Moroni, and even once by his less illustrious son Moronihah, the Zoramites, excepting a few haughty captains, exhibited little desire to join with the Lamanites on their occasional escapades into Nephite lands. And, since they feared no invasion by the defensive-minded Nephites, they hadn't kept their walls and other fortifications in great repair. In fact, as Kai approached it this time, it appeared they were transforming the walls and ditches into some sort of artistic manifestation. That seemed odd, but his taste for such things wasn't refined.

The gates had been removed—or had rotted away—replaced on one side by a large statue of a half-dressed man holding … a lightning bolt? Were they resurrecting the old Greek god Zeus? He remembered the man he had met in Gideon named Zeus. Good man. Great horseman, too, though he didn't look the part. It would be nice to find out how he was doing. Phinben as well. And Jeruzim, of course.

The merchant let him off near the center of the city with a hearty chuckle and insincere good wishes, and Kai made his way to the nearest inn. Nightfall would be coming soon. He would fish for some information and find a horse to rent—or better yet, a mule, so he could efficiently search the villages nearby without looking conspicuous. He fingered the purple merchant pin on his collar as he entered.

The great room was already loud and crowded, and he struggled to find a seat. He ended up next to a middle-aged woman and three men at a rectangular table, already enjoying drinks and a meal. The food didn't smell great. He sat meekly, picking up snatches of conversation. When one of the innkeepers came by, he asked for a simple meal and some water. She gave him a look of both pity and disdain, then ambled away.

"Just water?" said the woman at the table.

"I'm … here on business, um, for my master. Funds are tight."

She pursed her lips, eyes swimming in strong drink. "Cruel man, your master. I probably shouldn't be spending so much, though." After a hearty belch that seemed to take her by surprise, she frowned at her cup and plate, then sighed. "We were better off under the Nephites. This alliance with the Lamanites hasn't helped at all."

"But I saw the, um, beautification projects when I arrived. Like the statue at the main gate."

She gave a disgusted laugh. "That's the kind of idiocy our leaders spend money on. Better roads? No. Worthless statues of Zeus that the birds crap on? Sure!" She pounded the side of her fist on her breastbone to ease the passage of more noxious air.

"But—" he had to be careful, "as an independent city, you attract a wide variety of people ... and opportunities. And there's still trade with the Nephites."

She looked hard at him, her eyes clearing a little. "Are you a Nephite? I mean, is that your blood heritage?"

He shook his head, making something up. "No, I'm Mulekite. My name is Jerem. My father died in the Great War. My three brothers, too. I have a sister, though. She still lives in Nephihah."

"Hmmm ... well, I might move there. I'm tired of this place. I'm Isabel, by the way. My last husband died of a heart attack, and, quite frankly, there aren't a lot of good men left here. And by good, I mean rich." She smiled, eyes watering again as she picked up her drink and chugged back several large, loud swallows. Kai hid a smile as she hiccupped.

"Well," he proffered, "if I do well on this scouting trip, I hope to court my master's daughter. She has the most amazing auburn hair and violet eyes. You should see her eyes." He stared dreamily at one wall, wondering what kind of response he would get to that nonsense.

"Oh, I wish I was still young," came the breathy reply. "And that you were rich. Or that your father was, at least. I met a boy when I was barely older than you. Just visiting, but from a famous family. I thought I had him. And suddenly he left. And then—"

She was interrupted by a man with sunken jowls, standing on a table as he held aloft his tankard. He was clearly plastered. "Oh, holy God, we thank you for electing us. We are chosen!" Some of the fiery liquid sloshed out. "You have separated us from the foolish traditions of our brothers up north, who will be cast by your wrath down to hell." He wobbled, dangerously close to plunging off the table. "You were a spirit, you are a spirit, and you will be a spirit for—"

"Get off that table, Hezariah, or I'll knock you off it myself!" The innkeeper was back, and she appeared none too pleased. "You are blaspheming again. The Rameumptom—and the words proclaimed from its pinnacle—are sacred."

"Bollocks!" said the man, still wavering. "God only hears us when we're on that stand. When we're not, we can do and say whatever we want." He looked around, as if welcoming support from the crowd. The reaction was mixed, and his eyes crossed for a moment.

"Get off the table, Hezariah. I mean it. Last warning."

The man blinked, several times, then looked down, seeming confused about how he could accomplish her command. Finally, two of his comrades stood, reaching up and grabbing his arms to help him down to a bench, and then to the floor. He turned and sat heavily at the table, then looked at the innkeeper again.

"I say the words proper when I'm up there. I do. You're just cross because … well, I don't know why you're always so cross."

"I'm cross because of idiots like you," she said. She had been holding a plate and cup the whole time, and after growling at the man, she strode over to where Kai sat and deposited them in front of him. A chunk of dark bread, a meager bit of cheese, and a truly pathetic portion of mutton, half cooked. The water had a funny smell. He'd had worse, but not recently.

"Well, that was quite a scene," said Isabel, and suddenly Kai remembered where he'd heard that name. Could this be the same woman who had seduced Alma's son? What was his name? Oh, yes, Corianton. If he remembered right, Corianton had gone north on one of Hagoth's ships. He surely wouldn't have good memories of this place.

"I don't understand," said Kai. Actually, he did, at least a little.

"You haven't seen the Rameumptom? It's as dumb as the Zeus statue, but it makes people here feel superior, which I guess lets them put up with …" she glanced at his food with a half roll of her eyes "… things like this slop. I think I *will* move north. You haven't mentioned the name of your employer in … Nephihah, is it? Is he married?"

"Oh, um, yes, he is. To a goddess. Their daughter looks just like her."

Isabel frowned, her lips pouting. "Just my luck. That's okay. I don't like Nephihah much anyway. So, where will you be staying?"

The way she asked spiked the hair on the back of his neck. "Here,

I think," he replied. "If I can afford it. If not, I'll find a backup. I need some sleep. I have to make a very early start in the morning. My boss wants to find a particular man in one of the outlying villages."

"The villages? What would any of *them* have to trade? Maybe timber, I suppose, or some ore, if someone found a new vein?" She raised an eyebrow, waiting for him to respond.

He lowered his voice. "The latter, but it isn't confirmed yet, and he doesn't want other people knowing."

She nodded and winked. "I see. Well, your secret is safe with me."

Kai doubted that, and he glanced to either side before continuing. "Have you heard of any newcomers to the area? My boss thinks they might be looking for the same thing."

"Whoa, this is starting to sound like a complex situation. And he sent *you* to scout it out?"

Kai cleared his throat. "Well, not exactly. I'm, um, supposed to be on a slightly different mission."

"Define *slightly*."

"Like, in Jershon, looking at some new linens there. I got here before the other scout he's sending."

"That's a bit more than slightly. You must really like this daughter of his. You're trying to impress him?"

"Yes." He looked abashedly at the table. He still hadn't touched his food.

"Well, there are a couple of places I can think of that might be worth investigating, though I can't be sure. On the southwest side, near the bluffs along the river. But be careful. I've heard that some of the newcomers there aren't very friendly."

"Thank you." He tried not to sound surprised, but her information had come too easily. Unless he was overthinking it? Dan wasn't here to offer his opinion. Nor was Helaman. It was just him. And the Spirit. He knew that. But how much would God help him, especially given all his recent complaining, and even outright doubts?

He took a room at that inn, but only after leaving and coming back much later, when Isabel wasn't there. He also got some information from a different innkeeper on where he could rent a mule. Now, if he could only figure out how to offer up a decent prayer, one that might be answered, he would sleep easier.

———◇———

He left his room the next morning without a great deal of confidence. And he knew riding a mule all day wouldn't improve his mood. He hoped for a reasonably obedient one, but that hope was crucified in the first five minutes. He got a young mule, not well trained, with a stubborn streak as wide as the Sidon in spring. Fashioning a short riding crop out of a willow stick didn't work. Cajoling it with treats helped only occasionally. He almost took it back, but the old man who owned it had claimed it was his only one, and Kai didn't want to take the time to search for someone else who could rent one out.

At least the mule would let him jog in front of her sometimes. In fact, she seemed quite pleased by that. They made their way to the first village on the south side in decent time, though Kai certainly couldn't keep that up all day. Or at least, he didn't want to. Vyim truly had spoiled him.

Most people were out working fields or flocks, but he talked to a tanner and an artificer, along with a pair of mothers herding a gaggle of children in some daily chores. None were helpful, nor even seemed to want to be helpful. So he moved on, following narrow paths and trying to keep his bearings. He spooked a deer, which bounded off into the forest. The mule honked at that, apparently finding humor.

Three more villages came and went before midday, each less helpful than the last. After a light lunch, Kai pressed on, judging that he was more west than south of the city now, his relationship with the mule unimproved. She carried him about half the time, but her pace slowed as the day wore on. Unless, of course, he was jogging in front of her. Then she was happy to trot.

By the end of the day, he had visited ten villages, all within two miles of the city's newly artistic walls, circumnavigating about two-thirds of the boundary. He returned the mule to its owner, then his exhausted self to the inn, where he ordered some better food, claiming he had made a minor trade that day of some trinkets. Thankfully, Isabel wasn't there—and neither was the man who had pretended one of the tables was a Rameumptom. It was a relatively quiet crowd.

After eating, he decided to visit another couple of inns, and a shop or two that might still be open, to see what else he might be able to find out. Open shops he didn't find, but the inns were modestly busy. He met another Nephite trader in one of them, a man named Amnor. He dealt in silks, and he was on a mission to procure more raw materials, which Lamanite lands possessed in more abundance. He wasn't having as much luck as hoped, though. One of his regular suppliers had gone out of business and headed far to the west. It wasn't the first time Kai had heard something similar while in Lamanite lands.

"Do you know how far he was planning to go?" Kai asked as the man nursed a mild mead.

"Not sure, but perhaps as far as the Great Mountains. He wasn't alone, either. Two other men and their families went with him. It almost feels like the way so many of our people are emigrating north. They're tired of war, all the senseless conflict. It's been almost six hundred years since the brass plates were supposedly 'stolen' from Laman and Lemuel. Copies of them are available to anyone now. Why are we still fighting about them?"

"Why, indeed," agreed Kai. "And how can a right-of-rule claim from way back then still exist now? I don't get it. My parents don't, either."

"Unbridled greed drives this," said Amnor. "Lust for power. Excuses for perversions of the flesh, too. That's why Pahoran was murdered."

Kai nodded. He liked this man. "That's why that assassin … what was his name?"

"Kishkumen," answered Amnor with a hard glint in his eye, as if the name were an epithet.

"Yes. That's why Kishkumen tried to kill Helaman, too. I don't know how they caught him, but thank the Lord they did."

Amnor shook his head ruefully. "Some of the Lamanites are afraid that our problems will spill over into their lands. Directly, I mean, like with a retribution invasion. That's one reason more have been leaving."

Kai stared at his drink. "Well, I'm just a novice merchant scout. I don't know how to fix any of it. But hopefully Helaman does."

"Aye, I'll drink to that." Amnor lowered his voice, glancing furtively around. "To Helaman." They raised their cups, and then Amnor gazed into his, frowning. "Empty. I believe I'll ask for some wine this time."

As Amnor looked around for a server who could help him, it seemed as if Kai heard a bell, crystal clear, right next to his head. It was the word "wine." He was certain of it. Within seconds a server approached, and Amnor handed him his cup. "Some wine this time, please."

"Certainly," said the young man, taking the cup. Before he walked away, Kai asked, "Where does the best wine around here come from?"

Without hesitation, the young man answered, "Oh, that would be Achoakrim's vineyards, a few miles east of the city. Best grapes on Earth, so I'm told, and Master Achoakrim knows his business. He comes from far away, to the southeast, an exotic place where it rarely gets cold."

Amnor wrinkled his forehead. "Why, that sounds excellent. Do you have any of his wine in this establishment?"

The young man nodded. "We do. It's not cheap, though."

"That's all right. If it's as good as you say, it'll be worth it. Fill both our cups!"

Kai was about to object, but instead surrendered his cup, still half full. The young man bowed and retreated, returning shortly with the wine. Amnor took his with exaggerated pleasure, gave it a sniff, and then a sip. He looked approvingly at the young man. "Indeed, this is excellent. Thank you, son."

"My pleasure," said the young man, then turned his gaze to Kai.

Kai performed the same sniff and sip procedure. It tasted fine to him, but he was no connoisseur. "Yes, very good," he pronounced, and that bell rang again. He needed to find that winemaker.

It was hard to sleep that night. He kept pondering the strangeness of the experience with Amnor. Had it truly been the Spirit telling him to find Achoakrim? He didn't have another explanation, and he felt reasonably sure he wasn't losing his mind. East. Not southwest. Well, one thing he for sure felt good about was that he wouldn't be renting that useless mule again.

—◆—

He left well before sunrise the next morning. He had gotten some directions from the server the night before, after Amnor went up to his room, and while the trail wasn't easy, it wasn't difficult, either. Still, it was a little farther than expected, so it took him nearly four hours to reach the large barn with a half wall in front of it, the winepresses visible inside. He strode up to the first person he saw, doing maintenance on one of the presses.

"Are you Achoakrim?"

The man turned to peer at him, straightening his long, twisting beard. He looked neither Nephite nor Lamanite and was at least forty.

"Nah, he's traveling. Should be back in about a week."

Frustration crept into Kai's mind, but he could wait a week and come back, couldn't he? No, somehow that didn't feel right.

He sighed. "Oh. I was hoping to find him. I need to make contact with … someone very important, and I heard that I might be able to find him here, with Achoakrim. I've been gone a long time myself, traveling far to the northeast."

The man cocked his head. "Oh? Who were you hoping to find? We don't get a lot of visitors, besides traders. Our wine is very good, by the way."

Kai nodded. "I've tasted it, and that is true." He let out another heavy breath, looking around. "I really should only give this name to Achoakrim. A week, you said?"

The man stood straighter. "I'm his brother. We run this vineyard together."

Kai narrowed his eyes, considering, then plunged into the churning waters. "I'm looking for Imrahiel, who also goes by Chorinai. As I said, I've been gone quite a long while, but I heard he was chased out of

Zarahemla. He told me before I left that if I gave this sign to certain people—" he made a gesture with his left hand, the second sign he had given Kishkumen that fateful night, "they would help me."

The man stared silently at him for several moments, not as if what he had done was strange, but that it might be dangerous.

"You are in a real hurry," he finally said. "Otherwise you would have waited for my brother."

Kai nodded. "I am. Certain events are moving faster than anticipated."

"Fine. Follow me." He turned and proceeded farther into the building. Kai took a step after him, then stopped, the skin prickling on his arms. Was Imrahiel *here*? If so, he would have more protection than just one man. Kai hadn't seen any others close to the large barn, but the fields were close by, and men were surely working among the vines. How many were loyal to Gadianton, and how long had they been here?

He couldn't think of anything else to do, and he was desperate for information. He also reasoned that if the Spirit truly wanted him here, then the Spirit could protect him. He wasn't sure he was thinking about that right, especially given how unsteady he'd become, but he forged ahead.

The man stepped into what looked like a storage room on the other side of the building, with a small, dirty window filtering in the fitful light of a cloudy morning.

"Please, sit," said the man. There was only one chair, wedged in a corner. Pieces of wood and metal bands to make barrels competed with ropes and sacks and sundry other items to occupy most of the space. Dust motes floated erratically in the air.

Kai complied, and then the man moved to the door, closing it. When he turned, he had a long knife in his hand.

"The sign you gave me is old," he said, his voice cool.

"I know," said Kai, his mind running through various action scenarios. He had no idea how good this man was with his knife. Then again, the man had no idea of his abilities, either. "I said that."

"You need to show me one of the new signs. Second set of oaths, at least."

Kai shrugged. "I don't have those yet. I've been difficult to contact. Deep cover."

"I don't believe you."

Kai took a risk and stood. He needed his feet under him. The man raised the knife and set his own feet. "I understand," said Kai. "I can come back when your brother returns. He should have received a particular message, which he was not to share with *anyone*."

The man seemed to relax a little, but he adopted a confused look. "You're young. Very young."

Kai let his own look harden. "I have seen plenty. And I will see much more."

"Are you staying in Zoram?"

"Yes."

"Tell me where, and I'll arrange for a message to be sent to you when my brother returns."

"Very well. Address it to Jerem, at the *King's Harem*. You don't need to know my real name, and I don't need to know yours. Just your brother's."

That small slight, even though it was within Gadianton protocol, made the man frown, but he stepped away from the door. Kai moved forward and opened it, then turned and lunged low, tackling the man into a stack of barrel pieces and knocking the wind out of him. He grabbed the man's knife arm as he spun away, maneuvering behind and yanking his chin toward him with his other hand, taking them to the floor and bringing his legs around the man's waist. He increased tension on the chin to keep the man's mouth closed, causing him to struggle to bring in more air through his nose.

He realized he didn't have much leverage. And the man still gripped the knife. While Kai could keep him from yelling for help and wriggling out of his grasp, he couldn't make him do or say anything. The man tested his strength, even trying to use his legs to push them backward along the floor. Kai was stronger, and the man seemed to realize this. He relaxed a little, though he tried to growl his frustration.

"We're on the same side," whispered Kai into his ear. "But Imrahiel is not. Helaman got to him somehow, probably through one of Moronihah's spies. *That* is why Kishkumen failed. Gadianton knows this now. Your brother ..." Kai took a deep breath, preparing to embellish the lie "... is loyal to Imrahiel. At least, for now. Perhaps you can dissuade him from such a foolish, disastrous course. In the meantime, I need to know where Imrahiel went, because he clearly is not here."

He wasn't certain Imrahiel wasn't there, but the man tried to nod.

"Let go of the knife," Kai commanded, and the man complied. In one smooth movement, Kai grabbed the knife, pushed the man off, and got to his feet. The man rose slowly, rubbing his midsection and neck.

"This is why I was called back," said Kai. "We need to purge our ranks of any disloyalty before we make another try at Helaman and his corrupt government. You, by the way, never saw me today, but I will know if you or your brother betray the cause."

The man swallowed, his confusion deepening. "Imrahiel left two days ago with a small group. They were heading for Morianton."

Kai didn't have to pretend anger. "He is making his move. I must be on my way. Remember, brother, be careful who you trust." And with that, he tossed the man his knife and ran out the door. He didn't stop running until he was halfway back to Zoram.

CHAPTER 15

Yea, we see that whosoever will may lay hold upon the word of God,
which is quick and powerful, which shall divide asunder
all the cunning and the snares and the wiles of the devil,
and lead the man of Christ in a strait and narrow course across
that everlasting gulf of misery which is prepared to engulf the wicked—
And land their souls, yea, their immortal souls, at the right hand of God
in the kingdom of heaven, to sit down with Abraham, and Isaac,
and with Jacob, and with all our holy fathers, to go no more out.
—Helaman 3:29–30

Ara had never traveled outside Nephite lands before; she'd never even harbored strong desires to do so. The exotic lands to the east sounded interesting sometimes, but the north? Wasn't it filled mostly with ruins from the failed Jaredite civilization? Lots of ditches and large pits in places where they had mined vast amounts of metals, too, primarily copper, though she wasn't focused on those areas. The Gadiantons would be hovering within a few days' journey of the border, making their plans, biding their time.

She didn't feel unsafe, even knowing Gadiantons might be around, and even riding such a valuable horse as Shefah. She had dyed her hair obsidian black, adorning it with subtle ornaments to provoke curiosity without prolonging notice. She wore practical traveling pants, not often seen on women but not remarkable, either. Most of her Gadianton contacts were aware of how she liked to use her feminine wiles—and this outfit didn't fit that stereotype. The garments she'd acquired weren't the most comfortable, but she hadn't been able to afford nicer styles and cuts of cloth.

She kept diligently to her search pattern, though she varied her story. To some, she was a local runaway, though it was getting harder to pass as a teen. To others, a young widow looking for a new start outside Nephite lands. To yet others, she pretended to be an apprentice merchant scout, only she didn't have her pin yet. She tried to keep her flirting to a minimum, though to some degree it was necessary as she sought information.

She was good at serving food to people, thanks to her job at Zerahir's house, so she took a few jobs at inns. Most establishments were small, given the sparse population, and not very nice. The food was generally decent, though.

She finally reached a larger town, ostentatiously called the City of David. It seemed to be a growing crossroads of travel and trade, so she prepared to settle there for a short while. Surely, Kai and Dan had passed through here at some point, and someone would remember them. The two made a distinctive pair. She searched for women matching Siarah's description, too, but her focus remained almost solely on Kai. The longer she went without finding him, the greater the danger she imagined he was facing. She knew even better than he did how evil Gadianton and Imrahiel were. Like Kishkumen. She shivered every time she thought of that infernal creature, so amazed at how Kai had been able to stop him—permanently.

The man she approached for a job at David's newest inn looked like an older version of Kishkumen, and she almost retreated. The man gave her a funny look, half offended.

She recovered herself. "Oh, I'm sorry. You just … look like someone I knew."

The man cocked his head. "Knew?"

"He's dead."

After a knowing nod, he said, "All too common, down in Nephite lands. We're building something better here. You look newly arrived."

She glanced down at her clothes, which carried plenty of travel dust. "Is it that obvious?"

The man chuckled. "It is, but don't worry. All of us have been there. You wanted to ask me a question? That is, it appeared you did."

"Yes," she said, squaring her shoulders. "I'd like a job here, if you have one. I'm very good, having served at the house of a high judge in Zarahemla."

One eyebrow went up, followed by the other. "Is that so? Well, we don't have anyone that fancy here, and we don't aim to. But good service is always appreciated. I can't pay much, and I don't know how often I'll need you."

"That's all right. I can't promise how long I'll stay, either. I have a brother who came this way, with one of his friends. I'd like to find him. We'd be better off, I think, if we … you know … pooled our resources." She looked down, trying to look ashamed and vulnerable. Flirting wasn't her only weapon.

"Hmmm," said the man, rubbing his jaw. "Well, this *is* the largest town in the area, a natural place for people to visit. We're building a new road, if you noticed." She nodded. "Can you describe your brother to me? Perhaps I've seen him and his friend."

Ara gave a highly detailed description of Kai, less so of Dan. After pondering for just a moment, the man gave a sharp nod, accompanied by a frown. "I'm certain I met *those* two men, but they were part of a much larger company. They led it, in fact. Twenty men or so, and if I remember right, they were elites from Lehi's army."

Yes, that aligned, but she gave him a deeply confused look. "I'm … not sure how that could be. But I'm curious; do you know what they were doing here?"

"Looking for fugitives from Nephite justice, apparently. Though twenty soldiers seemed like overkill."

She meekly nodded agreement. "Did … they find them?"

The man shrugged. "Some say yes, some say no. But I heard they returned to Nephite lands after interrogating a few folks they found. That's been several weeks ago now."

She couldn't fully suppress her eagerness in receiving that tidbit. "Do you know where they went, exactly? I might be able to send him a letter ... if, you know, that's really him. He should be up here."

"No, I'm afraid I don't. Someone else might, though. You can ask around."

"Yes, I will. Thank you. And did you say I could have a job here?"

The man chuckled again. "Yes, we could use some help, and I believe you regarding your background. You can start this evening. Do you have a place to stay yet?"

She shook her head. "No, but the temporary camp at the edge of town will work just fine for the time being. That was a smart idea, by the way."

The man grinned. "It was mine. Refugees need a place to sleep and eat while they figure out what they're going to do long term. And putting such a camp next to the city means more of those refugees will likely stay in this area, helping drive our growth and prosperity. Our peace, too."

"Peace is what I want," said Ara, only half aware she said it. Her mind was spinning, trying to guess which Nephite city Kai and Dan had returned to. Had they found a good lead? They must have.

That evening was a slow one for the inn, and Ara picked up only two or three evenings a week for the next three weeks. At least she could preserve most of her aunt's money—and Jerena's—and still not starve, and she could spend the remainder of her time getting to know people and asking questions.

At last, she garnered a good location from a trader passing through to more northern lands. He had heard of the group Kai and Dan led. They had arrested several men east of Morianton before coming north, and rumor had it they were hot on the trail of more outlaws in that area. Ara questioned him carefully, trying to determine how reliable the rumor might be. She came away from the conversation satisfied enough to let the innkeeper know she was leaving. By morning she was back on the road with Shefah, heading straight as an arrow for Morianton, wishing she had just stayed there and kept digging, despite Osprey's advice.

She pushed hard, and in two days they were approaching Morianton from the northeast, late in the evening. She didn't want to try the inns that night, the feeling settling in her that she would need every bit of her remaining funds to make a new start somewhere, after all of this was done.

Nursing unpleasant thoughts of either never finding Kai or seeing him reunited with Siarah in such a notable morass as Morianton, she found a place to sleep under some trees a mile or more outside the walls, with brambles surrounding her. Exhaustion overwhelmed her into a sound sleep. By the time she awoke, the sun was already halfway through its climb, the air warm to the point of becoming stifling, given the lack of wind penetrating her resting place.

She scrambled to her feet and onto Shefah's back, then guided them out to the road leading into the city, noting how light her pack was now. She had little left of her travel rations, and she needed to refill her waterskin. But she felt refreshed, and the proximity of the city carried a glimmer of hope she was desperate to grasp. She would find Kai and figure out how to help him. And she would stop acting like a ninny and letting her emotions whipsaw her about. She wasn't twelve.

Grimly determined, she made her first priority finding that job. She tried four inns before she found success, and for meager pay. She would beg at the few synagogues in Morianton for leads on someone who could rent a room to her and also spare space for Shefah. They were *not* going to live out in the woods. She was putting out feelers, too, trying to determine where Kai and Dan might be. Unfortunately, promising leads eluded her.

She stayed away from the finer shops—particularly pottery shops—though Morianton had but few. Not like Zarahemla. She also avoided trolling the nicer parts of the city, including the one where her aunt lived. She didn't have the clothing for that anyway. No, it was the common shops and the inns for her. And the dirty streets ... how often were they cleaned?

———◇———

She was dragging herself to her tiny rented room near the walls very late one night, after a shift at the inn, when an arm snaked from the darkness, a hand gripping the top of her shoulder hard. It didn't hurt, but the voice did.

"My dear Raven, how good to see you again."

My Raven. Imrahiel had always seen her as his property. "I don't answer to that name."

"Oh? It is the name I gave you. Are you ungrateful?"

What kind of arrogant question was that? "What do you want, Imrahiel?" She turned toward him, ignoring the heavy pressure on her shoulder. She even put her hands on her hips. She was proud of herself for not trembling.

"Oh, I want a lot of things. First, I want to know why you betrayed me. Why you broke your oaths."

"Why do you think I broke them?"

"Oh, come now. Such a silly statement, from you? That's disappointing."

"Why did you kidnap Siarah?"

"You know that name? Well, I suppose *Kihoran* would have told you about her at some point."

Did he expect her to be surprised he knew Kai's real name? "Why did you kidnap her? Was it lust? Have you lost all self-control?"

The slap materialized out of the blackness, taking her by surprise, the other hand never leaving her shoulder. "You dare speak to me so? Do you think me devoid of power? Are you that much of a fool?"

She refused to show discomfort or fear. "I'll speak to you however I wish. I am not yours to command. Your precious oaths do not hold me. I was washed free of them."

The rich, hearty laugh startled her as much as the slap. "You let the Christians *baptize* you? Oh, that is rich. Indeed, it is." He pulled her deeper into the darkness. An alley swallowed them, and he pulled her through an open door into what smelled like an herbalist's shop. A candle was lit somewhere nearby, though she couldn't pinpoint the source of the meager light. Imrahiel shut the door with his foot. Then he let her go, pointing to a cushion on the floor. "Sit, my dear."

She took a step back, resisting the temptation to eye the door. "I'm not your dear. And I'll stand."

The laugh was softer this time. "Very well." Imrahiel took the only chair in the room, settling himself as if it were his throne. He had fancied a similar chair in that accursed pottery shop. "Why are you here in Morianton? What are you pretending at?"

"I'm working. Making a living as best I can. And looking for my father and brother. I don't care about my sister, in case you were wondering."

"Working," he deadpanned. "At perhaps the worst inn in all the region, for a dog's wages. I doubt that very much. Sources tell me you were living reasonably well in Gideon."

"You're rebuilding your network?"

"Of course. We have a lot of work to do."

She held back a sneer. She knew how deadly serious he was. "Where is Siarah? I'm sure you know."

"And why are you interested?" he asked, leaning forward and steepling his fingers under his chin, elbows on the armrests.

"She and Kai are betrothed."

"And what is that to you? A … finalization? Does that set you free to finally move on from him?" He leaned back suddenly, smiling. "Don't answer that. I can see it in your eyes. What a fascinating little love triangle. And here you are, trying to become some kind of heroine? Oh, my. I would not have predicted *this*."

"You haven't predicted a lot of things. That's why you're here, holed up in an herbalist's shop. And not a good one, based on the stench."

His gaze hardened, eyes narrowing. "Do you have a death wish? Are you that distraught over your beloved Kihoran? Where is *he*, by the way? We've lost track of him recently, though it appears he's at least no longer with that malicious group of Lehi's elites."

Her face heated, but she doubted he could notice that in the faint light. "I don't know. I went north looking for him, but he returned to Nephite lands."

Imrahiel gave a low growl. "Yes, he was traipsing around up north causing us some acute headaches. I'm anxious to find him again, isolate him, bring him in for a discussion."

"A *discussion?*" Her legs twitched involuntarily. "Why? What good would he be to you? He doesn't follow your oaths, either."

"He was there."

He didn't have to say where 'there' was. "So were a lot of people that night."

"He knows something that could be important. He's searching for Siarah, and we'll let him find her at the right time, once we figure out where he is now. Siarah herself doesn't appear to know anything."

"Why are you telling *me* all of this? Do you intend to 'disappear' me?" She shivered and swallowed as she said it.

He snorted. "I'm not that simple. Or crude. I'll get what I want first. Might it be that Kai has some feelings for you as well? What a lecher. I might be able to use that."

"You can try," she retorted, anger rising, "but you'll fail again. God is watching out for him, like he was that night."

His head tilted. "Oh, how so? Please, *do* tell."

"You already suspect he's the one who killed your precious Kishkumen, may the devil crap on his soul."

"Such colorful language. And did he?"

She lifted her chin. "I guess you'll have to ask him. When you're in prison."

"You can go now."

"What?"

"I said you can go now. Don't get any dumb ideas, but you're free to pursue this illustrious new career you've chosen … for now, that is."

It was her turn to narrow her eyes. "You'll have me watched."

"Of course."

"And tailed."

"I would be sloppy if I didn't."

"You're a monster."

"Depends on who's asking."

"Kai will destroy you."

"Oh, I look forward to that blunder."

— ◇ —

As Ara tried to rest that night, she couldn't believe she was still alive. She had no desire to sleep, but she didn't dare go anywhere outside the house that night, except to check on Shefah. How had she gotten herself trapped again? If she hadn't left Gideon, she would be … well, driving herself slowly insane worrying about what was happening to Kai. In the balance, she wasn't any worse off. And in the end, maybe Nephite lands weren't where she needed to be long term. The emigrants to the north had socialized another option for her. She had no true family any longer, and no real prospects for the future. She *would* help Kai and Siarah first, though. That inexplicable commitment burned in her chest.

Her resolve hardened, and she continued working at the inn and exploring various parts of the city. She even made a game of it, knowing she was always being followed. She would enter random shops, then return to them one or two days later. She would suddenly change directions, or pause for minutes at a time to study something, be it the people at an intersection, or an interesting building, or a group of homes tucked away in an obscure part of the city. She even convinced the city guards to let her take a stroll along the top of the city walls. One of them was cute, and seemed competent, but her notice was little more than passive.

Perhaps, she soon discovered, she had been playing the game a little *too* energetically. And it was increasingly just a game, as her hopes of ever finding Kai—much less of helping him in some way—faded more every day, despite her determination. She tried reconciling herself to the inevitable but had a hard time of it.

She was wandering the city again on a rare day off when two men began walking with her, one on either side. They were dressed better than commoners, but neither seemed to be carrying any weapons. She didn't sense immediate danger, but a wave of uncertainty swept through her mind.

"The chief judge would like to see you."

She looked sideways at the one who had spoken. "Excuse me? Did you say the chief judge of the city wants to talk to *me*?" That was either really good or really bad.

"Yes, and right now."

"Okay. Will he feed me? I've hardly eaten anything today."

"Don't be impertinent," said the other man, who seemed far more stoic, like Kishkumen had been in his frequent brooding moods.

"I'm not impertinent. I'm hungry. And tired. I'm also not important. Why would the chief judge want to see me? I don't even know his name." The last part was a lie, but the stoic man supplied it in a sourly arrogant tone.

"Chief Judge Tiberion has his reasons, which we need not question."

"But you question Chief Judge Helaman's decisions, am I right?"

The first man stifled a chuckle, then became serious again and let his companion respond.

"*You* don't have the right to question either of them."

"Oh, but I know Helaman. He's not so arrogant that he can't take criticism. I've witnessed it."

Silence followed, and she added, "You didn't know I knew him, did you. Your boss is probably aware, though." She gave an exaggerated har-rumph. Maybe she would be exiled from Morianton. That would most likely set her path to the north, which might be the right timing. "Fine, take me to him, and we can have whatever useless conversation he desires."

"Are you always this saucy?" asked the first man, and she glanced at his face to see genuine surprise.

"I told you, I'm hungry. Plus, my life isn't going where I wanted it to. So, I'm angry. There, are you happy?"

He rolled his eyes and shook his head, then grabbed her elbow to lead her to the right, down a different street. He didn't pull hard, but his grip was firm.

She followed, glancing at the other man. "Do I remind you of an old girlfriend who dumped you?"

The man's jaw hardened, and he didn't respond. They continued walking for several blocks, taking only two more turns. The first man's arm remained on her elbow, though with lighter pressure.

When they approached the Hall of Judgment, she took in its incon-gruous grandeur. Tiberion was happy to let his city slowly decay, but his judgment hall, probably with an attached residence, had to be lustrous and perfect. She nearly snorted her derision, but the guards out front looked dour enough to frighten a wild boar.

Her two escorts ushered her inside without a word to the guards, then up two flights of stairs to a broad foyer. There she was made to wait with the sulky one while the other disappeared down a hallway. He returned shortly and led them back down the stairs. Then they proceeded to the center of the building and into a large, ornate room, many of its surfaces either gilded or studded with precious metals and stones.

The chief judge sat in an overlarge chair on a short dais at one end. Several other guards lined the walls. Ara counted only a handful of other chairs on the intricate and sparkling mosaic floor. She studied the tiles further as she was led toward the pretend monarch, tilting her head more than once. Were the patterns supposed to depict Morianton himself subjecting the city of Lehi? He had tried that, of course. It had turned out horribly for him and his people.

She was halted about ten feet from the paunchy, middle-aged judge, who wore a thick, purple headband with various gems woven into it. His brown hair was long and shiny, his beard oiled to the point she feared it might start dripping. His clothes rivaled even those of the late Zerahir. She could live comfortably for a decade by selling his wardrobe alone. Add one or two of the gems, and she was set for life in her own small palace.

His smile oozed as much grease as his beard. "Master Imrahiel informs me you are something of a celebrity." His voice came out high and raspy, and the way his lips formed words made him look like a rat. It wasn't the face that chilled her, though. It was Imrahiel's name.

"I am not," she said with a slight shake of her head. Her two guards had moved to either side a couple of paces.

"But you have dined in the house of Chief Judge Helaman, and on more than one occasion. I cannot say that myself."

"I worked there."

He chuckled. "And dined with the family? I think not."

"Who says I actually dined with the family?" she asked, feigning confusion.

He pursed his lips in truly revolting fashion as he glanced away. When he refocused on her, his eyes cast daggers.

"You are a spy for Helaman, come to my city to determine how to overthrow me. Your boyfriend has caused trouble here, too, with a band of Lehi's men. He tried to undermine confidence in my leadership."

"I don't have a boyfriend." She wanted to add that Tiberion didn't possess *any* leadership skills, but she refrained.

"You will cease lying to me," he snapped. "You are only making matters worse for yourself."

She took a deep breath, letting it out slowly. "Someone is lying to you, that I agree with."

He pounded a fist on the arm of his chair, like an overgrown, petulant child. "I will not tolerate spies!"

She stood her ground, lifting her chin. "I came looking for the man you claim is my boyfriend, to help him. His betrothed was kidnapped by Imrahiel, and he is searching for her."

"Another lie," Tiberion snarled, though it came out more like a cat's hairball, which was amusing. She must be losing it if she found that funny. There was a good chance she was going to die this very hour … and it didn't bother her. Interesting.

"*You* are the liar," she said casually. "Helaman is an honest man who actually cares about the welfare of this people. You cannot defeat him."

Tiberion's eyes widened in shock. Doubtless, people didn't speak to him like that.

"And *you* are under arrest for high treason!" he pronounced, aiming a gem-bound finger at her. He looked at one of the guards. "Take her away. Give her the worst cell we have. And if she trips and falls a few times, so be it."

"Such a pathetic man," she said, fists clenched. "Beating and imprisoning women to protect your fragile ego. *You* are the traitor … and a coward." She didn't flinch as her two guards grabbed her roughly by the arms and hurried her out of the room.

When the large doors shut, the dour one grumbled to her, "That was one of the dumbest things I've ever seen anyone do."

"Wonderful," she responded. "I'm honored. So, are you going to start beating me now, or do you want to build up to it?"

He growled back, "I don't beat women."

"Nor do I," said the other, green eyes sparkling. "And we will make sure your accommodations aren't the worst we have."

She stared in surprise at each in turn. "You're tricking me," she finally said. "Psychological torture to go along with physical abuse. Nice. Gadianton has trained you well."

"We're not part of that group," the green-eyed one proclaimed.

"But your boss is," she declared with just as much certainty, "as is his pal Imrahiel, who I also used to work for in Zarahemla."

She caught a brief look of surprise on the dour one's face as she glanced back at the now closed doors. They started walking, keeping hold of her arms.

"Yes," she continued, staring forward, "I was a believer in their evil nonsense once. I am not now. I have no family because of them, and no future. So, throw me in whatever cell you wish." She increased her pace, pulling them along as old frustrations reasserted themselves.

Silence accompanied them until they reached a cross hallway near the front of the building.

"This way," said the mellower one, tugging her to the right. "We're not going to the underground cells."

She remained quiet until they reached a room at the far end of the building, its door adorned with a heavy lock. After they led her inside, she noticed it had a real bed, and even a small wash basin with a tall pitcher next to it. It also featured a window which, though barred, was graced by lacy curtains. The chamber pot wasn't disgusting, either. In fact, it didn't look like a removable pot at all, but emptied through the floor. And had a decent cover. This was far better than her rented room.

She turned to gaze at the two men with scrunched eyebrows. "You didn't beat me, as ordered, and you brought me *here*?"

"We're not uncivilized," said the dour one, though his demeanor seemed to be transforming before her eyes. He still wore that trademark frown.

"But won't Tiberion find out?"

He shrugged. "He never checks on things personally."

"Too lazy, huh? Imrahiel will come, though. I'm sure of it."

"Then we will show him to this room and claim we brought you here so that he could interview you in a better environment—out of respect for him, of course. And that you heal fast."

"Why? Why are you doing this?"

"I'm not sure," he said simply. "But we're not the terrible people you assume we are. And Morianton isn't as bad of a place as you think, either."

She nodded slowly. "Well, I doubt it's as good as *you* think, but thank you. I probably don't deserve to be treated this well. I've done bad things, and I've failed at many good ones. I think God might be done with me." She lowered her eyes and turned away, stepping toward the bed, where she sat and put her face in her hands.

Dour guard surprised her yet again. "God never abandons anyone."

She didn't look up, just listened as they exited and locked her door. Then she cried softly.

CHAPTER 16

Counsel with the Lord in all thy doings, and he will direct thee
for good; yea, when thou liest down at night lie down unto the Lord,
that he may watch over you in your sleep; and when thou risest
in the morning let thy heart be full of thanks unto God;
and if ye do these things, ye shall be lifted up at the last day.
—Alma 37:37

The field was sprinkled with so many white flowers it might have been a blanket of snow but for the green of the trees and the warm air, which Siarah felt even in the dream. Awareness that it was indeed a dream was rare for her. She looked down at her dress, a simple tan belted in rose. She couldn't see her feet, as the sea of blossoms reached past her knees. She spun, arms out and head tilted back, breathing deeply, soaking in the sunlight. Was this what heaven felt like? She could believe it. It was indescribable.

Sing the song of redeeming love.

Yes, she responded, *though my mouth isn't moving, I feel it. It's wonderful. Thank you.*

She felt a pinprick on her arm, so startling it was like lightning lancing from the clear, turquoise sky. Annoyance pierced her serenity, and she spun to identify the source of the vulgar intrusion.

Peace returned, and she heard the voice again.

Sing the song of redeeming love.

Yes, yes, so pure, so sweet. So peaceful and perfect.

"Siarah," came a disembodied voice, one she faintly recognized. But it couldn't be. She turned away, focusing all her mental dream energy on the flowers, the trees, the sky, the sun, the gentle breeze. She breathed in deeply again, savoring the scents. She could smell … *in her dream!* How glorious!

Don't forget the song.

I won't, I promise.

Something pinched her arm again, and anger flared. She turned and shouted, "Go away!"

The response was a thunderclap, then blackness. All the light, warmth, and joy disappeared, drawn through the eye of a needle. She was waking. She groaned, her eyes fluttering open to view the dim floor of her cell. She sighed and closed them again, trying to remember the vivid details of the dream, desperately hoping she could return to it.

"Siarah." The voice was slightly different, and more insistent.

She opened her eyes again, struggling to focus in the darkness. She caught a fuzzy outline of a person kneeling next to her. Her mind still half asleep, she said, "Zoram?"

"Yes, it's me," he whispered.

"Oh." She let every scintilla of sadness she felt at leaving the dream imbue her tone.

"I know. I'm not your favorite person. But I'm here to get you out."

Her mind lurched as the final vestiges of the dream shattered. "Get me out? How?" She frowned. "And *why*? Where are you taking me now?" Resentment and accusation punctuated her words.

He shook his head. "I'm not doing this for Gadianton. I'm doing it for you."

She struggled to push herself up to a sitting position, muscles resistant. His face was coming into better focus. "I don't believe you. This is another trick."

He closed his eyes and bowed his head for a moment, seeming to deflate. Then he looked up. "I was wrong. Gadianton is evil."

"You're just now figuring that out? Or did someone advise you that women like to hear the words 'I was wrong'—after which you can supposedly make them do anything you want?"

"I *was* wrong," he repeated, so earnestly she wanted to believe him. "He made his theories sound so attractive. He has fooled a great many people. When I received my orders—and not directly from him—to lead you away from Bountiful, to keep you moving and slowly try to turn you against Helaman, I believed your betrothed was the evil one. Helaman, too."

"By association, that made *me* evil as well." She clenched her jaw.

"Yes. But you are not. I know that in the deepest recesses of my soul."

She looked away, processing both words and emotion. "How do I know I can trust you?" she uttered into the still, dank air of the room.

"You can … pray, I guess. But I will also prove it to you." He swallowed. "I'll wait while you pray, but we need to leave soon. Your drunk guards will eventually wake up more sober."

She looked back at him. "What did you—?"

"Don't worry about it."

She studied his face while trying to sort out her feelings. She wasn't going to make him watch her pray about it, and she certainly wouldn't ask him to join her in such a prayer. Not after his betrayal. She also didn't want to stay in this place, her hopeless prison that wasn't even in Nephite lands.

"Where will you take me?" she finally asked.

"Wherever you want to go. We need to stop by Morianton first, though."

"Of course." It was her turn to deflate.

"No, it's not what you think. I can get some horses there, and other things you will need when you return to Zarahemla and I travel north."

"North? You're emigrating?"

"Yes. I am an enemy of both the government and Gadianton now."

She shook her head. "Why is everyone running? Why can't we work these things out?"

"Why, indeed. Do you need to pray?"

"No. I'll come with you, but only because I don't want to stay here." She tilted her head. "What if I bolt after we cross into Nephite lands?"

"You are free to do that. I won't pursue you."

"Right. Now I *really* don't believe you."

"I don't blame you," he said. "Now, can we go? We must be very quiet."

"Yes. Let me just gather my things." She got to her feet and looked around the cramped space. "Oh, that's right, I have *nothing*. So, I guess I'm ready."

"I'll replace your things in Morianton," he said, rising. "I give it as an oath."

"Don't con me with an oath. You lead, I'll follow." She waited until he stepped past her to the door before adding, "But God bless you if you *are* telling the truth."

He hitched a step, and without looking back slowly opened the door, pausing each time it creaked slightly. It took him a full minute to open it far enough for them to slip out into the front room of the house, where the guards lay passed out. The stench was horrific—how had she not smelled more of it in her room? A tender mercy from the Lord linked to her dream?

After another slow process at the front door, they were clear. Zoram led them around to the back of the house, through some trees, and to the edge of a field, which they skirted. He never said a word, and he didn't glance back. That gave her ample time to build up fears in her mind of what would happen next. She pictured them emerging into a clearing and discovering Gadianton and several of his minions, including the thoroughly frightening one. She could envision a tall post set in the ground, already piled about with wood to burn her alive. They would ask her to recant her faith, of course, and she would not. Zoram would laugh along with Gadianton at how gullible she was. They would celebrate her pain, glory in her last gasps of mortal breath. She would suffer as Abinadi. They were animals. Demons. Demon animals.

Zoram stopped after about an hour. The skies were beginning to lighten, showing their prettiest shades of bluish purple on the horizon.

After glancing around and listening, he crouched, finally facing her. "We are north of Zoram now, and away from the main roads. I don't know the minor roads here well, but I think we can make the border by sometime tomorrow."

"Jershon?"

"Yes. Then we can head straight for Morianton, get those horses, and have you on your way to Zarahemla."

"Are we safe for the moment?"

He cocked his head. "Yes."

"Good, because now I want to pray, and you can join me if you like. Then I'll tell you what I thought was going to happen back there, after we left, and how I hope I would have reacted."

His gaze intensified, but then he relaxed. "That is fine. Whatever you want. We can eat something, too. I brought food and water."

"Thank you, but spiritual food first."

———◇———

She made it through the late afternoon still breathing. Zoram had even wrapped pieces of cloth around her feet so she could walk better. He had only brought cheap, stolen sandals—worse even than the ones the Gadiantons had 'loaned' her for her walks—and they felt like they were worth what he had paid for them. Before the sun set, he made a small campsite in the midst of a stand of trees, near a gurgling brook. Then he announced he was going hunting.

"In the dark?" she asked, uncertainly.

"It isn't dark yet."

"But isn't early morning better? I'm no hunter, but that's what I've heard."

He shrugged. "The best hunters can bag prey any time, day or night. We're not starving—and we won't be any time soon—but it would be good to have some freshly cooked meat, don't you agree? I even brought a few spices."

She nodded, then raised an eyebrow. "Do you … want me to start a fire?"

"Sure." He handed her a small knife from his pack—he carried a larger one at his waist—plus a piece of flint, then set off with spear, bow, and a quiver full of arrows, leaving the pack and his sword behind. She followed the sound of his footsteps for about the first fifty yards, until they faded away to nothing.

She sat there with the knife for a while, doing nothing but pondering until the sun had almost set. Then she chided herself and began making preparations to start a fire while she still had a bit of light. It took fifteen minutes to get a good flame going with wood shavings and the flint, and by then it was hard to see. She found two large pieces of fallen wood nearby and dragged them to the fire, though she had no way to cut them shorter. She already had plenty of small sticks, though, and she shoved the end of one of the logs onto her small blaze, allowing it to grow. She sat on the other one.

She nearly fell off the withered wood when Zoram came tromping back into camp, carrying what looked like a small boar. Her eyes widened.

"Aren't boars dangerous to hunt?"

He plopped the animal on the ground, already gutted, and nodded toward it. "This one didn't know what hit it. He was alone, too."

"How many arrows did you use?"

"Just one."

"Really? That's impressive." She had no idea why she felt to tell him that.

"Not really. We'll eat well tonight, though, and we can save some meat to take with us. We just can't cure it very well, as I don't have the salt for that. We can get some in Jershon, I'm sure."

"All right." She lifted her little knife to prepare the boar meat for cooking. He stopped her, handing over his larger knife.

"This will make it easier."

"And you're not worried I'll stab you?"

He raised his eyebrows in plain confusion. "Um, no. Even though you hate me, you still won't stab me. You're too good."

"Too good?"

"You know what I mean."

"Do I? Good men have stabbed Lamanites, and justifiably so, in battle. Why not me?"

He remained perplexed. "I ... don't know. But please don't stab me."

She thought she caught the hint of a smile, but the flickering light might have been playing tricks.

"I could … if God wanted me to."

"I believe you, but I doubt God is ever going to want you to stab somebody."

She hoped he was right. Thirty minutes later, they were enjoying some of the most succulent meat she could ever remember tasting. It still paled against her dream of that morning, but it was *good*.

———◇———

She thought seriously about leaving Zoram after they crossed the border into Jershon. She was certain she could find someone else to help her, especially after telling her story. A kind priest or teacher, perhaps. The chief judge of Jershon was probably a good man. Zoram didn't say anything to her about the possibility, didn't even express surprise as she continued to trudge along beside him, mile after mile in the direction of Morianton. They still avoided people for the most part and slept under whatever canopy of foliage they could find to protect them from the scattered rains.

At one point, she wondered what was wrong with her. Why couldn't she just leave? She asked the Lord that question many times, but the answer remained mired in a quicksand of uncertainty. To lessen the impact, she kept preaching to Zoram. At least talking about God made her feel a little better.

"I'm sorry I haven't asked you this before, but what did your parents teach you about Jehovah?"

He rounded his shoulders as if she had just asked to be carried on his back. "They were Nehors."

"Nehors believe in the God of Abraham. At least, they say they do."

He was silent for several seconds as he led them along the side of a little-used road, the grass along its edges reaching a foot high. "You either believe in a god who cares what you do, or you don't believe one exists at all."

She pondered that. He didn't seem to notice when she hummed thoughtfully. "That's a profound point, Zoram."

He grunted an indeterminate acknowledgment.

"This earth didn't just pop into existence," she continued. "Like I said before, it isn't some random event. Someone created it, and why go to all that trouble without a purpose in mind? God does indeed care what we do, and what we are becoming. He also respects our agency. We get to choose how we behave, what opportunities we take advantage of. That is one of our greatest gifts—freedom to learn and progress."

He had gotten ahead of her, but he paused to let her catch up and walk beside him. He turned his head. "What if he isn't perfect? What if he gives us too much freedom? The world is a horrible place because we make so many bad choices. Why doesn't he take more control? Wouldn't you?" He stared forward again, face chiseled stone. Clearly, the question bothered him greatly.

She felt for him—for all who wandered in the darkness of agnosticism or superstition. And it *was* darkness. That was where Gadianton found most of his followers, she was certain. She thought carefully about her response.

"We aren't just casual creatures, Zoram. We aren't playthings. We are powerful beings, because we are literal sons and daughters of God, and Mother God. They respect us. They know our potential far better than we do, and they offer us all the help we need, even if it seems like they don't sometimes." She lowered her head, thinking about her own experiences.

"I'm glad you kidnapped me," she added.

He came to a dead stop, and she took another two steps before stumbling on something and turning to face him.

"Why?" he asked, brow as deeply furrowed as a new spring field, eyes narrowed like she was a hawk's prey ... or he was.

"Because my life was too easy. It made me ... spiritually lazy."

"You're not lazy."

She ignored his assertion. "I thought I would go and live blissfully in Zarahemla with Kai, and raise a family, and go to all the best parties, and be looked up to for being so close to the prophet. That's pride, which kills faith. I've never doubted God's existence—I guess that's just not in my nature—but I don't think I really knew him before. I still don't, to be honest. But at least I understand myself a little better now, and somehow that helps. Even if I'm still not free, and you're lying to me, and I end up back in the hands of Gadianton … even if I die today, or tomorrow, or next week, it will be okay. I'll return home to God, my Heavenly Father, and I'll be able to claim that I endured a *real* trial, that I did something hard. Maybe not all that well, but I think I'll get *some* credit for it."

His expression had transformed into a look of open astonishment. When his eyes weren't boring into her, they darted around the landscape behind her. His lips compressed as he worked the muscles of his jaw. He opened his mouth as if to speak, then clapped it shut again. Finally, he found the words of a reply. A question, actually.

"Who *are* you?"

She threw her shoulders back, feeling the onset of tears. "I am a daughter of God, made in the image of Mother God. I know they love me, because I have felt it many times. I am a dedicated follower of their beloved Son, the coming Messiah, even Jesus Christ. I have made covenants to trust him and obey his commandments. Those commandments bring me great peace and unspeakable joy as I strive to follow them. I have a good family, and I am a member of the Lord's church. I will do my best to keep my covenants until the time I pass from this life to the next, and then I will bathe the feet of my Savior, and my Heavenly Parents, with my tears—not out of sadness for the ordeals of this life, but for the hope and joy of eternal salvation."

Both tears and words flowed from a place she realized she had always had access to but had utilized too infrequently. She blinked rapidly, trying to discern his reaction. He was generally hard to read, but she could tell something had penetrated his armor. His mien became both troubled and amazed, as if he were realizing something and wasn't sure he wanted to.

She thought he was going to respond, but then he nodded sharply, eyes snapping back to the road ahead. He began walking again. She matched his stride, feeling lighter somehow. Her feet didn't hurt, either.

———◇———

After many days, they approached Morianton late in the afternoon. They hadn't spoken much the last two days—only out of basic necessity, really. He had been acting more respectful and deferential, though.

"I know you don't like this city," he said, "and I don't blame you, but it will be safer inside than out until I can get the horses and supplies. There are too many bandits in this area." He sighed as if conceding a point.

"We can leave for Zarahemla in the morning?"

"Yes. I'll be able to get some money for rooms at an inn. In fact, I'll take you to the common room of one I trust, while I gather everything. I wouldn't ask you to stay with anyone I know here."

She nodded. "All right. And thank you, Zoram."

"Don't thank me yet." That sounded ominous, but she shook it off.

They entered the city, the gate guards giving them the briefest of perusals. After a few minutes, they came to an inn, and Zoram led them inside. He showed her to a table, where she sat, then went and spoke in quiet tones with the innkeeper for a minute. Seeming satisfied, he nodded to her and exited.

Moments later, the innkeeper brought her a cup of mild mead and a plate of food, mostly dried fruits and crunchy bread, adding that dinner was being prepared. She was grateful for the meal and suddenly felt a lot hungrier.

Halfway through the plate, a different woman approached her table. It was hard to pin her age down, but the dark green eyes exuded a maturity and confidence born of long experience. She sat across from Siarah, taking a moment to settle her skirts.

"You are Siarah, I presume?"

Siarah's eyes widened, her face freezing mid-chew. She looked around, but nobody else seemed to be paying any attention. She hurriedly finished chewing and swallowed.

"Yes, I am. How … do you know my name?" She put her hands in her lap and clasped them tightly to keep them from shaking.

The woman's concerned smile came across as genuine—or as superb acting. "A great many people have been looking for you. Unfortunately, some of them—and not the good ones—are in Morianton, and they already know you're here."

Siarah squeezed her hands even more tightly. "What do you mean? What do I do? Can you help me? Please?"

Pity trickled from the woman's eyes. "There isn't much I can do at the moment, but don't lose hope."

Siarah looked down at the table. "I should have left. Before we got to the city, I should have left."

"Probably. But that man you're traveling with—Zeram?"

"Zoram."

"Yes, Zoram. I don't think he betrayed you, though he *was* Ahab's own fool to bring you here first. He didn't force you to come, did he?"

She blinked several times as she flagellated herself for her own stupidity. She *should* have set out on her own. *Oh, Father, why didn't I?* She shook her head as she looked up, eyes pleading. "Can you help me escape?"

The woman frowned as she gave a slight shake of her head. "Not yet. But, like I said, Siarah, don't give up hope." She rose abruptly, and Siarah wanted to reach across the table and grab her skirts to prevent her from leaving. Instead, she watched in profound sadness as the woman turned and walked toward the entrance, a sense of awful finality surging in her wake. Siarah blinked away tears, then spotted the slightest nod from a woman three tables away toward two men seated near the door. The men waited a few moments, then rose smoothly and approached Siarah. She thought she had learned some courage while a prisoner of Gadianton in Antionum, but it all fled. She visibly shook now, and the tears increased. What had she done? She should have been on her way to Zarahemla!

The men stood side by side across from her, both with mustaches— one black, one brown. The brown mustached one spoke. "You will come with us, Siarah, peacefully or trussed up."

His voice was cold, like the depths of hell without the fire. She rose slowly, her body feeling numb, all thoughts of the unfinished plate of food vanished from her mind. She stepped away from the table, then ignored the men completely as she began walking sedately toward the door. Surprisingly, her trembling had stopped, and her breaths came in a calm rhythm. The men fell in slightly behind her. She could feel their eyes on her back.

After she stepped outside, the same man said, "Turn left." She obeyed, and they moved up the street, half of her feeling somehow like a queen, the other like a dog meekly obeying its master, tail curled between its legs. They turned once more, then approached an imposing, ornate building that must be the Hall of Judgment. They steered her toward a side entrance, a guard barely glancing at them as they proceeded inside. They directed her down a hall, then up some stairs. At the end of a short hallway stood two stately doors, banded in brass and gilded with silver. She swallowed as she paused before them, and the man with the black mustache stepped by her to open it.

She entered. The room was empty except for a few chairs. She wasn't sure whether to be relieved by that or not. Her heart began beating a sporadic staccato.

"Wait here," ordered brown mustache, who then shut the door. The sound of its closing made her cringe—confirmation, perhaps, that her fate was sealed.

Sealed. As she had wanted so badly to be with Kai in the temple. She didn't even care which temple anymore. Zarahemla, Bountiful, or one of the others. The dream had died. God willed it, and it was so.

She found a chair against one of the walls and slumped into it. She tried to close her eyes and rest, but couldn't. All was still, like water before a dam's sudden breaking. Not knowing how long she would have to wait became a form of torture. Until she fell to her knees, then prostrated herself on the floor and supplicated the Lord.

She didn't know how much time had passed, but the sound of the door opening brought instant awareness. She scrambled to her feet, smoothing out her dress. A moment passed before Gadianton's Stormcloud entered the room, followed by the two men who had brought her from the inn—arrested her, really, and without any pretext of doing it lawfully. Gadianton himself, dressed in a complicated regalia of robes and sashes of many colors, highlighted with golden thread, then invaded the space.

He barely glanced at her as he strode regally across the room to sit in the large chair in the middle of the back wall, set on a narrow dais. At a flick of his wrist, brown and black mustaches hurried to her side and pulled her toward the center of the room, facing him. She stared down at the floor mosaic, but its confusing patterns caused her to look back up.

Gadianton sniffed. "So this is where you flew off to, little bird."

Her voice was soft in response. "I thought I was escaping. But I was lied to again." Something told her Zoram *hadn't* lied to her, but she didn't amend her comment. Perhaps it would give him some protection?

"Hmmm ... yes, that is an interesting situation. Zoram shows initiative, which can be good. But sometimes it is bad. He doesn't understand the whole picture, either. But ... what's done is done. You are here now. You will be a guest at Chief Judge Tiberion's home until we can set up the proper communications to lure your betrothed back here. We should have had him in Antionum—yes, he went there, looking for you and failing, which I imagine is a very frustrating thing for you to hear—but by dumb luck he eluded our grasp.

"Actually, this is good timing, with the potential for delightful drama. Our position in this city has been firmed up over the last several months. Helaman's law officers cannot touch us here—we have too many judges and local officers behind us. That is becoming true in other places as well, including Noah and Sidom. Zarahemla will come along again; I have no doubt of that."

He breathed deeply and clapped his hands, smiling like the devil himself. "I have someone I want you to meet. This will be ... quite delectable."

The door opened again behind her. She didn't look, just waited as someone else was brought in. Her two guards moved her over a couple of steps to make place for the other person to stand next to her before Gadianton. When she glanced over, she noted it was a woman, roughly dressed like her, but in pants, not skirts. Her reddish-brown hair, with streaks of black, seemed to defy the dullness of infrequent washing. Siarah didn't want to see her own hair.

"Siarah, betrothed of Kihoran, son of Gideon, of Bountiful. Meet Arayah, daughter of Lanaina, of Zarahemla, once of the oath but now a condemned betrayer. Also, Kihoran's *other* love interest."

He paused, leaning forward slightly, studying her reaction. She knew she blanched, and a tear leaked from the corner of one eye. But how could anything this man said matter?

"He is a liar," said Arayah, which earned her a strong cuff from behind. Siarah jumped, turning to see the woman regain her balance.

Gadianton waved a finger at Arayah. "You know to be more careful than that, clever Ara, clipped Raven. I don't really need you. At least, not to lure Kihoran here." His sordid smile made Siarah shiver. She experienced a flash of empathy for the other woman.

"You have been helpful, though, for now I know that it was Kihoran who broke his oaths and slew Kishkumen, interrupting our mission to fulfill the will of the true god of this world."

This time Siarah gave the other woman a look of horror and disdain. She herself had kept the secret, but this woman had not? And how had she even known?

"It won't do you any good," said Ara to Gadianton.

"Of course it will," he said, waving a dismissive hand. "You know nothing. And before long, you will pay for *all* of your insolence, which payment will serve an additional purpose."

Ara squinted at him. "What do you mean?"

"That you will die, of course," he replied, as if he had just decided what he wanted for breakfast the next morning. That rictus of a smile reappeared. "And by the hand of your own father."

Siarah would have fallen to the floor in a puddle at such a pronouncement made toward her, but Ara just lifted her chin and glared, making no response.

Gadianton's words strummed the tension. "I have recalled him from up north. He knows you are here. He doesn't yet know I will require him to kill you to seal his final set of oaths, but he will do it. Of that I am certain."

"You are a monster!" blurted Siarah before she could think.

Gadianton cast her a wicked snarl. "I am the savior of this nation—of Nephites and Lamanites alike. You—both of you—are nothing more than insects squatting in the road toward progress. You and that foolish boy of yours. His death will be just and holy retribution."

"He will kill you," said Ara calmly, and Siarah barely kept her jaw from dropping—not because the statement was so audacious, but because ... it felt true. Was that real, or just a wild imagining, borne on winds of desperation?

After another blow from behind nearly knocked Ara over, Gadianton erupted in laughter, the room ringing with his booming, maniacal timbre.

"Ah, Ara, Imrahiel has told me how feisty you can be—and how foolish. He will be here soon, by the way, to witness your final sacrifice for the cause. Afterward, we will have a mighty celebration—in your honor, of course!" He laughed again, and this time he definitely overdid it. It sounded utterly fake, hollow, and pathetic. Siarah lowered her eyes, doing her best to drown out the noise with another quick prayer.

"Well, this has been enjoyable," said Gadianton after letting his laughter fade. "If I didn't have other pressing matters to attend to ... well, it might be more enjoyable still." He addressed the guards standing behind her and Ara. "Take them to their rooms. And feed them well—we don't want either of them starving before our grand climax."

Ara was ushered out first, followed by Siarah, whose two guards led her along a serpentine path. She could tell when they passed from the main building into what appeared to be a palatial residence. This must be the chief judge's home. She was escorted to a bedroom and shoved inside. The lock clicked loudly behind her.

Chapter 17

There is nothing which is secret save it shall be revealed;
there is no work of darkness save it shall be made manifest
in the light; and there is nothing which is sealed upon
the earth save it shall be loosed.
—2 Nephi 30:17

Kai knew trouble awaited them in Morianton, but he didn't fear it. He tried not to be so brash as to welcome it, either. It was just him and Dan, but he was riding Vyim again, which almost made him feel like Samson.

"You're sure Helaman trusts this priest?" he asked as they followed a street near the inside of the eastern wall.

"Yes," said Dan. "And the opinion came recently enough that I'm not worried."

"How recent?"

"Two years."

Kai gave him a level look. "That's not very recent."

Dan shrugged. "We should be able to assess that for ourselves."

"You hope."

"Yes, I hope."

Kai let it drop, and eventually they arrived at a synagogue featuring a life-sized brazen serpent staff carved into the door.

"What is his name again?" Kai asked as he dismounted.

"Limher."

"And you're sure he wasn't one of Alma's army scouts?"

Dan chuckled. "Positive. Different Limher."

Kai secured Vyim's reins to a post, then led Dan inside. It was already evening, so the priest might be there. If not, someone else could direct them to his home.

They entered the main chamber, a room well lit by oil burning in various sconces. It was empty.

"Brother Limher?" Kai ventured in a voice he hoped wasn't too loud. They waited a few seconds, and he repeated the call.

After several more moments, a man trundled through a doorway from the back, a thick scroll tucked under one arm. His black beard was smartly trimmed, his eyes bright.

"May I help you, brothers?" His gaze darted to their military accoutrements, but he didn't comment on them.

"We are looking for a priest named Limher," said Kai. "Do you know where we might find him?"

"I am he." He glanced at their weapons again. "Is there some trouble?"

He seemed like a confident enough man—a point in his favor. Kai gestured toward Dan. "We are here on assignment from High Priest Helaman, and he has mentioned your name as someone he trusts." He could hear the skepticism in his own voice.

"Well, I can understand why Helaman would send someone here. I and a few others write the church leaders in Zarahemla regular letters, but it is good to see some things firsthand—or at least send others you trust to witness." He looked a little more closely at Dan, who wasn't wearing his distinctive headband, then asked, "You ... are a son of the elder Helaman? One of the two thousand?"

Dan nodded. "I am."

Limher bowed. "It is an honor. I know of none who live in this area ... though they would find ample missionary opportunity here." He made it sound like a plea, not a joke.

"That is true everywhere," said Dan, returning the bow, "fortunately or unfortunately. "We are spoiled and stubborn."

"You mean the Nephite people in general, right? Not the Ammonites, surely."

"Some of my people now, as well," said Dan sadly.

The air grew solemn, and several seconds passed. Finally, Kai cleared his throat.

"Is there a place we can speak with you in private? We have a few questions."

"Yes, of course." Limher turned, motioning them to follow him through the doorway to the back. They soon entered a cramped office space, with only two chairs.

"You both may sit. I will stand."

"I would prefer to stand at the moment," said Dan, closing the door, and the priest deferred with a nod of respect.

"So, what would you like to know?" Limher asked from behind a small, rickety desk. It reminded Kai of Shemnilom's dangerously decrepit counterpart, which perhaps had already given up the ghost. In fact, he hoped it had.

"The band of Gadianton is active in this area," Kai began, "and we have tracked several of them, looking for information on the abduction of my betrothed, named Siarah, and her location. We need your assistance in this matter."

"She was kidnapped? From where? From here?"

"No, Bountiful."

"Ah, that sounds audacious. Here, it is … unfortunately … more easily done. Many of our judges are corrupt, and if you know the right people, and have money, you can get away with almost anything. I fear deeply for the people of Morianton. There are still good people here, but they tire of the fight. Many of their faithful brothers and sisters have left for better opportunities and a safer environment. We are in danger of becoming the next Ammonihah, and I myself am torn."

"You might leave?" asked Dan.

Limher looked up at him, eyes expressive of great sorrow. "Part of me wishes to remain, to support our people still here and find those who are willing to accept the doctrine of Christ. But another part of me …" he took a deep breath, "wants to leave. I still desire to serve the Lord, don't get me wrong, but … in a happier place with better prospects." He lowered his head. "I fear I sin in that yearning."

Kai felt for the man. He probably had his own family to worry about, too. In his place, Kai couldn't say what he would do.

"Help us now," said Dan, his voice solemn, even reverent, "and perhaps the Lord will make things clear for you, one way or the other. Do not give audience to shame or fear. Just assist us. We were guided here by his hand."

Dan's words had a powerful effect on Limher. Kai could almost see the new strength infusing both body and spirit. The priest sat up straighter, his eyes clearing, and he said, "I will do that, brother. Thank you, most humbly, for coming."

"You're worried your family will be in danger if you're seen helping us," said Kai.

Limher blinked and swallowed, then nodded. "Yes. I am sorry."

Kai shook his head. "Don't be sorry. You have reason for concern."

"But reason to exercise your faith as well," added Dan. "If we are diligent in this, all will be well."

"I believe you," said Limher to Dan. Then he spoke to Kai. "I can feel the seriousness of your warning, but I will do what the Lord will have me do. And my wife is stronger than me."

Kai's chest warmed at the man's courageous expression of determination. "Well, thank you. We should start by trying to figure out where the Gadiantons—with Chief Judge Tiberion's help, most likely—might keep Siarah ... if she's here. Do you know anyone who might be in a position to hear or see something?"

Limher clasped his hands on the shaky desk and furrowed his brow, staring intently into the distance. After several seconds, he said, "I don't know anyone who might have direct knowledge, but we might get some indirect information. I would need to ask a few people to ... um, make some careful inquiries?" His eyes moved between Kai and Dan uncertainly.

"Yes," said Dan. "Just be careful. And prayerful. And caution those of your flock you speak with about this to do the same."

"Are there any particular places we should start searching?" asked Kai.

Limher shook his head. "Not that I know of. You can try the inns, of course, maybe speak with shopkeepers. I guess it depends on how low of a profile you want to keep."

Kai gave a grim smile. "I don't care if Gadianton knows I'm here. He probably already does anyway."

"Kai, we should take some precautions," warned Dan.

Kai offered a challenging stare in return. "It's time to confront him."

"He might not even be here."

"Then I guess I don't have much to worry about."

Dan's expression didn't change. "A lot of his band are here, though. And we don't have Lehi's men with us."

"Well," responded Kai, "as you have explained to me, we will need to rely on the Lord. It doesn't matter how much we're outnumbered."

Dan sighed. "The Lord still wants us to take precautions … or at least do our best in that regard."

"That time has passed. He will help us or he won't, but this is the end."

Limher's eyes widened to saucers as he bounced his gaze between them. Then he said in a timid voice, "You … can stay here instead of an inn. We have a guest room for the occasional visitor. Actually, it hasn't been used in quite some time. But it's safer. Even the Gadiantons hesitate to accost someone inside a synagogue, because of public reaction."

Kai thought about that. It was certainly better than camping outside the city or risking an inn. He glanced at Dan, then said, "Thank you. That is a gracious offer, and we accept."

"Will you preach to us, Master Dan, share some of your experiences?" asked Limher.

"Of course," responded Dan. "Kihoran, too, though he might object." He turned to Kai and quirked an eyebrow.

Kai felt pinned. He had no choice, so he nodded. He didn't care if he made a fool of himself preaching anyway. That didn't matter a speck of dust compared to his mission.

<hr />

Over the next few days, while Limher made his inquiries, Kai and Dan scoured the city. Dan had suggested they might disguise themselves, but Kai got the strong impression it wasn't necessary—and might even be counterproductive. In fact, as the days wore on, and nobody in the entire blasted city seemed to know anything, he became increasingly convinced that they just needed to confront Chief Judge Tiberion directly.

"We bear some of Helaman's authority as his emissaries," said Kai to Dan as they rode their horses to an outlying village to expand their search radius.

"And we have used it," said Dan.

"Have we? Certain people have cooperated, and with Lehi's men we were feared by most others, but we haven't truly exercised that authority."

"What are you thinking?" asked Dan with a skeptical look.

"That we should present ourselves to Chief Judge Tiberion, publicly and officially, and demand that he allow us to search the Hall of Judgment and his prisons. All of them."

He expected Dan to object, but instead the big man seemed to mull it over. "We use our real names?"

"Of course. He's already aware we're here."

"He might arrest us."

"He wouldn't dare … not yet."

Dan shrugged. "Maybe not. But he won't let us conduct those searches, either. He'll want an official document from Helaman, requiring that specific thing. And the high judges here will back him up on that."

Kai snorted. "The judges here would back him up on just about anything."

Dan smirked. "Like arresting us?"

Kai chuckled darkly. "I see your point. He still won't arrest us. It's too dangerous for him. He knows Lehi lurks nearby."

"And I still agree with you on that."

Kai pulled up on Vyim's reins, stopping him. Dan turned his horse across the path as he, too, halted, waiting for Kai to speak.

"Why waste time checking out the villages? We can go to the Hall of Judgment right now. In fact, we should run the horses there, not give anyone watching us time to warn Tiberion we're coming. I want to catch him by surprise."

Dan pondered only a moment before giving a sharp nod, and they were off. Kai was amazed he had agreed so easily, but Dan remained stubbornly hard to predict. As the wind whistled by his ears, Kai felt a sharp stab of guilt regarding his friend. How long had it been since he'd seen *his* family? He'd written many letters, but they needed him there with them, not traipsing around pursuing Kai's obsession. True, they were hunting Gadianton, which was an important purpose, but that's not what drove Kai. And Dan hadn't complained once. It was almost unbelievable.

Kai reluctantly pushed those thoughts to the back of his mind, though the determination to bring everything to a conclusion burned in his belly as Vyim flew toward the city, outpacing Dan's mount. Kai let him run, since they both knew their destination.

A guard at the city gates took notice, but barely had time to spit out a question, which Kai couldn't hear over the thunder and wind of Vyim's hooves. He soon had to slow the horse to avoid running innocent people down in the streets, which was frustrating. The Hall of Judgment called to him like a fiery beacon blazing from the top of a low hill at the center of the city. Dan caught up, and the closer they got, the more slowly they had to proceed, so that when they arrived Kai was ready to bite the head off the first guard he saw.

He leaped to the ground, then held the reins toward a surprised guard. "This horse is from Moronihah's stables—one of his most prized. He will have more than your hide if anything happens to him."

The man's knees seemed to shake, and a sheen of sweat burst onto his face. "Um, yes, uh, sir?"

"I am Kihoran, from the office of Chief Judge Helaman. Also one of Moronihah's elite scouts."

"Is something … happening?" the man stammered.

"Yes, but not what you think. I and my companion are here to see Chief Judge Tiberion on urgent business from Helaman. Captain Lehi may be joining us shortly."

That last part was a lie, but it had the desired effect. The poor guard, who looked barely older than Kai, gripped Vyim's reins like they were his only hope of life and salvation. Then he turned to shout over his shoulder, "High visitors from Zarahemla to see the chief judge! Apprise him at once!" His voice only broke twice. He faced Kai and gave a small bow, and then Kai stepped aside to allow Dan to pass his reins to another guard who had emerged from the building. From what Kai could tell through the doors and windows, the interior was already a hive of activity. He hadn't expected that quick of a reaction, but he hoped it boded well.

Without asking permission, he and Dan marched through the main doors and past several other newly arrived guards. Shouts began to precede them, and Kai ordered one of the guards to lead them to where Tiberion was giving audience that day. The stunned man complied without question. Even after more than two decades, it appeared the people of Morianton remembered what had happened when Nephite armies came to settle the violent land spat they had caused.

Kai felt surprise yet again when they were ushered immediately into a large, luxurious room where Tiberion sat with several aides and attendants. The chief judge rose calmly, eyeing both him and Dan speculatively until they stopped a few feet in front of him.

"How very kind of you to call on me unannounced," he said with a droll lilt.

"And we are grateful for your eagerness to see us on such short notice," replied Kai with a bite of sarcasm.

Tiberion glared at him for a few seconds in an obvious attempt at intimidation, then looked at one of his aides and waved a hand. "Get them chairs. And something to drink."

"Nothing to drink, thank you," said Dan, "though we appreciate the hospitality."

Tiberion frowned deeply at him. "You suspect us of some ill intent, Ammonite?"

Dan didn't back down. "Why would you assume that?"

"Why would—" Tiberion began, then waved his hand again, this time in disgust, and sat. The two chairs arrived for Kai and Dan.

Kai didn't let his body relax for even a moment in his seat. He stared hard at Tiberion, then said the words he had worked out on the fast ride over.

"You harbor people who are actively seeking to overthrow Helaman and the seat of government in Zarahemla."

After a brief display of shock, Tiberion laughed. "What kind of puffery is this? We are loyal citizens. We pay our portion for the public works. Our men fill positions in the army. We uphold the laws of the land. And we are *happy* to be Nephites."

"An impressive official statement," said Kai coolly, "but Gadianton—he who tried to have Helaman assassinated—is here in the city, as are some of his top lieutenants, such as Imrahiel, who I know personally."

Tiberion gave a throaty chuckle. "I'm not aware of every person who happens to be visiting my city," he rebutted. "And people are free to come and go. That is the law, is it not?"

"Unless those people have violated more serious laws, in which case you have a duty to apprehend them and either try them for crimes committed here, or hand them over to law officers from other cities."

"I am doing my duty to the people of Morianton and Nephi," Tiberion replied in a high dudgeon. "And if you believe you are doing yours by coming into my court and insulting me with such fantastical allegations, then I will be forced to draft a strong letter to Chief Judge Helaman so that he can disabuse you of that foolish notion."

It was a weak threat, and Tiberion probably knew it. Kai hardened his gaze further. "I'm not a diplomat. I'm not here to conduct flowery, pointless negotiations. You will hand over Gadianton and any others of his band who are here, and we will take them back to Zarahemla for trial. Lehi is on his way to help us do that."

He wasn't sure why he lied again about Lehi coming, but he needed to show a plausible way to transport multiple prisoners across the country. It was time to arrange for a message to be sent to Lehi anyway. In fact, he should have done it yesterday.

"Or," said Tiberion, "I will detain you here, and we will await Helaman's response to my missive."

Kai shook his head. "You're not that stupid."

Tiberion sat seething for long moments, then waved his hand a third time. "I cannot help you. Now get out of my sight."

Kai remained sitting, and Dan followed suit, apparently waiting to see if and how Tiberion might try to enforce such an edict. Kai had to admit that part of him wanted a stronger confrontation.

"Are you *deaf*, boy?" spat Tiberion. "Whatever authority you think you have, it doesn't extend to harassing me and my people here in the Hall of Judgment. Nothing prevents me from having you forcibly escorted out—in fetters, if need be."

Dan sniffed, and Kai took that as his cue that he had pushed hard enough. He and Dan rose as one, then turned. As they began walking, Kai kicked over his chair, knowing it was childish but feeling unable to fully contain his emotions. He was now more certain than ever that Tiberion was helping Gadianton, that he knew exactly where both the bandit leader and Siarah were. He strained mightily to resist the temptation to spin back around and sprint toward the corrupt chief judge, then strangle him until he confessed all his knowledge of the affair. Dan would have his back.

He started when he found himself back outside, with the nervous guard handing him Vyim's reins. He could barely remember the passage out, or if Dan had said anything.

Apparently, he hadn't, or maybe he just knew Kai was in another world, for he didn't speak the entire ride back to the synagogue.

When they had settled their horses behind the building and taken care of them, Dan finally broke the silence.

"We were followed."

"I figured that," said Kai. "They already knew we were staying here, though."

"The synagogue may be in danger now."

"With Tiberion on the judgment seat, it was already in danger. Limher knows that."

"We should tell him what happened today," said Dan.

"You mean, what I did."

"What *we* did. I am with you, Kai, and I did not feel like the Lord was displeased. It wasn't perfect, but God allows for our imperfections, especially when we do our best, and for the right reasons."

Kai paused at the back door to the synagogue and looked at Dan. The light of the day had nearly disappeared. "Are my motives pure, Dan? I don't think so. I'm discounting the lives of people like Limher and his family—and you—driven by my own desperate need."

Dan laid a hand on his shoulder. "You are doing this for Siarah and her family, too. And we have already weakened the Gadiantons in this area, at least temporarily. You take too much on yourself. Others must also do their part to prevent them from regaining their prior influence. And it must be done with respect for the agency of our brothers and sisters—under both our laws and the laws of God."

"I know," said Kai, sagging a bit as he closed his eyes. He was suddenly exhausted. He also felt the sharp edge of discouragement. "But if we could take out a few key people, like Tiberion, we could cripple the Gadiantons. Isn't that what Captain Moroni would have done? It's better that a few die than that an entire nation suffer."

Dan nodded. "The words of Nephi. The Lord had a very specific purpose in leading him to kill Laban, and Laban fully deserved his fate. The Lord knew that. Nephi didn't. We do not know what the Lord knows, Kai, so we need to trust him. Taking it all into our imperfect hands is too dangerous. Disastrous, even."

"Trust him. Yes, I know you're right. But I'm not sure how much longer I can trust *myself*." He pushed open the door and went inside, Dan following silently. He looked for Limher, but the priest wasn't there that evening. And they didn't dare go to his home, not with the extra scrutiny they had just gathered.

When they got to their room, Kai dropped his weapons and satchel on the floor. Even his bones felt tired, so his small, lumpy bed looked more inviting than the finest pile of goose feathers.

"We should not end this day without prayer, brother."

Kai took a deep breath, then nodded. "Fine." He followed Dan in kneeling. "Go ahead."

"I believe you should offer it," said Dan, respectfully but firmly.

Kai breathed deeply again, sighing this time. "I'm not sure how well he'll listen to me, Dan. But all right." A yawn overtook him, and after struggling to get his mind in the right place, he began.

"Father ..." He sighed again, laboring to find meaningful words. "I don't think I did very well today ... but we're here, and we're safe at the moment, and ... I know you have helped us, even though I'm not sure I fully understand how. I ..." He paused, working through his roiling emotions. "We need your help. I believe Gadianton is here and that Tiberion is working with him. Siarah is probably here, too. I know you love Siarah, your daughter. We're trying to help her, and stop Gadianton, and ... well, whatever else you want us to do. Please, Father, help us. Help *me*. I'm the one with weak faith. I'm grateful for Dan, and Helaman, and Lehi, and Jerid, and Moronihah, and all who have helped me. Let their efforts not be in vain because I am weak, in the name of your son." With a heavy exhale, he slapped his hands on the floor, then pushed to get his feet under him.

"Amen, my brother," said Dan. Kai waited for more, but the stalwart warrior merely got to his feet and prepared himself for bed, including scrubbing his teeth, which he kept remarkably clean and white—another gift from his mother, he had explained once.

When Kai lay down, he stared at the dark ceiling for at least an hour, his thoughts focusing and then jumbling, over and over, until his mind finally grew tired of it. Then he slipped into a calm, restful sleep.

———◇———

As Zoram stood in front of the synagogue door late at night, poised to knock, it unexpectedly opened. No light spilled from the interior. A man was leaving, eyes focused on the latch. He let out a gasp when he noticed Zoram.

"Oh ... oh! I'm sorry, you startled me. I just stopped by to retrieve some scrolls so I could study them at home. I'm Limher, by the way, one of the priests here. Are you are ... ?"

"My name is Zoram. Has a young woman come by here, alone, asking for sanctuary?"

"Sanctuary? Um, no, though I'm aware of certain men searching for a young woman they believe might, um, be in the city."

Zoram's eyes narrowed. "Who are these men? Do you know them?" His words barely made it through his clenched teeth, the angry thunderheads he cast from his face seeming to unnerve the priest.

"Um, well, no. I mean, this is a big city, and I didn't think their request odd. But I couldn't tell them anything about where this young woman might be. I don't know if it's the same one you're searching for anyway. How do you know her?" He had finally stepped outside and closed the door, a trio of scrolls clutched to his chest. The anxiety had completely left his eyes.

"She would have come here," Zoram said, "or to one of the other synagogues. I have been searching them. I didn't know about this one until today."

"Hmmm. You are not from here?"

Zoram shook his head.

"Are you Christian?"

Many people had asked him that question before, most recently Siarah. But this time … it sounded different. It *felt* different. Why? He shook his head again and frowned. "No, I am not. But she is, and probably one of the most faithful among you."

"I see," said Limher, nodding, his anxiety seeming to rise again. "Is she in trouble?"

"Yes, she is. More than she can possibly imagine."

Limher's eyes suddenly exuded a great sadness. "That is awful. I sorely wish I could help you, but no young woman has come by here seeking sanctuary."

"You are certain?"

"Quite. I would surely know of it. I am sorry. I must return to my home now. You can come by again tomorrow. It is the Sabbath. I would be happy to show you through the building, and perhaps others might know something."

"I will," said Zoram, contemplating as he studied the priest's eyes. Was he hiding something? He couldn't be sure. All these Christian priests seemed to hide things, or pretend they knew mysteries a common man couldn't hope to discern. He nearly growled, but only in part because of the annoyance of these Christian priests. Several days had passed since Siarah had disappeared from the common room of the inn. Nobody there would tell him anything, and he had gathered a whole host of varied rumors from other random people throughout the city. He had no idea where she might have gone ... or been taken ... and he was at his wit's end.

Chapter 18

And now, their preservation was astonishing to our whole army,
yea, that they should be spared while there was a thousand
of our brethren who were slain. And we do justly ascribe it
to the miraculous power of God, because of their exceeding faith
in that which they had been taught to believe—that there was
a just God, and whosoever did not doubt, that
they should be preserved by his marvelous power.
—Alma 57:26

Kai awoke early, staring again at the ceiling. Only the barest hint of the coming sunrise pierced the window. The first clear thought that came was that he needed to visit Tiberion's home. He and Dan had learned it was attached to the Hall of Judgment, with its own entrance.

He bolted upright, then swung his feet off the bed. "Dan?"

He heard a muffled breath, then Dan's voice. "An early start?"

"Yes. Tiberion's house, or palace, whatever it is."

Dan sat up, rubbing his eyes. "Are you sure?"

"I don't know. I think so?"

"That is a dangerous play. More so than what we did yesterday."

"I know. But … we can request breakfast from his household as Helaman's emissaries. It's plausible enough, isn't it?"

Dan raised his eyebrows. "Barely."

Kai frowned, undeterred. "But it's worth a try. I feel it. Or I really want to. How can I tell the difference?"

"A difficult question for all of us. But the Spirit isn't insisting I dissuade you, so there's that."

"Yeah, there's that." Doubts crept in, growing stronger by the second, until Dan stood.

"Well, let's be about it, then. We are still on the Lord's errand and worthy of his assistance."

Kai wanted to say, "Well, you're definitely worthy of it. As for me …" But he refrained as they prepared to depart the synagogue. They decided to leave the horses behind. Kai could use a vigorous walk.

The light grew as they marched along the awakening streets. A few shops were beginning to open, some receiving early deliveries of goods for the day, including various types of food that made Kai's stomach rumble. They hadn't eaten any dinner. Perhaps his *stomach* had come up with the idea of breakfast at Tiberion's.

He chuckled inwardly, while his face remained a mask of seriousness and determination. Dan's, too, and most people gave them a wide berth.

As they neared the dedicated entrance to Tiberion's house, the doubts returned in strength, causing his heart to pound in his ears. In response, he gritted his teeth and walked faster. Dan matched him, saying nothing.

A single guard patrolled near the front doors, which were tall and intricately carved in a precious and rare dark wood, the handles leafed in gold. The man took a defensive stance in response to a pair of armed men approaching at a serious pace.

"Identify yourselves," he demanded, a slight tremor in his voice.

"Relax," said Kai. "We're emissaries from Chief Judge Helaman. We've had a long night, and we humbly request a morning repast from the chief judge of the city."

The man looked confused for a moment, then stood straight. "Wait here." He turned and disappeared inside the doors, leaving them unguarded. Kai was tempted to just follow him inside. But, envoys from Helaman would respect the boundaries of a man's home, even if he was in league with a blood-soaked villain like Gadianton. At least, in most circumstances they would. The temptation came again, then several more times over the next few minutes.

Finally, when Kai was about to carry out his invasion plan, the guard appeared in the doorway and waved them forward. "Come, you are welcomed by the graciousness of Chief Judge Tiberion."

"Thank you," said Dan after a moment, since Kai didn't feel like offering thanks. They followed the guard inside, and Kai noted the many expensive decorations—curtains, carpets, sculptures, paintings. It was indeed a palace, and Tiberion obviously took great pride in it. How easy had it been for Gadianton to set his hooks in this man?

The guard led them straight down a broad passageway and into an expansive formal dining room, dominated by a long, darkwood table that could easily seat thirty people. Four tall windows in deep embrasures along the far wall provided light through lace curtains. An interior garden lay beyond. As they sat, facing the windows, Kai couldn't believe his ploy had actually worked. Sure, it accorded with polite tradition, but he had definitely *not* been polite during their visit to the adjoining Hall of Judgment.

"It should just be a few minutes. The cooks have been notified."

"Thank you again," said Dan, and the guard left. He didn't go far, though, based on the brief echoes of his footsteps.

"So," said Dan, "we are inside. Now what?"

Kai shrugged. "We speak with Tiberion again, if he deigns to greet us. I think he will, just to show his authority in his own home."

"I agree. His pride will drive him to that. And what will you ask him?"

"I don't know yet. We'll see where the conversation goes."

Dan smiled slightly. "Your plan is thin on details."

Kai shrugged. "I'm doing the best I can. And I feel ... an urgency."

Dan nodded slowly, then said in a low voice, "I feel it, too."

Breakfast was soon served by an elderly woman with her hair in a large bun. Eggs, some slices of smoked meat, toasted bread, and several kinds of fresh fruit. It all looked and smelled delicious. After she left, Dan whispered, "Me first."

Kai squinted, and then it dawned on him. He didn't bother trying to convince his friend to leave off sampling the food for poison. And so Dan's hands and mouth moved quickly as he tasted everything, washing the bites down with several swigs from both their cups. After about a minute, he looked at Kai and nodded.

"Nothing fast-acting, at least. I do not believe they have tried to poison us. Had we given them more time to prepare, they might have."

"Yes, they might have indeed," Kai agreed and then began partaking, filling his empty belly. After a few minutes, Tiberion and two aides swept into the room, looking like they had already been up for hours hosting a banquet of state.

"We are happy to be able to feed our esteemed guests," said Tiberion, his voice remaining within diplomatic bounds, unlike the day before. For some reason, Kai didn't like the change. He would have preferred a more combative opening from the chief judge.

Kai watched as he and his aides seated themselves across the table from him and Dan, then said, "We appreciate your hospitality." He, too, maintained a tone of proper decorum. "Your cooks are talented."

"I'm delighted they have pleased you. Your visit is a surprise, however. With some notice, we could have prepared something far better."

Better. There was no doubt of that. "I'm sure you could have. But we go where the Spirit leads us, and today that is here."

"Oh?" Tiberion twisted his head to glance at his aides, clearly suppressing a smile. "Why would the Spirit bring you *here* today?"

Kai took another bite, chewing and swallowing before responding. "Because you're hiding something important from us ... and from Helaman. From your own people, too."

"Hiding?" Tiberion splayed his hands in front of him. "You're here, in my dining room, enjoying my food ... and I'm *hiding* something? I'm trying to be a gracious host, but why should I accept insults from someone whose identity as an emissary from the Chief Judge of all the land cannot even be verified to me?"

Kai kept his tone even, his face a mask of calm hiding the churning of his blood. "You know I am who I say I am. Some of Gadianton's people have confirmed it to you, even warned you how dangerous I am to him. I pretended to be part of his murderous organization once, helping to expose his treachery in Zarahemla ... which *included* aiding the

Lamanites in their invasion and takeover of the city. You are fully aware how cruel and barbarous Coriantumr was, how many innocent people he callously slaughtered, all in the name of power. Not truth, not justice, not love, but naked power. By supporting Gadianton, you support people like Coriantumr."

"Bah!" replied Tiberion, the anger in his tone mixed with some uncertainty. "Coriantumr is dead. Soldiers from Morianton, serving in Lehi's army, helped put him down. And you have no proof that Gadianton was involved anyway."

"Actually, the proof exists, and once Gadianton is taken into custody, he will receive a fair trial under the law. I personally might wish for something ... more expedited, but our laws help protect us from the rampant evil of men's hearts. Men like Akish. Do you remember Akish?" The name had just popped into Kai's mind. He recalled the basics of the ancient story.

"The Jaredite?" Tiberion laughed. "What does he have to do with this?"

"Everything," said Kai. "He was a friend of King Omer, and yet his lust for Omer's granddaughter—and for the power she could promise him through her father Jared—led him to revive the ancient, dark oaths. Had Omer not been warned by the Lord in a dream to flee, Akish would have delivered his head to Jared, the once-before traitorous son who then obtained his father's kingdom again by wickedness. And what happened to Jared? Evil destroyed evil. Akish murdered him and took over the throne, eventually even slaughtering his own son to protect his power. You are familiar with the oaths administered by Gadianton to his followers, as am I. He will kill anyone that he *perceives* rivals him ... including you."

Tiberion glowered, and then Kai heard the treading of many pairs of feet. Gadianton himself—it had to be, though Kai had never seen him in person—swept into the room from an arched side entrance, accompanied by ten armed men who quickly surrounded the table. Another man slipped in a few seconds later and took a guarding position by the doorway.

"Is that so, you meddling, stupid boy?" said Gadianton as he planted himself across the table from Kai and Dan. "You who murdered one of our most stalwart patriots."

Kai half expected himself to fly from his chair in a tidal wave of adrenaline, leap across the table, and attack the malignant serpent before him. But instead, he felt ... calm? He looked at Dan, whose serene face exuded a peace and confidence he couldn't describe. And then he spotted a woman entering through the same arched doorway. That was when his heart skipped a beat.

Mistress Havah.

The soft swish of her skirts emphasized the elegant sway of her hips as she crossed the room through dappled light dancing through the embroidered curtains to take a position to the right of Gadianton. She smiled at Kai, giving him a slight nod. Kai didn't know how to react. Should he be confused or angry?

She preempted him. "It is good to see you again, Kihoran. And in good health. I must say, this little surprise party is most intriguing ... and I wouldn't have missed it for the world." She granted a smile of equals to Gadianton, who had turned to give her a slight bow.

Gadianton focused again on Kai, standing straighter as if to impress Mistress Havah. Kai again felt the urge to leap at him—at them both. Helaman had *trusted* her?

"We will indeed have a trial today," Gadianton said. "You and Master Dan here stand accused of treason, blasphemy, and murder. After I have laid out the case against you, you will have a chance to proclaim your innocence. And then I will pronounce judgment."

"And execute us," said Kai. He still felt strangely relaxed, despite the longing to strangle both the haughty thief and the double-crossing spymistress.

"Let's not be presumptuous," said Gadianton in a preening tone. "We have a pair of additional witnesses for the defense that demand to be heard." He looked to the doorway, one eyebrow rising slightly as he fixed his sight on the guard there. Then he raised a hand in that direction, and his voice boomed. "Bring them in."

Two more pairs of armed men entered, holding the arms of Siarah and Ara, both firmly blindfolded and gagged.

Kai felt the muscles in his jaw twitch, his calm eroding rapidly. Both heels started tapping under the table. His eyes darted between Siarah and Ara, heart tearing into so many pieces he wasn't sure it could ever be whole again. Of course, if Gadianton succeeded in executing him, it wouldn't matter.

Was it really still an "if"?

He agonized for Dan, too, who had faithfully followed him into this disaster. An utter, foolish calamity.

"Let them go," said Kai as smoothly as he could manage. "Do whatever you want with me, but let them go. Dan, too. He can carry a message for you to Helaman."

Gadianton laughed, the tones rich and mocking.

"Slow down, false hero. We haven't even conducted the trial yet. Don't you believe in the justice process? In law and order? There is entertainment value here as well. I will even have scribes convert it to verse for future generations to enjoy."

Kai just blinked in return, glancing again at Siarah and Ara, who were made to sit in chairs farther down the other side of the table. Gadianton gestured again, and the blindfolds were removed. Two sets of haunting, feminine eyes locked desperately, fearfully upon him, pleading in a way he couldn't fully comprehend.

"These two are just getting to know each other," said Gadianton as he began pacing the length of the table. "Only one is your betrothed, but I believe I may be so bold as to say that you have strong feelings for them both."

Kai watched as Siarah and Ara looked at each other, Siarah's eyes expressing a startling compassion, Ara's revealing a deep, fathomless pain.

Gadianton clucked his tongue. "These are your two witnesses, as fate would have it. I do so look forward to what they have to say now. One at a time, of course—I really don't want them to speak over each other. We have rules of procedure, after all, especially in a court of law."

"May God smite you," said Dan in a clear, cutting voice that made Kai shiver.

Gadianton paused his pacing. "Ah, my poor Ammonite brother. My master is greater than yours, at least in this place, so I would like to see your god try." His brazenness chilled the air. "And soon, very soon, I will occupy my rightful place at the head of this nation. Then, the *real* work can commence in earnest."

"Child and virgin sacrifice?" ventured Kai in a mocking tone. "Mindless, limitless debauchery? Debilitating taxes so you can build palaces for yourself and all your concubines across the country? A vicious contest of dominion that will eventually see someone you trust kill you and take your place? You will suffer the fate of Riplakish." Yet another Jaredite king's name had materialized in his head, and he wondered why. He glanced at Dan, who gave him a somewhat surprised but approving look.

Gadianton restarted his pacing as he clucked again. "My, you must really be desperate, dredging up old Jaredite histories. Riplakish was a fool. I am not. And you cannot understand the magnitude of the justified anger I feel for you. Not only did you murder Kishkumen, but I have learned a few other things about your exploits—being the first to raise the alarm about the Lamanite invasion, carrying orders to Lehi and then setting up the ambush of Coriantumr's army. Coriantumr, regrettably, *was* a fool, but had he taken Bountiful, our plans still would have worked out beautifully. The Nephite and Lamanite nations would already be one, with me as their benevolent king, presiding in peace."

"You mean Tubaloth," corrected Kai. "That's what you promised him."

Gadianton stopped again and laughed, the sound sharper this time. "Tubaloth is a full barrel of lard. He would have been dead within the year. He is incapable of running a unified empire. *I* am. Your actions have merely delayed the inevitable. I can promise you that."

Dan stood suddenly, causing Gadianton's men to shift their feet and unlimber weapons. "The Nephites and Lamanites will only be united in righteousness, under the Son of God, even Jesus Christ," he declared. "This has long been prophesied. And the only way the Lamanites will come to rule is when the Nephites have been destroyed because of their own wickedness. That time is not now, nor will it come soon."

He sat as abruptly as he had stood, eyes still locked on Gadianton, who raised his eyebrows, seeming confused at the strangely dramatic soliloquy.

"You are brave," said Gadianton finally, considering him. "I must admit that. You and your brothers are all fearless, beyond logic. You chase a fantasy, but you do so with unwavering obstinacy. Of course, I still don't believe the myth that none of you died in battle. Those records were doctored, I am sure. But, as I said, you *are* bold." He flicked a glance at Kai. "This one, too, though I think part of *his* problem is that he is not right in the head. A pity."

Kai didn't rise to the insult. He stared instead at Siarah and Ara, wondering if Gadianton hadn't been correct. He loved Siarah and wanted to marry her, but seeing Ara again stoked new fires. How? Why? Was there indeed something wrong with him?

"Now," continued Gadianton, having moved to stand next to Mistress Havah again, "let us lay out the evidence, which I have personally vetted. That is useful, as I am also the judge." He winked at Kai, then continued. "Shortly after the deserved demise of Pahoran the Younger, Kihoran arrived in Zarahemla under an assumed name. Adonihah, I believe it was. He took a room at the inn called *Jacob's Rest* and then began making contacts within the city."

He paused a moment, bringing a finger to his lips and assuming a look of concentration.

"Excuse me, Master Gadianton," interrupted Mistress Havah, "but I have a few things I need to discuss with Lady Machala. I will be back before you conclude."

Gadianton frowned at her, but then nodded. "Fine." He looked at the high ceiling and took a deep breath as she exited the room. "Now, where was I? Ah, yes. We should back up a step. Prior to arriving at Zarahemla, Kihoran had visited—"

"Lehi," came a deep, gravelly voice from the main entryway behind Kai and Dan. Kai whirled in his chair. He would know that voice if he were buried ten feet in the ground. Lehi, with Jerid and his elites arrayed behind him, filled the passage to the front doors.

Lehi didn't carry a sword, but a massive axe, the head of which he thumped to the fine stone floor, cracking the delicate surface. "I followed a rumor about another mangy dog needing to be put down. It appears the rumor was true." He didn't smile as he laid his other hand atop the axe handle.

Gadianton's men behind Kai had parted like the Red Sea, moving to the sides of the room, swords drawn, eyes darting to Gadianton for direction. Kai studied a couple of them. These were hard men, not easily cowed. But they were now outnumbered. And facing Captain Lehi.

Kai scooted back from the table, rising as he drew his sword. Dan did the same. Kai looked at Siarah and Ara, still sitting and still gagged. Siarah's eyes leaked tears, staring at Kai in a desperate plea to which she couldn't give voice. Ara had turned her head toward Gadianton, glaring daggers at him, one after another.

Gadianton didn't seem worried. He squared himself to Lehi and lifted his chin. "You will not find this mangy dog so easy to put down." He snapped his fingers, and at least two dozen more men rushed into the room from the door to the kitchens, the last being … Imrahiel. He wasn't a fighter, but Kai was certain he enjoyed watching people die. His evil grin widened as his eyes rested briefly on Kai; they narrowed with wicked intent upon finding Ara.

"You will find more of my men outside," stated Gadianton, "trapping you here. You hadn't planned for that, it seems. As usual, you rushed in expecting everyone to fall at your feet in fear before the legendary but … hmmm … *aging* general."

Kai heard whispers from Jerid and a few of his men, then movement as they positioned themselves better in the hallway and the adjoining rooms to meet attacks from multiple directions. Lehi took a step forward, and this time he smiled.

"It doesn't matter how many men you have, Gadianton. You will soon realize that. If we don't end up executing you today, it won't be delayed long. I'll drag you to Zarahemla behind my horse, if I have to, and apologize to Helaman personally if you don't survive the experience. The worst that will happen to me is he'll ask me to retire. And I welcome that. So, what will it be? Do you come with me peacefully—you and that pretty she-dog Imrahiel—or must we slice our way through this mess you've made first?"

"The mess *I've* made?" burst Gadianton, eyes burning in a reddening face. "I will parade your head on a pole throughout this city. The people will rejoice as they rally to *me*! It truly was stupid of you to come to a place you are not liked. And you've condemned a great many people to death ... including these two poor women."

A guttural scream ripped through the air as the last syllable faded. Kai jerked his head in the direction of the doorway Gadianton had appeared through. The man guarding it had already launched his spear. Kai watched in what seemed like slow motion as the missile flew toward Gadianton. But the rebel leader had stepped back in reaction to the scream, and the spear whistled past him. Kai's eyes widened as the tip impacted and penetrated flesh ... in the chest of Imrahiel, who had turned toward the sound. His face imploded in shock as his bejeweled hands grasped the shaft protruding from his heart. A dying whimper escaped his lips as he crumpled to the floor, and then time regained its normal course.

Silence reigned for two full seconds, and then the man who had thrown the spear leaped toward the guards nearest Siarah and Ara with a war shout, drawing a sword in the process.

"Clear the room!" bellowed Lehi, and quick as a wink that monstrous axe was swinging with terrifying grace. Jerid and several other elites charged into the room after Lehi, engaging the rebels in a whirling, mesmerizing dance of sharpened steel. Kai took his opportunity to do what he'd been hoping for—cross the table and attack Gadianton. But several of the rebel leader's men closed ranks around him, and before he knew it, Kai found himself in a pitched battle, Dan arriving an instant later to provide lifesaving relief.

The fight was instant, concentrated bedlam, unlike anything he had ever seen, much less experienced up close. While the dining room was indeed large, too many men battled in a space occupied mostly by the massive table. Within seconds, several had jumped on top of it, including Jerid, one of his men, and several of Gadianton's soldiers. Even considering its bulk, Kai wondered how long the table would hold up under so many grown men shifting their weight so violently.

The answer came quickly, as the table cracked in the middle, then broke, tumbling the occupants toward the center. Dan stumbled to his knees as a Gadianton slid into him, and Kai managed to deflect a sword blow aimed for his friend, spinning toward the attacker to strike in the void of his overswing. The man couldn't react in time, and Kai's sword edge sliced deeply into his ribs. The man screamed and stumbled backward, swinging wildly. Kai ignored him for the moment as he parried the thrust of a short spear and kicked another man in the knee. Dan was up, and he finished off the man Kai had wounded in the ribs with an expert thrust. Jerid and another elite joined them, and they cut their way through to the windows, effectively splitting the Gadiantons in half. Kai spared a glance toward Lehi, resisting the temptation to stop and drop his jaw in awe as the big man strummed that magnificent, musical axe amid bloodcurdling bellows. Three elites guarded his back, and a pair of Gadiantons fled in terror through the door to the kitchens.

Kai's group stayed on defense as the battle surged unpredictably around them. Kai kept an ear out for any enemies approaching through the beautiful garden courtyard beyond the windows. They could easily break the glass and gain access to the room—or fire arrows into the crowded space. They would just as likely hit friend as foe, but Kai was sure some of the Gadiantons didn't care about that. And in the heat of battle, some men would strike out at anything.

He signaled to Dan, and they began moving slowly along the wall in the direction of Siarah and Ara ... and the unknown man trying to protect them. Kai caught glimpses, and the man was skilled. He valiantly fended off Gadianton and Nephite alike and had taken at least one wound—a nasty gash on his off-sword arm. When Kai and Dan were within a few feet, an escape route through the side entrance suddenly opened up. The man saw it, eyes widening in surprise.

"Siarah, I'll get you to safety!" he yelled. Siarah, her back to Ara, both of them gagless and holding up broken bits of their chairs for protection, spotted Kai. She glanced at the man, then at the escape route, which could close at any moment, and then back at Kai. "Be safe," she mouthed to him before letting the man rush her out of the room.

"Stop! Siarah!" Kai's shouts barely reached above the din of clashing metal and struggling men, and then he and Dan had to deal with several more Gadiantons who spilled into the space before them. Kai's adrenaline surged, but there were too many to move through quickly, and this group ended up being better fighters. Kai took a minor wound on his thigh, and a desperate enemy thrust penetrated nearly an inch into the muscles of his stomach. Dan made sure that man lost the use of his arm.

The windows shattered, and the fight intensified. As Kai had feared, more enemies joined the fray, most of them guards from the Hall of Judgment. Fortunately, a few of them read the lay of the land—especially the presence of Lehi—and threw in with the Nephite general. Which only increased the confusion. At one point, a Gadianton tried to grab Ara and pull her through the same doorway the mysterious man had taken Siarah, but Kai reached them in time, shoving his sword deep into the man's side. He and Ara moved along the side wall, accompanied by Dan and Jerid. The other elite, unfortunately, had fallen.

Lehi's voice boomed throughout the room like a thunderstorm in a box canyon. "Surrender your weapons!"

Kai turned toward the sound, making sure no enemy threatened his back, and surveyed the room. The fighting had halted—partly in surprise at Lehi's ominous command, Kai surmised, but also because the battle had been so intense. It became clear that Lehi and his men held the upper hand, and that their work of killing had accelerated. The screams and moans of the wounded and dying children of God—the most horrible sounds on earth—continued. Kai looked down at the man he'd just pierced.

The robber stared at him with eyes nearly squeezed shut, trying to stop the bleeding with both hands. Kai doubted the man would live. Part of him pitied the injured demon, but then he thought of Siarah as the remaining Gadiantons began dropping swords and short spears. His anger surged as he rushed out of the room, leaving Ara, Dan, and Jerid behind. He barely heard the report from one of the elites that Gadianton had escaped with a few men through the back windows.

Kai's footsteps carried him down the halls like an angry west wind. He didn't encounter any more Gadiantons, or any guards, even when he passed from the residence into the Hall of Judgment. He startled several servants and aides, though, and even a pair of judges.

"Where did he take her?" he screamed at the judges.

One of them nearly fainted at the blood covering Kai from head to toe, while the other shook his head and said, voice quavering, "We haven't seen anything, I promise you."

"Is there a side door?" Kai raised the tip of his sword to emphasize his seriousness, and the man gave him simple directions. Kai raced off, leaving bloody footprints. When he neared the door, a lone guard made a move to confront him but then thought better of it. Kai skidded to a stop.

"Did anyone pass this way?" he asked, breathing heavily.

The guard shook his head, and Kai's shoulders slumped. He had been sure they would exit through the nearest side door. Had they used a window? He couldn't continue the search himself, and he had already lost too much time. He gave an elongated yell of frustration, causing the guard to back up a few steps, then turned and ran back into the interior.

He returned to the dining room of the residence to see fourteen Gadiantons sitting against one wall, hands tied behind them. Several of Lehi's men stood guard, while the remainder triaged the wounded, starting with their own. A few of the dead had already been lined up along the back wall, and Kai spotted both Imrahiel and Tiberion in that group. Ara stood with Dan in a corner. When her eyes met Kai's, he noted intense sorrow. Then one of Lehi's elites, along with an older woman, drew Ara away to tend to her.

"Did you find her, Kihoran?" asked Lehi, moving toward him, glistening red axe resting on his shoulder.

Kai took a moment before responding. "No. Someone took her. The man who killed Imrahiel."

"Oh?" Lehi stopped a few feet away. "Now why do you suppose he did that?"

Kai wasn't sure which part he was asking about, so he kept silent and just shook his head.

"Any guards left in the Hall of Judgment?" asked Lehi.

"Only a handful." Kai felt himself becoming numb. He had *seen* Siarah. He'd been within ten feet of her. And somehow she was gone again. How was that possible? He had been *promised* he would find her. His breath stopped as realization dawned, turning his heart cold. He *had* found her, as the prophet foretold. Alive and well. But for some reason, the Lord hadn't wanted him to save her. Was he no longer worthy of her? Had his faith faltered so profoundly?

"Kihoran, look at me, soldier."

Kai realized his head had dropped. His hands and knees felt weak, and it wasn't just post-battle fatigue. He raised his eyes to meet Captain Lehi's, but he didn't try to put on a resolute face. He was beyond that.

"We found her, Kihoran," said Lehi, "and she didn't leave with someone loyal to Gadianton … at least, not anymore. We'll get a search organized, and we'll find her again. I promise you that, whether you want to trust me or not."

Kai nodded, the numbness spreading. He glanced at Dan, who was approaching.

"No sign?" asked Dan.

Kai shook his head, eyes wandering back to the floor.

"Jerid and I will organize the first search parties … if that's all right with you, Captain Lehi."

"It is. Additional men are on the way. Omner and I anticipated something eventful happening after we received a report from one of our spies. The information was accurate. And it wasn't hard to discover where you'd gone this morning."

Kai looked up again as a memory flashed to the fore. "There was a woman here, with Gadianton. She left before you arrived."

Lehi nodded. "She got out in time."

Kai frowned. "You knew she would be here?"

"Of course. It was her report we read, just last night. She advised us to come to the city with all possible haste."

"Oh." Kai's newly kindled hatred for Mistress Havah dissipated like steam in a stiff breeze.

"You mentioned others coming," said Dan. "When will they arrive?"

"Before midday. In the meantime, I have a letter to present to the high judges of the city. Actually, I have five different letters—one for each of the plausible scenarios Omner and I could come up with. I will deliver the one that says I am sorry that Tiberion was tragically killed in an episode of civil strife and that Omner will step in temporarily as the chief administrator. It bears my seal, and only a rotten lemuelberry will publicly argue that I wrote it ahead of time."

"The people of Morianton won't like this situation," noted Dan.

Lehi cracked a grin. "No, they won't. Most here believe that everyone in Lehi resents them and is constantly looking for ways to exact revenge. Lehites don't actually think that way, though this one—" he put a thumb to his own chest, "is surely tempted to right now."

Kai didn't want to ponder any of that. When his mind wasn't buried in three feet of mud, it spun uncontrollably. He felt like vomiting, and it had nothing to do with the blood starting to cake on skin and clothing.

"We've called for some physicians and their assistants," continued Lehi, giving Kai a concerned appraisal. "Most of the household servants have fled, but we can seek help from local Christians to get people ... and this place ... cleaned up. I've already dispatched a message to the nearest synagogue, with a request to spread the word. You should sit, son."

"What?" asked Kai. It was then he noticed the room slanting. His thoughts labored as if through freezing molasses. He didn't resist when Dan grasped his upper arm and led him to one of the few functional chairs in the room. His body slumped as he sat, and then Dan put a hand on his shoulder.

"All will be well, Kai. All will be well."

Kai barely heard the words, wasn't sure what they meant. But another thought burst to the surface. "Where is Ara?"

"She's been taken to another room of the house to be tended," answered Dan. "She suffered a nasty blow to the head, but she'll be fine."

Kai rose shakily to his feet. "I need to see her."

Dan glanced at Lehi, who nodded. "All right, I'll take you to her. She's almost as out of it as you, though. I should write down the conversation so you'll both remember it later."

Dan's flat attempt at humor slid past Kai, who let the big Ammonite lead him down the main passage, then along a shorter hallway to a bedroom with a window. Thick curtains had been partly drawn to cut the light cascading through it.

Ara lay on a bed, its sheets stained with blood in several places. A woman ministered to her with damp cloths, a poultice, and bandages. Part of her head wound had already been bandaged, the hair cut neatly away. She wouldn't love that hairdo, part of him mused.

Her eyes had been closed, but they opened when Kai stood next to the bed, swimming for a moment and then fixing on him. Her expression mixed shock and shame, but she didn't look away.

Kai's mind was working a little better after the short walk … with Dan to steady him, of course. "I'm glad you're going to be all right."

She drew her lips into a tight line, then said, "You shouldn't be. I wasn't supposed to be here. I had three marriage proposals in Gideon, and I didn't take any of them. Instead, I pretended I could help you find Siarah, for some selfish reason I can't even begin to explain to myself, much less to you. I messed things up here for you. For both of you."

"How? I don't understand."

"Imrahiel found me, followed me. I think I'm the reason he was here, with so many men."

"Huh." Kai rubbed his chin, which was thick with stubble. "I doubt very much this is your fault. And Imrahiel got what he deserved." The muscles in his jaw tightened, and he nearly spat. "I wish we could've gotten Gadianton, too."

"So do I. But … Siarah is gone again. I'm so sorry, Kai." She finally looked away, her eyes moist.

The woman tending her looked up at Kai in annoyance. "You're making her move her head. Stop it." She was clearly accustomed to speaking to reckless, thick-minded soldiers.

"Sorry," said Kai, then addressed Ara again. "We'll find her. I'm not sure who took her, but he wasn't a friend of Gadianton. That's a good thing, right?"

She looked at him again, then shook her head ever so slightly. "There are factions within the Gadiantons, so probably not." Her face fell further. "I'm sorry. I shouldn't have said that."

"It's the truth, isn't it? Or at least one possible relevant truth."

She didn't respond, just held still and closed her eyes as the woman applied another poultice and some additional bandaging. She grimaced slightly as the woman finished up. Then she opened her eyes again.

"I truly am sorry, Kai."

"It's all right, Ara. You did your be—" His world spun violently, and it was a good thing Dan was there as blackness overtook him and he crumpled like an empty barley sack.

EPILOGUE

Wherefore, whoso believeth in God might with surety
hope for a better world, yea, even a place at the right hand of God,
which hope cometh of faith, maketh an anchor to the souls of men,
which would make them sure and steadfast, always
abounding in good works, being led to glorify God.
—Ether 12:4

Kai awoke in a strange room. One too nice for him, though at first he couldn't articulate why. Then, his mind started functioning, and recollection surfaced. His memories ended with a view of Ara watching him pass out. He looked around. The room had two large windows—two!—and it must have been about midday from the brightness enveloping him.

He stared at the ceiling for nearly a minute before realizing a mural had been painted on it. Only a high judge or a wealthy merchant could afford such. Had he been taken to Lehi, or even to Zarahemla? No, he couldn't have been out that long. His injuries weren't that severe. He scanned the rest of the room, noting the wide, artfully carved door and a couch so large it could serve as another bed. The couch, a table, and several chests framed in an area of the floor covered by an expensive rug, colorful and thickly woven. It was then that he noted the bed beneath him, so luxurious he might have been sleeping on a puffy cloud.

Someone had changed his clothes, which made sense—one would never lay a bloody, sweaty mess such as he had been in a pristine environment like this. He felt the pressure of bandages around his leg, his abdomen, and his left hand. He raised that hand from where it had rested on a coverlet of the finest linen, dyed a soft green. He lifted the other hand as well, abstractly noting he had all his fingers. He wiggled his toes, then checked his entire body, as a soldier often did. He was whole, as far as he could tell.

He pushed the blanket aside and sat up, nearly crying out in pain as stomach muscles objected to the exercise. His feet were bare, and they had put him in a robe, not shirt and breeches, the fabric of which was almost too soft. He needed to find proper clothes. And something edible to fill a gnawing pit.

He padded across the room and opened the door, then stood and stared for a moment. He was on a second story, looking through a balustrade at a lush, flowering garden, perfectly manicured. As he studied it further, however, flaws began to manifest themselves, caused by humans who had recently tramped through the foliage. Now he knew where he was. Tiberion's house. The scene of the battle. He spied the broken windows of the dining room. He squeezed his eyes shut in an attempt to force out the horrors, but was only partially successful. He needed to keep moving.

He looked both directions down the covered, open-sided hallway, noting a probable way down to his left. He stepped quietly along the polished wooden floor, not sure why he was trying to be so stealthy. He passed several other doors, all of them closed, before reaching a circular staircase that headed both up and down.

He descended the stairs slowly, feeling the strain in his wounded thigh muscle. Again he almost cried out. At the bottom, he followed the scents of food being prepared. Halfway toward what appeared to be a doorway leading to the kitchens, Dan's voice boomed from behind, nearly causing his bad leg to buckle.

"Kai, you're up! But you shouldn't be. Your body needs to rest and heal."

Kai turned, noting how refreshed the former stripling warrior looked. His eyes didn't carry the haunted expression his own probably did, either. Of course, Dan had experienced worse battles, and more of them. He also possessed true faith and trust in the Lord, and that made a difference.

"You must be famished, I know. I was just coming to get some food from the kitchens to bring up to you … and I was going to wake you up. You've been sleeping long enough."

Kai blinked. "How long?"

"Almost two days.

"Two days? I wasn't hurt *that* badly."

"That's what I thought," said Dan with a smile and a wink. "Come, there's a place we can sit in one of the kitchens, and I'll get you that food."

"How many kitchens are there?"

"Well, Tiberion enjoyed fine dining. And fancy guests. There are three kitchens. Two here, and another within the Hall of Judgment— presumably so he wouldn't have to wait the extra minute for his food, which would cool down too much in the transport." He chuckled as he shook his head.

Kai followed Dan through the doorway, noting the spacious area with three cooks hard at work. Two of four ovens were lit, one with a large kettle in it and the other roasting meat on a thin, flat stone. The aromas were heavenly.

They passed through that kitchen into a smaller one, where a single cook was preparing some dishes involving various fruits and vegetables.

"Did … the household return?" asked Kai.

"Yes, except for a pair of servants. There are also a dozen of Lehi's men staying here, so we have quite a few mouths to feed. Jerid took the rest—we lost two, sadly—to join the searches for Gadianton and Siarah."

Kai hesitated after Dan showed him a small table where they could sit in a corner. "Any news yet?" He tried to sound hopeful but failed.

"Not yet." Dan's tone held optimism, and Kai couldn't decide if he wanted to be annoyed by that or not. "Lehi is pretty sure Gadianton went east instead of north."

"And Siarah?"

Dan sat after Kai finally did. "They must be traveling at night. Jerid hasn't been able to pick up the trail. A few rumors of sightings, but nothing definitive ... and in three different directions."

Kai rested elbows on the table and lowered his head into his hands, reliving the scene of her sudden departure. Without looking up, he said, "She left willingly."

"She was offered an opportunity to escape a hellacious battle with an uncertain outcome, and she took it."

"But she knew him. I saw it in her eyes." He looked up at Dan, who gave a slight frown.

"Probably."

"We don't have *any* idea who he is?"

"Not yet, but we've been questioning the Gadiantons we captured. We'll learn some important things, I'm sure of it."

"Yeah, if you can get them to see past those silly, infernal oaths." Kai felt like strangling something. Part of him wished a hungry cat would walk by.

Dan hadn't said anything to the cooks, but they must have known who Kai was, and he had clearly just gotten out of bed. No fewer than three plates of food, along with an extra-large cup of water, appeared at the table, filling it.

"Eat," said Dan. "As much as you want. I'm not hungry."

Kai cocked an eyebrow at that but didn't say anything. He began picking at a few items, especially the tender, savory meat, trying a few bites.

"Maybe he was a spy," he said after a minute. "One of us."

"Perhaps."

"She might prefer him to me, either way."

"Now, Kai, don't—"

"I'm serious. What if she does? It's her choice to make."

"We don't know that."

"We don't *not* know it." Despite his glum mood, he kept eating, his stomach insistent. He took a long pull of the water, too. After several more bites, he gave Dan a plaintive look. "What should I do?"

"I don't know, Kai, but I'm with you. You know that."

He did, for truth. But he remembered again how much Dan had

already sacrificed for him, especially being away from his family. That decided it.

"We should return to Zarahemla, at least for a while, let Lehi organize the searches. I trust him and Jerid—more than I trust myself, actually."

Dan didn't respond immediately, though Kai caught a glimmer of anticipation in his eyes. Finally, he asked, "Are you sure?"

"Yes, I am. It will do me good to speak to Helaman again."

"Aye, you and me both. I believe Ara is already on her way there, by the way. She said something about wanting to see Jerena. And she asked me to ... apologize again."

Kai gave a vehement shake of his head. "She has nothing to apologize for. None of this was her fault. It was mine."

Dan frowned, but let Kai continue eating. At one point, Kai took notice of his plates ... they were nearly empty! He didn't *feel* like he had eaten that much. He pushed them toward Dan.

"I'm full, my friend. You finish them off."

Dan obliged, though he partook slowly.

"Can we leave tomorrow?" Kai asked.

"Whenever you'd like, once you've healed well enough to travel. I will insist that a physician examine you first. I've made sure our horses are well. Limher has been a great help. He came by to see you, actually."

"He did?"

Dan shrugged. "I think he feels some responsibility for us, since we're Christian and we're here."

"Doesn't that put him in more danger?"

"Ha. Not with Omner in charge now. He's coming personally in a week to meet with the judges and speak to the people. He's a great man, as you know, and he'll accomplish much good before they select a new chief judge."

"Hmmm ... have we found any more Gadiantons in the city?"

"Yes, several important characters. This was a big blow to Gadianton. A few of his people—even some we suspect of crimes—might be able to return to Nephite society and wriggle out of legal culpability, but Gadianton himself is finished. If he returns to Nephite lands, he will be arrested, no matter what arguments he comes up with. That is another victory."

"He can still control his group from afar."

"Not as well. And I'm sure many of his followers have lost confidence in him. We did some good things here, Kai, even if we didn't achieve our main objective."

"You may have done well, Dan, but I failed."

———◇———

"The City of David? That's what they call it?"

Zoram shrugged, meeting Siarah's skeptical gaze. "Yes, and it's more impressive than you think. Growing fast, too, if the people I've spoken to have their histories straight."

"And you think we'll be safe there for a while?"

He nodded confidently. "I do."

She stared into the trees surrounding their small camp, pondering everything that had happened the last two weeks. For the first few days, she had wanted desperately to go back to Morianton—to Kai, if he still lived—and Zoram hadn't tried to stop her. He didn't argue with her about it, either, just said it was her decision, even told her to follow her heart. He only asked that she be careful. She appreciated that, more than he knew. And her heart ... mystified her.

"Who do you think won?"

He shrugged uncomfortably as he scratched his jaw. "I don't know. News makes it to these parts slowly. We're outside Nephite lands and the official communications channels. I'm sure we'll hear something soon from a trader or traveler. It's hard to bet against Captain Lehi, though. And those were his elites, not common soldiers. The best of the best."

"Should I have stayed? Even if Kai was killed, would it have been better to die with him?" She had asked an indirect variation of that question once, and he hadn't responded. The direct version clearly pained him.

"I can't answer that. I'm sorry if I—"

She placed a hand on his arm as she sighed, noting its warmth. "You did what was right, Zoram. I'm glad I'm still alive. You saved me. And I'm sorry. I know I'm not sounding grateful for it."

He looked down, then away toward the north. Her eyes followed his. This City of David lay about ten miles distant, he had learned. They could find refuge there, learn what happened in Morianton, and then decide what to do next. She trusted the city had a good synagogue.

———◆———

Approaching Helaman and Jerena's home made butterflies frenzy in Ara's stomach. The Santorem itself ushered in an unwelcome host of stark memories. She had been tempted to stop by Lady Lianah's home to see how she was coping without her husband but had come straight here instead. Her desire to see Jerena burned like a bonfire.

She politely asked the guards at the front to announce her, then waited. Jerena burst through the front door a minute later, directing the guards to open the gate and take her horse. She embraced Ara like a long-lost sister—though her last visit had been relatively recent. Ara had never felt so loved.

After entering the house, they went to the main room on the lower floor, sitting on either end of a comfortable couch covered in smooth, supple sheepskin, stitched in artistic patterns.

"I'm so glad you came," said Jerena. "Not two days ago, we received word from Captain Lehi about what happened in Morianton."

"Well, Shefah is very fast … and I didn't linger."

"How are you? I detect a deep sadness in your eyes." She studied the bandages around Ara's head but didn't comment on them.

Ara felt suddenly conscious of not just her eyes, but her entire appearance. She was dusty and ragged and hadn't slept well the entire trip. She swallowed before responding. "I'll survive."

Jerena paused, then said, "If I have anything to say about it, indeed you will. I'd like you to tutor our children again. You can stay here, and—"

"I can't stay. I'll return to Gideon. I wanted to see you, though. The letters have been nice, and I can glimpse the light of your faith in them, but it wasn't the same. I just ..."

"It is wonderful to behold your face as well." Jerena reached over and squeezed her hand. "Stay at least tonight and tomorrow night. And then ... you know what, I'll go with you to Gideon. I and the children. It's been a while, like I said before. That will give us more time to talk, maybe do a few things together. We can travel in comfort, too."

"I can't impose on you like that."

Jerena raised her hands. "How are you imposing? *I'm* proposing it! And I'm accepting on your behalf." She winked and smiled, and Ara finally nodded, her inner elation at the idea not quite reaching her face.

"You are a brave woman," continued Jerena. "I know things didn't turn out as you had hoped, but—"

"Because I messed them up." She was surprised by the bitterness in her own tone; it had resurfaced in strength. "Kai would have been far better off if I hadn't interfered."

"But he's alive, and so is Siarah, from what we know at this point. Gadianton fled the city, his network in tatters again. All good things, and you witnessed them."

"As useless baggage."

"*Not* as useless baggage. Listen to me, Arayah. You are a daughter of God, as precious to him as I am. You did your best, and the Lord always recognizes sincere effort. Always. I don't know if you made any mistakes or not, but even if you did, you made them honestly, with the right motives in mind."

The dam of tears burst. "The right *motives*?! My motives were selfish. I wanted to help Kai because ... I love him. Subconsciously at least, I thought that somehow, maybe, I could steal him away from her. It was about *me*, not him. And it certainly was not about Siarah." Her voice approached a dry whisper at the end, and she stared down at trembling hands.

"It's all right," said Jerena softly. "I'm not unaware of how these things work. I also *know* you did your best. None of us are perfect. We're all learning in this great school of mortality. It's challenging sometimes—actually, most of the time—but the fight is worth it. And God doesn't ever abandon us. We can only abandon him."

Ara felt the sincerity of her friend's words. Her friend. Yes, she had a real friend. Not a fake, simpering one. Not one driven by greed or emotion. One who was strong and good. So very strong. So very good.

"I need you to help me find him again," she said, the tears continuing to flow.

"Kai?"

"No, God."

———◆———

Kai and Dan strolled with Helaman through the garden surrounding his house. Jerena and the children had left with Ara before they arrived. Helaman must have thought the serenity of the deep, well-manicured foliage would calm Kai's soul. So far, that was a resounding negative. Dan's companionship during the journey home—which they hadn't rushed—*had* helped, but only temporarily.

Home. Again he wondered at his reference to Zarahemla as home. He had grown up in Bountiful, though he had been born somewhere in the vicinity of Zarahemla. He had received his schooling in Bountiful. He had, for a while, apprenticed with his adoptive father Gideon there. He had joined the army there. He had met Siarah there. It all seemed impossibly distant now.

"As I was saying," said Helaman, "the unrest spreading from Morianton is minor. Omner is doing a skillful job refuting the specious claims of injustice from various citizens and judges. I will ask him in my next letter if he believes I should make an appearance there, but in his first report he anticipated that such a visit would not be necessary. Captain Lehi can effectively handle the more obstinate holdouts to peace, and Omner will take care of the rest. Such a good man, and a brilliant administrator—the best among the sons of Mosiah, I think. Ammon is the preacher, Aaron the scholar, Himni the negotiator, Omner the administrator. And their grandchildren are proving to be just as adept. I've hired several to serve in various capacities across the country. We're achieving a better mix, I hope, of young, middle-aged, and, um, *highly experienced* in our leadership, both politically and in the Church. The Lord is surely guiding us."

Kai enjoyed listening to Helaman, even if he wasn't interested in the topic. The young prophet's optimism wasn't faked or overdone, though it still didn't penetrate Kai deeply.

"A good number of people continue leaving the nation," commented Dan. "We overheard many conversations about it on our way here."

Helaman didn't seem troubled by the phenomenon. "Yes, though it isn't a mass exodus. Sometimes I feel like I should be more concerned, but how can I blame them? They seek a place of peace. We're all tired of war, of the senseless killing, of the illogical disputes regarding matters hundreds of years in the past, of the naked greed and lust for power. How are men so foolish and blind?" *Now* he seemed worried, his face marred by a deep, ragged frown. He stopped and looked at Dan. "There is one group that concerns me, though."

"Who is that?"

"Some of your people, the Ammonites, have decided to migrate northward."

Dan mirrored Helaman's frown. "How many?"

"I'm not certain yet, but several hundred, at least. Ammon sent me a letter. He and two of his sons have been trying to convince them to stay, but with little success."

Dan's brow furrowed in deep concentration. "Is there another factor involved? Who leads them?"

Helaman placed a hand on Dan's shoulder and started them all walking again, at a slower pace. "There are no political divisions that I'm aware of, no disagreements over mundane things. Heshlon leads those who desire to emigrate. He is, by all accounts, a decent, faithful man, dedicated to the Lord and to his people."

Dan stopped them this time, the worry lines more pronounced. "He is also my uncle. I know he is a good man, but even the best of men can be deceived if they are not watchful and diligent."

"I know, my friend," said Helaman with a reassuring nod. "Ammon guides his flock well, despite his greatly advanced years, and he senses nothing amiss in Heshlon's activities or motives. Heshlon and others simply want to organize themselves in a new place where they can worship and serve God in peace. Father Lehi desired the same thing, as did his most valiant son. They intend to maintain contact with the Church, and with me, the prophet. They are not renouncing or ignoring my authority from the Lord in any way, not seeking to set up something to compete with it. I … well, I trust them, Brother Dan. I cannot say the same about many other Nephites who have left. Some have already strayed far from ecclesiastical authority, setting up their own independent churches. That, my friend, disturbs me, though I still respect their agency and their longing for peace."

They started moving again, and Kai fell behind a pace, happy to let Helaman and Dan have their conversation. After a few minutes of the two discussing various details regarding the emigrants—including Dan's description of the new City of David—Helaman halted again and turned to Kai.

"You are quiet, my friend."

"I … don't have anything to add."

"Oh, but you do. Your valor, your loyalty, and, yes, your faith, add a great deal."

"I mean, to the conversation."

"I know what you meant. But I want you to understand how truly valuable you are to the Lord's cause. I've been studying some of the words of Ether recently. What an incredible man. Abandoned, alone, fated to witness the entire destruction of his people. I can't even fathom his situation. And yet his writings are filled with such unexpected ebullience. He knew God lives. He knew God's promises are real. He knew our hope rests in the eternal glory offered by Christ. I challenge myself every day to do a better job of focusing on that perspective. I strive to ponder the celestial, and I still have a long way to go. I'm relatively young, but that isn't an excuse. I am the prophet, duly called by God to watch over this people. Such a daunting responsibility, and yet I always have help—from angels, including my wife, from the Spirit, and from the Lord himself. I cannot afford to dwell on my weaknesses. Address them, yes; flounder in them, no. I have too much work to do."

He didn't add, "And you do, too," but Kai heard the words all the same. He was right. Kai couldn't allow sadness and frustration to cripple him. But … that would take some time. And patience, as the search for Siarah continued. Perhaps some distraction as well. He suddenly remembered how happy he had been training with Jeruzim and the Gideon militia. In fact, that memory sang to him, quickly reaching a crescendo.

"May I go to Gideon for a while? I want to train again with Jeruzim and the others, clear my mind if I can."

Helaman cocked his head slightly as he gazed at him. After a few seconds, he nodded. "I think that is a splendid idea. Godspeed, Brother Kihoran."

END

ABOUT THE AUTHOR

In late 2020, M.D. House semi-retired from a successful career in Corporate Finance and Business Leadership that allowed him to experience all facets of designing, producing, marketing and selling products to customers across the world. He enjoyed that career, and still consults part-time, but being able to pursue his passion for creative writing has been a tremendous blessing.

During that first career, he published one science fiction novel, called *Patriot Star*. Since embarking on his new journey with much more time and focus for writing, he's published a sequel (*Kindred Star*), along with seven religious historical fiction novels (which were a surprise) and his first fantasy novel, *Crossroads of Awakening Memory, Book 1* of the epic fantasy series called the End Times Convergence.

His docket is filled with new projects, including Book 3 in the Patriot Star series, more Barabbas spin-offs, and additional volumes in the End Times Convergence (plus some side projects, of course).

You can learn more about M.D. House, including interviews with people like Eric Metaxas, Tricia Goyer, Carmen LaBerge, Roger Marsh, Chautona Havig, Jaime Vaughn, and Dr. Paul Reeves, at mdhouselive.com.

Made in the USA
Middletown, DE
17 December 2024